AMID STARS AND DARKNESS

AMID STARS AND DARKNESS

CHANI LYNN FEENER

SQUARE
FISH

SWOON READS

NEW YORK

FOR MATT AND LISA

An imprint of Macmillan Publishing Group, LLC
175 Fifth Avenue, New York, NY 10010
swoonreads.com

Square Fish and the Square Fish logo are trademarks of Macmillan and are used by
Swoon Reads under license from Macmillan.

Our books may be purchased in bulk for promotional, educational, or business
use. Please contact your local bookseller or the Macmillan Corporate and
Premium Sales Department at (800) 221-7945 ext. 5442 or by e-mail at
MacmillanSpecialMarkets@macmillan.com.

Library of Congress Control Number: 2016953561
ISBN 978-1-250-15895-6 (paperback) ISBN 978-1-250-12375-6 (ebook)

Originally published in the United States by Swoon Reads
First Square Fish edition, 2018
Book designed by Liz Dresner
Square Fish logo designed by Filomena Tuosto

33614080709610

10 9 8 7 6 5 4 3 2 1

LEXILE: 830L

CHAPTER 1

D
o we really have to play this game?" Delaney asked, the question coming out halfheartedly. She already knew what the response would be.

"Come on," Mariana pushed. "I'm nervous."

"You're never nervous." The two of them had been friends for four years now, so she would know. "Besides, I'm terrible at this. You always win. Hence, why I'm here standing in line, waiting to get into a place I have no interest in."

"Don't be so dull, D." Mariana bumped Delaney's shoulder playfully. "Any time with me is fun time. Now"—her deep chocolate eyes homed in on a man standing five paces ahead of them—"us or them?"

Delaney made a big show of staring at the back of the guy's head before shrugging pointedly. "Us?"

Ignoring the fact that Delaney's heart clearly wasn't in it, Mariana pondered a moment before disagreeing. "Definitely a them."

"How can you even tell?" Because chances were very good that her friend was right.

"It's in the set of his shoulders."

"It is not." Or, if it truly was, Delaney couldn't see it.

The heavy thrum of music from inside the large warehouse building vibrated around them, the waves rumbling up through their feet. True to its name, club Star Light was a glittering beacon off the fringe of Portland, Maine. The building itself was made of faded brick, and had once been home to some sort of manufacturing company. That was many years prior, and it'd been renovated into one of the hottest dance clubs in the state about half a decade ago.

"Tell me again who you're hoping to meet up with?" Delaney asked as the line moved another foot closer.

Being that it was Friday night, it came as no surprise that the place was packed. A curvy stretch of people trailed from the two metal doors all the way to the start of the parking lot to the right. Because Mariana and Delaney had traveled the forty-five minutes from their small town, Cymbeline, to Portland earlier in the day, they'd snagged a prime parking spot in front of one of the buildings across the street. At least leaving would be easier. Too bad they'd spent so long at dinner that they hadn't gotten here at opening.

"I'm not *hoping* anything," Mariana answered, though her wide grin gave her away.

"Right." Delaney rolled her eyes jokingly. "That's why you're 'nervous.' What's this one's name again? Starts with an *O*? Owen? Otto?"

"Ottus," she corrected, a strand of annoyance slipping past her deep-red-painted lips. "Which you totally remembered. His name is Ottus. And you're supposed to be here for moral support. This is our first time meeting in person, and I want it to be perfect."

"Oat-us," Delaney sounded it out, and made a face. She remembered seeing the spelling of it flashing on Mariana's phone last week. It wasn't done in the traditional way; it was strange.

But of course it would be, considering Ottus was an alien.

It'd only been three years since the revelation of extraterrestrials. Apparently, they'd been visiting Earth for millennia, and no one knew quite why they'd decided to come out of hiding now, only that they had. After exposing their existence, there'd been talk of a merger, which of course the humans had protested. They'd attempted to fight, but their weapons were toys in comparison to the technology those from Xenith had.

"He's Vakar," her roommate said then, excitement brimming behind her smooth brown eyes. "He told me he used to be a soldier."

Mariana was obsessed with the aliens, who she'd dubbed Them. Like they were rock stars she couldn't get enough of. It was the one thing Delaney was looking forward to now that they'd graduated high school and moved into an apartment: separate rooms.

She loved Mariana, but she didn't share her interest in the otherworldly. Still, she was glad her friend was so excited to meet someone, even if he was an ex–alien soldier.

"And now he's a bartender," Delaney said, making sure the teasing lilt to her voice was apparent. "How impressive."

"Shut up." They moved less than a foot closer to the door. "If you'd just give him a chance, you would like him, I promise. But not too much. I don't want to share."

"I don't have anything against aliens," Delaney said for what felt like the millionth time. "I'm just not enthralled by them like you are. I'd prefer to go about my life per usual and pretend the invasion never happened."

Mariana was quick to defend them. "They didn't invade."

Done with this conversation, Delaney scanned her mind for anything else they could talk about. Literally anything. There was a bickering couple directly behind them, and for a moment their argument about whether or not waiting to get in was worth it was entertaining enough to hold her attention.

At this rate, they were never getting in and Mariana would never get to meet the bartender.

"Moral support, huh?"

"Yes," Mariana agreed.

"All right." She stepped to the side of the line. "This is taking forever."

Delaney ignored the six people who'd been standing in front of them, locking eyes with the bouncer. She'd watched him more closely over the past ten minutes and had noticed his bored expression and slouched shoulders. If she had to guess, he and his lack of enthusiasm were the main causes for the slow line movement.

Flashing a grin at him, she made sure to have his full attention before slipping a twenty from her pocket. Angling her body to keep the rest of the line from seeing, she held the bill out and motioned toward Mariana, who was still waiting in their spot.

"My friend is running late for a date," she told him. "Help a girl out?"

He was about three times her size and didn't appear to be the nicest of people, so she kept her smile firmly in place. He glanced between the two of them once before motioning Mariana forward with a finger.

Plucking the twenty from her hand, he absently asked for her ID, barely bothering to look down at it once she'd held it out.

She was a bit disappointed by that fact—the fake had cost her a decent amount of money, and using it had been the only part about coming to this club that had excited her. Then they were

4

through the doors and Mariana swung an arm over her shoulder and they both laughed.

THEY'D SQUISHED THEIR way into the center of the crowd, relishing the flashing of neon strobe lights and the surrounding heat from the other patrons. It smelled like sweat and beer, and Delaney's ears were already burning from the heavy beat that thrummed from large speakers situated all around the rectangular room.

The dance floor was a large fifty-by-fifty square dais at the very center of the club. A single step led down to the rest of the place, with a bar lining the entire right wall, and booths and tables taking up the left and front. At the way back, a DJ station towered over the dance floor. A man with a bright pink Mohawk was currently spinning, his hair and teeth glowing.

The black lights painted the world in a mysterious radiance, turning everyday objects—like Delaney's Converse—into flashy items. The entire high-rise ceiling was covered in tiny glow stars of all sizes.

Despite her reservations, Delaney loved that she could disappear here, blend in and become just another cog in the universe. It was liberating in an odd way, one she couldn't quite place her finger on. Word spread quickly in a small town, and the town her parents still occupied off the coast of Maine was as small as they came. Not for the first time, she inwardly rejoiced at the fact they'd agreed to send her to boarding school.

She'd spent the past four years at Cymbeline Academy, a good two hours from where her parents lived. Just enough distance for Delaney to feel independent.

Mariana leaned in and screamed against the curve of Delaney's ear, "I'm going to get a drink!" They'd spotted Ottus working the bar when they'd entered, but Mariana had insisted they dance first, no doubt to build up her nerve.

"Are you sure?" Delaney asked. "Do you want me to go with?"

She shook her head. "I don't want our first face-to-face to be with a third wheel, no offense."

Delaney held up her hands and kept dancing. She spun as her friend disappeared among the masses, and Delaney twisted her hips and waved her arms to the heavy thrum. The song changed and she loosened up, switching tactics with ease.

The crowd moved in on her, caging, and she laughed when a boy around her age made a really bad robot move to get her attention. He fell into step with her and they swayed to the beat, close, but still far enough apart for it to be appropriate. Another three people turned toward them and joined, two of them girls.

She didn't know how many songs passed with them, but when she realized it'd been a while since Mariana had gone, she waved at her new friends and stepped back to go find her.

For a moment there she'd been able to distract herself with the music, but now enough time had passed that she was starting to get tired. Mariana was the partier in their equation, with Delaney merely dragged along for the ride every once in a while.

Stepping down from the dance floor, she scanned the bar, which stretched across the entire wall, easily spotting Mariana in her red outfit.

Sure enough, she was leaning across the white bar top, laughing at something Ottus had said.

He was all height and muscle, hair a mix between blond and brunette, depending on which way he turned his head. He'd shaved it so that there wasn't much to see anyway, making it even harder to correctly guess the shade.

The two of them had connected on one of the many dating apps Mariana used. The apps helped connect humans and aliens who were looking to get to know one another better, so it wasn't too big of a surprise that Delaney's best friend had signed up.

With a shake of her head, she decided to walk over and let her friend know she was leaving. There were enough people there that she had to move through the throng cautiously, but she'd only made it a few steps before someone slammed into her from the side.

She almost lost her footing, and instinctually reached out, grasping on to the other person's arm. Once steady, she glanced up to find herself staring at one of the most beautiful girls she'd ever seen.

They were about the same height, with the same narrow shoulders and long legs. The other girl's hair was even cut practically the same length, to just past her chin. That was where the similarities ended, however. Where Delaney's hair was a vibrant red, this girl's was inky black and slick like silk.

"Are you all right?" Delaney asked, pulling back and straightening.

The other girl stared at her oddly for half a second before the lost, distracted expression on her face suddenly morphed into a large smile. It was almost a bit creepy how wide it was, and Delaney instantly distrusted it.

"I'm perfect," the girl said in a high voice. She reached out and rested her hand on Delaney's left shoulder, squeezing lightly. "You have a *fantastic* night."

"Um"—Delaney turned as the girl went to step by—"yeah, you, too."

The girl was swallowed back up by the crowd. She hadn't even apologized for walking into her. Suddenly Delaney was completely drained. The music was too loud and the air was too stifling with all these people. Deciding she'd definitely more than done her best-friend duties, she turned back toward the bar where she'd seen Mariana only a few minutes before.

Only Mariana was no longer at the bar. Neither was Ottus.

Frowning, Delaney pulled her cell phone out of her back pocket. There weren't any messages, so she tapped Mariana's number and lifted the phone to her ear. It was hard to hear anything over the music blaring from all directions, but she was calling mostly so that her friend's phone would ring long enough to get her attention.

As it continued to ring in her ear, Delaney moved toward the exit, eager to get out of the throng. Outside, the air was sharp, and she sucked in a deep, chilled breath. It was close to one in the morning, and the line they'd waited in earlier was gone. There weren't many people out, just one or two smokers tucked against the brick siding by the door.

She turned away from them, heading in the direction of her car.

Mariana's voicemail picked up, and Delaney decided to give it one more try. After that she was going to resort to texting and waiting in the car. They'd driven together, so she didn't want to leave without knowing where her friend was and if she'd need a ride or not.

Knowing Mariana, the answer to that was the latter.

Just as Mariana's voicemail picked up again, Delaney's phone dinged. She paused at the entrance to an alley between the club and the equally large brick monstrosity next to it. Her car was visible on the other side of the street, directly under a streetlamp, so she could easily see within. It was empty.

She moved her attention to the screen and sighed when she saw the text message was from Mariana. Her friend let her know that she'd grabbed a ride with Ottus and was heading back to his place for the night.

Mariana had ended the text with a kiss emoticon and a winky face that had Delaney rolling her eyes and laughing at the same time.

Relieved that it meant she could now head home without worry, Delaney went to take a step forward, checking both sides of the street for oncoming traffic.

Before she knew what was happening, a heavy hand slammed against her mouth, yanking her back against someone's solid chest. She dropped her phone and, in her shock, watched it ricochet off the cement ground.

It landed on its back, so that the smiling image on her home screen of Mariana hugging her was the last thing she noticed before being tugged into the dark alley.

CHAPTER 2

Delaney couldn't tear her gaze away from the phone as she was dragged back into the dark crevice between the club and the closed restaurant at its right. The sky was practically black overhead, and the second they were in the shadows, her brain finally registered what was going on.

Her struggling increased, and she shook her head back and forth to try to dislodge the hand on her mouth. The arm around her waist tightened, almost to the point of pain, and she was pressed flush against her captor.

"Stop it, Lissa," mumbled a deep male voice directly above her. "We need to go."

She tried to tell him that he had the wrong girl, but she couldn't even manage a muffled word past his hold. Frustration welled, and she took a stuttering breath to clear her head before reacting. Slamming her foot down on top of his, she dropped to her knees when his grip momentarily loosened, not waiting for him to regain his composure.

Twisting around so she was sitting on the cold ground, she kicked out with both legs, landing a blow to his stomach. It felt like she was hitting a rock wall. Flipping onto her feet, she bolted for the alley opening.

A growl sounded at her back, and right before she was about to make it into the light, she was grabbed again. This time he lifted her off her feet, letting out pained grunts when she repeatedly kicked him in the shins. He didn't loosen his hold again, and instead shifted her weight to his side.

He carried her as if she weighed nothing, toward the end of the alley and farther from the front of the club and any semblance of safety. His shoulders practically blocked out the building behind him, and she had to tip her head all the way back just to maintain eye contact. He wasn't bulky by any means, but he was fit and, judging by that kick she'd given him earlier, steady as a damn tree.

Which meant that the five measly self-defense classes she'd let Mariana drag her to weren't getting her out of this.

"I'll scream," she threatened, not really sure why she was telling him instead of doing just that.

"Then I'll silence you."

He dropped her suddenly and slammed her back against the frozen stone wall. His body settled around her, effectively pinning her in. Her head didn't even come up to his chin, but a couple of inches lower so that she was staring at the top of his chest. When she pressed her hands against him, he didn't budge, and there wasn't enough room for her to attempt kicking again.

She waited and, when nothing happened, risked glancing up at him.

"What's wrong with you?" he asked her, suddenly breaking the silence. His brows were creased, and he was inspecting her like he would an unruly animal.

"With me?" Her voice was incredulous. "I'm not the one who just kidnapped someone, buddy."

"I told you, it's time to leave. You're the one who's making this difficult."

"I'm the one—" She stopped, shoved down the fear, and held up her hand between them. "Okay, let's start again. First of all, dragging someone into an alley against her will constitutes kidnapping. Second of all, you also happened to *kidnap* the wrong person."

"We don't have time for this."

Seriously? What wasn't he getting?

"I'm not Lissa," she stated plainly, watching his face for the obvious to set in.

Which it never did.

If anything, he seemed more aggravated than he had before. Instead of pulling back or apologizing, he gritted his teeth and relinquished the small amount of space between them. Her hand was now stuck between their bodies, and she wiggled it to get free until his low growl had her freezing for what seemed like the millionth time that night.

"This isn't attractive," he sneered down at her. "I told you what would happen if you tested me again, Olena."

She blinked at him. What? So was the girl he was looking for named Lissa . . . or Olena? The realization that he was clearly insane actually gave her an inkling of relief. He was delusional, sure, but all she had to do was stall him a bit, and someone would eventually stumble upon them, right?

Did delusional people have actual plans? She assumed—hoped, really—not. Besides, this was a dead end. In order to get her anywhere from here, he'd have to lead her back out the opening on the other side. It was very early in the morning, but all she needed was for one person to be there so that she could call for help. Then it was only ten feet to her car and home free she'd be.

Having a plan, even one as dodgy as that, helped calm her nerves so she could think more clearly. She wasn't sure if one could actually get through to a delusional person, but what would be the harm in trying? It'd certainly fall under the category of stalling.

"Whoever you think I am," she said, making sure to ease her tone, "I promise you, I'm not her. Just let me go, and no one has to get in trouble here. I won't tell anyone about this, or you. You can go your way, and I can go mine."

She tried to look trustworthy, easing her features to hopefully cover her dread. She'd grab the first cop she could once she left this alley.

"Enough," he barked, slamming a fist against the wall a few inches from her head. Bits of the stone broke off and crumbled to the ground.

How the hell . . . ? Her eyes widened, and some of her panic returned.

"You aren't listening—" she tried again, only to be swiftly cut off by his face invading the personal space of her own.

"They're coming, Olena. We don't have time for any more of your games. You don't want to leave? I get it, but you have responsibilities, and it's time you owned up to who you are. Now"—he angled his head at her, his expression softening some—"stop playing. I'm trying to protect you."

She forced herself to look him dead in the eye. "I swear to god, I am not the girl you're looking for."

He let out a frustrated sigh and pulled back, wrapping a large hand around her thin arm to tug her after him. When she stumbled forward, he linked his other arm around her waist, keeping her securely upright with his large body.

Before her mind could filter through all the possible ways she could attempt getting loose, the sound of footsteps to her right caught her attention and she frowned.

That was the dead end. . . . How . . . ?

"Ander Ruckus." Another man, only slightly less imposing than the guy holding her to him, appeared in the darkness. He bowed his head, then straightened, nodding curtly toward Delaney. "Lissa Olena."

She didn't bother correcting this one when he called her the wrong name. She wouldn't be able to get through to him no matter what she said. Even now, the way he held himself across from them, legs spread, hands clasped and visible, like a soldier—

She gasped, and both of their eyes snapped in her direction, instantly confirming her suspicions.

Her body started shaking, and she was too shocked to realize how weak that would make her look. It'd been too dark to see before, but she could make out the color of her captor's eyes now, yellow with a ring of dark green.

Like an alien's.

"Oh shit," she said breathlessly, body going slightly lax so that he had to tighten his grip around her, practically holding her up now.

"What?" her captor snapped. "What happened?"

"Ruckus," the other soldier said, drawing his attention and pointing upward. "We should get to the ship. Fawna's detecting enemy soldiers approaching quickly. We don't have much time left before they're—" His words were abruptly cut off by the sound of gunfire.

Only it was a bit different, the sounds more like pings that whizzed through the air toward them. A few bullets embedded in the stone walls at either side, sending clouds of dust into the air.

Delaney regained herself, straightening and gripping the guy—Ruckus, she assumed—tightly. She couldn't muster enough guilt not to use him as a shield; it was either that or get shot herself. She tucked herself closer, risking a glance over his shoulder at the opening of the alley, where three men were slinking their way in.

Using her sudden compliance as an opportunity, Ruckus rushed them toward the dead end while the other guy opened fire on their pursuers. Lifting his arm, her captor gripped a black metal bar that she hadn't noticed hovering down from the sky, and tugged once.

"Hold on to me," he ordered against the crown of her head, bringing her up high enough so that she could wrap her arms around his neck. She hesitated and he shook her. "It's either this or die here, Olena," he hissed. "They will kill you."

"Thanks, Captain Obvious." They were shooting at them, after all. "I'm just not sure what makes you a safer option?"

Before he could respond, another round of gunfire went off, and Delaney's panic spread. She linked her arms around his neck without further protest, her only thought on getting out of there intact.

"Put your legs around my waist," he asserted, and this time she didn't hesitate. The second he was satisfied that she was secure, he pulled on the metal bar.

"Activate extraction shield and pull us up, Fawna," he said, and it took Delaney a second to realize he must have a communicator in his ear. A thin, see-through beam wrapped around them and the man still on the ground. It was green, and from the other side she saw the men shoot at it, bullets bouncing off as if hitting bulletproof glass.

When they started rising, she yelped and tightened her arms and legs around him. She thought she heard him chuckle, but she couldn't pull her eyes off the slowly receding ground to check.

They were high enough now that she could see over the tops of the buildings, and more soldiers dressed in all black were approaching the mouth of the alley. She counted a dozen before stopping, not wanting to waste her time. Another black bar on a long silver string zipped past her head, and she watched it drop to hover over the guy who was firing on their attackers.

Without looking, he reached up and grabbed on, yanking once before it started pulling him up toward them. He continued to fire his weapon, a gun she'd never seen before, the color of melted silver with a line of bright red lit up on its side.

"Hurry it up, Fawna," Ruckus growled.

This time she did look up, and sucked in a deep breath. The ropes were being drawn into the underside of a large ship she hadn't been able to make out from the ground. It reminded her a lot of a jet plane, except three times the size and with circular wings instead of sharp-tipped ones. It was black but had somehow been programmed to camouflage with the night sky. Stars winked back at her from its metallic surface as if really there.

A bottom hatch opened up when they were only a few feet away, metal doors sliding to the sides to expose a deep beige room. The ropes bringing them up were attached to the ceiling of this room, and instead of a crank rolling it, the line merely disappeared within the metal.

"Oh shit," she repeated, vaguely recalling she'd already said that. She was so distracted by the gaping mouth of the alien ship she was headed toward, she didn't notice the green force field around them flickering and then disappearing.

She totally felt the bullet that sliced through the side of her left arm, though. It was a searing sensation, like someone was branding her with a hot knife, and it shot bolts of fire that immediately spiked through her bloodstream.

She cried out, saw a burst of red stain the white leather of her jacket, and had one last moment of panic before her vision winked out and everything went black.

CHAPTER 3

Delaney moaned and shifted, wondering why she'd fallen asleep on the hard couch instead of going to bed; sometimes she fell asleep in front of the TV in the living room. Her mind searched for details of last night: she'd gone out with Mariana to celebrate, so she had to have been exhausted when they'd gotten—

She shot upright so quickly, she saw stars.

Mariana.

Last night.

It all rushed back to her. She hadn't made it home because she'd been frickin' kidnapped by aliens. And shot at. Her gaze went to her left arm, recalling the pain and the blood she'd seen before she'd passed out. Only, there wasn't so much as a scratch now.

Someone had removed her jacket, and she was left in her short-sleeved navy shirt. There wasn't a speck of blood on her bare flesh, no scar, nothing. It was as if it had never happened. Her gaze trailed over to the other side of the compartment, landing on her jacket. The left arm was shredded.

Confusion set in, and she was still rubbing at the spot when she stood and did a slow circle in the center of the room. It was white metal, with two cots on either side. She'd been sleeping on one of them, the thin pad so far from the comforts of a mattress, she actually snorted. Sure, they could travel across space but couldn't come up with a better version of a cot. That made sense.

There were no windows, but a small sink was built into one end of the room. On the wall across from it there was a wide door, big enough to fit two grown men shoulder to shoulder. She'd just taken a step toward it when a beeping sounded and the door whooshed to the right faster than she could blink.

The one who'd taken her stood there, watching. His oddly colored eyes scanned her once, as if searching for imperfections.

Damn, he was gorgeous. If not for the fact that the guy was a total psycho, she might have looked at her circumstances a bit differently. Unlike back in the alley, there was enough light here for her to get a good look at his features.

He had a strong jawline and a square chin. His hair was a warm chocolate shade, shorter on the sides, and long on the top. It was the type of cut generally kept swept back, but right now it was shaken loose, and it hung off to the right of his head. Some strands fell down his forehead all the way to his mouth, they were so long. A ruby glinted in his right ear—no, three rubies: one at the lobe, another at the center, and one at the top, settled against the inner curve.

If the eyes hadn't given him away, the outfit certainly would have. The shirt was sleeveless and zipped up the front with a golden zipper. The material appeared strange, thick and almost with a sheen to it. There was a short, stiff collar. His pants were form-fitting, tucked into large boots, and there were three strange black metal bands circling his wrists and upper arms.

The pants were charcoal. The uniform shirt forest green.

The color of Vakar.

She swallowed the lump in her throat, clutching her arm to her. Her feet were squared—as if there were anywhere she could run. She recalled how easy fighting him off had been. As in, not at all.

It took all her willpower not to cower when he took a single step forward, eating up one of the five paces between them.

He cocked his head, and she clenched her jaw so tightly, she felt the pressure in her teeth.

"You're still not talking to me," he concluded after another tense moment of silence. Nodding to himself as if it made perfect sense, he looked away, moving over to the cot across from her. He flicked her jacket off to the side and dropped down, stretching his long legs out in front of him.

The move forced her to retreat back to avoid him touching her, and he lifted a single brow, the corner of his mouth turning up at the same time.

"We're talking right now," she bit out, determined not to let him scare her. Or at least not to make it so obvious to him that he did.

Rubber squeaked against the floor, and then another man appeared in the doorway. He was smaller than Ruckus, with narrower shoulders, but still taller than her by at least half a foot. He was wearing the same charcoal military pants tucked into boots, but a forest-green lab coat was thrown over it and buttoned all the way up the front.

"Lissa Olena." He bowed his head.

"Olena—"

"Like I've already told you *a million times*," she spat, cutting Ruckus off, "I am *not* Olena. Or Lissa, for that matter. Whoever the hell you're looking for, I'm not her. How you can be so daft as to mix us up is beyond me, but I am not her, asshole. So, if you could just let me off this ship, we can go our separate ways."

She'd almost lost her resolve when she'd said *ship*, but she had managed to maintain her superior air at the last second. Thankfully. The way he was watching her, like if he told her to jump he fully expected her to comply, was really beginning to piss her off. She hated being told what to do.

"I must admit . . ." He settled more comfortably against the wall and crossed his arms over his chest. "The look in your eyes? Almost convincing. Of course, we both know you're being ridiculous. This is *me*. Not some easily manipulated Teller."

"Whoever this Olena person is, I really hope she's not your girlfriend, because if so, she really needs to reconsider her life choices."

"My *girlfriend*?" He made a face like he'd just eaten a lemon.

Wow, pretty insulting for this Olena chick, she noted. Until she realized that if he was that disgusted by *her*, and he thought *Delaney* was her . . .

New tactic.

"What happened to my arm?" She finally stopped rubbing at it and dropped her hand so he could see her unmarked flesh. No doubt he'd seen it already, but still.

"I healed it," he said, clearly thinking she was stupid for asking. "It wasn't deep. You were lucky. We were able to extract the poison before it could do permanent damage. You've only been out for three cycles."

"Wait," she held up a hand. "Three what now?"

"Cycles."

"What's a cycle?" She clenched her fists when he rolled his eyes.

"I'm serious! What the hell is a cycle?! How long have I been here?" Feeling the panic rising up once more, she dropped down onto the edge of the cot, careful to keep her feet far from his outstretched ones. "Mariana has to be freaking out," she said to herself. "She's probably called the police by now."

Unless, of course, she was still with Ottus.

Ruckus leaned forward, propping his arms on his knees. "They were going to kill you, Olena. The Tars are still upset about the arrangement. As soon as your parents and the Zane discovered they'd found you, they alerted my team and me."

When all she did was frown, he moved back. "I promised you space, Lissa—not that I'd let you get yourself killed by your stubbornness."

"Why does she have two names?" Delaney blurted, grasping on to the one part of the jumbled mess he'd just said that she could process. The rest of it was gibberish to her. "Is it like a nickname?" He'd said "your parents," so they weren't siblings. And they clearly weren't dating. "Are you two related?"

He looked at her like he had back in the alley, that mixture of confusion and surprise. Like he was seeing her for the first time.

"Okay, whatever, don't tell me," she sighed. "Look, I don't know much about aliens—Vakar," she corrected, not wanting to insult him while she was trying to bargain for her life. "And I most definitely don't know what a Tar is, but I do know that thing they shot me with hurt like hell. If they're after this Olena person, then she's still there. She's still in danger."

He continued to stare, and she fought the urge to stomp her foot like a child.

"Damn it, Ruckus—" She spun away and came face-to-face with the small rectangular mirror hanging over the sink. Only, it wasn't her face staring back at her. Her breath caught in her throat, and for a moment she completely forgot to breathe.

The girl staring back at her looked vaguely familiar. A dark-haired girl with milky skin. The same girl who'd bumped into her back at the club. Back in the dim lighting, Delaney hadn't been able to make out her eyes, but now, like with Ruckus, it was easy. Gold, with a rim of deep violet.

Delaney blinked, and the girl in the mirror did the same. Just to be sure, she lifted a hand and pressed her fingers against her cheek, almost painfully. Finally recalling that air was necessary, she gasped, the sudden intake making her feel light-headed and woozy. She stumbled back and dropped onto the cot, shaking her head.

"I think I'm having a panic attack," she admitted, though her voice came out breathy and weak, and she wasn't sure either of them could hear her. She wasn't sure she meant for them to. Her heart thumped wildly in her chest, to the point that it felt as if there were a vice gripping her tight. "Oh yeah, definitely a panic attack."

She'd never had one of those before; today was clearly a day of firsts.

She struggled to compose herself, keeping an eye trained between the two of them just in case. Now that she'd seen herself, she had a better understanding of why they were so adamant she was this Lissa person. But that didn't mean she trusted them.

A device in the pocket of the smaller one still by the open door beeped then. He pulled it out and then frowned over at Ruckus.

"Her vitals are spiking, Ander," he informed him, as if that weren't already completely obvious with the way she had practically curled into a ball.

"You're monitoring my vitals?" she asked, noting the hint of annoyance in her tone and grasping at it. Anger was easier to manage than fear, and right now she needed to be smart. In control. She narrowed her eyes at Ruckus, trying to see him in a different light. "So, you're a doctor?"

Was this Olena person sick, on top of being hunted by these Tars?

His whole body tensed, stilling to the point that she wasn't certain he was even breathing. Even from this distance, she could see his pupils dilating, felt the change of his emotions by the heaviness that entered the atmosphere. Whoever had come up with that saying about tension and a knife clearly hadn't met Ruckus.

You couldn't cut the tension in this room with a damn chainsaw.

"Look in the mirror again." His voice was steely, and the command was delivered low.

She shook her head. She wasn't ready to see that other face again just yet. If she did, she might *really* lose it, and then she'd be completely screwed. Pretty much the only thing she currently had going for her was the fact that she hadn't completely mentally checked out. What would they do to her if she did? If she wasn't conscious enough to defend herself because she was too busy weeping on the floor like an idiot?

A prospect that was seeming more likely as the seconds ticked by.

"Do it," he demanded. "Now."

"Um." She licked her lips and swallowed audibly. "Ruckus? That is your name, right? I just assumed because Ander is a title . . . Unless I got that part wrong, too?" For the first time, she wished she'd paid more attention to Mariana's alien obsession.

"I didn't mean to insult you, if you're not a doctor," she continued, opting to be truthful as a last attempt. "I'm just freaking out and—"

"Oh." The smaller one's voice shook and his eyes widened. "No."

"What does that mean?" Ruckus demanded. When he didn't immediately get a response, the muscles in his jaw visibly tightened. "Gibus."

"You aren't going to like it. . . ." He wrung his hands, but despite his words, there was a tiny bit of excitement behind his wide eyes.

"Answer me, Sutter." Before the smaller guy could, however, Ruckus swore and got to his feet so quickly that Delaney actually shot back.

Her skull rebounded off the wall, but he'd stopped paying attention to her already.

"The last time Olena was here," Ruckus declared, "she took something, didn't she?" The other man's face was answer enough. "What was it?"

"Ander—"

"What was it?"

She wanted to point out that he had a serious interrupting problem, but she smartly kept her mouth shut.

The smaller one, Gibus, dropped his gaze.

"It was the device you'd been working on, wasn't it?" Obviously, the question was rhetorical. "I told you to keep that thing safe! You call this"—he flung an arm out toward her—"safe?!"

Gibus suddenly found the slick white floor very interesting. He hung his head and kept his shoulders tense and squared. His silence spoke volumes.

"She got the damn thing to work," Ruckus said, then added another angry curse.

At least, Delaney assumed it was a curse; it sounded like one even though the word itself wasn't familiar.

"Someone gonna fill me in?" she asked, eyeing Ruckus warily. If he came at her, she was so going to knee him in the junk. She knew where that was, too, in the exact same place as a human male's. Another tidbit from Mariana.

"Who are you?" Gibus said breathlessly, maintaining his distance.

She felt a shred of hope, and dropped her guard a bit.

"Not Olena, that's for sure," she said smoothly.

"I was going to tell you. . . ." He glanced at Ruckus from the corner of his eye, and it was like watching a child interact with a teacher. "I'd hoped I'd merely misplaced it. I do that. Often. And even if she had taken it, I didn't think she'd be able to do"—he waved a hand at Delaney—"this. We're talking about *Olena*, after all. Technological genius, she is not, Ander. I didn't—"

"Dismissed," Ruckus growled. "You'll be dealt with accordingly later."

"What the hell is going on?" Delaney asked, moving to her feet. "Why do I look like someone else? You know what"—she held up a hand—"I don't even care. Now that we've established that you really do have the wrong person, can you reverse it and take me back already?"

Ruckus maintained eye contact, but Gibus looked away, clueing her in that something was wrong.

"What?" she said breathlessly, afraid to get an answer.

Gibus ran a hand through his scruffy chestnut hair. "The thing is—"

"You're *dismissed*," Ruckus told him before he could finish. When Gibus didn't move, Ruckus shot a death stare his way. "Leave—now. And do not report this to anyone except Pettus. Do you understand, Sutter?"

"Yes, Ander." He gave a curt nod.

"Good. Update Pettus and then send him here."

"Yes, Ander." Gibus turned away, and the door slid shut behind him.

She stared after him, feeling dread seep through her with every second that ticked by. She almost wanted to go after him. It seemed like he was willing to give her answers. Ruckus was a puzzle, and she really didn't like puzzles.

Finally she gave in and turned to look at him, finding his harsh gaze already on her. There were only three feet between them, but at least it didn't look like he was planning to bridge the gap.

"What's your name?" he asked, startling her with the gentleness there.

She tilted her head, preparing for a trap. "Delaney."

He nodded. "Delaney, I'm Ruckus."

"Got that much."

"Of course." He ran a hand through his hair. "My lolaura—" He stopped, took a breath. "Apologies for my mistake. If you knew what I do, you'd understand why it was so difficult for me to believe you."

"What do you know?" she inquired.

"The man you just met, Gibus, has made a terrible error in judgment. Olena, the real Olena, likes to hang around his workstation when she's on board. He'd shelved a project for our military some time ago, a device that could alter the appearance of someone. It was meant to be used to help my people in the war."

"But that's over now," she said, remembering something she'd absently caught on the news. "The Vakar and Kints are at peace. Right?"

He gritted his teeth but nodded nonetheless. "Yes, we are at peace. I ordered that project destroyed anyway, because if it fell into enemy hands, it would be catastrophic. Obviously, my order wasn't carried out."

"Go back." She was struggling to wrap her brain around this. "How would this device alter someone's appearance? I mean, how is that even possible?"

"By messing with the brain waves of a population with a specific gene. Gibus was unable to perfect the device, however. It alters the perspective of everyone, including those who've used the device, and had it used on them. This would have made it exceedingly difficult for us to trust what we saw. If the enemy realized what we were up to, for instance, all they had to do was switch out the double for the real person, and we would never know."

"I'm sorry." She rubbed at her temples. "I'm seriously slow right now."

"You still don't understand."

"No."

He tugged something out of his back pocket. It was a little larger than her iPhone, and square instead of rectangular. It looked more like a piece of glass, but when he tapped the center, it turned black. He pressed at it a few more times and then turned it around so she could see the screen.

A dark-haired girl smiled coyly at her from it.

"This is Lissa Olena," he said. "As the Ander, it is my job to ensure her safety."

"I walked into her," Delaney told him.

He actually looked sorry for her, putting the device back into his pocket. "She walked into you, more like."

"She did something to me." It wasn't a question, because that had already been established. Suddenly she was extremely tired. The warring emotions of panic and fear and anger had drained her.

"I imagine that's when she used the device to alter your appearance," he agreed, waving at her body.

"Oh shit." She slumped back down onto the cot, dropping her head into her hands. That explained so much, why he'd taken her, why he'd insisted that she was messing with him. Why those people had shot her.

"Why are the Tars after her again?" she asked.

"They don't agree with the peace treaty," he surprised her by answering. "They're a small rebellious group formed of Kints who disagree with their Rex's decision to end the war."

"Is a Rex like a president?"

"More like a king," he corrected. "We still operate as a monarchy of sorts."

"Okay, so Rex means king."

"Their king. Vakar and Kint, you would call them countries, with slightly differing languages. Our king, the Vakar king, is called a Basileus. Our queen is Basilissa. And our princess—"

"Is called Lissa." Delaney let out a slow breath and leaned back against the wall, drained. "I've been played by a goddamn alien princess." None of this made any sense. "Why?"

For a second it didn't seem like he was going to tell her, but he must have seen something on her face, because he gave in and came to sit next to her on the small cot. Settling, he angled his body so that his back was to the door and he could hold her gaze.

"The peace treaty between my people and the Kints was built

on an arranged marriage," he divulged. "Olena has been on Earth for the past five years, for her denzeration. It's a period in every Vakar's life when they come of age and are allowed to explore Earth. To get to know the planet, the primitive life-forms there, and decide if they'd like to stay as an analyst, or if they'd like to return to Xenith.

"Being our Lissa, Olena knew when she left that staying on Earth was never really an option for her, but she'd convinced her parents to allow her to take the right anyway. Last week marked the end of her denzeration, and she was supposed to meet me and come back home."

"Let me guess," she said, stopping him. "She never showed."

"No, she did not. Somehow the Tars discovered she was somewhere on Earth, unprotected, and sent assassins. I managed to track her to Portland. She clearly wanted me to find her so that she could lead me to you. She used you as a distraction, Delaney. I'm"—he hesitated—"sorry."

Despite everything going on, the corner of her mouth twitched. "Not something you say often, huh?"

"No," he admitted, smiling some himself. "If I had known she'd gotten her hands on Gibus's prototype, that it hadn't been destroyed like I'd ordered, I wouldn't have taken you the way that I did. I can tell this is all very frightening for you."

"I'm not frightened," she insisted, instantly switching from tired to defense mode.

"I don't blame you," he told her easily. "It's a scary situation. You said it yourself: You don't know much about my people." He cocked his head. "You aren't one of those humans who are fascinated by us."

She snorted. "Definitely not."

The door opened up at his back, and the other guy from the alley stepped inside. Closing the hatch behind him, he waited until Ruckus had turned on the cot so that he could easily look at them both.

"We have a problem, Ander." His voice was melodious, lighter than Ruckus's, and smooth. He glanced over at Delaney momentarily but didn't address her as Gibus had.

His long-sleeved green shirt was tucked into his pants, the zipper in the center done all the way up, closing the inch-wide collar around his neck. His hair was swiped back the same as the last time she'd seen him, held there by some sort of gel. It was a light brown, a match to his eyes, though when she looked closely, she could just make out the ring of dark blue around the outside of the otherwise tan irises.

"Pettus, you spoke to Gibus?" Ruckus asked.

"Yes—"

"How close are we to Xenith?"

"We've got an estimated three ticks till we breech the atmosphere. But"—his eyes trailed over to Delaney for a split second—"that isn't the problem I was referring to, Ander."

Suddenly a red light began flashing on the ceiling, and a loud beeping noise sounded.

Ruckus swore again, but Pettus was already continuing.

"It's the Zane, Ander." He paused and glanced between them. "He's here."

CHAPTER 4

Who's the Zane?" Delaney frowned, not liking the way they were looking at each other. Like something terrible was about to happen—something even more terrible than taking the wrong person from another planet.

"They're about to board," Ruckus said, ignoring her, his attention on Pettus. "We're out of options. She's going to need to convince him."

Pettus nodded, clearly understanding, and Ruckus moved over to the door, pressing a palm flat against a panel on the wall. Static crackled through it for a second, and then Gibus's voice filtered into the room.

"Bring me a hebi," Ruckus ordered.

Pettus stepped up to her. "Here's the thing: You look like Olena. Exactly like her. And, well, we sort of need you . . ." He waved both hands in air as if juggling invisible balls.

She tilted her head at him, scrunching up her face in the process. What was he going on about? Why the hell couldn't any of them just speak plainly?

"You need to pretend to be Olena," he stated.

She couldn't help it—she snorted. "Yeah, right."

"Right," he maintained. "We took you thinking that you were the Lissa, and we've just been informed that the Kints found out why her return home was delayed."

"You mean they found out she didn't want to be married off like cattle?" It was the only reason she could think of for anyone being desperate enough to do *this* to someone else. Not that that justified it. At all.

His eyes narrowed, but he continued. "They aren't happy. They don't believe that Olena really wants peace. Their Zane is boarding as we speak. If he discovers that Olena eluded us, that she went to such great lengths in order to do so, he'll reinstate the war." He paused, locking his odd-colored eyes on hers and holding them until he knew he had her complete attention. "They'll kill us, Delaney."

"Kill us . . . dead?"

"Pretty sure there's no other version of *kill*, even on Earth," he said dryly.

"But it's not my fault, or yours for that matter. It's Olena's."

"They're our enemies. They don't care. They're itching for a reason to go back to war. The Kints don't just want this planet; they want Earth as well, and my people and this treaty are the only things keeping them from enslaving yours."

The red light above them changed colors, flashing orange now. Pettus swore, using the same word as Ruckus had before, and opened his mouth to say something else when suddenly Gibus was at the door.

He handed a small square box over to Ruckus.

"Go," Ruckus ordered them. "Delay him."

They left without another word, and he twisted the top off of the small box Gibus had given him. Inside, there was an item that reminded Delaney of a circular bandage.

"I need you to do this," he told her, attention still on the small circle.

"I don't." She shook her head.

His eyes shot to hers, full of frustration. "They *want* to kill us, Delaney. They just need an excuse."

He moved toward her, motioning for her to angle her head. When she didn't immediately do so, he sighed again and held the circle up before her. "We call this a hebi. It's a translating device that's embedded into the side of the neck. We've been speaking English; the Kint will not do so."

"Sounds like I'd only need that if I planned on speaking to them then," she countered, "which I do not."

"Do you want to die?" he asked. "You do this, maybe we live. You don't, we definitely die. Choose."

"*Maybe?*" she repeated.

"You've done a good job of hiding your fear so far. Draw on that."

If the peace treaty between the aliens was broken, then the treaty between them and Earth would be as well. She knew Pettus was right about the Kints wanting her planet. And Ruckus was huge; she'd never seen anyone as strong or as tough looking as him. If he was worried . . . maybe she should be, too.

"Just this once, right?" Her voice was a bit weak, and she strengthened it. "I pretend to be her and get us out of this, then you guys tell your Basileus, or whatever, the truth and take me home."

"Yes." He made to lift the hebi closer, but she held up her hand.

"Promise." She didn't know if aliens made promises, or if they knew what they were, but desperate times and all that.

"I give you my word, Delaney. I'm the one who wrongly took you; I will return you to your rightful place."

She allowed herself one last deep breath and then straightened, coming to her full five-six height. She didn't have to say anything aloud, because he noted her silent agreement.

"So I'll be able to understand the Kints with this?" she asked, tilting her head to the left to give him better access.

"And Vakar," he confirmed. "It attaches to the brain and will allow you to instinctually speak our languages as well. It translates and deciphers so that words in our language that are similar to yours will be translated accordingly."

"To my brain?" Her nerves spiked up another notch.

"I'm not a Sutter," he stated, busy placing the hebi. "I don't know all the logistics."

"I'll speak a different language without knowing I'm doing it?" That seemed like a question he could answer.

"It calibrates to whatever language is first spoken to you. For example, if I spoke to you in Vakar, your reply would automatically come out as Vakar."

"Kind of takes away having to actually learn, huh?"

The hebi was practically see-through, and at first, when he placed it on her neck, it felt sticky. Then her skin tightened around the area, and a cooling sensation followed. Ruckus stepped back, and when Delaney touched the right side of her neck, she couldn't feel anything.

"It disappears into the skin," he informed her, already turning away. "Ensures it can't be removed accidentally or otherwise."

Guess that meant she was never taking it off, either.

"Wait," she said, stopping him just as he was about to open the door. "What's a Zane? Who is he?"

Amazingly, Ruckus actually looked a little guilty when he said, "He's their prince."

The door was open, exposing them to the long hallway before she could respond, which was probably a good thing, because the tightness that'd been in her chest turned to lead in her stomach.

Their prince.

Olena's betrothed, the one she didn't want to marry and the one who knew it.

Shit. Shit. Shit.

You can do this! she told herself as Ruckus motioned with a curve of his chin for her to follow him. She stepped out into the hallway, leaving the room for the first time and suddenly wishing she didn't have to. It was safe in that room, safer than out here, anyway, and she wanted desperately to turn around. She didn't, fighting against her flight instinct and focusing on the one that would get her out of this hellish situation.

Fight.

"Have they met before?" she asked him quietly, afraid someone might be ahead of them and overhear. Right now it was just the two of them in the long, winding white hallway, but she didn't know where they were going. As soon as they'd taken a few turns, she also didn't know the way back.

"A few times," he answered out of the corner of his mouth. "Don't be too nice, but don't be rude, either. Remember, all of our lives depend on you."

"They don't know about the device, right? The one that did this to me?"

He shook his head.

Well, that was something, at least. Even if she was a little odd during this meeting, there was no way the Zane could jump to the conclusion she was someone else posing as the Lissa. Only a crazy person would think of that.

They heard voices up ahead, and turned a corner, entering a large square room. It was the center of a crossway, halls branching off in all four directions. The group before her had obviously just come from the corridor directly across from them. When they came to the entryways, both parties halted.

Pettus was off to the side, with three men behind him. They all had stoic expressions and wore similar outfits to his, only in blue. They were tall, fit, but lacked the commanding air that Ruckus had in spades.

The man who'd clearly been leading the party toward them, however, didn't have the same problem as his men. He demanded attention, respect, instantly. It was clear in the way he held himself, the way he took up space and seemed to suck up all the oxygen in the room. His hair was light blond, more sunflower than honey. His uniform was different, the collar of his formfitting shirt an inch taller than the rest, the sleeves stopping at his elbows instead of covering his whole arm.

He was as tall as Ruckus, but his legs seemed longer somehow, and his eyes were cornflower blue rimmed in a deep crimson. They were a mixture of beautiful and creepy, especially with the burning way he had them currently set upon her.

She couldn't call him more attractive than Ruckus, just attractive in a different sort of way. There was no doubt in her mind that he was the Zane.

"I told them you were on your way, Ander Ruckus," Pettus was explaining the whole time she and the Zane stared at each other. "Zane Trystan couldn't wait."

"I think I've waited long enough," the Zane spoke, his voice cutting across the room like a blade. "Don't you agree, Lissa Olena?"

Her confidence had been waning since the moment she'd spotted him. He didn't appear to be the type of man who was easily manipulated. And he definitely looked like the type to kill the person attempting the manipulation.

"I apologize for my delay," she said; it was the first thing that had come to mind. "I was unforgivably detained."

"Unforgivably?" He took a step toward her and, if he noticed Ruckus tensing at her side like she did, he ignored it. "Indeed. What was it that detained you, Lissa, if you don't mind my asking?"

She wasn't one to be easily fooled, either. He wasn't asking.

"As I'm sure you're aware," she said, taking a risk, "Earth has many strange oddities to offer. I merely got caught up exploring the culture. There's a festival—it happens only once a year, in Maine—called the Summer Welcoming. It takes place in Seabrook, a very small town, and I'm afraid my curiosity got the best of me."

Silently, she prayed that he believed her, while simultaneously thanking her mini hometown for having at least one thing notable about it. It also happened to take place in May—last week, even. Her parents had been very upset with her for not coming home to celebrate it.

"Hmm." His eyes inspected her more closely. "Rumor has it your delay is due to other factors."

"Other factors?" she said, faking confusion. "What other factors could there be?" At his pointed look, she feigned indignation. "Are you implying that I intended to go back on my vow? I know my duty, Zane Trystan, same as you."

For a moment she feared he didn't believe her, that she'd stepped over a line or given some hint that she wasn't really who she said she was, but then he pulled his arms behind his back, his cold stance gentling some.

"Ander Ruckus, you and your men are free to leave us for a moment."

Her heart slammed into her chest, and it took everything in her not to show it. Her fingers twitched at her side, wanting to reach out and grab on to Ruckus before he could leave her alone. He might be an alien and a kidnapper, but at least she knew he'd listen to her. And frankly, she didn't trust the Zane. There was something about him, something dark that she couldn't quite place but knew well enough to avoid.

"With all due respect, Zane," Ruckus stated, clearly struggling himself, "Lissa Olena has had a long journey, and I'm under strict orders to return her to the castle. Already our arrival has been delayed due to your boarding."

"Surely she's not too exhausted to share a moment with her betrothed?" The Zane eyed her challengingly.

She rose to the occasion.

"It's fine, Ander." She never took her eyes from the Zane's stare. "I'm perfectly safe in the company of the Zane. Aren't I, Zane?" Game. Set. Match.

"Of course, Lissa." His lips twitched into a smirk, and his blue-and-crimson eyes glittered with humor. Turning, he extended an arm to her.

She forced herself to boldly step forward and take it. His arm was every bit as steel-like as Ruckus's were. She allowed the

Zane to angle her toward the hallway to his right as they began walking.

"My men will keep you company," the Zane called over his shoulder to Ruckus, before they turned a corner and went out of sight.

Taking even breaths, she glanced around their surroundings, having been rushed down the previous hallway with Ruckus. There really wasn't anything special about them, just pale white walls with doors scattered here and there and pipes lining the tops. Bright lights were set on the sides of both the floor and the ceiling.

"We talked about your silence last time we met, Olena," he told her suddenly in an even voice, "and how much I dislike it."

"Did we?" she asked, cocking a brow at him. "I don't recall."

"Don't you?" His tone was as hard as his arm and the metal all around them.

It was risky, but she was certain he'd found her return of his challenge back there amusing. If she could hold on to that amusement, at least long enough for them to dock the ship and her to exit safely, she might actually be able to pull this off.

She allowed her mouth to twitch and she dropped her gaze, saying volumes with the move.

"Ah," he said, "so you do remember."

"I doubt conversations had with you are easily forgotten," she told him.

"I know what you're doing." He'd led them down a labyrinth of hallways and then stopped, turning so that they were facing each other. "We were matched, Olena. How do you think it looks that my betrothed would rather stay on a primitive planet than return home to me?"

She bristled, noting the slight twinge in his voice when he'd mentioned their engagement. Going out on a limb, she dropped her arm from his and tilted up her chin defiantly.

"Let's not play games," she said. "Neither one of us wanted this. But that doesn't mean either of us would go back on our parents' word. We don't want to restart the war, do we?"

That glint returned, chasing away the anger that had threatened to spill into his eyes. "No, of course not."

"Exactly. I stayed away for the reason I gave."

"For a human celebration."

"Yes."

"I don't believe you." Before she could argue, he took a large step forward, forcing her back against the wall.

What was with aliens and crowding her?!

"You were honest about one thing, however," he told her, dipping his head low enough to keep the two of them at eye level. "I don't want to bind to you any more than you want to bind to me. You are a child, Olena, always have been, and while I see Earth has done you some good, given you at least a slightly more witty tongue, I doubt it's done enough to erase all of your many shortcomings."

He took another step closer. He'd kill her if he got the chance; that was so clear now that she wondered how he'd managed to mask it from everyone well enough for them to think betrothing him to Olena was a good idea. No wonder the girl had run.

"If I wasn't clear before, so long as the Rex is alive, I will follow through with his orders. I will bind my life to yours, but I won't enjoy it, and unless you do exactly as you're told, you won't, either."

He flicked at her navy T-shirt then, sneering. "Did you wear this as a peace offering, Olena? What a weak attempt to get me to believe your story. A festival? We both know you tried to run." He slammed both palms against the wall at either side of her head with enough force that she bounced against it. "You can't run from me, Lissa."

"Zane Trystan, Lissa Olena." Ruckus had appeared at the end of the hallway. He did not look happy, but he didn't attempt to approach them. "We've landed, and the Basileus is requesting his daughter's presence."

"Of course." Trystan smiled a wolfish grin and pulled back, straightening his shirt. He gave Delaney one last once-over, clearly not liking what he saw, and then stepped away. "I'm sure you can take her from here, Ander."

Ruckus didn't respond, and it didn't seem like the Zane really expected him to, because he kept on his way without a backward glance.

The second the sounds of his retreating footsteps were no longer audible, Delaney let out the breath she'd been holding and slid down the wall to the floor.

"Are you all right?" Ruckus was kneeling in front of her in a matter of seconds.

"He's"—she inhaled—"intense."

"That's one way of putting it," he growled. "Another would be saying he's an asshole."

Seeing that the subject disturbed her, he stood, holding down a hand for her to take. Once he had her back on her feet, he didn't let go, instead tightening his grip to keep her from pulling away.

With a frown, she met his gaze.

"We just need to meet with the Basileus, and then I'll be able to take you home," he promised. "All this will seem like a really bad dream in no time."

"Yeah?" She tried to focus on his words and not how comforting it was to have his hand holding hers. "That'd be good."

RUCKUS AND PETTUS led Delaney off the ship and down a long hallway that attached to the castle. They moved quickly, giving her only enough time to catch glimpses of the place as they wound their way through the vast halls.

The smell was strange, foreign, a bit like mothballs and evergreen, and she trailed after Ruckus quietly, checking out the guards they passed from the corners of her eyes. And they passed many.

At each entry and exit point, there were always at least two guards. They stood tall, shoulders back, sort of like the ones she'd seen guarding the queen of England in all the pictures. Except they didn't have poofy hats, and she found she sort of wished they did. It would certainly ease some of the tension.

Their uniforms were similar to Ruckus's in that they wore charcoal military pants tucked into boots. The buttoned-up jackets were different, however, skintight and the color of moss, with heavy gold accents strewn about. She'd expected to see more of the silver weapon Pettus had used back in the alley against the Tars, but if they had any weapons on them, they were well hidden.

Everyone dropped their chins to their chests in a bow when she passed, but the move was mechanical, like toy soldiers, and it creeped her out.

They finally stopped at a set of tall golden doors, and Ruckus reached for the handle.

"Wait here," he told her and Pettus, opening it just enough for him to slip through without exposing the inside of the room.

"He needs to brief them," Pettus explained quietly. "It's best that he does that alone first."

Right, because it was doubtful they'd react well to the news a human had been brought in their daughter's stead.

Delaney kept silent, partly because she was unable to think of anything to say, and partly because she was afraid that if she did, she'd lose it. The more details she paid attention to in this castle, the more it sunk in that she was no longer on Earth. The walls were a material that'd been made to appear like wood but wasn't. She could see the metallic sheen of it from where she stood, a few feet away.

Everything was done in earthy and metallic tones; even the lighting had a gold sheen to it.

The sudden opening of the door had her jumping, and she bit her bottom lip in embarrassment when she was met with Ruckus. His facial expression was tight, and he merely nodded at her and angled his head over his shoulder.

Taking a deep breath, she braced herself and then stepped beneath the archway.

The room was an office, with a fireplace to the right of the double doors and a small, round black table to the far right, big enough to seat five. At the center, positioned between two large bay windows that overlooked the sprawling yard, was a desk three times the size of any she'd seen before. Her gaze immediately landed on a tall man seated behind it; he had the same inky hair as Olena. A woman stood closely by his side, hands clasped before her.

There were no computers that she was used to, but a glass screen sat propped at an angle in front of where the man was sitting. She couldn't make out what he was watching, and there was no sound, but movement on the other side of the glass clued her in that it was a video of sorts.

Ruckus came up to her then, lightly touching her elbow as he held his other hand out toward the pair. "May I introduce the Basileus Magnus Ond, and the Basilissa Tilda Ond."

Delaney wasn't sure what to do, so she tried a bow, grateful for Ruckus's steadying grip on her arm when she almost wobbled. She wasn't sure how much longer she could stand there, pretending everything was fine, and hoped this conversation would end quickly.

She hoped they'd put her directly on a ship headed back home.

"Ander Ruckus tells us your name is Delaney." The Basileus's voice was sharp, though she got the feeling he was attempting—poorly—not to intimidate her.

"Delaney Grace, sir." Was it appropriate to call him sir? He didn't correct her.

Both he and the Basilissa took a moment to openly inspect her. There wasn't much to look at, of course, seeing as how she appeared exactly as their daughter did on the outside, but she held still and waited for them to finish.

"The Sutter did this?" The Basilissa, Tilda, pursed her lips in either disgust or confusion. Delaney couldn't tell which.

"It was his device," Ruckus said carefully, "but it was stolen by the Lissa, who used it without Sutter Gibus's knowledge."

"And Trystan doesn't seem to know?"

"If he did," the Basileus said with a grunt, "he would have declared war by now. No, she must have fooled him."

His stare was making her even more uncomfortable, and Delaney barely resisted the urge to clear her throat pointedly. Instead she held her head high and tried to make her voice as calm and respectful as possible.

"I'd just like to go home," she told them.

"This is not an ideal situation," the Basileus said then, "and I assure you we will be taking steps to right the wrong my daughter has done us all. However"—he folded his hands across the surface of his desk slowly—"it has also come to my attention that we have no real knowledge of where she is. As you know, Earth is a big planet. Therefore—"

She felt the blood draining from her face before he'd even finished his sentence.

"We simply cannot allow you to leave."

CHAPTER 5

With all due respect, we can't ask this of her," Ruckus said. He was deep in conversation with the Basileus and Basilissa, but Delaney barely registered anything they were saying.

She'd zoned out the second it'd been stated they weren't going to let her go home. Suddenly it was too hot in the room, despite its size and the open windows across from her that showed an almost pitch-black sky. At least she couldn't see any alien terrain through them; right now she didn't think she could handle that.

Mariana had to have realized by now that Delaney wasn't at home. She would have texted her as soon as she'd gotten to Ottus's house and expected a reply. They did that. Let each other know that they'd gotten to their destinations safely. It was nice, considering that Delaney had grown up in a large home with absentee parents.

Just like Olena's parents, they had no idea where their daughter currently was. The thought made her laugh, the sound strained even to her own ears.

Fingers tightened at her elbow and she glanced up, blinking to find them all staring at her. Ruckus was frowning, and there may have even been a dash of general concern, but the Basileus drew everyone's attention away before she could be certain.

"You understand the stakes," he asked curtly, "don't you, Delaney Grace? You've been told what will happen to your people should the Kints declare war on the Vakar, correct? If so, you understand why this decision has to be made. Neither one of us can risk the Zane discovering my daughter is still on Earth. Until we find her, you're our best chance at eluding him."

"If there were another option," Tilda said then, "believe that we would take it."

"Yes," Magnus agreed. "We know what we're asking of you is difficult to accept. But it is the only way, for now, to ensure the safety of everyone. Surely, put plainly, you agree, don't you, Ander?"

Ruckus wouldn't meet her gaze, but Delaney didn't need him to. She'd already caught the same glimmer in the Basileus's eyes that she had in Trystan's. He wasn't asking. He was telling.

She didn't really have a choice.

"This is a lot to take in," Tilda said. "Ander, please escort her to her rooms."

"We can discuss this further in the morning," Magnus added.

When they looked to her a final time, she nodded mutely, and from there Ruckus moved her out of the room rather quickly. She paid even less attention to her surroundings this time, not even noting the guards they passed or that the color of the walls had changed to light green until they were stopped at yet another door.

He pushed it open and then placed a hand at her back, easing her gently inside with more care than she would have expected. She was still too dazed to put up a fight, and entered without argument.

It was a bedroom with a king-sized bed set against the center of the right wall.

The room was shaped like an octagon, with each other side smaller than the one before it. The longer walls were about fifteen feet across, the shorter sides half that. Each of the four smaller walls had a door set in it, all closed.

Even still, the door on the far left obviously let out onto a balcony, because she could see it from the window that made up the entire wall directly across from the bed, floor to ceiling. The glass was sparkling and so clean, it was practically invisible. Outside, a deck painted white, like the walls inside, stretched out with a railing that would come up just beneath her chest. There was a patio set out there, a small circular glass table with only two metal chairs, also white. They were pristine; this whole place was pristine.

As if someone hadn't lived in it in quite a while.

How long had Ruckus said Olena had been gone? Five years?

She dropped her gaze to the carpet, running her foot over it. She was still wearing her Converse, and their neon-yellow color was a sharp contrast to the forest green beneath her. White walls with green molding, green bed frame, green vanity against the large far wall . . . She was sensing a theme here.

"How long?" She moved farther into the room and then turned to face Ruckus.

He'd come in behind her and shut the door, but was now running a hand through his dark hair and staring out the window.

"Presumably until Olena is found," he told her.

"I can't stay here," she snapped, the words coming out slightly hysterical.

"Lower your voice," he ordered, yellow-green eyes hardening

slightly. Easing forward, he approached as if she were a wounded animal he didn't want to spook. Once he was only a foot away, he halted, giving her a moment to adjust to his presence before speaking.

"I will get you home, Delaney," he told her softly. "I promised, and I meant it. It's just . . . I can't do it as soon as we'd hoped."

She was trapped here, and the only way out was by playing along. By pretending to be a person she knew nothing about, in a world she knew nothing about. Why was this happening?

He began leading her toward the bed, but she yanked herself free.

"I'm not a child," she spat, "and I don't need to sit down. You're going to hold me prisoner; just man up already and admit it. That's what this is." She took a shaky breath. "Tell me the truth, Ruckus. I know you have to find Olena. All right. Fine. But how long is that going to take? When can I go home?"

He opened his mouth, shut it again. Running his large hands through his hair, he knocked more dark strands loose so that he had to sweep them to the right instead of back in order to keep his hair out of his face. In this lighting, the green rim around his eyes forced the yellow to glow like shimmery coins at the bottom of a clear lake.

"I don't know," he admitted.

"Oh." It was all she could manage. She swallowed and glanced at the bed at his back. "I know I said I didn't need to sit, but . . ."

He moved to her, quickly helping her across the room and to the edge of the bed. Once she was on it, he stared down at her.

"Now I know you're in shock," he teased lightly, dipping his head so that she was forced to look at him instead of her lap like she had been. "You didn't put up a fight just now."

Realizing he was referencing helping her to the bed, she grunted and rolled her eyes for good measure. The corner of her mouth turned up, and she found even with everything going on, her smile was real.

"I don't really like getting help," she told him with a single shoulder shrug. "It's a personality flaw of mine."

"Yes," he agreed. "Along with stubbornness, and a poor temper."

"Jeez," she drawled, "tell me how you really feel, why don't you?"

It was meant as a joke, but he took it seriously, the easy playfulness dropping away as quickly as it'd come. He stiffened, suddenly seeming like a tree in front of her.

"I feel like what I did to you is unforgivable," he said.

He smelled like firewood, the kind that had been lit for a good while. Immediately she pictured the dying days of summer, those chilly nights when fall began to rear its head, and sweaters and bonfires abounded.

When their current positions started to make her uncomfortable, she bolted to her feet so fast, Ruckus needed to backtrack a few steps to avoid her slamming into him. She was already turning away, though, pacing the room, her hands on her hips.

"What do they want me to do?" she asked, barreling on when his eyes widened. "Whatever it is, I'll do it, but then I get to go home, right?"

He nodded.

"You're telling me the truth, aren't you?"

"Yes, Delaney." He gave her a comforting half smile. "You're very brave . . ."

"For a human," she filled in the blank he'd left open.

The corner of his mouth twitched. "Yes. There's that."

"Okay." She waved at him. "Tell me what it is I'm supposed to do."

"Simple," he said, his tone hinting that what he was about to say was anything but. "Convince the world that you are Lissa Olena."

She paused. "Oh, is that all?"

"Particularly"—he clenched his fists at his sides so hard, his knuckles turned bone white—"Zane Trystan."

"He's still here?" she said breathlessly. For some reason she'd thought he'd gone. He'd gotten what he wanted, hadn't he? Meeting her on the ship. He'd seen with his own eyes that they had Olena. Unless . . .

"Did he suspect something?"

"I don't think so," he assured her.

"Then what's he still doing here?"

"Apparently his father, Rex Hortan End—"

"His dad's name is Hortan?" she interrupted.

"Yes." He angled his head. "Why?"

"Nothing." She licked her lips. "It's just a stupid name, that's all. Not very intimidating, if you know what I mean."

"No, I do not know what you mean, because I've actually met him." He was in front of her again in half a second. "Promise me you won't underestimate him. That you'll avoid him. He isn't here, and there's no reason for him to come for a visit. Don't mention his name to anyone, and hopefully he won't find a reason to come."

She was on board with that plan. The less alien royalty she had to deal with, the better. She'd already hit her limit with Trystan; the last thing she wanted to do was meet the man who'd raised *that*.

Seeing that she understood, he stepped back.

"You feel responsible for me," she said, just coming to the conclusion herself, "don't you?"

"I have a responsibility as the man who took you to ensure your safe return," he replied.

"So I'm a responsibility." She nodded to herself and then continued before he could misunderstand her meaning. "That's good. Soldiers take their responsibilities very seriously. At least, the ones back on Earth do." This time it was a question, and one she let linger in her eyes when she set them on him.

"I'm an Ander, Delaney," he told her in a steady voice. "That's a commander. And more than that, I'm the Ander put in charge of Lissa Olena. I've been the Ander in charge of her since before she left for Earth."

All she wanted to do right now was curl up into a ball and have a complete meltdown, but where would that get her? Certainly not back home. So, she'd suck it up, try to do what she was told, and hopefully be out of here in . . .

"They can't keep me here forever; that's hardly a solution. And I doubt they've got enough confidence in me, a stranger, to be under the assumption I'll be able to pull this off for long."

"The Basileus has ordered another search team back to Earth. Fortunately, the device was a prototype, and therefore only works once. She used it up on you, so there won't be any more decoys for her to hide behind. They'll find her, discreetly, and bring her back. Once they do, you'll be free to go home."

"And what about"—she waved a hand in front of her face— "this? I really don't want to spend the rest of my life looking like her royal bitchness." Not to mention the fact that the thought of looking into a mirror again still made her queasy.

"Gibus is working on that now. He's confident he'll have a solution within a week."

Okay, so that wasn't too bad. They could find the real Olena in a week, couldn't they? It's not like there were many places for her to hide.

Only an entire damn planet.

"Delaney?" Ruckus rested a hand on her arm to steady her. "You've gone pale. What were you just thinking?"

"How long do you think it'll take for them to find her?" she demanded. "You said it took you a week? And you actually know her. How are they supposed to find her, Ruckus? And if you're the best, why aren't you going with them?"

"My leaving would be suspicious," he admitted. "I told you. I've been with the Lissa for many years. There is no good enough lie to tell that would convince the Zane that I needed to return to Earth when you're already here."

"Yeah, that's the thing." She stabbed her finger at the center of her chest. "*I'm* here."

"He doesn't know that, Delaney." His expression hardened. "And he's not going to. You understand what that would mean, don't you? If he were to find out? It wouldn't just mean war for my race, but yours as well. The Kints won't stop until they've got earthlings on their knees. Right now the Vakar are the only thing standing between you and slavery. Playing along benefits your kind just as much as it does mine."

"So," she said, and took a deep breath, "I can either be a slave now, or a slave later?"

"Try not to look at it that way."

"How would you look at it?" she asked. "If it were you in my shoes?"

"If it were me," he confessed. "I would have broken down by now." Smirking, he angled his head toward the window wall. "Or at the very least, have broken something."

"Hulk smash." She eyed his arms pointedly. "Makes sense."

"I'm afraid I don't get that reference."

"Probably for the best." She rubbed her face, drained.

"You're tired," he concluded, stepping back. "I don't have to remind you to be respectful tomorrow, do I?"

"That goes without saying," she said, and snorted. "It's not every day a lowly human such as I gets to meet with royalty."

"And tone down the misplaced humor." He paused, cocked his head. "On second thought, leave the humor altogether. The last thing we want is to annoy them. They're already upset enough as it is by their daughter's actions."

"I get the feeling you're implying you find me annoying, Ruckus." She eyed the bed and then sighed, resigned to agree with him on that much at least. She was exhausted, and sleep sounded really good right about now. It would give her a reprieve from all the crazy that had exploded into her life.

"For all you know," he said coyly, "annoying means something different on this planet."

"I doubt it." She smiled and shook her head at him, then glanced at the large bed yet again. She could probably sleep comfortably on that thing with nine other people. The silky green-and-white sheets looked like heaven, and she wanted desperately to get lost in them.

"Right," he said, moving toward the door. "I've placed Pettus on your protection detail for the night. He's right outside. If you need anything, ask him. Aside from the Basileus and Basilissa, he, Gibus, and I are the only ones who know about your identity, Delaney. It's imperative that we keep it that way."

"Where will you be?" She hated herself the moment she asked it, but she kept a straight face, hoping he wouldn't get the wrong idea.

"I still have to be briefed." He rubbed at the back of his neck, exposing for the first time that he was just as tired as she. "It could take a while. After that, my quarters are just down the hall."

Obviously, her poker face was better than she thought, because it became apparent he'd misinterpreted her reason for asking when he turned back to face her.

"I know this must be daunting, and that it can't be easy letting your guard down in a strange place but"—he held her gaze as if hoping she'd see the truth of it in his eyes—"you are safe here, Delaney. I won't let anything happen to you."

"Anything else," she said before she could stop herself, "you mean."

He flinched, nodded once, and then reached for the shiny silver door handle.

Alone, again, she decided to finally check out the bathroom. She didn't look at much, just went straight to what she thought was the sink. There weren't any knobs; instead there were large white buttons the size of her palm. When she tapped the one on the left with a red square painted in the center, a panel opened up before her, exposing an oval basin.

The countertops were made of a polished white stone that shone under the bright overhead light. When she tipped her head back, it was to find that, like in the bedroom, the ceiling here was a skylight. A thousand tiny winks of light flickered above.

Hot water had spilled into the basin, filling it halfway up, and after she hit the button to the right with blue, cold water poured to fill it the rest of the way. It resulted in the perfect temperature, and she dipped her hands in it and splashed warm water on her face—which she refused to meet in the mirror. Her eyes were starting to itch, and she knew she was about to cry.

Twisting, she quickly searched out the toilet, finding another button, this one a square, on the opposite wall of the sink. On it there was a silver rectangle. Clicking that, she let out a sigh of relief when another compartment on the wall, almost as big as she was, opened up and a toilet slid out toward her.

It looked almost exactly the same as the ones she was used to, only there was no back, and the flushing mechanism was down by her right foot.

Her business concluded, she washed her hands one last time, taking a moment to sniff the odd-smelling soap that'd been left out in a silver dish. It was sort of a mix of cotton candy and Red Hots.

She didn't bother with the closet, instead yanking the thick covers back on the bed and crawling in, fully clothed. Slumping back in the center of the large bed, she curled up and then risked a look upward at the night sky. A star rocketed across the inky black.

One definite good thing about having such a large bed: There were more than enough blankets and pillows to help muffle her sobs.

CHAPTER 6

Despite her exhaustion, there was no hope of her sleeping. Once her tears were spent, she drifted in and out for about an hour before finally giving into her frustration. Tossing the thick comforter off, she stood, mind already racing.

There might not be a way out of this that she could see, but that didn't mean she needed to wait in here by herself until someone told her what to do next. She'd been in charge of her own fate for so long, the last thing she was willing to do was allow someone else complete control over it. Which meant figuring this place out, and soon.

She wanted to be prepared for anything the Basileus and Basilissa threw at her, especially considering they were the ones who decided when, and whether, she could go home. Ever since waking up on the ship, she'd been in a floating state, allowing Ruckus to lead her where he may, but now that her nerves had—for the most part—settled, adrenaline coursed through her anew.

She'd never been one to sit on her hands.

Delaney glanced over at the door and took a deep breath. There were only two things standing in her immediate way: it and Pettus, whom Ruckus had left behind as a watchdog. She thought over her next course of action carefully before proceeding, moving across the room and twisting open the door quickly before she could think better of it.

Currently, her fear of the unknown vastly outweighed the fear of getting caught, and that was what drove her onward.

Pettus turned to her with a start the second she had the door open. He glanced over her shoulder as if afraid he'd find someone else in there, but then his brow furrowed into a deep frown and he turned to fully face her.

"Is everything all right?" he asked in a soft voice. There was a look in his eyes that sparked the already lit ember within her.

"I just can't sleep," she told him.

That look solidified, a mixture of kindness and pity. It was the latter that she latched on to. As far as she was concerned, he was almost every bit as much to blame for her being in this situation as Ruckus was.

"It's a lot to take in, I'm sure," he agreed, nodding as if there were any chance he could actually know what it was she was going through. "Do you need anything? Something to help you sleep, perhaps?"

Like a drug? She barely repressed a shiver. Pass.

"Pretty sure I've been out long enough, thanks." She saw him flinch at her reminder that she'd been unconscious on their ship. A tiny part of her felt bad for the jab, but only a tiny part. Stepping back, she made a gesture to indicate he should come in. She hadn't even thought to ask Ruckus any questions on Olena when he'd been there earlier, but now a million of them were circling her mind like rabid wolves. She needed answers or she'd go crazy.

He hesitated, however, searching the darkness at her back a second time, though now with a different sort of suspicion on his face.

"It's not a trap," she said with a snort. The idea that she could take on someone like him, a trained alien soldier, was laughable.

He must have realized the idiocy of it himself, for he cracked a sheepish smile and stepped in without further prompting. Pettus kept going until he was at the center of the room before the large window. True to his position as guard, he kept her in his line of sight the entire time, subtly watching her out of the corner of his eye while she shut the door.

She stopped about ten feet away, crossing her arms over her chest and propping a hip against the wall in a nonchalant move she'd perfected when she was thirteen and constantly annoying her father—on purpose.

"What is it you wished to speak about, Delaney?" Now that they were safely within the confines of the massive bedroom, it was apparently all right to call her by name.

"Can you tell me about her?" she asked. "Olena?"

His mouth twisted in displeasure, and he glanced back out the window.

"That part I already got," she stated dryly, and when he glanced back at her with another frown in place, she elaborated. "People don't like her very much."

"No," he agreed, "they don't."

"Why not?" she persisted. "If I'm going to pretend to be her, I should probably know a little more about her, don't you think?"

"Ruckus—"

"Isn't here," she cut him off. "So I'm asking you. Please."

She felt a little bad pressuring him into it, surprisingly. They may have even been friends under different circumstances. Met at the club, hung out. He didn't have the same magnetism that Ruckus did, which was actually a good thing, because it meant that she could think clearly in his presence, but he didn't instill in her wariness like Trystan did, either.

"She's extremely self-centered," he conceded on a massive sigh, "as I'm sure you've also gathered."

Oh yeah.

"I've never really seen her interested in much of anything. Except for parties—she loves those. And big, flashy events." He canted his head, gaze sharpening to search for her reaction to his next words. "That's why we were certain we'd find her at the club."

She lifted a challenging brow. "And here I thought you had aliens there spying for you."

He chuckled. "You're smarter than you look, Delaney Grace."

"Well, I look like Olena so . . ."

"Exactly."

She rolled her eyes, but she was smiling now as well. "What else?"

"There isn't much else, to be honest." He shrugged. "At least not much I could tell you. I rarely spoke to her, and when I did, it was only in passing, when Ruckus was too busy to do so himself. She didn't listen to anyone; it was a wonder that she bothered to take his advice as often as she did. Even her parents had trouble with her."

"So, you don't know any of her likes or dislikes?"

"She didn't like very much, as I've said," he reiterated. "As far as dislikes . . . does *everything* count? I mean, the girl literally abandoned her home planet. Doesn't that speak for itself? If there was anything here she cared about, she might have chosen otherwise."

Delaney quirked a single brow. "You're forgetting: I've met Trystan."

"You're saying you'd run, too?"

"I'm saying I don't know." And how had this conversation turned to her? She needed answers, and she found herself extremely dissatisfied with the ones Pettus had been able to offer.

"One time," he said, and his voice had lowered, as if he was afraid of being overheard even though it was still just the two of them, "a few years ago, she pretended to drown. Ruckus wasn't there; he had a meeting with the Basileus and had placed me in charge. I pulled her out of the pool and tried to revive her—at least that's what I thought I was doing. Turns out, she thought it'd be funny for Ruckus to walk in on me giving her mouth-to-mouth, and for her to pretend we were kissing."

That was pretty messed up. "Ruckus didn't really buy that you were making out, right?"

"No," he confirmed. "He's smarter than that. But there was no reason for her to do it in the first place. She could have gotten me in serious trouble, could have cost me my job, and she didn't care. All she thought about was that it'd be funny."

No wonder everyone thought she was bitch. Olena treated people like playthings. If that was what people expected of her, Delaney was in more trouble than she'd thought. She couldn't do stuff like that, fake her death for a laugh.

If this was the girl she was pretending to be, she needed to be on her A game, and she couldn't do that when she didn't know anything else about Vakar—or the Kints, for that matter. Somehow she needed to get answers, and after his reluctance to tell her anything about Olena without Ruckus there, she doubted Pettus would spill about how Vakar operated.

She was about to lie and say she was going to try to sleep after all when her stomach growled loudly. Which gave her an idea. She

couldn't make someone panic by faking her death, but a little trick-
ery? That her conscious would allow.

"You're hungry." Fortunately, Pettus had heard the sound as
well.

"It's been a while since I've eaten," she confirmed. Then she
pretended to hesitate before she asked, "Can you get me something
to eat? I don't think I'll make it to morning without."

"I'm not supposed to leave my post," he told her, though not
with very much conviction.

Her stomach growled again—she *was* actually hungry, but that
would have to wait.

"All right." He sighed. "Stay here and don't answer the door for
anyone. Understood?"

She nodded, only just catching his words through the pounding of her heart. He left and closed the door behind him, and she
waited, counting to ten under her breath. If they'd passed the kitchens on their way up to her room earlier, she hadn't seen them, so
she didn't know how far away they were. It was a matter of guess-
ing how long to wait so that she didn't accidentally run into him
leaving or returning, before going herself.

She felt a bit guilty, especially considering he'd just gotten done
telling her that horrible story about Olena and how she'd played
him. But this wasn't the same, right? She wasn't faking her death
or trying to trick him into making out with her so . . .

Yup, decidedly not the same.

Initially she'd only intended to lure him in and grill him for
information, but now . . . the opportunity to get out of this room,
to really explore and find the answers she so desperately needed,
was too great to pass up.

She moved to the door and slowly eased it open. It was dark in the hall, and it took a moment for her eyes to adjust. Once they had, she was left with the decision of which direction to go. She hadn't been paying enough attention when brought here to have any clear indicator of what side of the hall led where.

Throwing it to chance, she turned right, padding down the hallway swiftly but soundlessly. Some hallways were lit with dim orange lights pressed against the walls every few feet; others were almost pitch-black. She avoided those. She wasn't quite sure what she hoped to find, only that there had to be somewhere with answers out there. The castle was huge, after all.

Knowing that she didn't want to inadvertently run into the Basileus or Basilissa, however, had her also avoiding the hallways that seemed too lavish. The ones with even more gold trim running down them than the wing where Olena's bedroom was located were also all carefully avoided. That still left plenty of selections though, and with the place being built like a maze, it was easy enough for her to choose between one hall and another.

A brighter orange glow, more vibrant than any of the other lights she'd seen thus far, filtered in at the end of a hallway. It effectively drew her into the darkness, her curiosity overshadowing her fear.

Logically, her brain told her, if there'd been any true danger here, there'd surely be guards, right? As it was, she'd yet to stumble upon a single one. The castle itself seemed to stand still, the quiet thick and heavy, beating down on her like a live thing. Through her wanderings, she'd found a sort of twisted comfort from it, the silence allowing her mind to filter through the day's events without any interruptions.

The hallway stretched some thirty feet, not a single light aside from the one at the very end of it. The closer she got, the brighter it became, and she realized that it was a mere fraction of itself shown from beneath the crack of a very large door.

It wasn't just spilling through the bottom but the side of the door as well; someone had left it open a good half a foot. Through the gap she could make out rows of cherrywood shelves covered with books of all sizes. Despite her enjoyment of the quiet up to this point, the distinct sound of crackling wood attracted her, igniting a homesickness at the center of her chest that had her pushing open the door the rest of the way. The possible ramifications of her actions were a blurry thought in the back of her mind, easily shuffled aside to make room for her inquisitiveness.

She entered a massive library the likes of which she'd only ever dreamed of. The walls stretched so high, she couldn't even begin to guess where they stopped, the rows of books trailing up after them just as tall. The very top of the ceiling was a dome, lines of golden metal trailing from all edges to meet at the center, where they formed an odd shape she couldn't label.

Delaney tried though, for a while, standing there with her head tilted back so far, her neck began to ache from it. The night sky above was charcoal with flickers of neon blues, greens, and pinks. She wondered if the windows were special, if there was something about them that turned the tiny pinpricks of light coming from the stars those odd colors. She was once again reminded that everything here was foreign to her, that she was out of place.

Except for the smell.

She found the source of it on the other side of the room, against a wide wall nestled between two stacks of shelves. The floor was solid beneath her feet, and she padded across it silently in her socks. She'd taken off her shoes earlier when she'd attempted to sleep, and hadn't thought about putting them back on in her rush to beat Pettus's return.

The fireplace was big enough to fit three of her easily, set in stone that sparkled like gold glitter had been used to form the rock. Heat radiated, hot enough that ten feet was the closest she could get before drops of sweat prickled her brow.

Now that she was in front of the fireplace, she could note that the woodsy smell was different from any of the ones back on Earth. There was a sweetness to it along with the smokiness, almost like someone had tossed a vat of gummy bears in it only moments prior. The scent effectively overpowered any that the dusty old volumes flanking it might have given off themselves.

She moved over to the closest bookshelf, selecting a tome at random. It had a burgundy spine, and when she pulled it from the wall, she found that it also had gold-leaf edges. She traced them with her finger, picking a page and opening it. The writing was in a language she couldn't read, and with a heavy frown she replaced it, moving on to another. The next five volumes she chose were in the same foreign language.

Delaney was a bit disappointed that the hebi didn't also help translate the written word. She figured it probably had something to do with the fact the device translated sound specifically. Unfortunately, the writing wasn't even recognizable enough for her to attempt properly sounding it out.

The part of her that'd grown excited the moment she'd entered the library began to wither, as if under the heat of the fire. This would have been the perfect place to get her answers, so of course it had to be completely useless to her. A blatant taunt from an already bitter universe.

She turned away, spinning in a circle to better inspect the place. There was no telling how large it actually was, not when the stacks formed mazes of their own, rows creating passages that led deeper into the room in every given direction. Seeing as how she was already lost—there was no way she was going to be able to backtrack to Olena's bedroom—she tossed caution to the wind and went for it.

"There's got to be some English here somewhere," she mumbled to herself, continuing on. It was a safe bet, considering Ruckus and his men had originally been speaking English with her on the ship.

At this point, any information she could glean would be good information. She knew little to nothing about either Vakar or Kint—damn Mariana for not pressuring her more into learning about them—and absolutely jack about Olena, aside from her being a bitch.

There had to be *something* here that could help her develop a stronger understanding of just what she'd been dragged into.

Delaney traveled through another four rows before coming to a stop at a corner made by two connecting shelves. Some of the spines had words on them, and her gaze homed in on one eleven rows up, with *American Customs* distinctly set in shiny silver lettering.

There was a step stool directly beneath it, as if someone had only just recently been searching the contents of this section as well. She hypothesized that if this book was in English, the rest here probably were, too. The stool was about a foot high, circular, and made of thick glass.

She hesitated when she pressed her foot against the surface, lightly at first, testing to make sure it could actually support her weight before sucking in a breath and going for it. Even with the lift, she had to stretch all the way up onto her toes in order for the tips of her fingers to graze the edge of the spine.

It was a struggle, but after a long moment she was able to grab it, and the two books that had flanked it, dropping down with a huge huff of relief. Absently flipping through the first book, she lifted a single brow when she stopped at a page with a crudely drawn image of a girl in a poodle skirt on roller skates.

How old was this book?

Instead of checking, she carefully placed it onto the stool and selected one of the others. This one was a bit more helpful, written in English but clearly connecting Earth to Xenith. She scanned references to kings and queens, and their deciphering into the Vakar and Kint versions: *King: Basileus (Vakar), Rex (Kint),* etc.

She was in the process of flipping through in search of new information when she turned. And saw him in her peripheral vision.

CHAPTER 7

It was impossible to tell just how long he'd been there, but it was obviously long enough. The corner that the rows formed turned only the one way, right, and led to a reading nook of sorts, which had been created by another three shelves and was nestled directly after another right turn. A single armchair had been placed there, old burnt-brown leather with brass finishing. It'd been set at an angle, so that it faced both the opposite hallway and the stacks to its right, giving whoever sat there ample space to stretch out their legs.

At least, it would have for just about anyone else; Trystan, however, seemed to barely fit. He had his legs stretched out and his feet pressed against the very bottom shelf despite the fact that he was sitting in the chair and not lounging. His arms sat against the rests, hands holding a book three times the size of the one she had.

He was still dressed in his uniform, somehow managing to appear dignified even here, surrounded by yellowed pages and heavy dust motes. His light blond hair was perfect, not a strand out of place, and he had his head angled at her, watching through those cornflower-blue-and-crimson eyes with an interest that had her gut instantly twisting into knots.

He was so still, she may have been able to convince herself he was a mere statue of the Zane, if not for the slow rise of the corner of his firm mouth. The fact that he enjoyed catching her off guard was obvious, as was the fact that his pleasure only grew from the knowledge that she knew about his enjoyment.

The danger here became apparent so swiftly, it was a raw sensation, a primal one that had her spine instantly straightening and her mind racing to attempt retracing her steps. If she had to get out of there, would she be able to find the door?

"Lissa Olena," he said, finally breaking the silence, his voice a poisonous purr, "how odd to find you here."

"I believe"—she cleared her throat, reminding herself that running wasn't an option—"technically, I found you."

He canted his head, eyes narrowing, though he never lost the vicious half smirk. "So it would seem." His chin nodded toward the book she was now clutching. "I wasn't aware you could read."

"Come on," she snapped before she could catch herself, "you can do better."

Both of his brows arched in surprise, before slowly settling once more. Instead of rising to her blatant challenge, he closed the book and folded in on himself, dropping his legs and standing with a flourish.

Tucking the book he'd been reading under his right arm, he slid his left hand into the front pocket of his navy pants, the material so dark, it could easily be mistaken for black in this dim lighting.

"We didn't get to finish our conversation," he said then, but his voice was different, lower. "Back on the ship."

"I wouldn't really call that a conversation." Was she pushing it too much? Keeping herself together was taking a lot more out of her than she'd expected; at least on the ship, she'd been well rested.

Perhaps ditching Pettus in the middle of the night without getting in at least an hour's worth of sleep hadn't been such a good idea.

"I wouldn't really call conversations *with you* conversations."

"Good." She took a deliberate step back. "Then we can end this one and go our separate ways."

"The last time we did that," he pointed out, "you ran off."

"I didn't run." Olena had. "Besides, what does it matter? I'm here now, aren't I? I came back."

"Did you?" These words were whispered, his lips barely moving along with the almost inaudible sound. Louder he said, "You're not clever enough to be up to something, Lissa. Whatever it is you think you're doing, I advise you to end it now."

"I'm not up to anything," she stated matter-of-factly, hoping he'd buy it.

"Really?" He didn't. "You're holding books, standing in a library I'm fairly certain has never seen you before. You didn't seek me out—you're naive, not suicidal—so what else could you possibly be doing?"

She switched the book to one hand and waved it pointedly in the air. "Reading."

"In English," he noted.

"Got a problem with English?" Which she knew the second it was out was a stupid question. He was Kint, after all. He hated everything from Earth.

"I have a problem with your tone." His expression darkened, and he took a single step forward, a step that would have made up five of her own.

"Best way to solve that?" Maintaining her ground was taking all of her courage, and only because her instincts warned that he was the type of predator who chased when the prey ran. "Leave me alone. We can't bother each other if you're not here."

"I was here first," he reminded her.

She wished she could go, she really did, but knew that if she tried, it would become all too clear she had no clue which way was out. She was fairly certain she was tiptoeing on a thin line already; she needed to avoid doing anything that would tip him off.

Delaney must have taken too long to respond, because the next thing she knew, he was crowding her up against the side of the same bookshelf she'd pulled her books from. One of them dropped out of her arms, clattering to the ground like a slap. Her breath caught in her throat, and she tightened her grip on the book she'd been reading.

Could she use it as a weapon if she had to?

Against him? Yeah, right. She wasn't so sure a bazooka would be useful against the Zane.

"You're trembling," he said, that taunting purr back in full force. "That's more like you."

She narrowed her eyes but bit her tongue. There was less than a foot of space between them right now, and while he didn't seem in a rush to close the gap, she'd already gathered his was a mercurial nature.

Why couldn't Olena have been nice? Not that she thought his actually liking her would have made this ruse any easier, but she might not even be in this situation at all if Trystan and Olena had actually wanted to marry each other.

He reached out and plucked the end of her T-shirt, rubbing the soft material between his fingers. "You haven't changed clothing."

She snatched her shirt back and pressed it against her hip to keep him from grabbing at it again. Inwardly, she couldn't help but curse herself for the mistake. She hadn't even thought to change, but that was because she hadn't intended to sneak out, not until the opportunity had presented itself. It didn't make sense for Olena to continue wearing Kint colors, especially not here in her own castle.

"It's comfortable," she stated, which wasn't a lie. One hundred percent cotton all the way. "And I've got—"

"Gotten used to it?" he cut her off, a single blond brow lifting in challenge. His eyes homed in on her, the interest there more frightening than his ire from earlier on the ship had been.

The sound of approaching footsteps cut off anything else he was going to say, and he turned his head toward the direction she'd come. His expression altered, annoyance setting in and turning his gaze to ice. It was that frozen look that Gibus ended up turning the corner and walking in on.

The Sutter stilled instantly, eyes widening and then snapping between the two of them. He opened his mouth, shut it, opened it again. His lab coat was slightly wrinkled, and his curly hair was in disarray. He'd clearly been lost in thought just then, and it was taking him a moment to put the pieces together.

"I didn't realize there was anyone else here," he said finally, shaking himself out of his stupor. He bowed to them. "Apologies, Zane Trystan. Lissa Olena."

"That's all right, Gibus." Delaney moved to him, making sure to keep her steps brisk but as casual as she could manage at the same time. It was a struggle not to outright run. "I'm actually glad you're here. I was wondering if I could ask you a few questions." She waved a finger at their surroundings. "Save me from having to go through any more of these books."

"Questions?" He blinked at her, then understanding dawned

and he cleared his throat. "Yes, yes, of course. I'd be happy to help in any way I can."

"Wonderful." She stepped toward the row of stacks he'd just come from. "Why don't you escort me back to my rooms? We can talk as we go."

Trystan watched their exchange closely, moving to prop his shoulder against one of the stacks almost absently. He wasn't fooling anyone, though; the wired way he held himself, muscles tensed and ready, was indicator enough that he was prepared for anything.

"Off so soon, Lissa?" he asked evenly.

Now that escape was actually possible, she refrained from returning with a biting comment. Instead she nodded at Trystan and grabbed Gibus's arm in a silent plea to get on with it.

"Good night, Zane."

Without giving him a chance to respond, the two of them turned the corner and moved out of sight. She didn't breathe again until they were out in the dark hallway, leaving Trystan and the labyrinthine stacks far behind.

"WHAT ARE YOU doing out here?" Gibus asked five minutes later. He'd kindly given her time to collect herself, but was now full of questions; she could see them in the set of his mouth and the flare in his eyes.

"I told you," she said breathlessly, still a bit shaken from her encounter with the Zane. "I was looking for answers."

"Answers?" His frown deepened. "To anything specific?"

"To *everything*," she stated. After having been in the heated library all this time, the hallways were now like an icebox, and she rubbed at her arms. She had no clue where they were going, and was forced to trust that Gibus was leading her back to Olena's rooms, though she refused to ask outright. "I assume you've heard?"

"About your indefinite stay?" he guessed, and he at least had the decency to appear guilty. His cheeks even heated some, reddening enough that she noticed every time they passed under a light. "Yes."

"So then help me," she said, waving a hand at him, her frustration welling. "You are part of the reason I'm in this mess."

He couldn't argue with that.

"If I'm going to *be her*, I need to know her, at least a little. Who is she?" She stopped him when he went to speak. "Besides a raging bitch."

While he openly pondered this question, she inspected him. He wasn't like the others: He wore every thought and emotion that crossed through him on his face. She could see him going through the range of them: contemplation, distaste, eureka, etc.

He wasn't as tall, either, something she'd noticed before, but now, standing next to him, that fact became even more apparent. Probably around six feet, which still left him a few inches shorter than even Pettus. He smelled a bit like mint, though it was subtle and hit her only whenever they turned a corner, forcing them closer to each other.

"Ruckus said Olena was able to steal the device because she hung out with you in your lab on the ship," she reminded him, remembering this detail herself. "You had to have spent time with her."

He snorted. "She only went there to get away from him. She complained he pried too much, that he wouldn't give her space to breathe, which, you know, is pretty much his job. Sometimes she'd feign interest in my work, ask me things using big words she clearly didn't understand, but at least then I could talk and pretend like what I was saying wasn't falling on deaf ears. Otherwise, it was just my listening to her whine."

"Not the first person to tell me she's a whiner." Which wasn't good, because Delaney hadn't whined a day in her life. Tantrums, even as a child, hadn't been her thing. Her pride wouldn't allow it.

"If you can't do it," he said then, as if having read her mind, "that's okay. Five years away will change a person, even a person like Olena. None of us would have thought her capable of pulling something like"—he motioned at her body—"this off. Not in a billion years. Just don't show an interest in anyone. Let them approach you if they must, but never approach them."

"Yeah," she said with a grunt, "not a problem." The last thing she planned on was walking up to a random alien and starting a conversation.

"From what I'm gathering," she continued, "Olena doesn't have many friends. Should I even be concerned about people trying to talk to her?" Trystan's words about conversations not really even being conversations filtered through her mind. Hopefully that part had been true. If Olena was a terrible conversationalist, no one would expect much talking out of her.

"My guess is they'll avoid you as often as possible," he confirmed, smiling at her relieved exhale.

"Pettus told me a story," she suggested, hoping he'd get the hint.

"Well, she stole that device—an illegal prototype that no one was supposed to ever know about—knowing full well that it could get me killed for treason, so"—he stared at her pointedly—"you already know the worst she's done to me."

"Killed?" She hadn't realized it was that bad for him. Though a quick perusal showed he looked rather well for someone accused of treason.

He waved off her concern, turning them down yet another dark corridor. "Ruckus was able to convince the Basileus not to go that far. It took a while, from what I understand, but he managed it just the same. I did lose a large amount of my funding and now have to run every idea past the Basileus before I can start working on it, though."

"He's a good guy? Ruckus?" She didn't know why she was asking, and hated the unsure tone her voice took on at doing so. She knew Gibus was staring at her, but she refused to meet his gaze, finding sudden interest in the darkness stretched before them.

"He feels awful for allowing Olena to trick him into taking you. In his defense, Pettus and I bought it, too. I'd still be buying it now if I didn't know better. Unless . . ." He squinted his eyes at her jokingly. "How do I know you're not really Olena pretending to not be Olena?"

"Ha-ha," she drawled, but the corner of her mouth turned up.

"No, seriously. For all we know, she's really an evil genius." He couldn't hold his expression, and ended up laughing through the last two words of his sentence. Shaking his head, he sent his thick curls flying around his forehead until they settled back, covering his ears.

He came to an abrupt stop before she could ask him anything else. It took her half a second to recognize the large dark wood door as the one she'd been brought to earlier. Great, they were here. Time to pay the Pied Piper—or in her case, pissed-off alien soldier.

If Gibus noticed her bracing herself, he was kind enough not to point it out. Instead he lifted a hand to the door, waited a moment—possibly to give her more time—and then pulled it open. It didn't make a single sound, but the second it was cracked, the yelling from within hit them.

"You had one job, Pettus." Ruckus's voice was deep and threatening. *"One!"*

Delaney pushed past Gibus, moving into the main room. She spotted Pettus first on the other side of the room, his hand rubbing at his neck, head hung. There was sweat on his brow, and he looked very uncomfortable, maybe even a bit frazzled. She immediately regretted tricking him.

Ruckus caught her eye next, over by the side of the bed. He was seething, pacing back and forth so that the single orange lamp on her nightstand that had been turned on dashed his shadow across the window wall. He swung around and came to a stop when he noticed her, mouth dropping open as if he were about to turn his anger on her.

"I didn't mean to get you in trouble," she said to Pettus before anyone else could get a word out. She felt bad, but she wouldn't apologize.

"He's not in trouble," Ruckus practically growled. "You are. When I left you—"

"Exactly," she stopped him. "You left me. In here, alone, moments after telling me that my entire life had been hijacked by aliens I never wanted to know about much less actually know."

He sucked in a breath, but she wasn't done. The fear and the frustration she'd been holding in while in the company of Trystan burst out of her now that it had a safer outlet to aim for.

"You can't just expect me to be okay with this," she told him, dropping the single book she still carried onto the ground. "Any of this."

It took him longer to reply than usual, and it seemed like that was because he was trying really hard to choose his words. That guilt was back, swimming behind his eyes, mixed in with residual anger at her for leaving. They stood there glaring for what felt like hours but was really less than a handful of seconds.

"I don't expect that," he finally said in a breathy tone, "not at all. You have every right to be upset, to want to go off and do things on your own, but, Delaney"—he pressed his palms against his chest—"I'm trying to help you. I want to help you."

"And you can't do that when you don't know where I am," she finished for him when it became apparent he wasn't going to say anything else. Sighing, she rubbed at her face, all the energy she'd had a moment ago draining out of her. Was that going to be her new normal? Her own emotions playing tricks on her, roller-coastering up and down again on a whim?

"Precisely." Ruckus looked over to Pettus and then motioned absently to the closed door where Gibus still stood. "You can go, Teller. I'll take it from here."

"Sir—"

"Just," he said, appearing every bit as exhausted as she did then, "go. Be back here to relieve me in the morning."

Pettus hesitated, wringing his hands before giving a curt nod. "Yes, Ander."

"Wait." When Pettus went to breeze past, Delaney grabbed his arm. "I didn't do it because I thought it would be funny." She'd done it out of a misguided notion of self-preservation, but she kept that part to herself. She figured she'd insulted all of them enough for one night.

Pettus picked up on the reference she was making, and though it seemed like he wanted to stay mad at her, he ended up sighing instead. "How about next time you just tell me you'd like to go somewhere, all right?"

She nodded.

There was a lengthy awkward silence after Pettus and Gibus left, shutting the door behind them with a soft click. Fortunately, this room was warmer than the halls had been, so Delaney didn't feel the need to dive under the covers on the bed for warmth. That gave her a couple of extra minutes to just stand uncomfortably by the window. That sweet smell of the room was slowly being overpowered by Ruckus's.

It made her homesick, made her yearn for her parents' backyard in the fall the few occasions in her childhood when her dad had found the time to play with her. He'd pile leaves five feet high, and they'd spend the day jumping and crawling through them. Those moments, with the chilling breeze stinging her cheeks, the smell of dirt and browning leaves, the off taste of bitter air on her tongue, were some of the best of her entire life.

"I don't suppose you're going to apologize to me?" Ruckus asked, yet it was clear from the lightening tone of his voice that he already knew the answer. He'd relaxed some, not much, just enough to be noticeable because she was looking at him so closely.

"No," she clarified.

"Right." He hung his head, contemplating. "I was sleeping, you know? Pettus woke me up to tell me that you'd disappeared."

"I didn't disappear," she corrected him. "I walked out. And . . ." At the reminder of exactly where she'd ended up, she frowned. Two unpleasant encounters with the Zane were enough to last her a lifetime, and she was already dreading the possibility of having to experience another one with him tomorrow.

"What?" He went to move closer then stopped himself. It was

clearly a struggle for him to maintain his distance. She was beginning to understand that this was just the type of person he was. He took his responsibilities as seriously as he'd claimed earlier. "Tell me what happened."

"Gibus found me in time."

"In time for what?"

"To avert an even bigger disaster," she admitted. "I found a library."

He grimaced. "Olena hates the library. She says the smell of books reminds her of rotting wood."

"Which brings me to my main point." She crossed her arms over her chest, trying to ignore how out of place she looked in her T-shirt and jeans next to him. "If someone had just told me something useful about her, I wouldn't have ended up there in the first place."

"When you meet with the Basileus and Basilissa tomorrow," he told her, "they'll tell you things. Anything they think you'll need to know."

"Which could be nothing."

"It could be," he agreed, and for a moment she was just grateful that he hadn't bothered lying to her. "But again, that's why I'm here. If you have questions, ask me, Delaney. I'll do my best to give you answers. This isn't an ideal situation for either of us, and it certainly isn't going to be easy." He paused; then: "But there's something else you're not saying. The fact that you ended up in a library can't be the reason you went pale a second ago."

"It's not. Trystan saw me." She toed the book she'd taken. She didn't know why she'd even bothered; from the little she'd gleaned, it wasn't going to be very helpful. Taking the time to replace it though, with the Zane standing right there, hadn't seemed like a good idea. "He talked to me."

"Did he suspect something?" Her earlier question repeated back at her was somewhat ironic.

"I don't think so," she parroted in turn. "He noticed there were differences—the me-being-in-a-library thing wasn't lost on him, either—but aside from that . . . he was the same arrogant asshole I met on the ship."

Ruckus pressed his knuckles at the space between his eyes as if he had a headache. "This is exactly why I don't want you going off alone. I understand you're used to doing things on your own terms, but this isn't Earth."

"Gee," she drawled, "thanks for the reminder."

"I already apologized for taking you," he grated. "Do you need me to say it again?"

Childishly, she shrugged a single shoulder, but managed to keep from actually saying yes. It wouldn't hurt hearing him grovel, but unfortunately it wouldn't help, either.

He let out a heavy sigh. "All right, let's try this again. You should really get some rest. The Basileus isn't exactly known for his patience, so when you meet him for breakfast tomorrow, you're going to want to be at your best. Tonight I'm going to be right outside. Me. Not Pettus. Also me? Not getting any sleep now. I'd sarcastically thank you for that, but I fear you'd just—"

"You're welcome." She couldn't help the grin.

"Do that." He dropped his hand against his thigh and then made his way over to the door. It shut quietly behind him.

Once he'd left, she found her body going lax, and she climbed back into the bed like a zombie. Earlier it might not have been possible, but this time, she was out the second her head hit the pillow.

CHAPTER 8

I t was a struggle, and she had to force herself to do it, but once Delaney glanced in the mirror in the bathroom, she couldn't look away. She'd hoped that since she was prepared to see Olena looking back at her this time, it wouldn't be as startling. Nope, that was definitely not the case. Though their hair was basically the same length, the slick black strands were incredibly foreign, and the gold-and-violet eyes peering back creeped her out.

Of course, even with a different face, the effects of yesterday were visible.

There were bags under her eyes from lack of sleep, not to mention puffy red marks, proof that she'd been crying before last night's library excursion. If only she'd thought to have her purse on her instead of leaving it in the car that night at the club, then she'd be fine. Half of her makeup was in there; she didn't use much.

Dipping her hands into the water basin she'd already filled with cold water, she waited for her fingers to chill and then pressed them beneath her eyes. A few more times, and at least some of the swelling had gone down.

A knock on the bathroom door startled her, and she silently cursed her jumpiness. How was she supposed to convince an entire castle full of people she was a princess if she couldn't even get ahold of herself while alone? Expecting Ruckus, she didn't take the time to mask her frustration as she moved over and yanked the door open.

Only to be met with a petite blond girl in a forest-green dress with buttons all up the front. Her hair was pulled to the side in a single curly ponytail, and she held her hands clasped in front of her. She bowed the second their eyes met. Hers were an emerald with a ring of vibrant orange, and for a second Delaney stood there speechless, staring at her.

"Good daybreak, Lissa Olena." The girl bowed again and then glanced over her shoulder into the bathroom. A frown marred her otherwise cherubic face. She had to only be around a year or so younger than Delaney. "I was told by the Teller that you could accommodate yourself."

"Pettus?" She cleared her throat, and straightened some in the hopes it would help her appear more regal and less . . . well, like her. "Teller Pettus was mistaken. I'm afraid my trip to Earth has left me a bit muddled." Did they say things like muddled on Xenith?

"Would you like help getting ready, Lissa Olena?"

"If that wouldn't be too much trouble." Crap. "I mean, yes, please."

Forget this. Letting out another sigh, she spun on her heel, went to the sink, and threw out her arm toward it. Not knowing how to act—proper, friendly, etc.—was making things worse. She decided to go on instinct from here on out. Hopefully it wouldn't end up being the worst mistake—or the last, for that matter—she ever made.

"How the heck am I supposed to get makeup out of this thing?" she asked, exasperated.

With a slight giggle that she tried to hide, the girl stepped forward and reached beneath the outer lip of the stone counter. She must have pressed a hidden latch there, for a drawer sprung out.

It was about six feet long and four feet deep, and packed with more products than Delaney could use in her entire lifetime. Some of it looked slightly familiar, but for the most part, the items were foreign. Reaching in, she cautiously lifted a tube of pale pink. It was shaped sort of like lipstick, but when she pulled the top off, a wand with bristles on the end popped out.

"Did you want to go with pink today, Lissa?" the girl asked, already picking out a few matching items from the drawer to go along with the tube in Delaney's hand.

Back home, Delaney didn't bother much with makeup, but she recalled seeing differently of Olena in the photo Ruckus had shown her. Her eyes wandered back up to the mirror, and this time it was easy to quickly look away. Mariana would know what to do with a face like Olena's, just what shades to use, how much.

She gritted her teeth, upset over the fact that on top of everything else, she could also no longer confidently know what makeup to wear or not wear. She didn't even want to think about clothes.

"Um . . ." She squished the top back on the tube and dropped it into the first section she'd pulled it from. "That's okay."

The girl immediately began putting away the items she'd pulled out.

"Sorry."

"Don't be, Lissa." She beamed. "What about red? It goes so well with your jet-black hair."

"What about gold?" Delaney asked, noticing a shiny tube that very color.

"Gold?" The girl seemed surprised. "Forgive me, but I was told you hated the color."

"Were you?" Who hated gold? She glanced pointedly at the golden buttons on the girl's dress. There'd been accents of the same on all the other uniforms she'd seen here so far. Perhaps Olena hated it because of that? Was it meant as a tiny rebellion?

Kind of a pathetic one, if you asked her.

"I was told by Wilima that silver was your preferred metallic, Lissa."

"Wilima?"

"Your previous atteta."

She assumed "atteta" meant "helper." "Well, I've been away a long time, and my tastes have changed over my denzeration"—she was pleased when her voice didn't stumble over that word—"and now I also love gold."

"Very good, Lissa." The girl didn't seem the least bit concerned by this change, and began to take out various shades.

"What's your name?" Delaney asked, hoping she wasn't stepping over some line by doing so.

"I am Lura," she said with a friendly smile, "your new atteta."

"It's nice to meet you, Lura."

That gave the girl pause, and she stared at Delaney oddly out of the corner of her eye. After a moment, she continued with what she'd been doing, carefully placing each item on the surface of the counter with little more than a soft click.

"Thank you, Lissa. It's a pleasure to meet you as well."

Shit, had they met before? If so, why didn't she just say? Unless she now thought Delaney was a bitch for not remembering. That was a distinct possibility. Just to be sure, she asked, and when the other girl laughed, she pulled back slightly, even more confused.

"Oh no," Lura told her. "I'm new to the castle. I wasn't working here when you left for your denzeration." In the large bathroom, the girl looked even smaller than she had in the doorway. Her eyes were lined in black, and it became clear there was something on her mind when she found sudden interest in comparing two tiny cases with practically the exact same shade.

"You have a question," Delaney prodded. "Ask."

"I couldn't."

"It's all right. What is it?"

"Was Earth . . ." She cleared her throat. "What's it like?"

Delaney's tears threatened to spill all over again, so she forced herself to concentrate on the makeover. Tapping her finger against the small square case in Lura's left hand, she shrugged a shoulder.

"It's great. I'll tell you all about it sometime."

"Will you really?" Lura's excitement filled the room, and she clutched the tiny makeup case against her chest. "That would be amazing. Thank you, Lissa Olena!"

"No problem. Can we, uh"—Delaney motioned to her face—"do something about this now?"

"Oh!" She leaped into action. "Of course! Breakfast is in less than an hour now!"

Less than an hour before she'd have to face the alien regents who were holding her captive? Great.

Her last remaining shred of hope was that at least Trystan would not be there.

THE BASILEUS WAS seated at the head of the table to her right, the Basilissa at the other end. There were a few empty seats, including the entire row across from her, and it somehow managed to make the room both smaller and larger at the same time.

At least Ruckus had been allowed to join them, and was sitting at her left. There was about three feet of space between them, this table having been made to seat eight at the very least, but having a familiar face was a major relief.

He'd already been there when Pettus had led her to the dining room. Apparently, she was the last to arrive and everyone had been waiting. They stood in a flourish upon her entrance, but it was obvious Ruckus was the only one who wasn't annoyed with how long she'd taken to get there.

"We understand that this situation is less than ideal for you." Magnus lifted a glass similar to a coffee mug filled with dark black liquid to his lips. "For us as well. Our daughter has always been an independent spirit—"

At her side, Ruckus practically choked on his own drink, barely catching himself at the last minute. It didn't seem like anyone else noticed but Delaney. She had to agree that "independent spirit" was putting it lightly.

"But none of us would ever have expected anything like this. However, it is imperative that you play the hand you were dealt, and play it well. That means showing up where you are supposed to. On time."

She bit her tongue but outwardly nodded.

"Good." He motioned toward Ruckus. "The Ander here will be with you throughout this process. He knows my daughter better than anyone. If you have any questions, he should be able to answer them for you. Still, is there anything immediate you think you should know?"

Somehow, gaping at a king seemed like a bad idea, so she ended up biting her tongue even harder.

"There's a lot, actually," she ended up saying, unable to condense it like he clearly wanted her to do. How was she supposed to take everything she needed to know and shove it into one or two questions? Besides that, it wasn't like she could point out that everything she had heard so far about his daughter painted her more as spoiled than *independent*.

"Yes, well." He cleared his throat. "That's to be expected. We want you to succeed here, Delaney. It's important to all of us that you do. To make it easier, we've pushed all of Olena's planned appearances off, except for one, but there's no speaking involved, so you should be fine."

"The people need to see that our daughter has returned to fulfill her duty," Tilda added from her side of the table.

"If for any reason there's something that the Ander can't answer," Magnus said, making it very clear by his tone he doubted there was such a thing, "he's under orders to contact me."

"It's amazing how much you look like her." Tilda leaned forward. "Not even I would know." Her smile was forced, and tinged with a heavy sadness. "You'll do just fine, Miss Grace, so long as you follow the set of rules we've laid out for you."

"Which are?" She'd always rebelled against the mere concept of rules, but now part of her had to admit having them wouldn't necessarily be a bad thing. She didn't know this world or its people; anything they could tell her to do, or not to do, as the case may be, would be helpful. Her thoughts turned back to last night, and she was reminded how well going off script had gone for her.

If following their guidelines—as she was going to call them in her head—would keep her from any more scary run-ins with the Zane, then that was reason enough to do so.

"No traveling the castle without an escort . . . ," Magnus began. He straightened in his seat, shoulders broad and pulled back as if it were necessary for him to intimidate her now when he'd been trying so hard not to up until this point. "And absolutely no leaving the castle grounds. We're currently removing any political personnel who don't need to be here, making sure that there is less opportunity for you to fail."

She took offense to that, but he was already continuing.

"It is our hope that Olena will be found in a timely fashion, but until then you must limit the number of people you interact with. Fortunately, our daughter is . . . somewhat of a loner, so no one will expect you to make small talk with them."

Joy. Of course, parts of that statement matched up with the things Pettus and Gibus had told her last night, while others . . . Was one considered a loner when they were such a raging bitch that no one *wanted* to be around them? Or did that just make them a pariah? Not to mention the fact that everyone else seemed to think that Olena liked to party, whereas her father was painting her as a recluse.

"Now"—he folded his hands before him—"to get down to some of the basics. Our daughter is not fond—"

The double doors behind the Basilissa burst open then, cutting off anything the Basileus might have been about to divulge. Trystan appeared with two sentries at his back, their eyes sheepish and downcast. Clearly, he'd forced his way in despite their efforts to stop him.

He grabbed the edges of the doors before they could slam against the walls, standing there for a moment, eyeing them all. It was a bold move, being that he was in Vakar territory, but he didn't seem the least bit concerned by his show of rudeness. In the extremely green room, his blue uniform stood out like a beacon.

Green walls, table, chairs. Gold accents. Yup, definitely a pattern. She was actually slightly relieved she'd gone with gold; it helped her to blend in a bit more. Absently, she reached under the table and tugged at the strange shirt Lura had given her. It was tight, almost too much so, and pressed against her chest in a way that made her look like she had a lot more going on upstairs than she really did.

It was shorter in front, exposing an inch of bare skin at her stomach, and long at the back, reminding her a bit of the penguin suits with the tails that men used to have to wear. It was a dull gold, not too shiny but not bland enough to be considered brown, either. Her skirt, which she didn't really even consider a skirt so much as a dinky piece of cloth, barely covered her thighs, and even sitting, she tugged at the hem, desperate to lower it at least a centimeter.

Lura had insisted that both items of clothing matched and had to be worn together. The only thing Delaney actually liked about the outfit was the boots, which were a soft buttery brown that stretched a good three inches above her knees. They had a slight heel to them as well, which was great, because around these people she was beginning to feel short.

"Zane Trystan." Magnus didn't bother hiding his displeasure. "I trust you slept well."

"The room is to my liking," he agreed with a single nod. Stepping in the rest of the way, he finally let the doors swing shut, and moved over to the unoccupied side of the table. He chose the seat directly across from Delaney, though he didn't spare her so much as a glance. "You'll forgive my intrusion; I was told this was where breakfast was being served."

He was tiptoeing a fine line, balancing in that space between polite and rude. They had a treaty, but that didn't mean any of the royals currently in the room had to like it.

It became even more apparent in that moment how badly the

Vakar needed this merger to work. If they didn't, there was no way Magnus would allow Trystan to speak to him like that or barge in the way he had, especially because he was a prince, where Magnus was a king.

"Of course." Tilda was the one to reply, that small smile returning, though it didn't fool anyone. She tapped her hand against the tabletop, just a light rapping of her knuckles, but almost immediately the doors on either side of the room reopened.

Delaney inspected the staff as they whirled by, providing golden platters for each guest. They'd let them go in the air about three feet up, and the tray would then float at an angle downward, landing perfectly centered before each of them. It took all of her willpower not to gape stupidly at it.

The last golden tray floated down to land in front of Trystan, and then all at once the lids that covered them rose up into the air at the same slow pace. They twisted, doing a circle, and then eased backward. Once they were a foot behind each of them, the servers reached up and plucked them out of the air, turning and exiting through the four doors that led in and out of the green room.

The second her plate became fully visible, she blinked.

There were three different foods on it: One looked to be a vegetable of some kind, stringy and a vibrant green. Maybe sort of like green beans if they'd been pulled apart at the seams. Another was flat and solid, reminding her of very burned toast, and then what she figured had to be the main course, a chunky bright neon-pink piece of meat that smelled a lot like bologna.

She gulped, audibly, too, because both the king and Ruckus turned her way. Risking a glance up, she almost flinched when she realized she'd caught Trystan's attention as well.

He was frowning at her, just the corners of his rose-petal-pink lips turned downward. The furrow between his brows was minuscule. When their eyes met, his hardened, the blue lightening to the color of steel in an instant.

She really wished she knew what Olena had done to piss him off so badly.

"So, Olena"—the Basileus cleared his throat—"did you enjoy your denzeration?"

He picked up the gold utensils at the right of his plate, sneakily showing her that they were exactly the same as knives and forks back home. In her nervousness, she hadn't noticed.

Anything he'd been going to say to her before was now impossible in Trystan's presence, so they were all forced to act like everything was normal. This would be her first real test, made even more so because it was in front of the Basileus and Basilissa.

"I did," she said, following suit. She really didn't want to eat that pink stuff, but knew she had to eat something or else she'd cause suspicion. Cutting into the greens, she lifted a half-inch piece to her lips.

"A bit too much, it would seem," Trystan spoke, eyes still locked on her. "She almost didn't leave."

"Nonsense." Magnus waved him off. "She simply wanted to experience one last festival."

"Surely you remember your denzeration, Zane Trystan," Tilda joined in. Her smile was tight despite the lightness to her voice. She was beautiful, the kind that caused jaws to drop and people to stare stupidly after her.

Her skin was a deep shade, the look of someone who'd been in the sun for days, her blond hair long and swirling around her shoulders almost to her elbows. The dress she wore was every bit as formfitting as the one Delaney did, though it concealed a hell of a lot more skin. Her sleeves were long, but the front didn't dip quite so low, and when she'd been standing, Delaney had noted that the Basilissa was in a long green skirt that dropped to the ground.

Her eyes were almond shaped, like her daughter's, and the color of warm, freshly baked cookies. The ring around them was a shocking violet that was actually more pretty than freaky. She was thin, but tall, willowy. And the way she moved, almost as light as air. She came off so serene, it was hard to imagine she was the mother of someone as selfish as Olena.

That she was half the reason Delaney was being held there against her will.

"Certainly," the Zane sneered in response. Leaning back in his chair, he kept his gaze on Delaney as if hoping to jab her with his next words. "I'll never forget the stench of that planet. How anyone could live there among so much filth is beyond me. Let alone enjoy it."

"I take it Earth wasn't to your liking, Zane." Delaney boldly held his gaze, skewering another piece of the green stuff with her fork in the process. Weirdly, it wasn't bad. Sort of tasted like a mixture between sugarcane and sweet potatoes.

"Not at all, Lissa," he replied, though her statement had clearly been rhetorical.

"I suppose it wouldn't be." She shrugged a delicate shoulder and absently reached for the golden goblet at the left of her plate. Inwardly, she prayed she wasn't about to drink something that tasted like cat piss. Outwardly, she sipped at it, staring him down over the rim.

His eyes narrowed almost imperceptibly. "And just what do you mean by that?"

"Oh, nothing." She replaced the goblet with a steady click against the metal table. "Nothing at all."

He opened his mouth to argue but was cut off by the Basileus.

"Olena, have you been told about the Tandem yet? We're holding it explicitly in your honor. The Zane was kind enough to suggest it." He watched her through blue-and-green-rimmed eyes. Right now he knew she wasn't really his daughter, and yet all his senses were claiming otherwise. What must that be like?

"That was nice of him." She hoped. For all she knew, a Tandem was a ritual sacrifice. That definitely seemed like the sort of thing Trystan would be all for.

Tilda tried to cover up Delaney's obvious lack of enthusiasm. "It seems our daughter has spent so much time on Earth, she's no longer thrilled by the same things here as she once was."

"It's just hard getting interested in the same old things once you've pet a lion and gone parasailing." Delaney latched on and went with it. She took another sip of her drink, deciding she liked the almost-fruit-punch flavor. "They also let you bungee-jump," she went on, not sure how much they really knew about Earth activities and not wanting to push her luck. "It's a lot of fun."

"Isn't that where they dive off cliffs with only a string to hold them?" Ruckus asked, addressing her for the first time that morning.

She glanced his way and couldn't help the mischievous smile. "Oh yeah."

"You did that?" This came from Trystan. He was skeptical but also curious. She'd take either of those things over anger from him any day.

She had to admit, when he wasn't pounding walls and standing close enough for it to be impossible not to note he was a giant, he was attractive. His hair wasn't shaved on the sides like Ruckus's and Pettus's, which she'd gathered was their version of a military look. Though it was still thick on the top and shorter on the sides.

He was wearing the same navy uniform he'd been in yesterday, and seemed really at ease in it. He certainly wasn't having the same issues as she was with her clothing, anyway.

"Twice." She beamed at him, and relished his surprise because it meant he hadn't thought she was capable. Perhaps Olena wasn't the type to take risks? She mentally snorted. If that'd been the case before, it definitely wasn't now. Forcing her identity on a human? Probably the biggest risk of them all.

Especially considering there were two possible wars resting on the deception.

The Kints couldn't figure out what Olena had done, and they couldn't discover what Delaney was doing now. Who she really was. She wondered what would happen to her if they did. Would the Basileus still uphold his end of the deal? Send her back to Earth in time for the war with the Kints to begin? Or would they even get the chance to make that decision?

Trystan didn't strike her as the type of guy to forgive and forget. He'd probably kill her.

"We should make our way outside," Magnus stated then, sliding his chair back to stand. When he did, the rest of them got up as well, Delaney scrambling to follow suit.

Someone really should have filled her in on the etiquette before putting her out there in the open. It was hard to keep up with all the rules when she didn't even know what they were. She assumed that was what they'd been hoping to get into, but Trystan had to go and ruin it.

Ruckus should have filled her in last night, but they'd both been distracted and tired. And honestly, part of her had seriously hoped she wouldn't be around long enough for an alien etiquette lesson to be necessary.

But what if she was trapped here for months and had to learn all their customs? The world dimmed around the edges for a moment, and she stopped breathing.

"Olena?" Magnus called her.

"Lissa Olena?" Ruckus touched the side of her arm, and she immediately snapped out of it.

Swallowing, she glanced over at Magnus and tried a shaky smile. "Sorry. Daydreaming for a moment. What did you say?"

"I asked if you minded Ander Ruckus accompanying you outside. Your mother and I have some more preparing to do for the Tandem."

"Of course, Father. That's no problem at all."

She wondered if the Zane found Magnus's request odd. Technically, seeing as how they were betrothed, shouldn't he be the one accompanying her to events?

She guessed not, because when she risked looking over, Trystan was already moving toward the door closest to his left, not even giving her a backward glance.

Maybe he'd make this easy on her after all.

CHAPTER 9

I t's a game," Ruckus told her as he led her through the metallic castle toward the back.

She'd never been this way before, but she was too caught up in his explanation of what a Tandem was to pay much attention. From what little she did process, this part of the castle looked exactly the same as the part she'd entered through yesterday. There wasn't a single doorway without a soldier flanking it, each dressed in the forest green and gold, and black pants tucked into boots.

She was tempted to ask where the hell they'd all been last night, but decided it wasn't worth reminding him of what she'd done.

"More like a sport," he went on. He kept his eyes on the Zane, who walked in front of them a good thirty or so feet away, too far to overhear. "There are two teams, with six members on each. Every player rides his own ung."

"What's an ung?"

"Do you know what an emu is?"

"Like the bird?"

"Yes. Ungs are similar, except that along with their feathers, they also have scales and tusks."

"Tusks?"

"Big ones. And very sharp, which makes it easy for them to crack the jewbie egg."

"The *what*?" She got a little too loud there, and pulled back, dropping her arms to her sides. She thought she saw Trystan slow a bit and cock his head to the side as if trying to listen, but she must have been wrong, because Ruckus carried on.

"The players toss the egg backward to their teammates while riding the ungs. There are several obstacle courses, and they lose points and have to start an obstacle over every time a team member drops an egg. Or if it gets cracked by one of the ung tusks."

"This is seriously the weirdest game I have ever heard of." She couldn't believe these people were more technologically advanced than hers. Seriously? A sport where you rode animals and tried to catch an egg without breaking it? Sounded like something someone would do before the written word, let alone the Internet.

"Olena would agree, though she wouldn't put it so nicely." He reached out and rested the tips of his fingers against her arm. "The Zane insisted on this, otherwise we wouldn't be risking it."

She filled in the blanks. "Make sure I'm careful. Got it."

They were coming to the end of the wide hall now, and she tilted her head to hear better when pounding sounds started drifting their way. The closer they got, the louder the sounds, and mingled with them was a cacophony of voices and cheers.

"Ruckus?" she said, a bad feeling starting to settle in the pit of her stomach. "Just how big of an event is this, exactly?"

Up ahead, Trystan made it to the doors. The two guards at the sides opened them for him, exposing bright sunlight and a field of green. That, and a massive tentlike fixture set up to the right and already crowded with people.

It didn't take them long to get there, and the second she stepped outside, she wanted to turn around and run back in.

Ruckus leaned down and whispered into her ear, "Relax." His hand went to her lower back. "You might actually enjoy it, Delaney."

At his touch, her body settled some, most of the tension in her shoulders dissipating. Surprised by her reaction to him, she momentarily allowed herself to be distracted before she felt brave enough to continue.

She took a deep, steadying breath and nodded, determined to get on with it before she lost her newfound nerve. The tented area was actually on the other side of what she assumed was the playing field. While she could make out most of their faces already staring, it was somewhat comforting to know she wouldn't need to get too close to any of them.

"The main event is held there." Ruckus pointed ahead where an area had been boarded off with a thin golden wire. It stretched up and over a brilliant green hill and disappeared out of sight. "It starts here, at the first obstacle, and makes its way down. Sort of like . . . golf. You do know golf, correct?"

She nodded again, a bit distracted now by the sights.

The sky was a frothy light green, but the ground was the same as it was back on Earth, with healthy green grass and trees. There weren't a lot of them, more like one or two planted sporadically, probably because the space was used as a Tandem course.

They happened by one of the trees, and upon closer inspection she realized there were minor differences. The leaves, for one, were all veined yellow, and ribbons of cerulean blue shot up the trunks and through the bark like lightning bolts.

She couldn't see an end to the property from where they were, as she was so focused on the crowd. A large tent had been positioned a ways away from the mass of people, and was sectioned off with more gold wire and even a few guards. The yellow tent flaps had been pulled back to expose the inside, and she came to a halt when she caught her first sight of what must have been an ung.

Ruckus had made a good comparison when he'd mentioned emus, though she imagined the ung would be the result of an emu falling into a vat of toxic waste and coming out a mutant. It was at least four times the size of one of the birds back home, more around that of a Clydesdale horse.

One of the riders shot out from beneath the tent, clearly doing a warm-up, and brought the ung closer to them. Its skin was covered in gray scales of various shades, so that it looked like an odd shadow twisting in the light. There were feathers, green ones, poofing out of the sides of its narrow head in place of ears, and large wings were tucked into its sides. From the bottom of its five-inch pointy black beak, two daggerlike tusks jutted upward.

The creature's legs were as thick as bowling balls, with massive three-toed feet that had Delaney picturing the Velociraptors from _Jurassic Park_. The same gray scales covered each foot, and when they hit the ground, they actually left behind footprints in the otherwise pristine grass.

"The footprints add an extra layer of difficulty," Ruckus said, noticing what she was paying attention to. Five other riders came out to join the first. "It's about to start."

The first obstacle wasn't much of one. There were a few thin poles that they needed to steer their ungs around, as well as a flat black object that stood three feet off the ground. The course wasn't cordoned off into two sections, but there was a clear split, with one team on the side nearest her and the other closer to the crowd.

"Do you want to sit?" Ruckus tapped the side of her arm.

"No, I'm fine here." She watched in fascination as the teams got in order, one rider positioned in front of the other, with two feet of empty space between them.

On this side, there weren't many people, and she got the impression that only those trusted by the Basileus and those who worked in the castle were allowed. It gave her the perfect view of the course without making her feel squished or crowded by anyone. Because of it, she was able to let her guard down a bit. Let some of her amazement show. Which was good, seeing as how she didn't think she'd have been able to hide it.

The players all wore uniforms similar to jockeys back on Earth, though their shirts had octagons on them and not triangles or diamonds. On some, the shape was painted yellow; on others, it was green. Their tight riding pants alternated as well, with the lead player in green, the one behind him in yellow, and so on.

On the other side, the other team's colors were different. They were all dressed in navy blue and light gray.

Two men walked onto the field, stopping five feet in front of the leads of each team. Each man held up a ball—the egg—the color of coffee, high enough for everyone to see.

For a second there was total silence, and then a loud horn blew, the eggs were tossed to the first team members, and the men dove out of the way as the ungs shot forward. The first member twisted his ung around one of the thin gold poles that stretched higher than he did, then he tossed the egg over his shoulder without looking and continued on. The second, who was already moving on his heels, caught the egg, moved around the pole, and repeated the motion by chucking it to the guy behind him.

A few times she thought for sure someone was going to drop it, but their deft fingers managed to clasp it in midair, or stroke the side so that it rolled into their palms as if coaxed there. By the time the last team member had the egg, the first three had already disappeared over the rise of the hill, no doubt moving on to the second course.

The last member rose up so that he was standing in his saddle—which she noted was exactly like the kind for a horse—and tossed the egg over the rise. A moment later excited shouts came from the crowd below, who could see the second course.

"He caught it," Ruckus said with a chuckle, then pointed to the Kint team who was a half minute behind. Their final rider was now doing the same, tossing the ball over. Another cheer sounded and he grunted. "They did, too."

"We are the best." The new voice caused Delaney's spine to tingle, and she twisted her head to find Trystan approaching. There was a glint in his eyes she couldn't place, and she wasn't sure she actually even wanted to.

"We'll see," Ruckus replied in a tight voice, then added, "Zane Trystan."

"I'll escort Lissa Olena from here, Ander." He came to a stop at her side, close enough that the tips of her fingers almost touched his thigh.

"With all due respect—"

"You can follow at an appropriate distance." Trystan waved him off, signaling that he should fall back.

Ruckus held her gaze for a moment before obeying. It was clear by the way his jaw clenched that he didn't like it. He didn't have any say in the matter though; he was only a commanding officer, while Trystan was a prince.

Steeling herself for another conversation with him, Delaney forced her gaze away from the safety of Ruckus and faced the Zane.

He was watching her closely and with interest. Offering up the curve of his arm, he smiled wickedly. "Shall we, Lissa?"

Her hand was tiny against his arm, and as they started walking toward the hill that would lead to the second course, her heart began to thump. Needing to keep her cool, she reminded herself that there was nothing he could do to her out here. Not with all these witnesses. Besides, he wasn't stupid. He hated Olena, sure, but he had to know hurting her would only cause him more trouble, especially when he was currently in Vakar territory and not Kint.

He led her over the small rise to the second part of the course, which looked very similar to the first. There were a few extra poles for obstacles, and the teams were already halfway through them. Without a word, he picked up the pace, almost tugging her along before she managed to find her footing.

Delaney's fingers inched toward the hem of her skirt, finally giving in and tugging it down. She managed to get it half an inch, but within three steps it'd ridden up again. The faster they walked, the quicker it rose, and she inwardly cursed for what felt like the millionth time that she'd allowed Lura to convince her that wearing it was a good idea.

Then an odd sense of awareness had her turning her head slowly toward the man at her right.

Trystan was watching her, but more so, he was looking at where her hand was still pressed against the end of the gold cloth and her thigh in a poor attempt to keep the skirt in place. Sensing she was now looking his way, he glanced up.

"Uncomfortable, Lissa?" he asked in a husky voice.

The crowd to the right cheered, and a breeze blew by, bringing with it a hint of roses and sweat. She'd stopped paying attention to where they were going, knowing only that they were following the trail of the course, but suddenly she was uneasy. It was bad enough that she had to be here with him; now she was also missing the actual event.

Ruckus had been right, too. She'd been enjoying it up until Trystan had appeared.

"I'm fine, Zane." She cocked her head. "You?"

He chuckled. "What reason would I have to be uncomfortable?"

Not having a good enough response to that, she shrugged a delicate shoulder and returned her attention to the game.

"It's a bit curious what you'd want with a book comparing human and Vakar customs," he said, breaking the silence when it became apparent she wasn't going to. He didn't look at her when he did it, letting this information sink in.

He'd been paying way more attention to her at the library than she'd even guessed.

"It contains Kint customs, too," she said, spitting out the first thing that came to mind. Which apparently wasn't the right thing.

"First the shirt, now this?" He quirked a blond brow. "Careful, I might start to think you're trying."

They'd caught up to the game and were close enough that she could pointedly turn her attention its way. She watched as the players swerved through the obstacles, fascinated by how swiftly they were able to do so.

"Do they learn how to ride at an early age?" she asked, momentarily forgetting in her curiosity that she shouldn't.

Trystan, who'd still been moving them briskly along, paused and glanced down at her.

"Never mind," she blurted before he could respond. A second later one of the Vakar players fumbled, and she sucked in a breath.

The egg dropped to the ground with a vicious splat, releasing a thick perfume of cloves into the air. The innards were a milky white, which the clawed feet of the ung smashed farther into the ground as the creature wobbled. The Vakar player was half out of his seat, trying, and failing, to right himself. After a short struggle, he fell out completely, landing with a sharp sound on his shoulder.

Delaney winced, watching as the Kint team continued on to the other course even as a few Vakar came running onto the field to check on the fallen player. He was sitting up, but he clutched at his left shoulder, clearly in pain.

When she finally pulled her eyes away and looked back at him, Trystan was grinning ear to ear. It wasn't the boyish and innocent kind of smile, though. There was something darker lurking just beneath the surface, and before she could fully place her finger on it, he was bringing them to a stop.

They'd moved away from the wire by some ten feet, putting more space between them and the few others watching on this side. There was another tree ahead a few yards, short and stubby, maybe only a foot or so taller than the Zane. Its leaves tinkled when a warm breeze blew by, like pennies being dropped into a glass jar.

"Should we continue on, Lissa Olena?" he asked her, indicating the next course. "Or would you prefer we stay behind and watch the Vakar attempt to catch up?"

He tried to pull her forward, but she stalled by slowly removing her arm from his. When his hand settled at her elbow, lightly urging her now, she ignored it. Delaney searched for Ruckus out of the corner of her eye, realizing with a start that he wasn't behind them. At least, not close enough for her to see. Where'd he go? He wouldn't have left her alone with the Zane, would he?

"Do you think he'll be all right?" she asked, voicing the first thing that came to mind.

On the field, two Vakar were helping ease the injured player to his feet.

Trystan frowned at her, dropping the hand he'd still had on her arm. "Do you care?"

Because Olena was a self-centered brat who wouldn't, Delaney recalled too late.

"I'm just concerned we might not win now," she said in a poor attempt to save face. "His clumsiness cost us."

If anything, this only caused his frown to deepen.

"Did you develop a liking for sports while you were away as well then?" he wondered, and it was clear from his tone that she'd piqued his interest. Which was the exact opposite of what she was trying to accomplish.

"Right," she drawled, "along with my newly acquired witty tongue." Deliberately, she took a step back the way they'd come. "As great as this has been, Trystan, I'm afraid I must excuse myself."

She was a bit surprised when he didn't immediately try to stop her, yet he didn't have too long to ponder over it. Hearing her name, she glanced toward the beginning of the course, squinting against the harsh glare of yellow sunlight. Weird, that the sky was a different color, but the sun and the ground were the same.

"Olena." Ruckus was quickly making his way toward her.

She took a step in his direction, about to call back, when suddenly an explosion rent the air. The blast came from behind, and she was knocked off her feet and tossed a good ways forward. The motion ended up bringing her closer to Ruckus, who was upon her in a matter of seconds.

Her head rang and her vision winked in and out. Disoriented, she clung to his wrists when he dropped to his knees and reached for her. An acrid smell filled the air, like burning rubber, and she managed to swivel her head around to see that the tree she'd been so close to had blown up.

The tree she'd been close to . . . but not close enough.

She gasped, and as if of their own accord, her eyes sought out Trystan.

He must have gotten on the ground right away. Aside from his hair being a little mussed up, it didn't seem like he'd been affected by the blast at all. Their eyes met, and there was no denying the feral look in his icy blue gaze.

He'd tried to kill her.

The Zane, Olena's—meaning *her*—fiancé, had just tried to kill her!

"IT WAS TRYSTAN," she whispered as Ruckus rushed her down yet another hallway in that godforsaken labyrinthine nightmare of a building.

He'd lifted her into his arms and carried her all the way back to the castle, his men falling in around him. Now the other five guards had dropped back, trailing behind while keeping watch. As if they were afraid of another attack.

"Did you hear me?" she asked, tightening her arms around his neck. She'd protested initially when he'd lifted her, but truth be told, she wasn't sure she could get her legs to work right now anyway. "Ruckus?"

"Are you hurt?" His tone was gruff, leaving no room to discuss anything else. "I don't see any blood. Are you hurt, Delaney?" Her real name had been uttered under his breath.

"No." She shook her head, and when he didn't look at her to see, she answered again, "No." She licked her dry lips. "Where were you?"

His face remained stoic and his steps steady. Wherever they were going, he was determined to get there as quickly as possible. Even having carried her a good half mile now, he didn't seem out of breath. His grip around her back and beneath her thighs never wavered or loosened.

"We received an anonymous tip," he revealed, as if unsure whether or not he really wanted to tell her. "I had to step away to take it. I was only gone a second, but you must have picked up the pace, because by the time I got back, you'd moved farther down the course than I'd expected."

"What was the tip?" She was pretty sure she already knew.

"An assassination attempt." He took a deep breath. "On the Lissa. I was on my way back to get you. The tip claimed the Tars hoped to catch Olena off guard."

"But that's not what you think." She wasn't asking.

Finally his eyes met hers. "That's not what you think, either."

"It was him," she insisted. "I know it. He led me straight there, and why place a bomb unless you can anticipate knowing where and when the target will be?" She shook her head. "It was him."

"Yes," he agreed. "I believe it was. But that doesn't matter."

"What?" She gaped at him. "He tried to kill me, Ruckus."

"We don't have any proof," he pointed out. They turned down another hallway, their surroundings immediately changing. Here, instead of fake wooden walls, the hallway took on a similar feel to that of the ship. White walls loomed around, and while there were still windows sporadically placed, there was no longer any furniture.

Deciding to shelve the subject until they'd both cooled off a bit, she tightened the hand she held at the center of his chest.

"Where are we going?"

"To get you fitted," he snapped, as if it were a stupid question. "It's what I should have done the second we landed here."

"I don't understand."

"Of course you don't."

"There's no reason to be a dick about it," she said, bristling. "I was the one almost blown up, remember?"

Without another word, he pushed them through two light-gray swinging doors, entering a large lab complete with metal work-benches and broken machinery parts. At the way back there was another set of doors, and he shoved his way past just as easily, turning his body so that no part of hers ever took the brunt force of them.

She spotted Gibus in the far corner of this room, fiddling with strange dials on the arm of a padded chair. She vaguely wondered if they went to the dentist on Xenith, or if they were spared that special kind of torture.

A second later it became painfully apparent Ruckus planned on putting her in the chair, and she struggled for the first time, forcing him to pause in his haste to get there.

"Stop it," he said.

"Put me down."

"I'm about to."

"Not in that, you aren't."

Sensing her fear, his expression eased, some of the anger dropping away. "It's not going to hurt you, Delaney," he said calmly, holding her gaze. "I'm not going to hurt you."

She tried to look away but couldn't.

He must have mistaken her silence for acceptance, and he had her in the seat before she could even begin another protest, his hands pressing down on her shoulders when she tried to stand. Letting out a low growl, he motioned for Gibus to hurry up with whatever his part in this was.

"Okay." Gibus cleared his throat and winced when she shot a glare his way. "I can't do it with her moving like that."

"Damn it, Delaney. Stay still."

"Absolutely not."

"And just why not?"

She eased her struggles long enough to chuck her chin out toward Gibus's right arm, which he was not so discreetly holding behind his back. "I totally saw the needle."

"It's not a needle," Gibus corrected her. "More like a tagger. Sort of like they do with dogs on your planet."

Her mouth dropped open. "Oh, *hell* no."

Ruckus shoved her down with a tad more force this time, shooting daggers over at the other Vakar while doing so. Leaning over, he pinned her to the chair by crowding her in, so that she was blocked by his massive form on all three sides. His head lowered, their foreheads almost touching.

"We need to get you fitted . . . ," he began, rushing on when she would have argued again. "It's not up for discussion. If we'd done this earlier, I might have been able to get you away from the blast before it went off."

"I'm fine," she said, and her struggles had ceased.

"This time." He clenched his jaw. "What about next time?"

"If we tell on Trystan, there won't be a next time."

"Don't act naive, Delaney; it's unattractive."

Before she could get offended, he motioned to Gibus. The large metallic object that was exposed wiped her mind clear of anything other than the threatening tip. It looked sort of like a cross between a stapler and a tattoo gun. There was a sharp blade at the bottom, about a quarter of an inch long, and a small flat square piece directly above it.

"This part makes a thin cut," Gibus began to explain, bringing it closer to her and pointing to the blade, "and this part deposits the chip." He tapped the square. "It'll only sting for a minute, and it takes less than a second. We've all done it."

"Done what, exactly?" She nibbled on her bottom lip, torn between trying to feign toughness and just allowing her fear to show.

"How much do you know about brain waves?"

She frowned, taken aback by the odd question. Here she was, in an alien workshop, surrounded by torn metal parts that smelled like oil and acid, and he was asking her about brains? Though, it did clue her in on where exactly they planned on sticking that thing. Her hand automatically went to the back of her neck.

Gibus smiled approvingly. "Good. See? Not as clueless as you thought. We've found a way to tap into brain waves, deciphering and tuning into them sort of like radio frequencies. Connecting certain frequencies allows two parties to communicate with each other through it without having to speak out loud."

"You're talking about telepathy."

"Yes."

She was in the last of a row of seven chairs. They all looked exactly the same, with a space between the headrest and the actual backing. It left a good foot of empty space where someone from behind could access the person sitting. More aptly, access their neck.

"That's what you meant, wasn't it?" She caught Ruckus's gaze again, putting the pieces together. "When you said I still wasn't talking to you back on the ship. You thought I was Olena. The two of you"—she motioned toward his head—"can communicate telepathically?"

"Yes," he said. "Only a select few are allowed to do that with any of the royal family. As the head of the Lissa's personal guard, being able to connect with her in that way is an immensely important tool."

"So," she said, scrambling to follow what he was saying, "I couldn't talk to everybody mentally? Even if I'm fitted?"

"No," he said, shaking his head, sending some of the long brunette tendrils loose to cascade over the side of his face. His yellow-and-green eyes held her captive, as if hoping that she'd be able to see he was telling her the truth. "Only those who've been tuned into your frequency can hear and share thoughts with you. The chip has already been programmed to work with a human brain; we just have to dial my frequency in."

"You'll be able to get into my head." She did not like the sound of that.

"I'm the only one who will be able to," he assured her. "You need this, Delaney. Today was a close call: Ten more feet, and you would have been dead."

Somehow she knew what he was really saying, what went unsaid between the lines.

She needed *him*.

And he wasn't wrong. Who else did she have here? There were only five people on this entire planet who knew her true identity, and out of them, she'd only had a full conversation with three:

Pettus, Gibus, and Ruckus. The first she'd recently tricked, the second was already walking a thin line with the Basileus, and the last . . .

He might have taken her against her will, but he hadn't known what he was doing at the time, and ever since he'd discovered his mistake, he'd done nothing but try to keep her safe. Startled, she realized she trusted him. If he said this was something she needed to do, then she'd take his word for it.

"All right." She licked her lips and took a deep breath. "Do it before I come to my senses and change my mind."

He nodded over to Gibus, and she shook her head quickly.

"No, you do it." She stretched her fingers around the ends of the armrests and squeezed the soft white material.

Ruckus hesitated but ended up taking the device. Switching places with Gibus, he stepped first to her side and then behind her, out of sight. She felt him brush the strands of her hair out of the way, baring the center of her neck right beneath the base of her skull. His fingers were warm, reassuring when they rubbed to give her an idea of where she'd feel the cold metal a second before she did.

"Ready?" he asked, and at her nod, he pressed the lever on the gun. The blade sliced her skin and something slid beneath it.

She hissed in a breath and cursed, finding it difficult to stay still. Her whole neck burned like it was on fire, and the chip they'd inserted felt like a lump pressing down on her skull despite the fact that it couldn't be bigger than her pinky nail.

When he was in front of her again, she reached back and pressed her fingers against the cut. The spot was wet with blood. Her hand was brushed aside, and she realized Gibus was the one behind her now, applying a small bandage over the entrance wound.

"Your idea and my idea of *sting* are very different," she grumbled. Her fingertips were stained red, and she glowered at them. If she ever got her hands on that stupid alien princess . . .

"That was nothing," Ruckus admitted sheepishly. "This next part's the rough one."

Strike that: The second her neck stopped burning, she was going after him.

CHAPTER 10

Her head was going to explode, she was sure of it, and tried to tell them as much, but she couldn't get her teeth to unclench long enough to get a word out.

"Hurry it up," Ruckus growled. He was kneeling in front of her, one hand on her arm, the other on her bare thigh. When he wasn't yelling at Gibus, he was whispering words of encouragement to her that she couldn't process in her current state.

Because her brain wasn't used to having a foreign piece of machinery attached to it, her synapses were firing at random, trying to relay information that the rest of her brain couldn't yet comprehend. One of the men had said something about that being the telepathic connection they were attempting to form, but she'd stopped listening when Gibus had pulled out a flat piece of glass similar to what Ruckus had used to show her the picture of Olena.

He'd tapped a few buttons, and the next thing she knew: agony.

"Why's this taking so long?" Ruckus snapped for what felt like the hundredth time when she started to writhe. "Can you make the connection or not?!"

"Almost," Gibus assured him, though he was sweating and his

voice shook a little at the end of the word. "Her human brain is rebelling. It's going to take another minute."

"She can't withstand this another minute!"

Delaney would have agreed if her tongue hadn't swollen in her mouth. Positive she was about to break a tooth with how tightly she was grinding her jaws, she was already plotting both of their murders when Gibus let out a cry of success and slammed his finger down on the screen a final time.

"Her head's going to explode," a voice filtered through, panicked and rambling. *"First I kidnap her; now I'm going to kill her! This was a bad idea. None of the other humans reacted this way. I'm going to end up—"*

"Driving me absolutely crazy if you keep up the yelling," Delaney hissed through thin lips. She pressed her palms over her eyes and focused on evening out her breathing. The pounding in her head was still there, but it no longer felt like there was a vice squeezing it, which was something.

Ruckus's eyes widened. *"Were you just—"*

"Hearing your thoughts?" she said, cutting him off again, and risked slitting her eyes open to glare at him. "And just because I thought the same thing about my head going boom, doesn't mean I needed to hear you thinking it, too."

"I'm sorry." He looked like the uncomfortable one now. "I hadn't realized the connection had opened up."

"Does that mean it can be controlled?" Because that would be a plus. Already the thought of always being able to hear what he was thinking, and vice versa, gave her the creeps. It was hard enough being around him on an alien planet without his being able to read her mind.

Right now it was easier for her to keep up a strong front because she knew he believed she was feeling strong. If he knew just how terrified she really was by all this . . . She didn't need to know his opinion of her when that happened.

"It won't take long to adjust. For the next few hours you'll feel warmth where the chip is right before I lock on to your frequency. The sensation will fade," Ruckus explained. "You can prevent your thoughts from filtering into my head if you want, but anything I want to say to you, you can't stop. I control my side of the connection; therefore, I'm the only one who can cut it. The same way you control your end of it.

"If you don't want me to hear you"—obviously he'd been paying attention—"erect a barrier. It's different for everyone, but for me, picturing a glass box around my mind works. After a few times it'll come naturally to you; the chip will learn your cues and adjust accordingly."

"It's sort of like my iPhone," she said in a poor attempt to mask how freaked out she still was. "Only instead of learning the word *LOL*, it's learning how to mentally tell someone to fuck off."

He grunted, but the humor glimmering in his eyes gave him away. "Focus. You connected with me before because Gibus activated the chip and sent it my frequency. You're not tapped into me anymore. To get it back, think of a thought, and imagine pushing it toward me. You'll feel the burn again, signaling the chip activating; once it does, anything you think you can send directly to me. Understand?"

"Not in the least." She adjusted herself on the seat, getting more comfortable, and then clasped her hands in her lap. "All right, let's do this."

She didn't know what to think about, so she just let a jumbled mess fill her head as she concentrated on the hot alien across from her. Shaking those thoughts from her mind until she could dissect them during a more private moment, she imagined a slew of words filling the air, trailing from her head to his. It would have been quite comical even, if it hadn't felt like someone was putting out a cigarette on the back of her neck.

She was glad that sensation wouldn't last, at least.

Ruckus scrunched up his face at her.

"What?" she asked, worried she hadn't covered up her trailing thoughts about his attractiveness fast enough.

"What is a tamale?"

She laughed, glancing between him and Gibus to see that the other Vakar was just as clueless.

Meeting his gaze, she beamed. "My favorite food."

"STOP." SHE GRINNED over at him when he froze for the third time since leaving the lab. *"Can you hear me now?"*

"Seriously, Delaney," he said, and ground his teeth so hard, she heard the sound.

"What?" She shrugged innocently. "I think it's funny."

"That's a phone commercial?" He started walking again, leading them through the castle. They'd already passed through the white portion of the place, clearly the science wing, and he'd brought them back to the fake wooden rooms. So far she had yet to see a guard, so they must not be in a popular area.

Gibus had stayed behind to continue working on . . . whatever it was he was working on.

"It was," she told Ruckus out loud. Then, telepathically: *"It's not anymore."*

"This isn't a toy," he scolded. "I didn't get you fitted so you could play around."

"Oh, relax." They turned another corner, and the flooring changed from hardwood to carpeting the color of cream. "I'm practicing. You said the chip had to be conditioned to pick up on my cues, right? Well, this is me conditioning. The last thing I want is you getting in my head and overhearing something you shouldn't all because I didn't know what I was doing."

His pace slowed down, and it took her a moment to realize. He was a few steps back when she finally turned to him, a questioning look in her eye.

The place had clearly been built for Ruckus's kind, with high ceilings and hallways wide enough to fit six of him shoulder to shoulder. There were no windows in this portion of the castle, so the only lighting came from a row of white lights strung up at the center directly above them. It smelled like a mixture of burned firewood and bleach, the first coming from him while the second was the hall itself.

Not wanting to dwell on why she could smell him from a distance away, she angled her hips and sighed exasperatedly, laying it on a bit thick even in her own mind. A grin split across his handsome face, and she knew she'd made an error somewhere.

"What don't you want me to overhear?" he asked, voice dropping an octave, as if they were sharing a secret between them even though they were the only ones around. He pulled back his shoulders and tucked his hands into his front pockets, rocking back on his heels. The whole pose was too relaxed, the sudden change in him coming off almost cocky.

"Pretty much everything," she said cautiously. "Can we keep going now?"

"Why? Are you already done concentrating on 'the hot alien'?"

She felt her face go red. "I hate mind reading."

His chuckle was warm, real, and his body seemed to ease even more. "There's nothing to be embarrassed about."

"Oh? Because you're so hot and you know it?"

"I've never thought about it before." He shrugged. "Appearance has never really mattered to me."

"That's easy enough to say when you look like *that*." She waved a hand, indicating all of him.

His brow furrowed in an obvious mixture of confusion and surprise.

"Olena!" The Basileus's call carried down the hall, and they both turned in his direction.

Guiltily, though not really having a reason to be, they both stepped away from each other, watching as he approached, Pettus and three other guards on his heels.

"I heard about what happened." Magnus reached them and came to a sudden stop, just short of reaching out to touch her arm. His hand hesitated in the air for another second or so before he dropped it back to his side. "Are you all right?"

"Yes." She wrung her hands and forced a small smile. "I'm fine, thank you."

"We've caught the men responsible," he said, fury lacing his tone. "Don't worry. They will be dealt with accordingly. If something had happened to you . . ." Magnus glanced over his shoulder at the three unknown guards and then waved them back down the hall.

They did as ordered, stopping where they could keep an eye on him but could no longer overhear.

Not that there was much to overhear, for the four of them stood around in an awkward silence for a long moment. Pettus and Ruckus both kept their arms in front of themselves, clasped, while the Basileus seemed to struggle with whether or not to speak and, if the former, what to say.

Sick of the stalling, Delaney came right out with it. "Trystan was involved."

Magnus's eyes went wide, and his mouth thinned. "That is not an accusation you should make lightly, or at all. Especially out loud."

"He was luring me to the tree," she insisted, though she smartly kept her voice down.

"Coincidence," he stated. "He was in every bit as much danger there as you were, was he not?"

Well . . . yes, actually. She hadn't thought of that. She'd been so surprised and freaked out that she hadn't really stopped to think about the fact that he'd been closer to the explosion than she had. He'd gotten to the ground quickly, sure, but she'd seen them move. Aliens were faster than humans.

Perhaps she'd jumped to conclusions?

"Besides," Magnus added, seeing her internal struggle, "like I already told you, we caught the bombers. They're Tars who hoped ruining the celebration would cause a panic. It seems like you were never actually their intended target; it just happened to work out that way. They're more upset now knowing that they could have killed you, even accidentally, than they are that their plan failed. No one is panicking. We're Vakar. We don't scare lightly."

She couldn't really argue with him, his being the Basileus and all. Not to mention, he was making valid points. What did she really know about their politics anyway? Hell, she hadn't even known the Tars existed until yesterday.

"I'm sorry you got mixed up in all this," Magnus said, swiftly putting an end to the discussion.

"If you were really sorry," she couldn't help but say, "you'd send me home."

The darkening of the blue in his irises was the only outward sign of his anger. His voice, while clipped, remained even, and his shoulders hadn't so much as tensed. Being that he was a king, it shouldn't have been surprising that he had such strong control over his body and its reactions.

"Delaney," Ruckus urged telepathically, but she didn't look at him, keeping her attention on the Basileus.

"The reason why that's impossible has already been explained to you, Miss Grace. Please, don't mistake my pity for stupidity. I won't risk my people so that one human girl can go back to her bland life."

Okay . . . were all aliens assholes? Because she was seriously starting to get that vibe. Also, did they all have to look so . . . perfect? She'd been so nervous this morning at breakfast, she hadn't really taken the time to observe just how vital the Basileus looked. In comparison to the Basilissa, he was a hard yet handsome man; on his own, however, the full extent of his attractiveness stood out.

He was maybe an inch shorter than Ruckus, so probably around six four, and his inky black hair was thicker, and wavy. She'd peg him as a surfer back home with locks like those.

"With all due respect"—she held tightly to her anger, making sure to only allow part of it to show—"you don't know anything about me, or my life. Just because I'm not a Lissa back on Earth doesn't mean that my day-to-day life is any less eventful."

"Yes." He nodded snidely. "That's right, isn't it? Parasailing and bungee jumping, correct?"

"You forgot about petting the lion," she bit out.

"Careful, Miss Grace," he warned, and at her side Ruckus's fists clenched. "If that's true, you've already survived one encounter with a predator. Do you really want to try your luck at another?"

"She's not well, Basileus," Ruckus said, coming to her defense. "Not only did she hit her head during the explosion, but we just came from her fitting."

"You had her fitted?" Magnus glanced between the two of them, wearing a deep frown.

"She's unaware of our customs and our policies," Ruckus stated. This last part was said with more force and a pointed look her way. "Getting fitted was the best way to feed her information while concealing her identity."

"Hmm." Satisfied with that, the Basileus moved to leave. "Smart decision, Ander. Keep up the good work. And you, Miss Grace"—there was clear warning all over his face—"watch your step. Remember, the Vakar aren't the only ones who will suffer should the Kints discover what's really going on here."

"You mean what your daughter's done?" She quirked a brow, but before he could verbally—or worse, physically—attack her, she followed up with, "I know how important maintaining my cover is. For both of our people. I'll do my job of convincing them, but I want your word that the second you get Olena back, I get to go home safely."

He eyed her, and she couldn't tell if he was impressed or simply still annoyed by her boldness. The former must have won out, however, because he ended up giving her a half smile that appeared to be legitimate.

"You've got my word, Miss Grace. Play your part, and in the end we'll both get what we want."

"Good." He could be lying, that was always a possibility, but there was no real reason for him to bother. He needed her cooperation, sure, yet that could be forced out of her any number of ways, and he didn't come off like the type who lacked imagination.

"I have prisoners to attend to." He bowed his head to her and then acknowledged Ruckus and Pettus. "I'll see you at dinner tonight, Miss Grace." He didn't stick around for a reply.

"What do you think you're doing?" Ruckus demanded once the Basileus had disappeared down the hall. He yanked on her arm until she glared back at him. He was pissed, nostrils flaring and everything. "Are you trying to get yourself killed?"

"I'll excuse myself, Ander." Pettus sent her an apologetic look and then hastened away, heading toward the science wing.

"He can't hurt me," she reminded him when they were alone. "He needs me."

"For now," he snapped. "What about tomorrow? Or the day after? The second he finds his daughter, do you really think he'll let you leave if you've insulted him? He's a king, Delaney! There are rules here just as there are on Earth, the most important being: Don't make an enemy of the man in charge."

She couldn't help her grunt. If only he knew about her rebellious stage a few years ago, then he'd realize what he was saying fell on deaf ears. Her entire freshman summer of high school had been spent conducting ways to raise her father's blood pressure whenever she was home on break. Mariana had even helped with a few of those ideas.

At the thought of her best friend, her anger dwindled, leaving her empty. Wrapping her arms around herself, she took a shaky breath. She hated all these highs and lows, the way she'd feel like she'd finally gotten ahold of herself only for something to remind her that she was, in more ways than one, a prisoner here.

"What's a cycle?" she asked suddenly, recalling she'd never gotten an answer about that.

Her change of subject confused him, but he answered anyway. "It's our word for *day*."

Her eyes bugged. "Day? Back on the ship you said I'd been out for three cycles! I was unconscious for three days?!"

This was not happening. First, she was kidnapped, then she was almost murdered right after breakfast. Next she gets a painful and terrifying alien computer-type chip installed into her brain, and now Ruckus was telling her that she'd been missing for not two days but five!

"It's almost been a week," she said breathlessly, backpedaling so that she could lean against the brown metal wall for support. "They must be going crazy. Mariana probably thinks I'm dead."

"Delaney—"

"I need to contact them." She'd barely heard him call her name. "Mariana and my parents. They need to know that I'm all right."

"You can't do that," he told her.

"Why not?" It wouldn't affect what she was doing here. No one knew who Delaney Grace was; they'd never make the connection if she reached out to her friends and family.

"You're on another planet, for one." He ran a hand through his brunette hair, leaving his heavy palm at the base of his skull. "You can't just call them on the telephone, Delaney."

"So have them send an e-mail," she said, scrambling to come up with a solution.

He gave her a pointed stare. "We both know that would only exacerbate the situation. Even if the e-mail wasn't somehow intercepted by the Kint, which is likely, if your roommate thinks something bad has happened to you—"

"You mean like a kidnapping?"

"Then she would have called the police," he went on, the only sign he'd heard her a slight narrowing of his eyes. "Any contact you make now will be investigated. The bigger the investigation, the more news coverage. And the more news coverage—"

"The more likely it is one of the Kints will notice something is off," she said, putting it together. Slumping against the wall, she squeezed her eyes shut. There were aliens of both groups on Earth; some even stayed permanently. There was always the chance that they'd tune in at an inopportune time and see that a recently graduated high school student had gone missing in the exact same place the Lissa had been found.

It was a stretch, of course, that they'd even begin to guess what had really happened, that Olena had switched planets with Delaney, but could they risk it? No.

"This is a nightmare," she whispered, not really meaning to. A second later she felt Ruckus's warm breath fan against her cheeks, and her eyes snapped open, going wide at his nearness.

He'd moved so that he was standing toe-to-toe with her, arms up at the sides of her head in a similar pose to the one Trystan had used to intimidate her last night. This was different, however, because there was no threat in the way he held his body around hers. It was more like protection, and it caused a strange warmth to pool in the center of her chest.

"Tell me something," he said breathlessly, the words so low that someone standing even half a foot away wouldn't be able to hear.

"Something," she found herself answering, absently licking her lips.

His gaze trailed down and followed the move, and she sucked in a breath when the yellow in his eyes began to glimmer gold. He caught himself, matched her stare again, and shifted his feet, the move bringing him half an inch closer to her. No part of them actually touched, but the heat transferring back and forth was palpable.

Delaney didn't understand this. She knew what attraction was, of course, but couldn't comprehend how she could be feeling it toward him. Not only was he of a different species, but he'd also dragged her into this mess, and they hardly knew each other.

"I'm trying to get to know you," he said then, remaining where he was even when she stilled.

Oh shit.

"How much of that did you hear?" she asked, immediately picturing the clear box around her mind like he'd told her to do. She hadn't even been aware of the slight burning at the back of her neck. He'd just connected with her telepathically, read her mind, and she'd been too distracted to notice.

Stupid.

"Just the part about us not knowing each other," he said, easing some of her embarrassment. It would have really sucked if he'd caught the part about her finding him gorgeous.

She was still embarrassed about the hot alien comment from earlier.

"That's what I'm trying to do right now, Delaney"—he looked at her full lips again as if compelled to—"get to know you."

She didn't know how to respond so ended up not saying anything.

"I know your favorite food." The corner of his mouth turned up in an interested half smile. "Tell me something else."

"I'm a cat person," she managed, though the husky way she spoke made her wish she'd stuck with the silence thing a little longer. Her palms flattened against the surface of the wall. "Do you have cats on Xenith?"

"No," he divulged, "but I've seen them on your planet." His smile grew. "What else?"

"What else do you want to know?"

"Whatever you want to tell me."

This was seriously weird. Yet it was working: He'd successfully gotten her mind off her worry for Mariana and her parents. She was grateful for the distraction, and found that it made her want to oblige him and his game of twenty questions. But only if she got something out of it as well.

"I'll tell you mine if you tell me yours," she teased, surprised that she was able to with him still so close, invading her senses. His scent reminded her again of sitting around bonfires—which was giving her a serious craving for marshmallows—and made her want to do the oddest things. Like rub her cheek against the mus-cled curve of his neck.

She'd always been a sucker for fall, it was her favorite season, and if she'd been home right then, she'd no doubt be at one of the end-of-the-school-year fire pit parties. It was still spring there, but a bonfire always took her back to brisk autumn air and bursts of colorful leaves. That must be one of the reasons she felt so com-fortable around him. His smell was so familiar.

"All right," he agreed, pulling away. "But we should return to Olena's room first."

Not being out in the open seemed like a good plan, so she silently agreed and fell into step at his side.

CHAPTER 11

ell me what your favorite thing to do is," he persisted the moment they were back inside Olena's bedroom. "It's obviously not attending Tandem games."

"No," she said, and laughed, "definitely not. I like bowling."

"Bowling?" He pursed his lips. "Is that the sport where you knock things down?"

"Pins." She nodded. "You roll a ball down a lane and try to take out as many pins as you can. I'm fairly good, not to brag or anything. I spent a lot of time hiding out in the bowling alley in my town to avoid going home to an empty house. My parents both have strenuous jobs."

"We don't have anything like that here. But we do have movies. They're played on a stage and broadcast in actual 3-D. Perhaps we can go to one soon. Do you like movies?"

"Love them."

He was standing with his back to the window wall, hands tucked casually into the front pockets of his charcoal pants. Unlike in the hall, he maintained his distance, keeping a polite five feet between him and where she stood at the edge of the bed.

"Have you always wanted to be an Ander?" she asked.

"Yes," he replied, then glanced away. "Though it's not what I expected."

"How so?" She found she didn't like the unsure look in his eyes. She wanted to make it go away.

"No one wants to be around Olena," he offered, "and I am always around her. It makes . . . having other relations difficult. It doesn't help that I spent the last five years circling Earth's orbit. I needed to stay close in case there was an emergency and she needed me."

Delaney scanned his features, taking in the way his shoulders had slumped and how tired he suddenly appeared. She'd been so focused on herself, she hadn't noticed how much this situation had taken out of him as well.

"You're lonely." She felt bad the second she pointed it out, but he only chuckled.

"I have an important job," he said, as if that should be enough explanation.

The sound of approaching footsteps cut off anything else they were about to say. A second later a heavy fist knocked against the door.

Ruckus glanced at her, and it was clear he hadn't been expecting anyone. Another knock came, this one more impatient than the last, and he moved to answer. His spine stiffened as soon as he had it open.

Trystan was standing in the hall, head bowed down as he listened intently to the hushed whispers of a Kint soldier. A second after the door was opened, however, he held up three fingers, instantly hushing his companion and stared pointedly at the Ander.

Ruckus stiffly stepped to the side, allowing him entrance, but stopped the other Kint soldier at the doorway.

"Lissa Olena." Trystan approached and came to an easy stop before her. "I was looking for you earlier. I wanted to know how you were doing after the attack. Clearly my worry was misplaced." He glanced between her and Ruckus, staring a bit too intensely at her guard. "The Ander seems to have kept you in good health."

"And I see you survived as well." She ran her eyes from his toes upward, making sure to let her lips twist slightly, a small sign of her ire. She couldn't come outright and say that she hated him—that was obvious—especially with his man standing in the hallway over his shoulder. Didn't mean she had to be the epitome of polite, either.

Still, her reaction gave him pause.

"Don't push him, Delaney." Ruckus's warning echoed through her mind as if he were speaking directly into the curve of her ear.

The sudden intrusion caused her to shiver, a move that of course the Zane picked up on, because his surprised expression immediately morphed into one of satisfaction.

"I'm curious, Lissa Olena, what it is exactly you did on Earth all these years." He angled his head at her. "Surely it wasn't merely extreme sports and risks with jungle animals."

"Savanna, actually," she corrected coolly. "They're called the king of the jungle, but lions don't actually live there. Tigers do, as well as some other large feline species." At this point she didn't know why she was still talking, but figured it had something to do with her not wanting to hear the sound of his voice any longer.

There was a smooth timber to it that always sent her entire body into alert mode, as if her brain didn't know if it liked the way he spoke or not. She hated everything he said; that was a certainty at least. And the less time she spent in his presence, the better for everyone. Her hope from earlier that his hatred of Olena would keep him away dwindled. Obviously, his feelings were only going to make this harder.

"She's developed a fondness for cats," Ruckus divulged with a bored shrug, as if it were of very little importance.

"And here I thought you hated animals," he replied. "We should get together, talk more about your travels." He didn't bother looking Ruckus's way, but it was clear his next words indicated him: "In private."

"I'm not sure that's necessary . . . ," she began, but the rest of her sentence died in her throat when he took a single step closer, invading her personal space. Even knowing Ruckus was right there wasn't a huge comfort.

Unbidden, her gaze slid over to him, and she bit her tongue when she noted the fury burning through his eyes. Ruckus's hands were clenched once more into fists at his sides, a similar reaction to the one he'd had when the Basileus had threatened her earlier.

"It wasn't a request." Trystan brought her attention back to him. "We'll dine alone tonight. In my rooms."

"I've already promised to eat with the Basileus."

He nodded, but before she could feel even an inkling of relief, he followed it with, "I'm sure your father will understand that I'd want to check on you after the scare this morning. Brightan," he addressed the tall brunette man over his shoulder, "be sure to speak with the Basileus about his daughter's new evening schedule."

"Right away, Zane." The man, Brightan, bowed low, and then turned quickly on his heel. His shoulders were every bit as broad as the other two men still with her, with defined muscle to boot, but she knew he was only meant to carry out the appearance of a bodyguard.

Trystan didn't need anyone to protect him; that was painfully obvious.

"There, now that that's taken care of"—he moved around her stealthily, finding humor when she turned with him to keep her body facing his—"you no longer have a decent excuse as to why you shouldn't share a meal with your intended."

Her eyes narrowed, really hating the smug look that passed over his belying angelic features.

"Maybe I don't want to make your poisoning me any easier," she stated dryly.

He grinned. "You think I tried to kill you? What, this morning?" At her silence, he chuckled. "What a fascinating possibility. I would never stoop to poison, though, Lissa. It's a cowardly way to take a life, don't you agree?"

"No more so than a bomb."

If anything, her jab only caused his mirth to grow, and he openly laughed. "You're definitely going to have to tell me how you spent your time on Earth." Moving backward, he headed for the door, all the while perusing her from top to bottom. Just as he was about to reach the door, he twisted around and called over his shoulder, "Until tonight, Lissa."

It didn't pass her notice that he didn't deny involvement in the attack.

"You shouldn't be so quick with your tongue," Ruckus growled, shutting the door with a bit more force than necessary. "How many times do I need to repeat myself on this?"

She rolled her eyes. "Please, as if I stood a chance against the Basileus, or the Zane for that matter. Neither of them likes me very much, in case you didn't notice."

"The Basileus is fearful for his daughter," he pointed out, "and the Zane—"

"Hates me?" She held out her hands. "Yeah, I got that much. Who thought pairing the two of them up would be a good idea again? There's got to be an easier way to find peace. The way I see it, those two will end up killing each other before the honeymoon is over."

"We don't honeymoon here." He moved across the room toward the door in the nearest right corner. "And no one would suspect Olena of being capable of murder. Which is mostly what the problem is. You are far too outspoken to pass for her. She's a snob, yes, but no one would ever accuse the Lissa of being strong."

"Well"—she batted her lashes at him—"they will now."

"This isn't funny, Delaney," he said, and came back, spinning her around and pinning her to the wall so quickly, she sucked in a breath. Gone was the playful man he'd been before the Zane's arrival. This was the fierce Ander who'd taken her from that alley against her will. "I've asked you before and I'll ask you again. Are you trying to get yourself killed?"

"Of course not."

"Then stop baiting the people who could easily take your life."

"It's fine," she insisted. "You heard him. He thinks my change in personality has to do with five years spent on Earth, and he wouldn't be wrong. The Olena you're describing, the meek one who couldn't kill someone? Yeah, that's the same one who did this to me."

He opened his mouth to argue, but she pressed a firm finger to his lips. His eyes widened, but he didn't try to speak again.

"Would you want to be married off to a tyrant like Trystan," she asked, "or would you rather be dead? Olena found an option around those two. Pinning her misfortune on me is every bit as bad as if she'd attempted murder. I'm not just the wrong person, aka not her; I also happen to be *human*. One who knows nothing about your culture or your language, or your planet for that matter. I was just the girl she happened to bump into."

She took a deep breath. "I'm doing the best I can, Ruckus, but I've got to do this my way. I'll go crazy if I don't."

He squeezed his eyes shut and thought it over for a moment. It was obvious he was torn between being frustrated and understanding.

"Promise me you'll at least attempt to be more careful," he mumbled. "I can't get you home safely if you're dead, Delaney."

"If I die, there's war, right?" She waited until he'd opened his yellow-green eyes again and latched them on to her once more. "So I won't die. Wars are never fun."

He pulled back with a humorless grunt and ran a hand down his face. Sunlight streamed through the window to his right, and his shadow splayed across the soft carpet, stretching all the way to partially climb the opposite wall.

"What the hell is wrong with me?" he said, though it seemed to be to himself and not her.

Still, she frowned. "What do you mean?"

"Nothing."

"Got any ideas on how to get me out of dinner?" she asked after a moment of silence.

"No," he admitted, "but I've got a few on how to get you out of that skirt." At her look, he moved for the right-side door a second time. "I meant, I've got a more appropriate outfit in mind. Unless you want to wear that skimpy thing in front of the Zane again?"

She groaned and followed him, noting it led to a massive closet. "Has it really only been a day?"

"An eventful one, that's for certain." He started riffling through the outfits that were hung up, clearly seeking out something specific.

"Have you gone through her clothes before?" she asked. Why did that make her uncomfortable?

"I've gone through all her things," he replied. "It's my job."

"But you didn't go to Earth with her?" There was a round white ottoman situated in the center of the room, big enough to seat five. Going to it, she sat as she watched him move around the room like it was his instead of Olena's.

"The whole point of a denzeration is to go alone. That way there's no pressure from an outside force."

"Okay," she drawled, "but she's the princess. One who had no say in whether or not she actually got to stay at the end of her five-year trip, so wouldn't her situation have called for different rules? You on a ship staying in orbit doesn't seem like enough. I mean, what if the Kints had gotten her?"

"We were in a shaky peace with them already when she left," he said. "And we had weekly face-to-face check-ins. She lived in secure buildings with guards, and had a phone I could connect to whenever I wanted."

"If not the Kints, what about the Tars?" She leaned back on her arms, getting comfortable. "You had to think there was a chance they'd make it to Earth and try something."

"It's not as easy to get to your planet as you believe, Delaney." He smiled over at her. "Not even the Kints allow unauthorized personnel into space, and if they happened to let a group of Tars through, they'd easily be found out. It would have meant war."

"Why don't the Kints want war again?" She'd never really been told. Seemed to her if they wanted Earth so badly, they wouldn't just roll over. "Trystan despises Olena, and he really doesn't like the fact that he has to marry her. Why would he agree to that?"

"Because his father told him to," he explained, as if the answer were obvious. "He's the Rex, remember? As a Kint, you don't defy your Rex, even if you're the Zane. Especially then, really."

"Okay." She could buy that. "So then does Trystan have any siblings?"

"No, why?"

"Then he's the heir?"

"Yes . . ."

"And the Rex is fine with forcing his only child, and the future ruler of his people, into marrying a woman he hates?"

Heaving a sigh, Ruckus detached himself from his search and came over to sit next to her. Their knees bumped when he turned to better face her, but if he noticed, he made no sign of it.

"The Rex knows that war would mean great losses on both sides. He doesn't want to risk the lives of his people. It's his hope that by forcing a merger between us, his son will come to this conclusion as well."

"You're saying he does know how Trystan feels; he just doesn't care?"

"Once they're bound, it'll be Trystan's duty, by both Vakar and Kint law, to protect her. Because she's a Lissa, that protection must also fall on her people. By making them marry, the Rex is ensuring that his wish for peace is upheld. Even once he's gone, and Trystan takes the throne, he'll still be constrained by the binding law."

"That's what it's called here?" She quirked a brow. "A binding? Gee, how romantic. What do you guys call divorce?"

"We don't." He shook his head. "We don't have it. We mate for life."

She stared, suddenly feeling her cheeks begin to color.

Knowing her train of thought, he chuckled and stood to return to his task of finding her something else to wear. "I don't mean sex, Delaney. We can have sex before being bound to someone."

She couldn't see his face now, but she thought she heard a note of humor in his voice.

"We just take our vows more seriously than humans do. For us, a binding is more than merely marriage. Our species isn't as fertile as yours. When we bind with someone, we also undergo a practice that syncs our bodies together, sort of calibrating them to fit reproductively."

Um, what? She sat up and dropped her chin against her palm. "As in, you have to be programmed to have children with some-one? That's what you're saying?"

"Yes," he agreed. "Unless we decide to choose a human to bind with, we do."

She shifted in her seat, suddenly uncomfortable. "So . . . if you wanted to procreate with a human . . . ?"

"We wouldn't need to worry about the genetic programming," he confirmed, not nearly as bothered by this conversation as she was. "It's only difficult for us if it's a coupling with our own people. Human biology seems to accept us without the need for such extremes. It's one reason many of us have chosen to remain on Earth. Here, your only option is to sync your body with another. And it can only be programmed into our systems once."

"You'll only be able to procreate with one person?!" She didn't know why she felt so grossed out by that. Wasn't it technically the point? You married someone with the intention of being with them and only them for the rest of your life. You wouldn't even need to think about having children with someone else. Unless . . ."

"What if one of them dies?"

He ran a hand through his hair in frustration. "We don't age the same way as humans. Our life-span is longer, and our medicine has advanced to the point where we virtually can't get sick."

"But you can still die, right?" She shifted to the edge of her seat. "In an accident, or in battle." Otherwise, why be so freaked out about the possibility of a war?

"Yes," he clarified. "We can still die. To answer your question, if one person bound to another does so, then the one left living is, for all intents and purposes, considered barren."

"Well," she said, and let out a slow breath, "that's shitty."

"*That's* why we take binding with someone very seriously."

"Not if you're the Rex," she corrected, shrugging when he glared. "What? He's forcing his son to marry a woman he hates, *and* taking his chance of having children with someone he actually cares about. That sucks."

He narrowed his eyes at her. "Please tell me that's not sympathy I hear in your voice."

"Of course not." She waved him off. "It's pity."

"Delaney—"

"I feel bad for him," she said. "Come on, in light of what you just told me, how can you expect me not to? And I thought I was the prisoner here. Nope. That guy is as screwed as I am. No wonder he's such a jerk." She held up a hand to stop his approach. "I'm not saying his being a total douche bag is justified, only that I see where he's coming from, that's all."

"Trust me," he assured. "once you get to know him better, you won't feel that way anymore."

"Yeah," she said, letting the word drag on pointedly, "I really have no intention of getting to know him better."

"Finally." He sighed dramatically. "You say something intelligent."

"Hey!"

Finding what he'd been looking for, he tugged a garment off a rack and turned to hold it out to her.

"Here. Go put this on."

She stood and gave a mock salute before snatching it from his hand and leaving for the bathroom. His rich chuckle followed her.

CHAPTER 12

The Zane's rooms were all the way on the other side of the castle. It felt like they had to leave a half hour early just to make it on time, not that it mattered, because Trystan wasn't even there.

Instead his man, Brightan, had let her in, ordering that Ruckus was to remain outside. The only reason either of them had agreed was because Brightan would be waiting, too. The Kint had mumbled something about the Zane being delayed and then had swiftly sealed her in the massive suite alone.

They'd given the Zane a room similar in size to her own, with the same strange octagon shape. There was even a balcony. However, that was where the similarities ended. For one, this first room wasn't the bedroom, more a sitting room that had been decked out to look like an intimate dining area for the night. A round glass table big enough to seat four was situated right in front of the window, with a shallow glass bowl set in the center.

When she glanced inside the bowl, she found a single pale pink floating candle, the wick alight with an equally pink glow. Vaguely, she wondered how they got the flame to do that, but curiosity about the rest of her surroundings had her moving on.

Against the wall across from the window overlooking his balcony was a long silver table. An assortment of glass and metal bottles was scattered across it, the liquids sorted from light gold to dark amber.

"He color-coded his liquor." She sent the thought to Ruckus with a shake of her head. What a freak.

They'd agreed he'd remain close enough for their fittings to connect. They wouldn't keep the channel open but wouldn't ignore each other, either. That last part was mostly Ruckus's stipulation. He was worried about her and what would happen tonight. Since she was worried about the same things, she decided she was okay with having him in her head.

"This brown stuff in tall bottles is alcohol, right?" she added, absently touching the crystal topper of a bottle filled with mud-dark liquid.

"Not the same stuff you're used to," Ruckus replied, *"but yes, basically. If he offers, decline."*

She snorted. Obviously. Not that Trystan seemed like the type to "offer" often. He'd demand.

The walls here were painted pale gray, and the floor was black. It was almost like the room had been made for Trystan, with its monochrome coloring and cold, steel-like exterior. There were no pictures on the walls, and despite the tables that had been set up, the room felt empty.

Having already explored the sitting room, and assuming that the closet and bathroom were in the same places as in her own rooms, Delaney found herself drawn toward the last door.

It was painted a darker shade of gray than the walls, with a handle such a bright silver, it glinted in the lamplight. She pushed the door open and stepped inside the new room, reaching around the inner wall for a switch to help chase away the darkness. There was no point to that, however, because a moment later a single bulb at the very center flickered and painted the room in a golden hue.

"*Delaney*," Ruckus spoke, but she was too distracted.

She'd walked into Trystan's bedroom.

The bed was neatly made, the silky navy-blue bedspread so dark, it was practically black, and was without a single wrinkle. There was carpet in here, dark and thick so that her heel-covered feet sunk in.

Unfortunately, that was all she got to see before she heard someone shifting at her back.

"They're motion sensored," Trystan's smooth voice said. "The lights."

She spun around to find he was watching her from less than ten feet away. He'd stopped near the table, the pink glow from the candle casting wicked shadows across his angelic features. He appeared more the devil in disguise here than she'd ever seen him before, and a tingle swept up her spine.

This was dangerous, her snooping, and as if to reinforce her thoughts, he spoke again.

"But you knew that." He tilted his head. "Didn't you?"

Tugging the door to his room shut with a bit more force than necessary, she crossed her arms defiantly over her chest. She knew how ridiculous it was, trying to look intimidating to an alien twice her size, but pride wouldn't let her back down, or show how embarrassed she really felt at having been caught snooping. And in his bedroom, no less.

"You're late," she stated coolly.

"You waited." His eyes scanned her body languidly. "Interesting."

She had no idea what he was implying, but there was something. Not wanting to dwell on what she couldn't figure out, she motioned toward the still unset table. The quicker they got this started, the faster she could leave. She already didn't like the way he was looking at her, different from the steady hatred he'd carried during their past encounters. No, there was something else there, and the fact that she couldn't tell if it was suspicion made her even more uncomfortable.

"Are we going to do this or what?" she said with a huff. It wasn't hard playing the spoiled princess when she didn't like the guy in the room with her.

If he'd expected a different reaction to his tardiness, he didn't show it.

"Why don't you sit down?" he suggested in an almost purr. "I'll get dinner."

She chose the chair closest to the exit. It meant she'd have her back to the door and wouldn't be able to see who entered, but she knew that Ruckus was on the other side and would stop anyone who was a threat to her.

Except, of course, for the Zane, who he'd let right in.

Her choice also meant she had to pass the Zane to sit down, and though she kept as much space between them as possible, he seemed to touch her with his trailing gaze alone. The second she was tucked into the glass chair, her legs beneath the table, he gave a satisfied nod and moved for the bar. His deft fingers reached under the lip, and he pressed a hidden button.

The bottom of the bar opened up, the flat sides pulling to the right and left to expose a hidden inner chamber. There were two wide shelves within, each with two golden trays identical to the ones from breakfast.

Taking a tray in each of his large hands, Trystan slid them out and then brought them over. One tray floated into place in front of her, while the other slid into the empty spot directly across from her. But Trystan had already turned back to the bar, returning with two tall glasses that reminded her of champagne flutes. He held the one with the lighter amber-colored liquid out to her.

"Bergozy is your favorite, right?" he asked, settling into his seat. He lifted his own darker drink, sipping it and eyeing her over the rim.

She placed the glass down to the left of her tray without tasting it. "I didn't think you paid attention."

"To your likes and dislikes?" He quirked a thin blond brow. The setting sun outside the large window wall to his right cast a sparkling array of warm tones across his already golden skin. His sky-blue eyes were bright, the ring of crimson around them a beautiful contrasting color closer to burgundy right then.

He'd changed his outfit from before, so that he was wearing an all-blue suit that looked like it'd come straight from a fashion runway. He'd paired the dark navy suit jacket and pants with a crisp shirt that matched the main sky color of his eyes, and had left the first three buttons undone to show an inch of bare chest.

"I don't," he finished, draining his glass before dropping it down to the surface of the table with a click. "I assumed dressing as someone from Earth would make you more comfortable, seeing as how you enjoyed your time there so much."

Great, so he'd caught her eyeing him. Awesome.

"Picking my favorite drink and dressing to impress?" She made a tsk. "Careful, seems like you're paying attention to my likes and dislikes now."

"Is it your favorite, though?" He motioned to her untouched

glass. "You haven't even tried it yet." It was a clear challenge, and he waited patiently for her to rise to the occasion.

She knew she'd agreed not to drink any of the alcohol, but there was no way she could turn Trystan down now. It would be way too suspicious for her to refuse, and would also lead to his thinking she wanted to keep a clear head in order to stay on her toes. The last thing she needed was his knowing how nervous he made her.

Lifting the drink, she took a tentative sip, almost giving herself away when a burst of fruit flavors surprised her. It was sort of like grapefruit and lemons, a combination she would have thought too citrusy but that somehow worked.

She swallowed down another sip and then returned it to the table. A rush of warmth spread through her, and she immediately felt some of the tension ease from her muscles. Which wasn't good, because she needed to keep her wits about her in order to survive this—possibly even literally.

"You like it." He grinned then like the cat that ate the canary.

"Did you expect me not to?" Okay, now she was confused. . . .

"It's just"—he propped his elbows on the table—"you used to hate it. After seeing you clearly enjoy the Tandem this morning, I was curious to discover what else is different. As I've already admitted, I know next to nothing about you, Lissa, other than of course the fact that you're an indulgent—"

"Child?" she cut him off, quickly taking another sip despite knowing it was a bad idea. "Hmm, so you've mentioned." It didn't pass by her notice that he'd purposefully left out the part about almost being blown up at said Tandem this morning.

He'd tricked her, telling her that it was something she liked and then divulging that Olena hated it. The real question was why?

"Which makes me curious," she went on, hoping to get to the heart of the situation, "why I'm here right now. What's the purpose of us eating together when there's nothing to do but trade insults?"

Instead of answering, he motioned to the tray in front of her. "You should eat. Go ahead." His eyes glimmered. "I made sure not to order crumvit."

Shit. He'd noticed her avoiding the pink stuff on her plate this morning, which she assumed was called crumvit. Just how attentive had he secretly been?

She forced herself to reach out and lift the lid like he'd suggested. "My tastes have changed since my trip."

"It seems a lot has with you." He nodded, removing the top to his own dinner.

Delaney blinked down at her plate, at first thinking she must be hallucinating. A glance over at the dish in front of him, however, proved otherwise. A cheeseburger with a fluffy toasted bun and a piece of crisp, vibrant green lettuce sat next to a heaping pile of crispy, browned French fries. There was a dollop of ketchup to the side, as well as another darker one she recognized as barbeque sauce.

The smell was a fresh mixture of tangy spices and medium-cooked meat, almost like she'd just ordered it straight from a restaurant on Earth.

Unable to cover her frown this time, she met his gaze. "What is this?"

"Don't you know?"

"Obviously—"

"Then that's a pretty stupid question, don't you think?"

"Where did you get this?" she bit out, clenching her hands

under the table. The see-through table, so of course he saw, and the corner of his mouth turned up mockingly.

"I instructed the cooks to make it," he said. "After your reaction to breakfast this morning, I assumed you could use something more familiar. Five years is a long time to be away from home; it's really not that surprising you've developed a taste for Earth food. I myself have never tried"—he circled a finger over his own burger—"this before, so I'm warning you now, if I don't like it, I'll be very cross with you."

"It's not like I ordered you to get it," she pointed out, narrowing her eyes.

He chuckled. "You couldn't order me to do anything, Lissa. Let's not forget that."

"That's right. I'm not the Rex." She realized mentioning his father was a huge mistake a second later when his eyes heated like daggers and his shoulders tensed to the point that he looked twice the size he'd been a moment prior.

"Neither of us is pleased about this," she carried on, easing her voice some so that it was no longer taunting or accusatory. She hoped it didn't noticeably shake. "Is goading each other really the best solution?"

Instinct told her that pushing him right now would be the worst mistake of her life. As pissed as he'd just made her, only one of them was an alien capable of choking the life out of the other.

"We're both slaves to our king's will," he stated. "For now, the Rex dictates my life, and the Basileus dictates yours. It doesn't mean I have to like it, or you for that matter."

"I can say the same," she pointed out. "It's clear we're a terrible match."

"But we *were* matched." He picked up his cheeseburger. "And in less than two months we'll be bound if our fathers have their way."

She reached for Ruckus, felt the now familiar burn at her neck. *"They're getting married in two months?!"*

"That is the current plan," Ruckus confirmed.

Before she could respond, Trystan made a sound in the back of his throat, something akin to a moan. His eyes were closed, and he was slowly chewing the bite he'd just taken, clearly savoring it.

"It appears I won't have to punish you after all," he told her once he'd swallowed. "This is actually very good."

"Being here is punishment enough," she expressed. She'd tried to ease the tension, tried being passably nice, and he'd wanted none of it. Sure, he was scary and could kill her bare-handed, but one attempt at being the voice of reason here was enough for her.

He didn't get angry by her words anyway, motioning to her own untouched food instead and ordered, "Eat."

Not having a good enough reason not to, she did as he said. They settled into a reasonably tolerable silence, both of them diving into their food. And why not? It was the only thing in the room either of them actually liked.

For the second time that day Delaney felt bad for Olena—and for Trystan. It must suck being told you were going to share your life with someone you couldn't even share a single meal with. If she'd been in Olena's shoes, she'd have wanted an out as well; though, she liked to believe she was a better person and wouldn't have screwed over some innocent in order to save her own skin.

Trystan got up suddenly, startling her from her musings. Even more surprising, she noticed that they'd both finished eating. At some point, she must have sipped more of the bergozy as well, for the glass that'd been mostly full was more than half empty.

That explained the fuzzy feeling in her head.

Grabbing the last two trays on the bottom rack, he brought them over and placed them on top of their empty dinner plates. Without waiting for her this time, he lifted the lid on his and picked up a golden fork to his left. Still, he didn't take a bite, but met her gaze across the table. During the silence, some of his insufferable humor had come back, and along with it the challenging glint.

Opening her tray, she couldn't help the slight smile at what she found.

A single slice of pumpkin pie was displayed, perfectly positioned in the center of the gold plate. It was roughly four inches across at the crust, tapering down to a perfect point. A huge swirl of lightly whipped cream topped it off.

The dessert on Trystan's plate was different, a chocolate brownie-type pie with a chocolate crumble crust and a matching heaping of cream. He twirled the fork in his left hand, the light in his eyes only brightening with her reaction.

"I chose the right one," he said, and nodded, pleased with himself. He must have noted the way she'd all but overlooked his pie for her own.

"Pumpkin pie is my favorite," she tentatively divulged. Unable to resist, she picked up her own fork and cut a decent chunk off the end. "All fall things, really."

It tasted like bliss in her mouth, and she struggled not to make the same moaning sound he had when he'd bitten into his burger. It was hard though, really hard, especially because he'd somehow managed to find the best damn pumpkin pie she'd ever had in her entire life. And she'd eaten a lot of pumpkin pie over the years.

She wanted to stop him when his arm stretched across the table, but figured he'd been the one to get the pie in the first place, so . . .

She leaned back as he scooped some with his own fork, and watched as he brought it to his mouth. The widening of his eyes actually made her laugh.

"It's good, right?" She took another bite. The sliding of metal across glass had her glancing up a second time, and she blinked when she found he'd pushed his plate toward her.

"So is this," he said, as if she needed prompting, then waited patiently for her to try his dessert. When she had, he pulled it back, continuing to eat.

Slowly, she placed the fork into her mouth, the bittersweet taste of dark chocolate coating her tongue. She had to admit he was right: It was also very good. She wanted to ask where they'd gotten the ingredients, whether or not they actually had pumpkins and cocoa beans here on Xenith, but refrained. Making a note to ask Ruckus about it later, she finished off her pie.

"You should ask for it at your Uprising," Trystan suggested, smirking at her now empty plate. "It's still two weeks away; I'm sure the Basileus won't mind changing the menu. I believe I was told the Basilissa had chosen gremming in your absence." He made a face. "Dreadful. How they even call that a dessert here in Vakar is beyond me."

She was still caught on the Uprising portion of his speech. What was it, and why was it happening in two weeks? Surely, if it was still on, the Basileus thought they'd have found Olena by then. That was good, wasn't it?

That was all she'd have to survive, another two weeks at most, and then she could go back to Earth. That wasn't so bad. She could manage until then, especially now that she'd gotten a burst of fresh hope.

"That's an interesting choice." Finished now with his dessert as well, he'd leaned back in his chair and was eyeing her outfit.

She'd worn what Ruckus had pulled from the closet, a ruby-red dress that hugged her curves in all the right ways. There was a layer of lace that made up the sleeves that went to her elbows, and while the original material only dropped a few inches down her thighs, a sheer skirt went the rest of the way, long enough to practically trail on the floor even in her three-inch black heels. The bottom part of the sheer material turned red once more, with it trailing upward to her shins in patterns that reminded her of flames.

While she'd been a bit uncomfortable with it at first, after Ruckus had shown her a few pieces from the rest of Olena's closet, she'd immediately agreed with him. Apparently, the Lissa didn't own anything longer than mid-thigh, and not a single pair of pants. There were a couple of shorts, but those were even shorter than the dresses had been.

Because of the type of table, Trystan was getting a perfect view of what might as well have been bare thigh, considering the sheer material. The neckline was also low enough that every time she'd bent toward her dish, she'd probably given him a decent look down the front. He knew about her black bra at that point, that was for sure.

Back home, Delaney hadn't been a prude by any standard, but she wouldn't have been caught dead in something this revealing, either. She'd even worn decent clothing to the club the other night. Up until this point, the room and the meal had distracted her, but now she felt her cheeks staining, and she uselessly smoothed her hands over her lap, leaving them there to cover as much bare skin as possible. Which wasn't much at all.

If anything, her tiny hands only managed to make her legs appear longer, and she gritted her teeth, wondering if he saw the same thing.

The sudden spark of heat in his eyes killed any hope of that not being the case.

"Not any more so than what you went with," she said, indicating his suit and trying to regain control of the situation.

"Are you a wolf in sheep's clothing then, Lissa?" he asked. "That is how the Earth saying goes, isn't it?"

For once his underlying threat actually made her more comfortable. They needed to get back to the two of them trading barbs, forget that this odd moment had ever happened.

"Well." She pushed her chair back and stood, hoping her legs weren't visibly shaking. "As great as this has been—"

"You're afraid you must excuse yourself?" he teased, throwing her words from earlier at the Tandem back at her. He didn't rise, remaining calm and relaxed in his seat. He was almost too relaxed.

"Are you mocking me?" she asked, despite the pressure in her chest urging her to just let it go and leave.

"Not at all." He shook his head. "It took you longer than I expected to run."

She bristled. "I'm not running."

"Of course not," he agreed in a tone that was clearly disingenuous. "You'd have nowhere to go, and you're smart enough to know not to bother trying. Aren't you, Lissa?"

"You're threatening me." Oh yeah, she totally should have left a minute ago instead of starting down this path. For a moment things between them hadn't been so bad, but now that stealthy Zane from before had returned in full force.

This had been a mistake, a huge mistake. She needed to get out of there.

"I'm merely pointing out what you astutely did earlier," he explained. "That so long as the Rex and the Basileus continue to seek out this ridiculous merger, you and I are stuck here. I can't escape any more than you can."

She froze, panic momentarily buzzing in her ears so loudly, she couldn't hear anything else.

"What do you mean by that?" she said breathlessly, hating how her voice quavered.

"Only that you can't hide"—he leaned forward, though he still didn't rise—"not even on Earth."

She thought of something, grasped on to it like a lifeline. "You still don't believe I went to a fair."

"No." He shook his head. "I do not. The Lissa Olena I know wouldn't be caught dead at a grungy human fair."

"Well, I'm clearly not the Olena you think you know."

"Clearly," he repeated, angling his head at her.

When he didn't say anything more, she gulped and took a step back. He didn't stop her, so she moved all the way to the door, turning with her hand already on the handle to glance back at him over her shoulder.

He was still watching her, but she couldn't read his expression, and she didn't like the way his lips were curved up in a knowing half smirk that turned her blood to ice.

"Have a nice evening, Lissa," he murmured, and despite being on the other side of the room, she heard him clear as day. "We'll do this again." He caught her gaze, smirk broadening. "Soon."

She wasn't proud of it, but she threw the door open and fled.

CHAPTER 13

She'd been—not so proudly—spending the morning hiding away in her room when the brisk knock came at her door. Ignoring it, Delaney remained where she was, lying back on the bed, looking up at the skylight. Above, the sky was a mixture of sea green and grayish blue; she'd been staring at it for the past hour.

The sound of the door opening had her stiffening, but she still didn't move. A second later Ruckus's face hovered above hers, forcing her to acknowledge his presence. He shook his head and pulled back, silently waiting.

With a groan of annoyance, she sat up and glared at him. "What?"

"Get dressed." He tossed a bundle of clothing onto the bed at her side and crossed his arms. There was a patient but steady look about him, like he was prepared to wait all day if he had to, but he fully intended to get his way.

She fingered the bundle to give her a moment to stall, then asked, "Why?"

"I have a surprise for you." The corner of his mouth turned up, but aside from that, it was the only part of him that budged.

"I'm good, thanks." She pushed the clothing away.

"Delaney." He sighed, dropping his arms to his sides. "I understand you need some time after dealing with the Zane last night, but I'd like to show you something good about my planet. Something to remind you that we aren't all bad."

She hesitated. It wasn't as if staying here could actually keep Trystan away from her; the fact that he'd barged in yesterday was proof of that. At least if she went now, she'd be with Ruckus, whom she trusted a hell of a lot more than anyone else on Xenith. Seeing no other good option, she stood and snatched the bundle off the bed before heading toward the bathroom.

A few minutes later she came out and lifted a brow at him.

The swimsuit looked exactly like the ones back home, and she wondered if that was where it had originally come from. The bottoms were gold, and hung a few inches below her navel. Apparently, the Vakar hadn't gotten the memo that high-waist bottoms were back in. The top was a shade lighter, with a glittery material that tied behind her back. A mint-green sundress had been given to her to put over it.

"Swimming?" She crossed the room to the closet and grabbed a pair of white wedges off the nearest shelf.

"It's much more than that." He waited until she'd slipped the shoes on and then asked, "What's wrong?" Now he was watching her with a slight frown, an odd expression on someone always so put together.

And he was. His spine was always straight, shoulders always back. His gaze assessed everything at once, and even when he appeared relaxed, she could tell his body was ready to snap into action at a moment's notice.

It was clear he could be hard, but ever since discovering her true identity, he'd been, for the most part, gentle with her. He certainly hadn't treated her like the Basileus had.

At his pressing look, she sighed.

"You mean besides the fact that I feel half naked in front of you? I'm not used to wearing a bikini in front of aliens."

He chuckled and she narrowed her eyes. "Don't worry. I'll be in a similar situation once we get there." There was a suggestive note in his tone, and she quickly looked away.

"Where are we going, anyway?" she asked the second they were out in the hall.

"You'll see," his words trickled into her head.

"That's never gonna stop being creepy," she told him aloud. Unable to keep her own smirk at bay, however, she added, "And awesome."

"It can be annoying," he confessed. "Imagine over a dozen people trying to speak to you telepathically all at once."

"You have that many people dialed in to your frequency?" That seemed like way too many. She was already uncomfortable with just the one. *"Can* they talk to you all at once?"

"In a way." He pursed his lips, clearly trying to think up the best way to explain. "It's more like voicemail. I receive the first one sent, and then it continues to play the rest. But I can't pause to respond, so if I have five messages, I have to wait until I've listened to them all and then remember what they said before I can answer. I can turn the setting off, but being connected to so many people is risky without the delay. All those voices reaching my head at the same time could cause an overload in the system."

"What would happen to you?"

"Basically, I'd have an aneurism." He shrugged like it was no big deal.

"Let's just keep that setting on"—she patted the side of his arm—"forever."

Passing her a sly look, he asked, "Why? Would that bother you?"

"If something in your brain pretty much exploded? Yeah." Okay, she was being a bit dramatic, but picturing it, a strong guy like him helpless to stop something like that, made her queasy.

"You're worried about me." He flashed her a smile, then pressed a flat palm against the double doors in front of them.

There were no guards in this section of the castle—she couldn't remember the last time she'd seen someone—and these doors were unlocked. Made from a flimsier material, they swung inward at just the slightest push.

Ruckus entered first, then held them open for her, a challenging light in his eyes that she couldn't resist.

It was an indoor pool, but nothing like what one would find at a hotel or a mansion back home.

There wasn't sand, or traditional tile; instead the ground was covered with a fluffy plant, almost like grass that'd been given a perm. The pool itself was an odd shape that curved in some places and went straight in others, flowing around the bumpy walls made of various stones, and swirling around the three large stone columns that sprouted upward toward the ceiling.

In the center of the pool was another smaller pool, perfectly circular, that stood at least a yard higher than the original, with a set of winding stone steps that curled from the edge of the main pool around the left side of the rise to disappear in the back.

There was a green tint to the water, and a sweet smell of almonds permeated the air. She would have believed they were outside on some jungle island if it weren't for the skylight above, a clear glass bubble that shielded them, curving down to meet walls covered with climbing vines and other foliage.

She moved over to the edge of the pool and reached up to touch a tiny white star-shaped flower. There were seemingly billions of them, sprouting from the vines in scattered pinpricks of white and pale yellow. Their petals were silky soft but were pointed in five directions. The almond smell was coming from them.

"Stellaperier. The best translation I can think of would be 'star climbers.'" Ruckus had stepped up behind her, close enough so that his warm breath blew against her neck, causing the petals of the nearest flowers to flutter. "There's a story to them, where it's said that each bloom was really a star reborn. They reach for the sky because they remember their old lives and wish to return."

Sounded familiar.

"Ruckus," she said, "I want to go home."

"I'll get you back there," he assured her. "I promise."

"I shouldn't keep making you tell me that." She forced a smile. "But it helps to hear it."

"At night the flowers glow," he told her after a pause.

"They do not." Then she spun around quickly, too quickly, and almost tripped. His hands at her arms stopped her, and she sucked in a breath at their proximity. She took a moment where all she did was stare at his chest, the part that came at her eye level. Then she risked a glance up, and her heart rate increased.

Oh no. His attractiveness was starting to work on her.

He grinned knowingly and released her, moving over to the edge of the pool. Then he reached back and tugged off his black T-shirt in one swoop. He tossed it onto the strange ground without a care, deft fingers already moving to undo the button of his pants.

She turned, pretending to find something interesting across the room, but his barely restrained laugh clued her in that he knew exactly what she was doing. She'd never been shy around the opposite sex before—didn't have a ton of experience with them, either, but enough not to blush every time a guy dropped his pants.

He'd come prepared, having put swim trunks on underneath. They were a bright ruby red, a sharp contrast to his golden complexion. Hell, to his golden everything.

A real golden boy," she thought, not really meaning to, and froze when she realized what she'd done. Her hand slapped against the back of her neck, cheeks staining the same shade as his suit, and a wide grin split across his gorgeous face.

"Golden boy, huh?" he preened.

"It must have mistaken my thought process as activation," she cursed. "Stupid alien technology."

"So you were thinking about me?"

She threw her arm out pointedly toward the water. "Are we going in or what?"

Ruckus openly laughed, seemingly finding great pleasure in her frazzled state. He began wading into the pool, and her traitorous thoughts homed in on the contours of his back and the way his spine arched, and brought her gaze down to his tapered waist. His arms were corded muscle, his legs and torso long. She'd thought he was hot with clothes on, but seeing him like this . . .

He spun around once he was up to his chin, the grin still in place. No doubt he knew she'd just been ogling him some more. So far his people were an attractive species, reminding her of models back on her planet. He'd probably discovered the effect he had on the opposite sex years ago.

"Delaney," he said, "come in."

She licked her lips, stubbornly crossing her arms and cocking out a hip. She was still wearing the green dress and the shoes. The air here was getting crisp, licking against her skin in a way that left chills behind. The water looked like it'd be the perfect temperature, not too warm, not too cold.

"What if I promise to show you sometime? Will you come in then?" he said, and she blinked.

"What?"

"The flowers," he said, and chuckled, clearly knowing where her mind had just been. "I'll bring you here one of these nights and show you. You've never seen anything like it." He held her gaze. "They used to be the only thing in this entire castle I actually enjoyed being around."

A bitter taste rose in her mouth, and the warm feeling that'd been collecting in her lower belly vanished.

"Ruck—"

"What color is your hair?"

She frowned. "My hair? It's red."

"Red." The corner of his mouth turned up in an interested half smile. "We don't have redheads here. You'd be a commodity. Everyone would stare."

"So it's a good thing I look like Olena then, huh?" she managed.

"What color are your eyes?" Obviously, he was determined.

"They're green," she said. Then she added, "I got them from my grandmother."

"What shade of green?" he asked.

"I've been told they look exactly like a cat's."

"You and cats." He tilted his head, eyes roaming over her as if trying to picture what she'd look like as someone else. He'd see the black-haired girl he'd known for years, Olena. It was her body right now shoved into the sundress. Her eyes he saw rolling, her arms. Her legs. Her lips.

"You can stare all you like." Even to her own ears, she sounded deflated. "You'll never really see me."

Ruckus flinched and was standing less than an inch in front of her before she could blink. Taking her by the elbows, he held her steady until she met his gaze, staring up at him from under her long lashes.

Were her lashes even long to him? She couldn't recall what Olena's looked like, if they were long or short and stumpy. Black, or dark brown.

"I'll never really see me," she pondered, pursing her lips. "At least, not the me that you're seeing. Does that make sense?" When he didn't respond, she elaborated. "I don't know what I look like to you, Ruckus. I don't know if when I make a sad face, that's what everyone here actually sees. I don't know Olena's expressions or her mannerisms, or if any of my own carry over correctly."

And, considering how hard it still was for her to look in the mirror, she didn't really see that changing anytime soon.

"You arch your brow when you think someone has said something stupid," he told her quietly. "When you're nervous, you chew on the side of your cheek. It's almost imperceptible; I wouldn't have even picked up on it if I hadn't been watching you so closely during breakfast. And when you're angry"—he reached out and brushed his thumb lightly between her brows—"your eyes harden, and a tiny crease forms right here."

He smoothed his thumbs over the curves of her elbows. "Olena never did any of those things. Really, she only had the two settings: pouty and bitchy. Though, now that I'm thinking about it, she could really pull off spacey as well."

"I'm pretty sure you're not supposed to be saying stuff like that about your Lissa," she said for lack of a better thing to say.

"Until this is all sorted, you're my Lissa." The tiny V formed between his thick brows once more. "You wear her so differently."

"That is seriously disgusting," she told him honestly. "It sounds like I skinned her and made a suit. Really, there was no other way you could have put that? Maybe even just not saying anything would have worked."

Instead of apologizing, he lifted a hand to brush aside a strand of her hair, still frowning. "I wish I could see you."

"I wish you could see me, too," she whispered, surprised to find she meant it. Pulling away, she made a big show of rolling her eyes, then bent to undo the straps of her wedges. Kicking those off, she took a moment to relish the soft spongy feel of the odd grass between her toes, then yanked the sundress over her head.

With a start, she realized there were actually perks to looking like someone else. If he had been able to see the real her, she might have been more self-conscious. As it was, Olena had a great form, and one that he apparently knew well. There wasn't anything Delaney could do that he hadn't already seen from the actual Lissa.

There was a certain freedom in that.

To his credit, he kept his eyes locked on hers, not taking in her body—aka Olena's body. When he offered his hand, she took it, and he moved backward, never once breaking eye contact. It was deeper the farther in they went, and closer to the center where he could still stand, her feet hovered over the bottom.

A glance toward the doors showed her that there was a hallway that overlooked the pool. The side that faced them was all glass, so that whoever walked by could look down and see the swimmers.

She didn't know why, but it creeped her out. There was a distinct fishbowl feeling to it.

She'd been swimming since she was four, so she let go of him and began enjoying the warm water. Her skin tingled slightly whenever she moved, and she shot him a questioning look.

"It's got healing properties," he explained. "The green tint is a type of algae found on remote parts of Xenith. A Sutter"—the Vakar word for scientist—"discovered it about five hundred years ago. It's very expensive and hard to come by, but the Basileus insisted on having it added to this place. It's a less aggressive version of the Alter Pool, which is a healing source of water that can mend even bone. Only the royal family is allowed access to it. But this will do, and we're allowed to be here. It'll heal your cuts and bruises, ease headaches, the like."

"Is that why you brought me here?" She'd ask more about the Alter Pool later.

"I figured you could use some relief from all the stress," he confessed. "Don't Earth girls like spa days? That's what you call them there, correct?"

"My mother loves them." She started swimming slow, leisurely circles around him as she spoke. "She goes twice a month. I was invited along once, before my senior prom. It was supposed to be a special treat, so that I'd look and feel my best at the dance. I thought we'd get to spend some time together, but we didn't. She went off and had a private massage, scheduled me for a mud bath. Suffice it to say, not my thing."

"And what is your thing?" Before she could answer, he reached out, hooking his arm around her small waist and pulling her in.

Her body slapped against his hard chest, and she instinctually wrapped her arms around his neck. She could feel the thumping of his heart where her breasts were pressed tightly against him, and realized that her own was beating to the same frantic rhythm. Their mouths were mere centimeters apart, and the algae-laced water had done nothing to diminish his firewood scent from this close.

"Um, I like"—she had to pause and re-wet her throat—"bowling." Her mind latched on to the first thing she could think of, and she realized the second his lips turned up how stupid that was. "But I already told you that."

"Yes," he agreed, "you did."

"I also like—"

"Tamales," he interrupted. "And movies."

She narrowed her eyes in mock annoyance. "You trying to impress me or something, Ruck?"

"Ruck?" He canted his head as if thinking it over. "I preferred the nickname Golden Boy, but I guess I'll take what I can get."

She hadn't even noticed she'd shortened his name. It was a bad habit of hers, something she did with all the people in her life she felt comfortable with. There wasn't a friend she'd had in her lifetime that was without a nickname.

"Olena had one of those for the Zane, you know," he added.

"She had a nickname for the guy she hated? Was it 'Asshole'?"

"No," he said, and laughed, "though that one's much better. It was Tryst. She said he was physically everything anyone could ever want in a guy, so she'd love to have a tryst with him. That was before their first conversation, of course. Up until then, she used to pine for him in the back of the room."

"Should we be doing this?" she asked then, not wanting to think about Trystan anymore.

"What?" He lifted a brow. "Having fun?"

"Sure." She shrugged. "That. And this." She waved in the tiny bit of space left between them. "Is this something that you and Olena usually did? Get this close?"

"I've seen her naked," he confessed. Then, before she could process how she felt about that, he said, "But she's never seen me naked. We weren't together, Delaney, and I told you the truth before. I've never been attracted to her."

"But you are now?" In his eyes, he was currently holding Olena's body flush against his, after all. It was her mouth he kept sneaking glances at, her eyes, not Delaney's green ones, that he was staring into.

His grip around her waist tightened, and he cupped her head in his hand, holding her steady. "No. She isn't who I'm attracted to. You are."

She allowed herself a moment to enjoy the feel of his hands on her, the heat sparking between them. There was a comfort whenever they were together, as if she knew, despite his being the one who'd taken her, that he would keep her safe. That he would keep his promise to get her back home.

Pulling away was hard, but she disengaged their bodies and floated back a few feet to create space. At his confused and hurt look, she shook her head. She wanted him to keep holding her, and that was scary.

"I wish I could believe that," she ended up saying. "That you really are feeling this way because of me . . ."

"But you don't," he said, catching on. "Because I don't know what you look like?"

"Because to you I look like her." She wanted to try to get him to understand, yet she didn't know how to. It was simple in her mind, but clearly he didn't feel the same way, because his frustration was apparent.

Suddenly he cocked his head to the side, listening to something she couldn't hear. It took her a moment to realize someone must have connected with him telepathically. She thought about asking how far the connection stretched but figured now wasn't the right time. That was even more apparent when he started for the shore.

"Something's come up," he told her, already dressed by the time she'd joined him. Bending down, he snatched her dress and held it out to her, avoiding looking her way. "I'm needed back in the joint room."

She'd ask what a joint room was later as well. It took her longer to strap her shoes back on than it did to pull the dress over her wet suit. Either Ruckus hadn't thought about bringing towels, or in his haste to get away from her, he just didn't want to bother with them. He was waiting by the door when she finished, and she walked over.

There was no real reason for her to do it, but at the last moment she found herself looking up. Her heart froze in her chest when her eyes locked on cornflower-blue-and-crimson ones.

Trystan was standing in the glass hallway, staring down at her.

CHAPTER 14

O lena!"

Delaney rolled over, swatting at the hands shaking her arms. In her groggy dream state, she couldn't understand the words, but she knew she wanted to be left alone.

"Olena!" The person shook her harder, cursed, and then yanked her off the bed and onto her feet.

Letting out a yelp, she snapped fully awake and blinked up at a pair of yellow-green eyes. Strong arms banded around her, one at her waist and the other around her shoulders, holding her up. He wasn't dressed in his uniform, and even though that confused her, for a second she didn't understand who he was or where she was.

Then he shook her again, and she gripped his shoulders to keep her head from snapping back by the force.

"Damn it, Ruckus," she growled, it all rushing back to her.

He'd brought her back from the pool and had left her in Olena's rooms without a word. She'd spent the rest of the night pacing. Glancing up, she saw that it still wasn't fully morning, a shadowy glow cast around the room. She couldn't have been asleep for more than two hours.

"We need to go, now," he bit out, turning to drag her toward the door.

That was when she noticed Lura was also standing there, wearing a thin silver nightgown that barely reached her knees. That explained why Ruckus had been calling her Olena. The other girl was pale, and was wringing her hands in front of her. Her gaze kept shifting from them to the open door where Pettus was waiting.

Delaney could hear shouts from the hall, and every few seconds a group of soldiers rushed by.

"What's going on?" She tried to loosen his hold as he practically dragged her away from the bed. She'd gone to sleep in one of the gold nightgowns from Olena's closet. The damn thing was even shorter than Lura's, and barely covered anything.

"We're under attack," he growled.

"What?!"

"Just get moving, Olena!" Ruckus got them out the door and moved his grip to her arm so that she was standing on her own feet. Without sparing her a glance, he began leading them down the hall, trailing her behind him so quickly, she kept almost tripping.

"Report?" he asked Pettus, the other soldier moving up to the right.

"They've been held back at the entrance. After the explosion security swarmed in. Tellers are holding them off as we speak. It shouldn't be long," Pettus informed him. They reached a four-way stop, and Pettus took a step to the right, giving a nod, before heading away and blending in with another group of soldiers dressed in forest green.

"There's been *another* explosion?" She hadn't understood anything else he'd said, but she was pretty sure that was the most important part anyway.

"Yes." Ruckus pulled them down another hall, this one narrower than the rest. "At the front of the building. A supply craft had a bomb hidden on it. By the time the men at the gate picked up on the device's signature, it was too late. It took out the fountain."

"There's a fountain?" She hadn't seen the front of the castle yet, the only time she'd been outside being at the Tandem game. Now that she was thinking about it, though, all the explosions seemed to be happening out there. Maybe sticking indoors was the smartest way to go.

"There was."

They came to a sudden stop in front of a painting of a tall man with blond hair dressed similarly to how the Basileus was dressed yesterday. Curling his fingers around the left edge of the gold frame, Ruckus unhooked a latch and the painting swung outward.

"This is you." He motioned toward Lura, who'd been following quietly behind them.

She moved forward and reached up to pull herself into the dark cavern that the painting had revealed. It was another hallway of a sort, with no lighting. There was no way of telling how deep it went.

"Wait." Delaney stopped him when he went to close the painting after Lura. "We're leaving her?"

"This leads straight to the basement," he explained, shrugging off her hold so he could finish.

She and Lura stared at each other until the hidden door clicked shut once more.

"Shouldn't she stay with us?" she couldn't help but ask, thinking that being with him was safer than anywhere Lura could be going.

"No," he said, and started forward again. "The royal family has a different security location. That's where we're going. I'll drop you off and then—"

"Absolutely not." She dug her heels into the floor so that he'd either stop or drag her. He stopped. "I want to stay with you."

Another blast went off before he could respond, and this time she felt it. The walls actually shook around them, and her eyes widened. Without knowing what she was doing, she'd stepped closer to him, allowing him to wrap his arms around her tinier form for the second time. Huddled against his chest, surrounded by him, she was able to take a breath.

"Something else just happened," he told her, as if she hadn't already figured that out. "I need to go out and check on it, help my men. I'm the Ander, Delaney. It's my job."

"I thought your job was to keep me safe," she mumbled against the smooth black cloth of his shirt. She inhaled deeply, letting his familiar scent of crackling firewood comfort her. On some level she knew she was being childish, asking him to stick around, clinging to him like she was.

"It is," he said calmly. She felt him hesitate, then his chin dropped to the top of her head and his voice lowered huskily. "I'm going to bring you to the Basileus. His security team is made up of the strongest and best-trained soldiers in Vakar. They'll protect you until I come back for you."

She didn't say anything, allowing him to tip her head up toward him after a moment.

"I have to do this, Delaney," he reminded her, scanning her face for understanding. "I don't have a choice."

She licked her lips, not liking the flash of fear in her chest. "And if you did?"

He let out a stuttering breath and ran the knuckles of his right hand across her cheek. The caress was featherlight and over in a matter of seconds. The sun was coming up now, so the hallway was starting to turn umber and dust motes danced around them like specks of glitter.

"I'd stay with you," he whispered, almost too low for her to hear. Another boom rent the air, this one closer than the last. The glass in the panes across from them shook from the force. Grabbing her hand, he rushed them on their way. "Come on!"

There wasn't anything else she could do but try to keep up. It wasn't right of her to ask him to hang around because she was scared, not when he was supposed to be out there putting a stop to whoever was currently attacking them. Could it be the Tars? What were they trying to do, get their people back? She recalled the Basileus mentioning earlier that he'd caught them.

"Olena!" a sharp voice called out at their backs. Trystan was making his way toward them, not quite running but certainly not taking his sweet time, either. His long legs seemed to eat up the space, so that he'd reached her even without them having slowed.

His large hand wrapped around the wrist of her free arm, holding on when Ruckus would have continued to pull her away.

She froze between them.

"Let go," Ruckus growled out the warning, lifting his left hand into the air in a whip of motion. There was a thick metal band, like a bracelet, that extended into his palm when he tapped the edge with the tips of his fingers.

Before her eyes, a gun formed, four flashing green lights flickering at the side. He curled his pointer finger, and a loop dropped from the base of the metal, circling, while another curved piece slid down so that he was now holding the trigger. She didn't know much about weapons, but this didn't look like any type of gun she'd seen before.

That explained why she'd never seen any of the guards armed. They actually had been.

Ruckus kept the gun aimed at Trystan, his other hand squeezing hers with a mixture of assurance and possessiveness. Another blast went off, and while he didn't waver, the Zane's eyes flared.

"What the hell do you think you're doing, Ander?"

"Let her go," Ruckus repeated. "Right now."

He didn't. Instead he took a threatening step, so that they were all close enough to one another to look like a group having a private conversation. His blond hair was rumpled, long strands in disarray around his stern face. He'd missed the top button on his jeanlike gray pants, and the blue shirt he'd thrown on was wrinkled and torn an inch at the collar.

With a frown, she realized his feet were also bare.

"As the Zane," he said, his tone barely restraining his fury, "I am ordering you to drop your weapon and back away." Nothing happened. "Do it now, Ander Ruckus."

"Ruckus." Delaney squeezed his hand back, waiting for him to dart his gaze sideways at her. His eyes didn't linger long before shooting back over to Trystan. They'd literally just had a conversation about things he couldn't do without getting in trouble, and yet here he was, holding a gun against a regent.

"If you won't listen to me," Trystan said, his voice tightening, "then you should at least listen to the Lissa."

"I'll lower the fritz the second you let go of her arm."

It was obvious he did not want to do that, but after a moment, when Ruckus didn't so much as flinch, Trystan finally released her and took a step back, putting both hands in the air, palms toward them.

"Have you lost your mind?" he growled.

"Until I know exactly what is happening," Ruckus informed him, "no one touches the Lissa except me. As her head of guard, I'm clear of all political laws in regard to treatment or station. From here, until I know without a shadow of a doubt that she is safe, I am the one who calls the shots. So, when I say get your hands off her, you do it."

Wrapping his arm around her shoulders, Ruckus eased Delaney to the side and waved his gun at the Zane. Being that he was royalty, he'd clearly been going to the same place, and though he didn't like it, he started walking, leaving the two of them at his back.

"I could have shot him," Ruckus said directly into her mind. *"I get political asylum when it comes to protecting you."*

"Sure," she drawled, *"until the Kints got pissed because of their dead Zane and called the war back on. Just"*—she mentally sighed, not sure if he could hear it—*"don't point that thing at him again."*

"It's a fritz," he told her, voice finally starting to calm some. *"It blasts apart particles. Would have blown a hole straight through his chest so you could have seen to the other side."*

"Lovely."

With quick steps, he led them down the corridor and around a sharp corner. At the end there was another portrait, this one of an animal she didn't recognize; it was somewhere between a bear and a rabbit. She wanted to take a better look, but before they'd even made it halfway there, it opened from the inside.

A man poked his head out, checking over their shoulders before waving them frantically toward him. He was dressed like the other Vakar soldiers, and addressed Ruckus by title once they'd reached him. Stepping back, he allowed them to pass, inclining his head toward both her and Trystan.

The entrance didn't lead to a stairwell like it had with the one Lura had passed through. Instead there was a small square room about ten by ten, with four bulky doors, including the one that doubled as the painting.

Ruckus moved to the one on the left, rapping his knuckles against it in a discernible pattern. Almost before he'd finished, it was thrown open, a gust of stale air spewing toward them, kicking up the dust at their feet. He yanked on it, stepped through, and pressed a hand against her lower back to urge her forward into the darkness.

And it was seriously dark.

Unable to see a thing, she instinctually reached out to feel the sides, slinking to the right and waiting for him to direct. A light snapped to life, spilling a vibrant orange hue throughout to expose a room almost identical to the one they'd just vacated.

Frowning, she glanced over at him.

"This way." He motioned toward the door across the room this time.

Trystan stepped in after them, suddenly a towering presence at her back. Her spine stiffened, and the words she'd been about to speak aloud died on her tongue. Instead she reached out with her fitting. There was no longer a burning sensation when it activated. It was so easy, much more so than yesterday when they'd implanted it. Almost as simple as breathing. She merely thought about talking to Ruckus, and she did.

"It's a labyrinth," she said.

"A maze," he corrected her. *"Labyrinths always have a distinct*

center; this does not. The goal is to keep enemies away from you, not help them get closer."

She counted another five rooms, passing through silently and following his direction whenever he motioned her one way or the other. Surprisingly, Trystan remained quiet as well, though he kept close. He didn't touch her again, but his body was always there, at what felt like less than a centimeter from her back whenever they paused and waited for another door.

Finally a door opened, and they were met with a different view. The room inside was three times as big as all the rest, and wasn't empty. There were piles of packaged foods she didn't recognize to the left, and a few jugs of water in the far right corner. There were also about a dozen people, including the Basileus and Basilissa.

When she entered, the latter spotted her first and rushed over, taking her up into her arms as if she were really her daughter. No doubt because she'd also seen Trystan over her shoulder.

"Thank the stars you're all right," the Basilissa said breathlessly, and pretty convincingly. Her arms tightened around her back, and her chin rested on her shoulder. Her silky blond hair cascaded around her. "I was so worried they'd gotten to you."

"I'm fine," she said, caught off guard.

"Are the outer doors secured?" Ruckus was asking a tall willowy soldier with light brown hair.

"Yes, Ander," the soldier replied before she nodded toward the opening. "Shall I escort you out and check on the other locations?"

"Let's do that." He glanced over at Delaney and cleared his throat. "Give me one second, Teller. Wait outside."

"Yes, Ander."

He approached her and the Basilissa, who'd let her go but hadn't moved away. His greeting was brief, and then he turned his attention fully on Delaney.

"You'll be careful," she found herself saying before he could get a word out. "Right?"

"Of course." He took a step closer, then hesitated and clearly thought better of it. Stopping a little over two feet away, he rested his hands on the gold square at his belt. There was a click, and he pulled away a piece of it, handing it over.

She viewed the small golden circle in her palm and winged a brow in question at him.

"It's a tracking device," he told her softly, ignoring the Basilissa and Trystan, who hadn't moved nearly as far off as either of them would have liked. "Keep it on you. Don't lose it."

"I won't," she promised, slipping the tiny disk, no bigger than a dime, into the curve of her bra. Thankfully she'd been too exhausted to remove it, leaving it on underneath the skimpy nightgown. Now, being in so many people's company, she was glad for it. It provided at least a bit more cover.

Ruckus's face scrunched up at the move, and the next thing she knew, he was removing his green jacket.

"What are you—"

He wrapped it around her shoulders, tugging it sharply so that it instantly secured her in its thick warmth. On him, the garment was formfitting; on her, it was about three sizes too big. Popping the collar around her neck, he studied his handiwork, fingers remaining close to her jaw just a little longer than appropriate.

It was the Basilissa clearing her throat that finally snapped him out of it.

He was only wearing a black tank top now, painting him in all dark colors. She was worried that he wouldn't be recognized, that someone on their side might mistake him for the enemy. He must have seen this written on her face, because he made a shushing sound and smiled softly.

"I'll be fine," he reassured her, pulling back. "Promise you will be, too."

"Yes," she agreed, hugging his jacket closer to her body in a completely instinctual move. She stood there and watched him leave, flinching a little when the heavy foot-thick metal door shut behind him.

She couldn't recall ever feeling so alone before.

There were only a few lights in the room, all of them pretty dim. Over by the Basileus in the corner with the water was the brightest one, and Delaney certainly didn't want to go anywhere near him.

"Are you sure you're all right?" Tilda asked. The way her eyes shone, it looked like she really meant it. "What with what happened the other day, and now this . . ." She allowed her sentence to trail off pointedly.

And Delaney understood. The Basilissa was trying to confirm that she was still up for the job; she just couldn't say as much with Trystan hovering over their shoulders like a shadow.

"It'll take a lot more than a few pesky assassination attempts to jar me," she told her, trying to make her tone light despite the way her stomach clenched at the notion. She never would have guessed that one day she'd act so flip about someone trying to kill her, even if she was faking it.

Tilda must have bought it, though, because she nodded, glancing back over at Trystan quickly. A slight frown marred her dark skin.

"I need to go back to your father," she said. There was a look in her eyes, almost like she was sorry for something. Maybe for putting her in this situation. "We're discussing what's going on with Trump Haggar. Would you like to join us?"

"No, thank you. I was in the middle of sleeping. I think I'll just go rest"—she pointed at the opposite corner, where there was a single cot and no one else around—"over there."

"Sure, darling." She placed a hand on her cheek momentarily, then moved away. It was dark enough that for a few seconds she was no longer visible, until she stepped into the circle of light provided by the lantern hung over the Basileus's dark head.

Delaney was already lowering herself down to the secluded cot when she realized with a sick twist in her gut that Trystan had followed her. When he eased down next to her, she squished over as far as space would allow, pressing her shoulder up against the freezing wall. It was cold down here, even with Ruckus's uniform jacket.

The room smelled of frost. That bitter, biting kind that only came around sunrise, while most people were still sleeping.

In the distance, she could hear the blasts of more explosions, and fear at the thought of Ruckus out in that gripped her. She should have tried harder to make him stay, have thrown a Lissa-sized fit, the kind that these people would believe. They all thought Olena was a spoiled brat anyway. This was one time she really should have owned up to that image.

How were the Tars managing such a large-scale attack? She couldn't count further than six without hearing another shaking boom, and if that was possible from where she was tucked away in a metal room . . .

"You're putting on a brave front," Trystan spoke then, eyeing her coyly in the dark. "How unlike you."

She just *had* to choose the darker, secluded corner.

"Seriously?" This was not the time or place for one of his rambles. "You didn't know me all that well. Quit acting like you did so we can move past your being surprised every time I open my mouth."

"I knew you well enough," he countered. "You were vapid before, a coward. Now . . . You never did tell me about your time on Earth."

"Veni, vidi, vici," she mumbled under her breath, only half paying attention to him. It was dangerous, *he* was dangerous, but Ruckus was out there, and she didn't know what was happening to him.

"'I came, I saw, I conquered'?" A single golden brow winged up. "How very Kint of you."

That got her attention. She glared at him, making sure to push all her annoyance into that one look.

"I am not a Kint. I'll never be a Kint." It was probably wrong of her to be so prejudiced against his people. She didn't actually know anything about them except what she'd been told. The only two she'd ever even spoken with had been him and Brightan, neither of whom had helped boost her opinion.

"You will be," Trystan said then, voice cutting through the tight darkness. She could make out the outline of his large body, see the contours of his face and his eyes. He was close enough that his expressions were as visible to her as if the two of them had been in broad daylight. "Once the binding ceremony has been completed, you will be."

Great, now they were talking about marriage again. The arrangement never made either of them happy, and caught in this confined space, it really wasn't a good topic to discuss.

Still, she couldn't help but rise to the bait, adding, "Well, then that will also make you a Vakar."

"We'd be responsible for each other's people, yes." He didn't appear the least bit upset.

Which made her suspicious.

"Trystan," she said, somehow managing to keep her tone as sweet and even as possible, "do you actually intend for us to be bound?"

His grin was wicked, the kind you'd expect to see on a serial killer right before he added another trophy to his collection.

"Vapid before," he repeated, leaning in a bit closer. "Not anymore."

"Perhaps we should all take a trip to Earth," she stated, for lack of a better response. His reaction to her question unsettled her, and she was all about covering it up. "Go ahead. Take five years, or ten. I'll wait."

"If I went, you'd go."

"And why is that?"

"Because neither of us is leaving here without the other. Not until this whole thing gets settled."

"Not until you find a way out of our binding, you mean." Why she pressed it was beyond her. Maybe it was morbid curiosity; maybe it was her need for preparation. She couldn't prepare for the worst if she didn't know all he was capable of.

"Smart girl." He inched toward her even more. "Except, you're off about one detail."

"What's that?" Blood rushed through her ears, and it was obvious when he smirked that he knew he'd finally gotten to her.

He brought his head down to hers conspiratorially. "I already found a way."

She froze, unable to breathe.

"A couple, actually. I'm the type of man who likes to keep his options open."

"Always have a plan B," she found herself murmuring.

"Precisely."

Because he hadn't said it in so many words, she couldn't prove it, but she was positive he'd just admitted to trying to kill her the other day. Was that what was going on outside right now? Were all the explosions an attempt to get a lucky shot and blow her up?

For some reason, it felt like they'd been doing this dance for a lifetime. At the very least, a week, not the mere few days that had actually passed.

Another explosion ripped through the air, dimmed from where they were but still discernible.

"Seems like you aren't receiving a very warm welcome home, are you?" He reached up and swept a loose strand of hair out of her eyes.

She couldn't help it—she shivered. He could break her with that hand. A glance over his massive form showed only blurry outlines of the others. If she couldn't see them, they certainly were unable to see her.

You'd think with her being the Lissa—false or not—they'd be paying better attention. Her life right now was the deciding factor in a war, after all.

"It appears I'm not the only one who dislikes you," Trystan continued, though he kept his hand in her hair, fingers sweeping back until he was cupping her skull.

With one swift tug, he had her on her knees, kneeling on the cot, pressed against his front so tightly, it was momentarily hard for her to breathe. Forcing her head back with a yank, he kept her gaze pinned to his own, a mocking half smirk playing at his firm pink lips.

"My father might be king right now, but *I* am the future Rex. The hatred I have for you is far from secret. It really isn't all that surprising that my people rebel against our binding." The hand he held at her lower back tightened, fingers splaying out as if needing to touch more of her despite his words. "If I accepted you, they probably wouldn't react this way."

"Are you admitting the Tars work for you?" She tried to keep her body lax. Tensing would only give him more pleasure and probably would result in another painful tug of her hair.

"Don't be silly," he scolded, like he would a child.

She licked her lips and his gaze followed.

"Okay," she said, switching tactics, "but you don't, do you?" At his raised brow, she elaborated. "Approve of our merger? You don't accept me."

"*Merging* with you was never the issue," he said crassly. "You have a mildly attractive outer shell."

Wow. If he thought the gorgeous princess was only decent looking, he'd probably chuck her away in revulsion if he could see Delaney's true face. She didn't have low self-esteem or anything like that, but Delaney couldn't hold a candle to a girl like Olena.

"But once would be enough," he went on. "Enough to settle my curiosity, and enough to grow infinitely more tired of you. My children are going to be kings and queens. You really think I'd sully them with your DNA?"

"I have royal blood," she managed, "same as you."

"Blood has very little to do with it." His eyes trailed languidly down the curve of her pale throat. "Unfortunately."

There was little doubt in her mind he was imagining slitting it.

"You don't like me," she stated, trying to get his attention away from blatantly murderous thoughts. "I don't like you. Glad we settled that."

"We haven't settled anything," he disagreed. Suddenly he cocked his head, listening, and with a start, she realized the blasts outside had stopped at some point. "It seems, however, Ander Ruckus has. Pity."

He let her go so quickly, she dropped, glaring up at him as he stood. He smirked at her again, his gaze roaming her body.

"Hmm, I think I like you like this, though," he practically purred, "splayed out before me. At my mercy."

She took her time getting to her feet, attempting to cling to some semblance of dignity. Besides, running from predators was never a wise choice. It only excited them more. She thought about slapping him, but you only got one freebee slap against a psycho and she didn't want to waste hers.

"That"—she forced her spine straight and took a threatening step toward him—"is never going to happen."

His eyes widened in shock at her boldness. Had he thought he'd scared her into submission already?

"Like I said," she growled, "you don't know me. I'm not the meek pushover Lissa you remember."

People were starting to move toward the door that had just been reopened, and she turned to go. At the last second she spun back.

"Oh, and by the way," she told him, "*I* don't want *my* future children to be *sullied* with the douche bag gene, asshole."

She left before she could do or say anything else suicidal.

CHAPTER 15

Of course, she had no idea where she was going. Outside of the bunker was the first of many square rooms she'd have to pass through in order to make it out. She'd managed to keep up with the first four or five turns, but that was way back at the beginning. She didn't have to look to know the exact moment Trystan stepped up behind her; she felt him there, burning at her back like a flame. It occurred to her with a sick twist in her stomach that the members of the royal family probably all knew the way.

Was he waiting on her to show him? Obviously, as the Zane of what had for so long been a warring country, he wouldn't have been privy to the way out. The Basileus didn't strike her as the type of man who'd leave the well-being of his family in the hands of others, so they had to know which direction to go themselves, which doors to choose.

Which meant so would Olena.

"Lissa Olena." A soldier she'd never seen before stepped forward, bowing his sandy-blond head. "Ander Ruckus sent me to escort you out."

"He did?" She tried to hold back the frown but couldn't. Why would he send someone she didn't know? And, more important, who didn't know her? How did he explain to this soldier that she didn't know her way out of the maze?

"Yes, Lissa." He bowed his head again. "He said to tell you that he'll meet you in your chambers as soon as he's able."

"All right . . ." Crossing her arms over her chest, she indicated with a half wave that he should begin leading the way. Hopefully he'd take that as a sign she was allowing him to escort her and not that she didn't know where she was going.

Fortunately, Trystan hadn't said anything, though she felt him moving along with them. After a while he fell behind a few steps, but she doubted it was to give her space. Sure enough, when she risked a glance back, it was to find he'd been detained at the opening of one of the rooms.

He watched her over the shoulders of the two soldiers blocking him as she passed into another hallway and out of sight. She wasn't sure, but he looked pissed at being held back, and she wondered what it was the Vakar soldiers could possibly want from him to risk his wrath.

"Watch your step, Lissa," the guard leading her said, offering a hand to help her over the lip of the doorway.

"Thank you." She walked with him toward a door on the left. "What's your name?"

"Teller Dreadus," he told her.

"On Earth, *dread*'s not exactly the best word," she joked, smiling so that he'd know that was all it was. She was looking at him when he opened the next door, stepping through when he motioned her before him.

If she'd been paying attention, she probably would have realized something was off. Ruckus never let her walk into a room first. It was apparently too risky.

She felt the punch to her side before her senses picked up on the other presence. The blow was strong enough that it sent her sailing to the right, slamming into the metal wall with a heavy *oof*. Her head ricocheted off, and for a second she saw dancing black spots. Once her vision had cleared, she was able to make out three soldiers, including the one who'd led her there. They were surrounding her, crowding her into the corner.

Her anger rose and she stubbornly got to her feet, ignoring the sharp pain from her left ribs, where one of them had just hit her.

They were the same massive alien size as the rest, tall and fit, but not bulky. The smell of sweat surrounded them, and tension was a thick cloud in the tiny box of a room. It was somewhat comforting, knowing they were nervous, worried. It probably wouldn't help her, but at least they'd suffer from anxiety after they killed her.

And it was clear that was what they were going to do.

"Don't be stupid," she said, trying to reason with them anyway. "Pretty sure this is subversion."

They gave her funny looks and she cursed. *Subversion* probably wasn't a word they had here. But seeing as how they were going to kill her anyway . . .

"Mutiny?" she tried again. More confused looks. "Damn. I'm calling you traitors, idiots. Get it?"

Not the right thing to do. A pissed-off soldier lunged for her, and she dropped to a crouch so that he ended up hitting the same wall she had. Scurrying out from beneath him before he could regain his balance, she twisted onto her butt and kicked out against the next soldier's thighs.

It didn't move him enough, but it caught him off guard and she was able to scramble to her feet. Frantically, she looked around for anything that could be useful. It being an empty room, however, there was nothing.

"Ruckus!" She really wished she'd asked how far that connection reached now.

Stupid.

The soldier who'd lured her here, Dreadus, moved toward her, coming close enough for her to lash out. Curving her hands, she used the only weapon she had, raking her nails across his soft cheek.

Four thick welts instantly formed from his brow to the point of his chin, red welling. A couple of beads of blood rolled down his jaw and plopped onto the cold, gray stone floor.

So aliens bled red. Who knew?

He made the mistake of freezing, probably surprised that cowardly Olena had struck him. Had they expected her to huddle in a corner and beg?

Taking advantage of his hesitation, she kicked out, landing a blow to his right kneecap. She heard and felt the pop, and rushed out of the way when he toppled with a howl.

The man who'd hit the wall earlier stood, preparing to lunge at her again. She was in the process of backing away when suddenly the door to her right opened and Trystan was standing there. He was staring at Dreadus, who was still on the ground, clutching his leg, and didn't seem to notice there were two other soldiers in the room.

He'd partially blocked her view, but she saw the man against the wall push forward, still intent on attacking despite the Zane's arrival.

"Trystan!" The warning instinctually slipped past her lips, and she pushed him aside. He was so surprised by her outburst that he was easy to move, and once he was out of the way, she was close enough to intercept. Her fisted hand slammed against the soldier's cheek, the first real punch she'd thrown since those self-defense classes years ago. The pain in her knuckles directly after caused her to hiss, but the soldier recovered quickly.

His hand burrowed in her short hair and tugged. He let out a grunt when she brought her heel down on his toes, and then again when her elbow found his solar plexus. He was doubling over while she was practically tripping in her haste to get away, when the door on the other side of the room opened.

For a split second, her eyes met Pettus's and she held her breath. He glanced around, clearly unsure what he was seeing, and then snapped into action. Relief swept through her so strong that it was all she could do to press against the wall in order to stay upright.

A gun—a fritz—identical to the one she'd seen Ruckus with earlier, formed in his hand, and he shot one in the shoulder when he came at him. The blast wasn't loud, more like a ping and a blast of heat in the air. The green lights on the weapon flashed distractingly as Pettus turned to aim at the man who'd just been holding her.

She stared at the first soldier, or more aptly, the gaping hole in him, unable to look away. It was like someone had taken a circular cookie cutter and pressed down on the spot between his shoulder and chest. His body had dropped after the shot so that he was leaning against the wall, and she could see the metal right through him. There wasn't any blood; the heat from the blast had cauterized the wound. But he was definitely dead.

"You're going to kill him." Pettus's harsh words snapped her out of it, and she twisted around.

Trystan was holding Dreadus by the neck.

The soldier was kicking his feet in the air, his toes hovering a few inches above the ground. He had both hands wrapped around Trystan's wrists, trying to get him to loosen his hold, but the Zane didn't seem to notice. Instead he angled the other man's head with a thumb, all while clenching tighter around his windpipe.

Getting a better look at the scratches, Trystan arched his brows and sent her a look over his shoulder. She gritted her teeth when she saw surprise on his face, but there was something else, too, and she thought it might be pride.

For some reason, that made her even more uncomfortable, and she quickly looked away.

"We only need the one for questioning," he said, finally responding to Pettus's comment just as the soldier in his hands began to lose consciousness.

Delaney braced when three more Vakar soldiers came through the same door as Pettus had.

"Alert the Ander that the Lissa was attacked," Pettus ordered them, easing her mind that these guys weren't enemies. "Tell him we've got it under control for now"—he cast her a sideways glance—"but that he should probably get to her as soon as possible."

One of them went off to follow the command, the other two coming in closer.

"Take care of the bodies," Pettus told them a second before Trystan dropped the now dead Dreadus to the ground.

Dusting off his hands, he inclined his head toward the still open door at his back. "There are two more in the next room."

"Lissa Olena," Pettus called to her, and she tore her gaze away from the Zane. "Are you all right? Did they hurt you?"

Idly, her fingers lifted to her ribs, touching the spot tenderly. It hurt, but nothing was broken, so she shook her head.

"She's lying," Trystan growled, and was upon her within the next instant, tugging her hand away. He shoved the thick material of Ruckus's jacket out of the way and went to lift the flimsy nightgown.

"Hey!" She grabbed his hands, pushing them off her before he could get them more than an inch up her thigh. She looked pointedly around at the other three men in the room. "Hello?"

He blinked. "Modesty?"

Great, if Olena's closet hadn't been a clear indicator she was loose, his reaction certainly was. Still, there were lines she refused to cross, no matter how out of character for the Lissa it was. Getting naked in front of a bunch of random guys was definitely one of them.

Fortunately, Ruckus appeared at that moment, bursting through the door with such force, the metal clattered back against the wall. His eyes found her in a matter of seconds, and he was next to her, taking her hand and tugging her away from the Zane in a flash.

"Take a look at her side," Trystan ordered him coldly, then turned and left without a backward glance. She heard him in the next room over, ordering a Vakar soldier to lead him out of the maze, and then nothing.

Ruckus urged her toward one of the closed doors, opening and shutting it behind the two of them. His hand paused less than an inch from the end of her nightgown.

"May I?"

He'd seen her in a bathing suit yesterday, so she didn't know why she was so nervous. When she nodded, he began easing the material up over her hip. Maybe it was how slowly he was going, carefully, drawing it out. It was almost akin to torture, and she sort of wanted to snap at him to hurry it up. But she didn't. She was on edge because of everything that had happened, and it wasn't cool to take it out on him.

Ruckus let out a growl, causing her to glance down. A large bruise the size of a softball was forming directly below her left breast. It was already an ugly purplish-blue, and she winced when he skated his fingers around the edge of it.

"Apologies," he said, pulling back. He didn't, however, let go of her nightgown, keeping the material bunched in his hand and leaving her exposed to his view. He glanced at their clasped hands. That was when she noticed the blood on his arm, streaking its way up and around.

She gasped and tugged on him to get a better look.

"It's not mine," he assured her, bringing her back around so they were standing in front of each other once more. "I'm all right. I didn't get hit. Not like you did, apparently. I'm so sorry, Delaney."

"Why?" She pursed her lips. "It's not your fault."

"You were right," he disagreed. "I shouldn't have left you alone. If I had been here, they wouldn't have dared try something."

"I don't know about that," she said honestly. "Trystan was there, and they managed to section him off pretty easily."

He frowned. "You don't think he had something to do with this?"

"I'm not sure." Oddly, she wasn't. After everything he'd said to her, especially today, she should have been. She should have been certain he had everything to do with it, in fact, but . . . there'd been something in his eyes when he'd been detained and watched her leave without him. Something there when he'd been strangling that man.

Could be he was just upset that they'd botched the job—again—yet part of her didn't believe it.

"One of them was going to attack him from behind. Trystan

didn't see him coming. Besides, he doesn't strike me as sloppy," she said aloud, trying to explain it for the both of them, "and this was the epitome of it."

He thought it over then nodded. "We'll figure it out."

A knock sounded at the door, and he finally dropped her nightgown. He turned to block her from view as she smoothed it down again, and the door opened to expose Brightan.

The Kint soldier glanced between the two of them and then settled on a glare. He tensed in the doorway, and when he spoke, his voice was clipped. "The Zane?"

"He just left," Delaney said, wondering how he'd managed not to pass by him. From the annoyed look on Brightan's face, she guessed he'd probably lost his way in the maze. "He was all right."

The Kint lifted his upper lip in what could only constitute a sneer, and then motioned toward the room at his back, where Pettus and the others were still dealing with the bodies.

"If you'll show me the way out then, Ander," he said, confirming her suspicions that he'd gotten lost. "I'm sure you're eager to get the Lissa the proper medical attention."

Ruckus stiffened almost imperceptibly. If she hadn't been standing directly behind him, close enough to his spine to actually see, she would have missed it. His voice, however, was even when he addressed Brightan, agreeing with him.

Delaney tried not to look as they passed through the room, but her eyes were drawn one last time to the soldier Pettus had shot.

She couldn't get out of there fast enough.

CHAPTER 16

S he managed to stave off the Tars," Pettus said from where he huddled with Ruckus less than five feet away from her. He kept his voice down, almost as if he were attempting to keep her from overhearing.

"I am standing right here," Delaney pointed out, shaking her head. Feigning disinterest even though they were still talking about her, she turned in a slow circle, taking in her new surroundings.

The room was large, around the same size as her high school gym, with a few areas sectioned off with different-colored floor mats. The forest-green mat she was currently standing on squished beneath her as she turned back around to face the Vakar still deep in debate. Neither had said as much aloud, but it was pretty obvious why they'd brought her here.

"I took a few self-defense classes," she informed them, waiting for both of them to glance up at her. "But it was a couple of years ago, and like I said, it was only a few."

"Did they teach you how to fight aliens?" Ruckus asked.

"Nope"—she rocked back on her heels—"but a dick's a dick, right?"

He blinked at her and she felt her cheeks heating, already wishing she'd kept her mouth shut and just let them continue their little debate about her "skills," or lack thereof.

"That came out wrong," she tried, but it was too late.

"As adorably awkward as this just became," Pettus said, and clapped his hands loudly, causing her shoulders to stiffen, "we don't have all day."

Ruckus turned to him. "I'm pretty certain that's my call."

Pettus nodded once in agreement, then stepped over to Delaney. Once in front of her, he lifted his arms, placing both fists before his face. His feet shifted, and within a second it looked like he was going to attempt boxing with her.

"I assume they taught you as much in self-defense class?" he asked. When she agreed, he added, "Show me."

Feeling a bit ridiculous, she did as told, trying not to glance over his shoulder at Ruckus.

"Our physiology is very similar to humans," Pettus went on, either unaware of her discomfort or outright ignoring it. "Almost the exact same, in fact."

"So if I wanted to knock you out, I'd hit your temple or your jaw," she said, thinking it over, "really, really hard."

"Let's stick with attempting to disable," Ruckus said. "You won't be left like you were in the shelter again. I don't intend for you to be alone long enough to need to worry about knocking an attacker unconscious. Only holding them off long enough for Pettus or me to get to you."

"By the time I got there, you already had two of them on the ground." Pettus lifted his chin. "Show me how."

"Well, I scratched one of their faces. Like a girl." He probably didn't want her to demonstrate that part.

"Like a cat," Ruckus corrected, the corner of his mouth turning up slightly.

"You have to use what you can." Pettus nodded. "Claws work. What next?"

"I took out his knee. And then with the other guy . . ." She moved forward and demonstrated what she'd done, careful not to actually punch Pettus or step on his toes. Once she'd fully executed the move, she pulled back and waited for his input. Admittedly, when she'd been dragged to the classes by Mariana, she hadn't actually believed for a second she'd ever need what she'd learned.

"That's good." Pettus reached for her and then repositioned her arms and legs back into a fighting stance. Then, without warning, he brought his knee into an arch toward her side.

Instinctually, her hands slammed down, shoving his knee away. But before she could blink, he had his right fist pressed against the curve of her jaw. If this had been real, he would surely have taken her out of commission with that one.

She pulled back and grimaced.

"Here." Ruckus motioned for Pettus to step aside and then took his place. "Let me show you."

A couple of hours later she'd learned enough to be moderately more sure of herself or, at least, of the fact that she could successfully get away if attacked. So long as it was hand-to-hand combat. Ruckus had attempted to teach her a few moves to avoid the sharp edge of a knife or the barrel of a firearm, but she hadn't picked up on those techniques as easily.

Between the two of them, however, she was starting to get a better picture of the Vakar army, and why they were so willing to allow their Lissa to spend her denzeration virtually alone.

"Does Olena know how to do all this?" She blocked one of

Ruckus's punches and ducked his swinging arm. They were moving at a quicker pace now, not needing to slo-mo every move to avoid hurting her.

"She was taught," he confirmed, shifting back onto his right foot so that her elbow met with air. "Regents are trained at a very young age. It's important that members of the royal family are capable of defending themselves. Of course, even though she knows how to, she rarely bothers. Olena isn't the type to enjoy fighting her own battles."

Delaney snorted and twisted to the left, out of striking distance. "Tell me something I don't know."

"The Basileus and Basilissa would like a word with the Lissa," Pettus told them, giving her an apologetic look. His head was cocked to the side, and he appeared to be listening to something. Obviously someone was contacting him through his fitting. "They've already been escorted to the Green Room and are awaiting your arrival."

"Now?" Ruckus straightened. "I alerted the Basileus earlier about my training intentions for the day. He agreed it was important that she be prepared."

"I tried to explain that you weren't done with your session, Ander," he said, "but they insisted."

Of course they did; they were assholes.

"I'm not going to like this conversation, am I?" She looked up at Ruckus, noting the thin line his mouth had become and the way he was clenching his jaw.

"Honestly," he said, and sighed, "I'm not sure."

"It's doubtful," Pettus added, then held up both hands and quickly left when Ruckus glared.

Awesome.

WHY THEY BOTHERED to call it the Green Room was beyond her, considering that almost all the rooms in this place were painted the same damn color. She was even starting to get sick of the gold. Maybe after all this was done, she'd go home and toss all but her silver jewelry.

Which made her feel like she had a twisted connection to Olena. One she didn't like.

This happened to be the same room she'd first been brought to after leaving the ship, and the Basileus was seated once more behind his desk. The only major difference was that Magnus and Tilda weren't alone; occupying two of the leather chairs positioned to the left were Trystan and another man Delaney had never seen before.

He was dressed in dark blues and silver, a clear indicator that he was also a Kint. The way he sat stiffly with a blank expression clued her in that he was probably also a high-standing member. Military, more than likely.

The Basilissa was off to the side, watching the flickering lime-green flames in the fireplace. It happened to be large enough to fit Trystan in, and Delaney momentarily contemplated it.

"You wanted to see us, sir?" Ruckus broke the silence. He'd taken her hand to lead her from the training room, but he had to let it go as soon as they'd entered a more populated section of the castle. The gesture had been sweet.

She rubbed her palms together, finding she missed the feel of him. Truth be told, she was more shaken up by the past events than she'd initially believed.

"That's the second attack this week," the Basileus stated finally. With a twist of his expression, he flicked his wrist. "And it is no surprise that Rex Hortan shares in our concerns." He motioned absently over toward Trystan and the other Kint, as if that were enough explanation.

"Trump Jackan is one of the Rex's most trusted royal advisers," Ruckus said, filling her in through the fitting. *"His presence means the Rex has a demand."*

"Rex Hortan has requested that your Uprising be rescheduled," the Basileus said then. He set his blue-green eyes on her, and she realized they were same dark navy as the Kint colors.

She couldn't help but wonder if he ever wished that the blue had switched with the ring of deep green that circled it. Funny, that he had both Vakar and Kint in his eyes, though she doubted he'd find it so.

"To when?" Ruckus asked at her side. His expression was tight.

"Four days," Tilda responded, turning from the fire. Her hands were clasped before her, and she at least had the decency to glance away guiltily when Delaney looked at her. "It's our best chance of putting a stop to these attacks. Once our daughter has Uprisen, the Tars won't be able to say or do anything."

Her wording made Delaney pause.

"You don't seem very excited, Lissa Olena," Trystan pointed out. He was sitting back in his chair, his legs crossed, as if he hadn't a care in the world.

She knew better. He had to be hating this every bit as much as she did. Even not knowing exactly what the Uprising was, having it sooner had to imply the timetable for their binding had also been moved up.

"Haven't you been waiting for this since you were a child?" he added.

Had she?

"Yes," Ruckus answered even though she was pretty sure she hadn't actually sent the question to him.

"Of course," she stated, making her tone as nonchalant as possible to mask her growing doubts. They couldn't actually want her to go through with this, could they? "It caught me off guard, that's all."

"We've already taken care of most of the details," Tilda said, and for a moment Delaney was actually grateful to her for attempting to ease some of her worries. Even if she had to do it via cryptic phrasing. "Fortunately, you selected almost everything before leaving for your denzeration. I imagine you feel relieved now, knowing you won't need to find a dress on such short notice."

"Yes," she said, bobbing her head like an idiot, and stopped the moment she realized as much. "That is a relief."

"What the hell is an Uprising?" she sent to Ruckus, but before he could answer, Trystan abruptly stood.

He adjusted his uniform and motioned at Trump Jackan to rise as well. Once the two of them were standing, his eyes sought hers and the corner of his mouth turned up in what could only be considered an evil smirk.

Like, villainously so. She'd mentally paint on a mustache and imagine him twirling it if it weren't for the fact that he was legitimately terrifying.

"I'll be escorting you during the ceremony," he told her. "As your betrothed, it's only fitting. Unless you have a different selection in mind?"

It took all her willpower not to glance at Ruckus.

"No, you're right, of course." She almost threw up right then and there. The last thing she wanted to do was *anything* with Trystan.

"This being a Vakar Uprising," Trump Jackan said, speaking for the first time, the word *Vakar* coming off almost as a sneer, "the Rex doesn't feel his presence is necessary. Surely you agree, Basileus Magnus."

"Absolutely." The Basileus stood, resting his fingers on the top of his desk.

"Perfect." Trystan angled his head in a slight bow toward both of the regents before settling back on Delaney. "I'll see you soon then, Lissa Olena."

They waited for him and the Trump to go, not risking another sentence until the door had clicked shut behind them. Then the Basileus ran a hand through his hair, and the Basilissa leaned against the fireplace. Their reactions did not help ease Delaney's tumultuous feelings.

"There was nothing we could do," the Basileus said a moment later on a heavy sigh. "Turning down the Rex's suggestion would have drawn too much suspicion. Especially when he'd gone through the trouble of sending one of his advisers with the message, instead of merely having his son inform us."

"So Trump Jackan's presence was a power play?" Delaney asked.

"This entire thing is a power play, Miss Grace," he corrected her sternly. "Unfortunately, having the Uprising sooner is a good plan. It should cease these constant assassination attempts, for one."

"Why? What will make the Tars stop trying to kill Olena?"

"They could still try." Magnus shook his head, sending dark black tendrils around his sharp cheeks. "But it'll be even harder. She'll have access to the Alter Pool; killing her would be next to impossible so long as she remains close to the castle where she can get to it in time. Generally, once a regent is Uprisen, those against him or her realize that the odds are too low to bother attempting murder."

"*There's only so much water left in the Alter Pool,*" Ruckus explained. "*About a hundred years ago a new law was implemented by the Basileus stating that once a new ruler was Uprisen, the old would stop using it to heal.*"

"*Surely they could just do it anyway,*" she posed.

"*Not without breaking the law,*" he informed her, "*and even the king has laws he must follow. Once you're Uprisen, you're the only one here who will be able to use the pool's healing properties. It doesn't slow down aging, but the Basileus and Basilissa don't have to worry about that anyway. If, however, one of them is shot with a fritz, or worse . . .*"

They'd be screwed, would most likely die, and then she'd be the surviving ruler. The new Basilissa. Which was so not an option.

Tilda moved over to her, taking Delaney's hands in her own and squeezing lightly. "Please try to understand. We're doing this for our people, and for our daughter."

Delaney sighed. "I just want to go home."

"And you will," Magnus promised. "As soon as Olena is found, we will honor our agreement. Until then, however, you will be standing in her place for the Uprising. I'm sure Ruckus can show you what to do, what's expected. It's not very complex, so you shouldn't worry about screwing it up. But it is important that you pull it off without mistakes."

"If she's already the Lissa . . . ," Delaney started. She kept her attention on Tilda, seeing that she was the only one of the two who actually seemed to care what they were putting her through. "Then what's the actual purpose of an Uprising anyway? She's already the heir, isn't she?"

Hadn't she asked if Olena had siblings and been told no?

"It's sort of like an exchanging of power . . . ," Tilda began, clearly struggling to find the right words. "It's more than simply telling the universe that she's our heir; it's expressing that we're prepared to step aside for her. Once she's Uprisen, we"—she glanced at her husband—"will stop using the Alter Pool ourselves. It will be her decision then, if one of us should be fatally wounded, whether or not to allow us entrance."

"You're going to give *Olena* that kind of control?" Delaney yanked her hands out of the Basilissa's grasp. "Look, no disrespect or anything, but I have yet to hear one good thing about your daughter, and are you forgetting? She did *this* to me!"

"And she's about to be bound to the Zane of Kint," Magnus reminded her. "Who also happens to be the heir to his father. We're well aware of who our children are, Miss Grace, but together they'll be forced to grow up."

"Because if they don't, they'll never have children." She was still disgusted by that notion, and after this conversation, she was even more so with the Basileus. "You don't care whether or not she's happy, do you? She ran, and you still don't care."

"Delaney," Ruckus said, giving her a low warning and reaching out to touch her elbow.

"She's allowed to speak her mind." Magnus waved him off while maintaining eye contact with her. "So long as she does so here, behind closed doors. If anyone outside this room should discover your true identity, Miss Grace, let me remind you—"

"Don't bother," she cut him off. "I know the stakes. I don't want war for my people any more than you want it for yours."

"Ah." His eyes lost some of their edge, though the calculation remained. "So you think I'm a terrible father, but you believe I want what's best for my people? Has it not occurred to you then, that those things conflict? I can't have both my daughter's happiness and the safety of Vakar. I must choose. Should I place the well-being of my single daughter above that of the thousands who live here in Vakar?"

She really hated it when people she was arguing with made valid points. It was so much harder for her to continue to discredit them, to hate them. And she found she really wanted to hate the Basileus right now.

"Fine." She crossed her arms over her chest. "So I'll do the Uprising ceremony. Then what? We can't keep this up forever."

"We won't have to." Satisfied, Magnus went back around his desk, lowering himself dignifiedly back into his black leather chair. "They're close to finding my daughter. Who knows? They might end up bringing her back here the day after the Uprising, and then you'll get to return to your family." He smiled, but it was less than kind. "To your loving *father*."

Had she been thinking about fitting Trystan in the fireplace? Forget that. Burning Magnus alive was starting to have a certain appeal.

CHAPTER 17

They're scared, Delaney," Ruckus told her the next day. He'd brought her to another section of the castle, this one filled with weapons, none of which were recognizable. Explaining some of them to her, he'd walked her through the room, pointing out the most popular technology, including a spray that apparently melted through flesh.

Awesome.

The room housed most of the castle's main weapons. The floors were slick and onyx, the ceiling high. There were no windows, and two doors, one leading in from the main hall and another he'd told her led up a stairwell to another part of the castle.

There were four long tables, two on either side positioned with about six feet between them and the walls where more weapons hung. To the right was a sectioned-off area surrounded on one side by glass.

Many of the weapons here seemed extreme, but recalling that they'd been at war for many generations up until five years ago eased some of her judgment. She certainly didn't know what that was like, living in constant fear, always afraid a Kint ship was going to come up over the horizon and attack.

He told her about one of the worst attacks, something that happened ten years ago, not long before the shaky peace talks had begun. They'd bombed an entire Vakar city, killing thousands in a matter of minutes. There'd been nothing that the Basileus could do to stop it.

And that'd just been the beginning.

"We've gotten word that they're working on something," he was telling her now. "Something big. Worse than the tech they used on the city. It could destroy huge chucks of Vakar. Kill millions. We might not survive it if the intel is true."

"Is that why this peace treaty is so important?" she asked, walking around to the other side of a table. There were guns hanging on the wall behind it, some of which looked very similar to rifles back on Earth. How strange, that all this existed and she'd gone her whole life without knowing it.

"Partly," he said as he slowly trailed her, "yes. The Rex denies these claims, of course. He says there are no mass weapons being built."

"Do you believe him?"

"The Basileus—"

"No," she interrupted, turning in time to see him step up to her. "Do *you* believe him?"

"I believe if there are weapons being created of that caliber, the Rex doesn't know about it."

"How's that possible? He's the king."

"Who runs an entire population," he pointed out. "A lot can happen in a day, let alone a few years."

"All right." She began moving down the line, taking in more of the weapons on the wall. "But this peace treaty? It'll stop whoever's building from actually using them?"

"That's the hope," he admitted. "They'd be committing mass treason, and you've met Trystan. He's not exactly the type you want to anger. After he and Olena are bound, our people will be his people. If the Kints kill the Vakar, or even if the Vakar kill the Kints, they'll have to deal with him."

"Unless he's the one building." She shrugged when he paused. "What? Don't tell me you haven't thought about it. Who better than Trystan to slink behind his dad's back? Who, by the way, he has to hate just as much as Olena right now. You're right: He's not someone you want to piss off, and I guarantee the Rex has seriously pissed him off by taking his freedom away."

"That's not—"

"Yes," she insisted. "that's exactly what he's doing. Take it from me. I know a prisoner when I see one."

"You're not a prisoner, Delaney," he said softly, though there was little conviction in his tone.

"Tell me that again after you get me home."

He reached for her, linking their fingers together and tugging her closer. "The second your feet touch Earth ground," he promised.

There was a single table in front of the sectioned-off area, and he led her toward it. A couple dozen bracelet-shaped devices like the ones he and Pettus wore were arranged in neat rows on top of it. She recalled how it'd turned into a gun when Trystan had come upon them heading to the bunker.

"I want to teach you how to use a fritz," he told her, lifting a silver band off the table. Then he brought her around the sectioned area and swung open a clear door, waving her into the room.

"Bulletproof glass"—he rapped his knuckles against the wall to the left—"just in case. This area was made for target practice."

The far wall was blank, a white slate; facing it was an odd black rectangular thing set in the center of the room. It came up to her chin.

Ruckus moved toward the rectangle, flicking a switch at the side. A keyboard slid out of the bottom, and a screen flickered to life on one of the shiny black surfaces. It was clearly a computer, and he began typing away at it, glancing over at the blank wall when he was done.

Five holograms suddenly appeared before the wall, all forming the outlines of people. They were various sizes, some distinctly male, others female. The holograms glowed dark blue around the edges.

"No one's gotten around to changing the color setting since the peace treaty," Ruckus explained, noticing her thoughtful stare.

Clearly, the holograms were meant as murky representations of Kint soldiers.

"Here." He handed over the bracelet, waiting for her to daintily slip it from his fingers. The corner of his mouth curved up, but that was the only sign he gave that he knew she was nervous. "Put it on."

She slid it onto her left wrist, watching as it shrunk down to fit snugly. It wasn't tight, but it wasn't loose enough to even spin a centimeter on its own. She allowed him to take her hand and turn it over so she could see the bottom of it over her pulse point. There was an almost imperceptible circular hole there, like a pinprick.

"This is a sensor," he explained, taking her middle finger and easing it down toward the hole. "They're programmed to react only to a specific user's fingerprint. I reset this one this morning and adjusted it to fit you."

"How'd you do that?" She frowned up at him, narrowing her eyes when he smirked.

"Stealthily, that's how," was all he said, then returned to showing her how to activate it.

She wasn't capable of touching her wrist, but found it wasn't necessary. The second her finger hovered a few inches away, the device activated. A soft hum came from it, and then the metal began to change, extending outward the same way she'd seen his do.

He readjusted her arm so that she was no longer facing him, aiming it toward the middle hologram target. The fritz had fully formed now, still attached at the metal band that had narrowed some but otherwise remained unchanged.

He tapped it. "This is so you can't lose your weapon. It becomes an extension of you, so the only way to lose it is if someone cuts off your arm."

"Brilliant," she drawled, ignoring the rush of heat skittering down her spine when he chuckled.

"Don't worry," he said. "I don't actually intend for you to ever need this. It's just a precaution. I don't want what happened the other day to ever happen to you again. At least with this, you'll be better prepared to defend yourself."

"Speaking of, why didn't they just shoot me?" she asked. If they had, there wouldn't have been anything she could have done to stop them.

"We would have been able to trace which weapon fired the shot," Ruckus divulged. "They all have monitoring devices inside, so we know the exact time they were fired, how far, how strong the setting was, et cetera. I've set yours to light, for example. It'll stun people, not blast through them."

"It's not like I'm made of china," she stated dryly.

"So seeing Pettus blast a hole clean through that Teller didn't bother you at all?" he said, his sarcasm apparent.

"Okay," she admitted, "but the guy was trying to kill me, and I'd probably have to see it eventually."

"If I have my way," he said, and readjusted her arm a second time, "you'll never have to see anything like that again. But just in case . . . Now curve your finger inward. Yes, just like that."

A trigger formed within the space between her hand and pointer finger. She didn't touch it, afraid the thing would go off before either of them was ready. Even knowing it'd been set to the lowest setting and she couldn't accidentally kill someone, holding a weapon like this made her uncomfortable.

"You're going to aim at the big blue guy's head." He lifted her arm up an inch, until her line of sight was straight from the tip of her gun to the tall hologram in the middle. "And then inhale slowly and gently press down on the trigger."

She sucked in a shaky breath and did as he said.

A thin green beam shot forward, heading straight for the hologram. When it reached it, the outline slammed back as if it'd actually been hit, bursting into a thousand tiny sparks of blue light when it came against the wall. They rained down and petered out of existence, leaving behind four remaining unaffected holograms.

"Whoa," she said breathlessly. Then she brought her arm to the left, aiming at a shorter female target. "Let's do that again."

He laughed. "All right."

SHE WAS PLEASED to find she was a natural, and by the time they'd reset the holograms for the twentieth round, she could hit all the targets on the head one after the other without a pause. It was very Wild West feeling, and she found herself more and more comfortable with the fritz in her hand with every calculated shot.

He let her keep the fritz, and she ran the fingers of her right hand over it as she and Ruckus walked down the hall toward her room hours later. It could only be activated by her left hand, so there was no risk of her smoothing over the thin metal now. The band was smaller than his, only about a third-of-an-inch wide, more chic than the one on his wrist.

She'd been so excited and high off the rush the fritz had brought, she'd actually forgotten about the Uprising.

The moment she started thinking about it again, her excitement ebbed, and by the time they came to her door, she was sick to her stomach. When she stepped into the room, he was close at her heels, and she moved over to the window, taking a deep breath.

"Delaney." He moved up behind her. "What's wrong?"

"I forgot about the ceremony for a while there," she admitted. "And now I'm back to freaking out about it, that's all." She tried to laugh it off, but the sound was forced even to her own ears.

"So, you're saying I made you forget?" There was a hint of a smile in his voice, and when she turned, it was to find him standing less than an inch away. "Mission accomplished then."

She frowned, trying not to stare, even though it was impossible with his yellow-green eyes so close. "I thought the point was to teach me how to use a fritz?"

"That, too." He intensely held her gaze. "I also wanted to get close to you. Take your mind off the responsibilities you've been forced to have."

"And you thought getting close to me would do it? Distract me for a few hours?"

"Don't look so surprised," he drawled. "I know you feel it, too. Every time I do this"—he eased into her personal space even more so that she was forced to press herself flush against the window—"get close to you, your body reacts."

"Uh, duh." She swallowed, forcing her breathing to remain even despite the heavy thumping of her heart. "There's a massive alien crowding my space. You wouldn't react any differently."

"Not to you," he replied smoothly, "no. No, I wouldn't. My body does the same thing when I"—he smirked—"crowd your space, as you so delicately put it."

"I'm pretty sure this"—she waved a finger between them—"is a big Ander no-no."

"You aren't actually my Lissa, Delaney," he reminded her, "and we aren't doing anything wrong."

"Not yet," she mumbled, realizing her mistake when his grin turned wolfish. Had she thought Trystan the more dangerous of the two? How had she overlooked that Ruckus was just as feral as the Zane? And possibly even more of a threat to her, because what he was saying wasn't wrong.

She did feel something when she was around him. She just didn't quite know what that was yet.

"So you admit it." He reached up and brushed a strand of hair out of her face. "You do want something to happen between the two of us."

"We hardly know one another," she pointed out. "Remember? This is insane."

"Doesn't make it any less real. I like you, Delaney."

And then he kissed her.

It shouldn't have, but it caught her off guard. For a moment all she could do was stand there, frozen in his arms while his firm lips pressed against her own. When his tongue darted out, demanding entrance, she came out of it, responding with a fervor she hadn't known she was capable of. Maybe it was the need for contact; maybe it was simply the need for him. Either way, she welcomed it, linking her arms around his neck to pull him closer.

His tongue grazed the roof of her mouth, and she sucked on it when he went to retreat, holding him in for another few precious seconds.

He was an inferno around her, setting her skin ablaze everywhere their bodies touched. Her front was squished to his, her breasts rubbing against his solid chest in a way that made her moan.

The next thing she knew, she was sitting on the edge of the bed, not recalling how she'd gotten there. He'd settled himself between her spread legs, pinning her to him as his hands roamed up her back frantically and his mouth devoured hers feverishly. He was breathing hard, and she was panting, thighs squeezing around his hips to keep him close.

He ran a hand through her hair then, and she remembered Olena.

Even so, pulling away was a struggle. She pressed her hands against his chest and turned her head sharply to the side, separating them.

"You don't even know what I look like," she said, annoyed when her voice came out husky. His brow furrowed, and she shoved him away. *"This"*—she waved a hand down her body—"isn't me."

"I've never been attracted to the Lissa before," he told her.

"That doesn't make it better. And besides," she rushed on, "the second the real Lissa is found, I'm going home."

He reached for her, taking her hands in his larger ones. "Hey, I'm not asking you to be my girlfriend." She made a face and he paused. "That is what it's called on Earth, right?"

She nodded.

"Okay, well good. I'm not asking you to be mine; I'm only asking that you let this play out between us. Let us see where it goes."

"Ruckus—"

"I don't care," he said, stopping her, his voice firming some. "I don't care that I don't know what you really look like, don't you get that? It's not the package that I'm interested in here. It's *you*. The girl who fought off three Tellers with nothing but her smarts. And who stood up to the Basileus."

"Yeah?" She lifted a brow. "Pretty sure you hate whenever I do that."

"That is also the case," he agreed, struggling, and failing, to hold back a smile. "But the fact that you're constantly willing to fight past your fear? That I like. A lot."

Delaney closed her eyes, and his grip tightened. When she reopened her eyes to look at him again, it was obvious that he was worried. About her rejecting him? Or about her ability to continue this ruse, to convincingly be Olena?

"I'm not doing the best job being the Lissa," she pointed out. "I'm too brash."

"Everyone attributes that to your time spent on Earth," he said, shrugging it off. "Just"—he lowered his head closer to hers—"tell me you'll give it a try. You'll give *us* a try. If you're lucky, you'll only have a few more days here anyway, and then it's back home for you. What do you have to lose?"

He was right, wasn't he? If everything worked out, she'd get to leave soon and then nothing that happened here would matter. At least, she hoped it wouldn't.

Before she could let her doubts get in the way again, she gave a single nod and then sucked in a breath when his mouth dropped to hers once more.

CHAPTER 18

Delaney's hands gripped the railing of the balcony. She'd come out needing fresh air, and stared over the expanse of green. If she didn't look up at the sky, she could almost pretend she was at a manor somewhere back at home, and not on an alien planet.

There really wasn't all that much involved in the Uprising ceremony. Ruckus had explained it to her, and apparently the Lissa only had two lines to say in the whole thing. Total, the ceremony would last less than five minutes, which seemed like a huge waste to her, considering every important person in Vakar had been invited. The entire main hall—which he'd shown to her last night—was going to be decked out for the celebration.

Five minutes and two lines. Olena seriously sucked for blowing that off and sending her here to pick up the pieces.

As well as everyone claimed she was playing the part, Delaney knew the truth. Everything she did or said was based purely on survival instincts. She just wanted to make it through this. To make it back home.

The thought of Mariana and her parents, who were without a doubt completely going crazy with worry now, made tears burn at the corners of her eyes. She quickly brushed them away, refusing to give in to the hopelessness that threatened to creep up on her. Believing that the Basileus would follow up on his promise, that Ruckus would in fact bring her back to Earth, was the only thing keeping her going.

Well, that and her confusing new feelings for the Vakar soldier.

Tonight was it, the big ceremony, and they'd spent every day since that second kiss in her room getting to know each other. The whole time he'd walked her through the ceremony, he'd touched her.

It was in little ways when they were around others, a brush of his fingertips against her arm, the press of his thigh against hers under a table. He always seemed to be touching her, and with each touch, her feelings grew. She didn't know what she was doing when it came to him. It couldn't work out, and they both knew it. She'd tried explaining that once more, but he'd swiftly shut her down with another searing kiss.

And that was the other thing. She'd never been kissed like that. It had her wondering if there was something special about his kind in general, if maybe the human boys she'd kissed before couldn't measure up because of something simple like biology, and not something complicated.

The two of them having crazy chemistry would be complicated.

"Here's your teekee." Lura had appeared in the doorway leading to the balcony.

"Thank you." Delaney turned from the railing and forced a smile to her lips. She didn't walk over when the atteta moved to place the steaming green—shocker—mug on the glass table. She'd tried it for the first time last night after Ruckus had ordered it, and had found it very similar to tea, only with a fruitier aftertaste.

Wisps of white twirled up into the air, and the almost-berry scent drifted to her, cutting across the chilly breeze. Deciding it was too hot to drink right away, she remained where she was, against the railing. She debated whether or not to go back inside to get a sweatshirt—or at least the Vakar equivalent to one if she could find it—but chose not to. A little chill was good, helped keep her in the now, keep her focused.

"Will there be anything else, Lissa Olena?" Lura asked, wringing her hands.

Taking that as a sign that the girl had somewhere else she wanted to be, Delaney waved dismissively. "No, that's all right. Go on. Enjoy your day."

"Thank you, Lissa." She bowed and disappeared without any more preamble.

Delaney turned to gaze back out over the grounds, noticing a cropping of trees over toward the left. Had that been where the Tandem game had been held? She couldn't tell.

That first attack from the Tars felt like a lifetime ago. In the two weeks since Ruckus had first taken her from the club, so much had happened. Again, her thoughts turned dark as she thought of her parents and roommate. Up until now, whenever they'd come to mind, she'd dashed their images away. Thinking about them only made it worse, and besides, there was nothing she could do.

She needed to stay on track, work on the things she actually could change and control. Doing anything less would only make her go crazy, and there were too many people counting on her to pull this whole Lissa thing off for that to be acceptable.

The white metal railing circled the entire balcony and came up to just below her chest. She needed to lift onto the very tips of her toes in order to peer over it, finding nothing of interest for her efforts. Just more grass, or whatever they called the stuff here.

"Thinking of jumping?"

Startled, she dropped to her feet and twisted to face the new arrival.

Trystan had come up to her side and was resting his elbows on the top of the railing. At his height, he could see the bottom easily enough, and raised a questioning brow at her. She had no idea when he'd gotten there, or how long he'd been watching.

"And give you the satisfaction?" She snorted. "Hardly."

Had Lura let him in before leaving? If so, why hadn't she announced him? Wasn't that the proper thing to do? She resisted the urge to turn tail and run back inside, not wanting to be alone with him, yet not wanting to show weakness even more.

Trystan gazed out over the grounds, seemingly at ease, like this was a normal thing, the two of them enjoying some fresh air together.

"If you'd said that to me a few weeks ago—hell," he said, chuckling humorlessly, "if we were up here alone like this a few days ago, even, you'd be right. I might have even contemplated pushing you."

She angled her head and rethought that whole fleeing plan. "That's . . . comforting. . . ."

"It wasn't meant to be." He laughed darkly. "But it was honest."

She couldn't argue with him there, so she looked away, pretending to find interest in the rolling hills.

"It's the big day," he said, breaching the silence again. "Are you ready?"

"Absolutely," she lied. Her sarcasm had been too apparent for him to miss, so she added, "Who doesn't look forward to signing their future away?"

He was watching her intently out of narrowed eyes, as if trying to read her mind or something equally intrusive. He was dressed more casually today than she'd ever seen him, the tight navy shirt leaving his arms bare to expose corded muscle. His pants were just as formfitting, tucked into black boots.

It was a sharp contrast to her own clothing, the bronze dress flaring out at the hips so the skirts twirled when she moved, and bare feet. She hadn't intended on going anywhere today, not after Ruckus had told her this morning that he was needed to help set up security measures for tonight's event.

Pettus had offered to walk her around, but she'd politely declined. She'd gotten to know him a little better as well over the past couple of days, but it still wasn't the same. Truth was, Ruckus was the only one she felt 100 percent comfortable around. They'd come a long way since he'd come up behind her in that alley back in Maine.

"It does mark a certain turning point for the both of us," he said quietly, breaking into her thoughts. "It'll be our first official public appearance together. I'm sure the masses will eat that up."

"How are the plans coming?" she asked, unable to look him in the eye when she did. She felt him though, staring at her. "To stop the binding?" she elaborated. "Personally, I'm hoping since the last time we spoke, you've come up with something better than killing me."

The corner of his mouth twitched, but instead of responding, he motioned toward her side. "How is the bruise?"

"All better," she said between clenched teeth. "As if you really care. Ruckus took me back to the pool this morning—way to be a creepy Peeping Tom, by the way—and it was gone within an hour. Gotta admit: That's one thing I'd miss being on Earth. No magic healing water there."

"I've been told the healing effects of the Alter Pool are ten times more effective. *I've* got to admit that's one thing I'd like about being the leader of the Vakar."

"*Joint* leader," she reminded him, and the corner of his mouth twitched again.

"Of course." He shifted then, turning so that his towering body faced her. The wind picked up, blowing strands of his almost platinum blond hair around his face, and he absently smoothed them back with a large palm.

"What are you doing here, Trystan?" she asked then with a sigh. She didn't want to keep doing this. As far as she was concerned, she had tonight to get through and then hopefully the Basileus's estimation would come true and they'd find Olena by the day after.

"Can't your betrothed come and see you?" he replied. "Especially when you speak to him so informally. I'm not sure when we reached casual greetings with each other, but this isn't your first slip."

Shit, he was right. She'd dropped his title, having never needed to address someone of his station, or any station for that matter, before.

Turning her head away to hide the blanching of her already pale complexion, she tried to appear calm. The Olena he remembered from five years ago was afraid of him, sure, but now he was used to the version she'd been portraying since her arrival. In order to keep up appearances, her best option would be finding a happy medium between the two.

That was easier said than done, considering her massive pride and inability to cower.

"I'm not the only one," she said, latching on to the only memory she had of him doing so. "Back in the hallway, before we were brought to safety, you called me by my name alone."

"So I did," he confessed, not seeming the least bit annoyed she'd remembered. "That had more to do with your relation to who you were with than your relation to me, however."

She didn't understand, and he must have seen that, because he continued.

"It is important as your betrothed that I exude a certain closeness and"—he paused, definitely smirking this time—"possessiveness toward you. You being with the Ander, a man who spends more time with you than anyone else, this became even more imperative." He took a step closer, suddenly crowding her space. "He needs to understand that you belong to someone else."

It was getting hard to breathe, and she realized she most definitely should have taken the opportunity to go inside when she'd had the chance. Conversations with Trystan never went well, and if she hadn't been too distracted by her worry for her family and trepidation for tonight, she might have been able to put her pride aside and go. Sometimes flight was the smartest option, no matter whom it was you were running from.

Let him have the upper hand this once, so long as she got away to live another day.

She moved back from the railing, sucking in a breath when he took a deliberate step after her. She wasn't proud of it, but she froze. How had she missed that familiar glimmer in his icy blue-and-crimson eyes? The one that distinctly placed him in predator mode.

"Until a better option comes along, right?" she said, forcing the words past her lips, thankful when her voice didn't shake nearly as much as she'd feared. "We both want out of this arrangement, Zane. Why don't we come up with something together? A way where neither of us has to worry about more assassination attempts."

"Have you tried assassinating me then, Lissa?" he said, drawling out her title pointedly, making it clear he knew what she was doing. "I doubt it." He took another step, forcing her to retreat one herself. "If you had, I'd be aware of it. Something tells me you're smarter than I initially believed, though. More capable. Sounds like you've been racking that pretty little brain of yours for a way out. So, let's hear it. Come up with anything feasible?"

She gulped, then slid her right foot farther back, attempting a slow withdrawal from his hovering presence.

It'd be great if she had something to offer him, a solution, but she'd been so busy trying to keep her head afloat with this pretend Lissa act, she hadn't really been thinking about how to get Olena out of her arranged marriage. She'd sort of just assumed by then that it would no longer be her problem, and while she felt for the girl, she had to admit she didn't like her any more than anyone else seemed to.

Olena was the reason she was here, after all, being cornered by an alien three times her size out on some stupid balcony overlooking another damn planet.

"Haven't been thinking about it too hard then, huh?" He smirked again, shifting closer still. "What's wrong? Other things on your mind? I feel like getting out of this would be your number one priority, same as me. What on Earth could be more important than that?"

Her heart stopped. It'd been a clear jab, but what had he meant

by it? Mentioning Earth like that, using a clear Earth phrase . . .
He couldn't know.

"What are you trying to imply?" she found herself asking, despite knowing she shouldn't.

"You're hiding something." He lifted a finger, pressing it against her lips when she went to speak. "It doesn't matter if you tell me."

She slapped his hand away. "Then why bring it up at all?"

"To see your reaction." He grinned, herding her backward more quickly than before. "To get confirmation. Now I know I'm right. There is something. That's what I'm seeing in your eyes, what I've been seeing ever since you got back. You try to hide the differences." He clucked his tongue. "Oh, you try so hard. But I see through you, Lissa. Something's changed."

"That's ridiculous," she said, but even she had to admit there was little conviction in her tone. It was getting harder to think, with his body less than an inch from hers. She could even smell him, a strange clean scent, almost like freshly cut cucumbers and basil. How wrong, that he should smell like that, instead of something dangerous and masculine.

It seemed the more she tried to get away, the faster he advanced, intent on crowding her. Already the broad span of his shoulders blocked out most of the sky.

"It's not. I've been baiting you since the beginning, pulling out all the stops, and you still have yet to cry. In fact, quite the opposite seems to happen every time I attempt to push you too far. You don't cower like you used to; you actually flourish. Our arguments bring out the heat in you." He tipped her chin up with a single yet firm finger. "Secretly, you're a wild thing."

She pulled back sharply, coming up against the table hard enough to rattle it. She hadn't been aware he'd moved her so far back, and she heard the mug that Lura had placed there shatter against the glass surface.

She was in the process of turning to assess the mess when Trystan yanked her away so hard, she let out a cry of pain. It was a wonder he hadn't dislocated her shoulder with the amount of force he'd used. And he didn't let go, his grip tightening as if he thought she was going to try to pull away from him.

Which he'd be right about, but she couldn't so much as budge.

"Who brought you that?"

It was the tone of his voice had that her stilling her struggles. Slowly, she lifted her head to look at him, though, with how closely he had her pinned to his chest, all she could really see was the bottom of his chin. Still, she could make out the tightness of his jaw and the direction of his intense gaze.

With a frown, she turned to see why a little spilled teekee bothered him so much, then gasped all over again.

Smoky tendrils rose from the once slick surface. There were gaping craters and holes that burrowed straight through the three-inch-thick glass. Everywhere the teekee had touched was melted, a charred smell rising in the air along with the burning tendrils of whatever had actually been in the mug. The pieces of the cup remained oddly unaffected.

"Olena." He shook her, snapping her attention back his way. His eyes were as hard as ice on her. "Who. Brought. You. That?" It was the slow way he said it that hinted at how angry he was.

She blinked, trying to understand his odd behavior in relation to yet another attempt on her life. He'd killed that soldier, Dreadus, but part of her had assumed it was to save face. He'd even just brought up how important keeping up appearances was. But this . . . He was five times more pissed than he'd been that night in the bunker. Hell, she didn't think she'd ever seen anyone so angry before in her entire life.

Which didn't add up, and she really did hate when puzzle pieces refused to fit.

"My atteta," she answered before he could shake her again. She wasn't sure her arm could take it. "Lura. Right before you got here."

He let her go so suddenly, she stumbled. With a curse, he grabbed her again, righting her and then dragging her along with him through the balcony doors and back into her bedroom. He shoved her onto the bed, though a tad bit more gently, and without pausing, went straight to the door, tossing it open so hard, it almost came off the hinges.

"Get me the atteta," he demanded of Pettus, who stood guard outside. "Now, Teller!"

"I'm under orders not to leave the Lissa alone," Pettus informed him, holding his own despite how terrifying Trystan currently looked.

Bringing himself to his entire scary height, the Zane loomed over him in a much more threatening way than he just had with Delaney. It was good to note the difference, so that next time she'd be able to gauge how upset he was.

"Does it look like the Lissa is alone?" he growled so low, she barely caught it from where she still sat on the edge of the bed. "Do as I order, Teller, or I promise you, the atteta won't be the only one who pays in blood today."

He opened his mouth to argue, but Delaney stopped him.

"Pettus." She waited until he met her gaze, and then shook her head. "It's all right."

He could tell it wasn't—that was probably pretty obvious by the way she was shaking—but smartly, he didn't press her. Waiting for a moment to see if she'd change her mind, he consented and glared Trystan's way.

"I'll be back with the Ander soon," he stated.

"Be back with the atteta like I've instructed," Trystan hissed, "or the next murder attempt won't be against the Lissa; it'll be against you. And it will be a successful one."

Pettus's eyes widened, and he took off without more prompting. He must not have realized what had taken place out on the balcony, had only seen how pissed the Zane was and hadn't wanted to leave her alone with him.

She didn't really want that, either. Right now the Zane was the scariest thing she'd ever encountered, but she knew Trystan hadn't been lying. He would have hurt Pettus without hesitation, and she liked the Teller enough to spare him suffering at the risk of gaining a little of her own.

Trystan slammed the door shut and paced back toward her, running furious hands through his hair. She'd thought the room was big, but now, seeing him in it, prowling like a caged beast, she was forced to reassess.

Her hands clenched the comforter beneath her tightly, eyes locked on to his every movement. She couldn't help the fear in her chest, the cold chill in her veins, or the blood rushing through her head so loudly, she couldn't make out the words he was mumbling under his breath.

Okay, she thought to herself, *don't freak out*.

The sweet, timid girl who'd been helping her get dressed every morning since her arrival had just tried to murder her. No big. Assuming that it actually had been Lura. There was a chance it hadn't. She could have gone to the kitchens or whatever they called them and gotten it from someone else.

That had to be it, right? There was no way Lura would have done something like this. The way the liquid in that mug had eaten through the glass table . . . How could anyone do that to another person? Ever?

Her stomach tightened painfully, and she clasped a hand over it. Part of her wanted to throw up, and she had to squeeze her eyes shut in order to bank the sensation. Three. Three times someone had tried to kill her. And the attempts had all been different.

An explosion, a beatdown, and now poisoning . . . The Tars were seriously pulling all the stops to get her out of the way. She wasn't safe there, no matter what Ruckus and the Basileus believed. She wasn't safe.

She needed to go home.

"Hey." Trystan dropped before her, cupping her cheeks firmly. Once she'd opened her eyes again, he went on. "Don't do that," he said. "Don't cave in on yourself. Not when I'm just starting to be impressed with you. I'll find who did this and I'll make them suffer—you have my word. There's nothing to fear, Olena. I won't let anyone hurt you."

"Why?" she said on a shaky breath. Out of all the attacks, this one messed with her the most. She guessed everyone had their limits, and she'd merely hit hers.

He ran the pad of his thumb under her right eye. "I'm not sure," he admitted. "I just know that I won't."

"This wasn't you." She shut her eyes again, but he forced them open by tilting her chin up with the hands he still held her head with. It wasn't a question, and in truth she hadn't really meant to say it aloud at all.

"The Tandem game," he told her quietly, "that was me. I was going to lead you there and be done with it. Be free."

"But you didn't get me close enough." She frowned, unsure why his admission made her less afraid of him instead of more. Maybe she was going into shock? That made sense after everything she'd been through.

"No." He shook his head. "I didn't."

She had no idea if he was telling her that was done on purpose, if he'd let her walk away, or if it'd merely been a miscalculation on his part. Before she could even think to ask, his smooth voice was surrounding her once more.

"I had nothing to do with the other night," he assured her, "or with what just took place here. If I still wanted to kill you, you'd be dead. Some part of you knows that's true."

"Why are you telling me this?"

The look he gave her then was piercing—so much so, she felt it down to her toes.

"Because," he said breathlessly, "I want you to understand that I mean it when I tell you I won't let anyone else hurt you. The only person on this planet you have to fear, Olena, is me. *I* could have killed you on the field. *I* chose not to. The only reason you were even still alive long enough for those other attempts to be made is because I allowed it. And to answer your earlier question"—his hands slipped down to the base of her skull, holding her more securely—"no, I haven't come up with a solution that doesn't involve my killing you."

Oh yeah, she was pretty sure she was going to throw up. With any luck, he'd still be kneeling in front of her when it happened.

"But I am trying to," he shocked her by adding.

What shocked her even more was that she believed him.

CHAPTER 19

Ruckus showed up a few minutes later, Pettus and Lura close behind him. By then Trystan had already moved to the other side of the room to continue his pacing, so Ruckus was able to get close to her. He wrapped his arms around her as she stood, holding her against him gently but tightly. His warm breath fanned against the crown of her head, and for a moment neither of them spoke.

"I found her fleeing the grounds," Pettus said then, loud enough for them all to hear, though he was looking at Trystan when he did so. "She was about to board a hover car."

Those things still amazed Delaney. Ruckus had finally gotten around to showing her some of their vehicles. On Xenith none of the cars had wheels; they all floated. He'd begun to explain how the science of it all worked, but she'd quickly shut him down.

Some things were just information overload at that point.

"Still think she's innocent?" Trystan asked, staring at Delaney.

She hadn't said as much aloud, but he must have been able to figure out the direction of her thoughts. That was unnerving, because when she'd been having them, he'd been busy pacing.

Yet again, she hadn't realized he was paying such close attention to her.

"What happened?" Ruckus demanded, shifting so that he had all four of them in his line of sight.

"Someone put toxic in her teekee." Trystan curled two of his fingers toward Pettus and pointed out the side door that led to the balcony. "Put the atteta in one of the chairs. Maybe she'll smartly be more cooperative if she sees what she almost did to the Lissa."

Lura already looked sick, paler than snow, her emerald eyes as round as saucers. There were bags under her eyes that Delaney hadn't noticed earlier, and her whole body was quaking in Pettus's arms. She was afraid, yet another sign that attested to her guilt. She'd changed out of her uniform in a hurry, the pale yellow shirt she was wearing not buttoned up all the way. The buttons that were had been done haphazardly, and one leg of her black pants was tucked into a boot that had been left unzipped, while the other leg hung loose over the zipped boot.

"What happened?" Ruckus asked Delaney then as they watched Pettus lead the girl outside as he'd been instructed.

"I knocked the mug over, and Trystan stopped me from touching it," she said. *"If he hadn't been here, I probably would have drunk it."*

"What was he doing here?" Ruckus frowned over at her, then began to head after the Zane and the Teller, keeping Delaney securely at his back as he did so. It didn't seem necessary; Lura was too terrified to try anything here in front of them.

Delaney couldn't decide who Lura was more afraid of: Trystan or Ruckus. She kept ducking glances between the two of them, flinching whenever she caught one of their eyes.

"He wanted to talk." She didn't know how else to explain, so she kept it simple.

"Have the Basileus and Basilissa been notified?" Trystan was asking Pettus, who stood behind Lura, holding her down in one of the metal chairs on the balcony. Trystan stood on the other side of the table, his arms crossed, cocking his head in an intimidating manner.

"Yes, I informed them. They said to allow the Ander to handle it," Pettus said.

Of course they did.

"Wouldn't expect them to want to check on their only child or anything," she grumbled, then realized it was out loud when three sets of eyes darted her way. She'd sounded bitter, and for all she knew, Olena couldn't give two shits about her parents.

"Why'd you do it?" Delaney turned her attention to Lura, taking charge. Moving around Ruckus so she could get a better look, she carefully avoided getting close to the melted table.

Lura closed her eyes and inhaled shakily. When Pettus's hands clenched harder on her shoulders, she winced and then reopened her eyes on Delaney. It wasn't comforting to know that Olena was the only one on the balcony the atteta wasn't afraid of.

"No one wants you here." Her voice was soft, low, but there was a distinct underlying layer of hatred. "You should have stayed on Earth."

"On that we agree." She shrugged when Ruckus glared. There was no point pretending otherwise on that aspect; Trystan already knew how she felt about him.

"Linking you to the Zane will only result in the end of our people," Lura continued. "You're no leader. He'll be the one taking control, with you a mere armpiece. You'll be the death of Vakar society, and he'll be the weapon you use."

Delaney's brows winged up, and she gaped for a moment before regaining control. "You're serious?"

At Lura's silence, it became apparent she was.

"That's what this whole thing has been about? The Tars—it is safe to say you're with the Tars, right? Yeah? Brilliant—think I'll be a trophy wife who sits back and lets the Zane destroy Vakar? Did you all forget the only reason either of us"—she waved a finger between her and Trystan—"are doing this is for peace?"

Okay, well, in reality he was doing it because he'd been ordered to. She had no clue what his stance on peace was, but now wasn't really the time to ask.

"And what's up with trying to kill me?" She threw her arms out. "I'm the Vakar here; he's the Kint. Shouldn't you all be attempting to murder him?" She turned to Trystan. "No offense."

"None taken," he surprised her by saying, not the least bit offended by her words. He actually waved her on. "Please, continue."

"I think I'm done." She slammed her hands on her hips, felt the telltale tingle of anger rise up in her chest. "You know what? No, I'm not. I trusted you." She took a step closer to Lura. "I actually liked you, even. What kind of sick, pathetic snake does *this* to someone?!" She pointed to the destroyed table.

"Understand"—Lura licked her lips and held her gaze—"it's nothing personal. I actually found myself liking you as well. You're nothing like what the others told me." She frowned, but shook her head, sending her blond ponytail flying. "But that doesn't change the facts. You're no good for Vakar. Your merger will not result in peace, but war."

"You'll have war without it," Trystan reminded. "Right now the only reason Vakar is still breathing is because of my father's agreement with your Basileus."

"Until you actually follow through with the binding," Lura spoke to him, yet couldn't meet his gaze head on, "there's no guarantee of peace, of your cooperation."

They all heard the bedroom door being opened, and a second later Brighton could be seen through the glass, crossing to the balcony. He paused in the doorway, glancing between them all, then settled a look on Trystan.

Delaney assumed they were having a mental conversation through the fittings, as the two of them remained silent.

Ruckus walked over to where Pettus held Lura, to take the Teller's place. Once his hands were on her shoulders, he brought her down against the tabletop, her cheek a few inches from a small dime-sized puddle that had yet to evaporate. It was slowly eating its way through the glass but must have been too small to work as quickly as the rest had.

Her eyes went wide, and he ignored her gasps and struggles, holding her steady.

"Are there any other attempts we should know about?" he asked her coldly, and Delaney got why Lura had seemed so afraid of both him and the Zane instead of just the latter.

Trystan wore it more obviously, but Ruckus was every bit as capable of being a stone-cold killer.

Which had her thinking, how well did she really know him? What if she'd allowed her feelings for Ruckus to grow because part of her actually liked being here?

Being with him?

Earth was where she belonged, but she had to admit, if only to

235

herself, Xenith wasn't all that bad when you didn't consider the assassination attempts, the weird food, or the asshole regents trying to control her life.

The healing pool was nice, and then there was bergozy. . . . She'd seriously debated whether or not to ask if Ruckus could find her a bottle of that stuff to take home with her. The biggest perk, the Ander himself . . .

The Ander, who was currently holding a girl pinned to a table, close to a flesh-eating substance.

"I don't know," Lura was mumbling. She let out a cry when she was forced closer, so that the puff of her exhales had the surface of the puddle dancing. "I swear I don't!" Thick tears began to flow from her cheeks, dripping precariously close to the substance. Her eyes sought out Delaney, and she sobbed. "Please."

"Stop." The order was out of her mouth before she could think how it would look. When they all stared at her, she pulled back her shoulders. "Let her up."

"Olena . . ." Trystan seemed disappointed.

"Melting a hole in her cheek isn't going to help get us answers," she snapped. "Ruckus, you know that's true. Let her up."

He hesitated then complied, slowly lifting Lura and pressing her against the back of the chair again. Continuing to hold her securely, he motioned Pettus toward the balcony door where Brightan still stood.

"Ready a cell," he ordered, "and inform the Barer his services are requested."

Pettus left quickly. Seemed he was always running off to do an errand or two.

Delaney didn't know what a Barer was, but it couldn't have been good, because if at all possible, Lura became even more frightened. Her eyes were still huge, almost looking like they were going to pop right out of her head, and her tearstained cheeks were turning red and puffy.

"We could always partake ourselves," Trystan told Ruckus, angling his head at Lura in that familiar predatory way that had even Delaney shivering. "There are a few tricks I've recently learned that I'd love to get a chance to try out. What better subject than a traitor?"

"I don't know of any other attacks," Lura tried again, turning to Delaney. "Please, you've got to believe me."

"The Lissa doesn't have to do anything," Trystan corrected. "And stop looking at her. You don't have any right to it. The Lissa might not want to see your flesh eaten away, but I assure you, I have no such qualms. I will take you apart bit by bit unless you tell me exactly what it is we want to know. Nod once if you understand. Lose a finger now if you don't."

She nodded frantically.

"Good." He moved closer, stopping to press his palms flat against the edge of the table across from her. It was untouched by the substance so it was safe for him. "Who else was in on this? Are there others currently in the castle? On the staff?"

Her sobbing increased, and it was hard to understand her, but she was clearly giving him names. The list wasn't too long, yet there were at least five other people involved, enough to make Delaney seriously uncomfortable. Lura didn't want to give them up, that was clear, but her fear of the Zane pushed her into it.

"Did you get all that?" Trystan glanced at Ruckus over Lura's shoulder.

"Yes." He tilted his head upward. "I'm alerting my men now. They should have the others in custody within a few minutes."

"Once they're apprehended, then what?" Delaney asked, glancing between Trystan and Ruckus.

"Then they'll suffer the same fate as this one." Trystan straightened from the table. "Let me just make sure I've got this correct . . . ," he began. "The reason for this"—he indicated the table—"is because the Tars believe Olena won't make a good Regina?"

"The fact that you call it a Regina," Lura sneered through the snot now running down her nose, "proves we were right. This is Vakar; here we have a Basilissa. Here we have a Lew, not a *Zane*."

What was with the sudden burst of bravery? She'd been a sniveling mess up until this point; now she was talking back to the man who'd just threatened to cut her up?

"I've called her Lissa since my arrival," he argued. "I've done nothing to dishonor the Vakar ways."

"Zane—" Brightan began, speaking aloud for the first time, but Trystan swiftly cut him off.

"You think I'll control her, is that it?" he snapped at Lura. "That she'll bend to my will and I'll be able to wipe the Vakar culture clean off Xenith without so much as a protest from her?"

He chuckled darkly, the sound deep and reverberating from the very back of his throat. "You clearly haven't been paying attention. This isn't the same Lissa as the one who left five years ago. It would be a waste of my valuable time to convince her to forsake her people." His head turned in Delaney's direction so that he was watching her out of the corner of his eye. "And I have other things in mind I'd like to convince her to do. Better things. Far more interesting things."

His gaze roamed down her body pointedly, and she barely held back a shudder. The way he'd angled himself, she doubted Ruckus could see where he was actually looking, and not wanting to start the two of them off, she didn't want to give away that his last words were meant for her and not Lura.

"The names you gave us," Ruckus chimed in, pulling Lura's head back slightly so that she was forced to acknowledge him, "are those the only ones? The only Vakar involved?"

"The only ones in the castle," she divulged, "who I know about."

"How else do you think they were able to pull off the mass bombing the other night?" Trystan stated. "They had to have had Vakar on their side. Did you really think they were all disgruntled Kints, Ander?"

"No, the other night proved that," Ruckus admitted through clenched teeth. "Though I had hoped."

Trystan's response was a grunt, and surprisingly he didn't press any more than that.

Delaney crossed her arms over her chest and moved to lean back against the railing. This whole thing was such a mess. She'd known after those Vakar soldiers had attacked her that some of Olena's own people were involved; she just hadn't realized how deeply it ran. Trystan hadn't been kidding when he'd said people didn't like her.

Vapid had probably been the nicer way of putting it, even.

Which made her even more confused, because how had someone described as a weak pushover been able to come up with a plan the likes of which Olena had? Using a device to make someone look like her, luring her guards after the fake version of herself . . .

These types of things took smarts and planning. Sure, Gibus had been the one to create the device, and she must have merely stumbled upon it and used the find to her advantage, but still.

Either they were all wrong about her, and Olena wasn't as dim-witted as they believed, or she'd gotten seriously lucky on this one. Making Delaney seriously unlucky.

"At least the Uprising is tonight," Trystan told Ruckus.

"Still?" Delaney gaped at him, straightening from the railing. Part of her had sort of hoped they'd postpone it, considering the trauma she'd obviously just endured.

"It's our best chance of keeping you safe," Trystan informed her as if he thought she was stupid for not realizing it on her own. "Once you're Uprisen, the punishment for attempting assassination will be raised, and without access to the Alter Pool, the Basileus and Basilissa will be vulnerable to attack. No Vakar would risk losing their rulers for a chance at stopping your reign."

"He's right," Ruckus agreed.

She thought she was beginning to understand the Tars' predicament, recalling what she'd been told about the Alter Pool. If the Tars killed her prior to the ceremony, then the Basileus would be forced to choose a new heir, despite his not having any other children. He could perhaps try again with his wife, or he could probably choose someone else.

Case in point, there were options. If she went through with the ceremony, however, the Tars would lose their window. After that, if they killed her, they risked their Basileus and Basilissa being murdered before a new regent could even be discussed. The Kint members probably wouldn't care, so she assumed this fear stemmed solely from those Vakar members.

"If the Kints want war so badly, wouldn't that be ideal?" she asked boldly. "Get me out of the way then go for Mom and Pops?"

"Mom and—" Ruckus stopped himself, then took a deep steadying breath.

"Who says the Kints want war?" Trystan asked her, voice low. If he'd noticed her slip, he didn't point it out. Instead he seemed caught up on the first aspect of her statement. "The Rex is the one who posed this asinine alliance in the first place."

Oh. She really wished she'd known that the Rex had been the one to initially propose peace between them.

"Just because he wants peace doesn't mean the rest of your people do," she pointed out. There was definitely a line, and she was close to crossing it, but she needed some time to think over the upcoming ceremony, and distracting them seemed to be the best way to get it.

She'd thought she'd have the morning to mentally prepare, to steady her racing heart and figure out how she was going to get through this without completely losing it. It wasn't a big deal, she kept trying to convince herself. Again, there were only those two lines. The real issue was standing up there in front of all those people, pretending to be someone else.

A lot could give her away: body language, the way she greeted people, and apparently her damn eyes, if anyone was as observant as Trystan apparently was.

"Is this assumption based on the knowledge that we would win in a war?" Trystan asked, the corner of his mouth turning up. It was a trick, however, an attempt to mask his residual anger. He did not like her accusations, apparently.

Ironic.

"I am not going to stand here and listen to this," Ruckus stated.

"That's because you know I'm right," Trystan said, goading him. "Face it, Ander. You need me to bind myself to the Lissa every bit as much as the rest of the Vakar. It's true, many of the Kints don't agree with peace, but most do. We might have a better chance of winning, but the losses on both sides would be astronomical. This may surprise you," he said, and glanced at her, "both of you, but I don't want to throw my people's lives away any more than my father does."

Ruckus held up a hand when Delaney went to speak, stilling her. After a moment he nodded and addressed the Zane.

"Pettus just told me the Barer is prepared," he informed them. Telepathic communication sure made gaining information a lot easier. It may even be faster than the cell phones she was used to.

Though she still did miss her phone.

"We should get ready for the ceremony." Trystan moved to gently touch the curve of Delaney's elbow. As he glanced at the atteta, his gaze hardened. "Get her to the prison. We both should have time to witness her interrogation before the start of the Uprising."

Clearly annoyed that he was forced to take orders from the Zane, Ruckus took his time lifting Lura out of the chair. He was in the process of bringing her toward the doors when the girl burst out of his arms in a shocking display of speed and strength. Caught off guard, he didn't have a chance to grab her.

She was on her way toward Delaney, swiping her hand across the puddle on the table as she went. The smell of burning flesh instantly permeated the air, and she let out a cry of pain. It didn't slow her, however. She continued forward, now holding her blackening fingers extended, her intent obvious.

She was going to rub whatever hadn't already eaten through her onto Delaney.

Lura still didn't pause when Trystan stepped in her way, clearly not caring at this point which of them she hurt. She let out a scream, vicious-sounding and full of agony, but with her hand only a few inches away from Trystan's throat, her body jerked.

For a frozen moment everyone was still, and then her body slumped to the side, slowly, toppling like a marionette whose strings had just been cut. Once she was sprawled facedown on the ground, the gaping hole at the center of her back became visible.

Brighton held a fritz out in front of him.

"You just—" Delaney was having trouble processing.

"Protected my Zane," he interrupted. Finally Brighton lowered his arm back to his side, and the gun re-formed so that only the metal band around his wrist remained.

"Come away." Ruckus was there suddenly, urging her past Trystan's large form and toward the door. He had her inside and sitting on her bed again in a matter of seconds. "Damn it, you shouldn't have seen that."

Trystan had followed them and was casually leaning, a shoulder propped against the doorframe. He watched her curiously over the top of the Ander's head, not the least bit affected by what had just happened.

"Brighton was doing his job," he said with a shrug, having obviously seen something on her face he felt the need to address. "It happens."

"Get out." She gripped Ruckus's hand where he'd placed it on her thigh, and glared over at the Zane. She'd had enough, and if he stayed there one more moment, she was going to lose it. A girl had just died, and his response was that "it happens"?

His entire body tensed, but he didn't straighten right away. With those narrowed blue-and-crimson eyes he watched her closely, as if silently daring her to order him to go again. Considering who he was, he wasn't used to being told what to do, and seeing as how he looked like *that*, she was certain he also wasn't used to women kicking him out of their bedrooms.

"Careful, Lissa," he drawled.

"She said get out," Ruckus said over his shoulder. He'd been kneeling in front of her but now stood, keeping close. His move exposed their still held hands, and he realized his mistake too late.

Trystan's gaze homed in on their intertwined fingers, and his jaw clenched so tightly, she thought he'd pop it. He did pull back from the frame now, holding himself steady for a few breaths as if needing to regain his composure. When he raised his eyes to hers a final time, there was so much fury there, her heart stopped.

That, and the promise of retaliation. The kind she was most certain she would not like coming from him.

"I'll be back in five hours to escort you to the ceremony," he said in a clear warning. "Be ready when I do."

Brighton had already lifted Lura's body, and now carried it across the room without so much as glancing in either her or Ruckus's direction. Without a sound, he left, waiting in the hall for the Zane to follow.

For the second time that day, Trystan slammed the door behind him.

"You've got to get me out of here," she whispered to Ruckus once they were alone. She wasn't afraid of anyone magically overhearing; it was just the loudest she could manage to get her voice.

"Delaney." He sat down next to her, pulling her close so that his arms were wrapped securely around her body and she was cradled in his lap. "You know I want to."

"I'm not safe here," she insisted. "Everyone keeps trying to kill me. And now . . . I'm not Olena. I shouldn't have to go through with this, take this stupid oath. I'm not her. This isn't my life or my destiny or whatever you guys call fate here."

"It's just this one more thing," he assured her.

"Is it?" She pulled back so that she could look up at him. "Have they found Olena yet?" His glance away was answer enough. "Then you don't know that. What do they expect? For me to marry Trystan as their daughter as well?"

"Absolutely not," he growled, arms tightening. "I'd never let that happen."

"You wouldn't really have much of a say though, would you?" she stated. He was bound by their laws, by the Basileus's will.

Though, she figured, right now she was in the same boat, whether or not she was a real citizen of Xenith. She couldn't get home until Magnus gave his permission, after all.

"We'd leave," he told her firmly. It'd only taken him a second to come to that decision. "If Olena's not found by then and they try to make you do that, I'll take you and my ship and we'll go."

"And risk war?" She didn't want to nurture that spark of hope igniting in her chest at his words.

"Like you said"—he brushed a strand of hair off her face and cupped her cheek, dropping his forehead to hers—"you are not Olena. This isn't your responsibility; it's hers. If there is a war, it'll be because of her cowardice, not yours. You can't be expected to marry someone you don't want to, Delaney."

She swallowed the lump in her throat, wishing that they could remain here like this. Everything else in the world was harsh and unknown, but there between them something was forming, something that was starting to become familiar.

"Why not?" She met his yellow-green gaze, feeling the tears finally beat her and slip past her defenses to roll down her cheeks. "It's what they were going to make Olena do."

He didn't have a response to that.

"ou can do this," Ruckus told her. He adjusted his military jacket, the one with the long sleeves, eyes scanning each and every soldier they passed.

Within the next ten minutes, she'd be Uprisen and the Tars would lose their prime window. Because of this, he'd refused to leave her side, even when the Zane—the still sulky, broody Zane, who was currently on her right side—had made his stance on the matter perfectly clear.

Together they flanked her as they moved down the hall toward the large ballroom where the ceremony would take place. Like the Ander, the Zane was dressed to impress, though his outfit was navy blue and he'd chosen to go with the sleeveless version of the jacket.

"The Ander's right," Trystan reluctantly agreed. "You'll do fine." His gaze also roamed over the guards they passed, though not a single one of them returned his look.

They came to the end of the hall, where a set of double doors stood before them. They were wide enough that the three of them could fit through shoulder to shoulder with ease; however, protocol stated that she and the Zane needed to enter alone. It made a statement to the higher-ups on the other side.

Ruckus hesitated, holding out a hand so that the two sentries at either door paused, already in the process of reaching for the handles.

"I'm going to be right behind you," he promised her, running a finger down her forearm. It was clear he wanted to do more, touch her more, but he couldn't risk it.

"She'll be fine," Trystan bit out, this time glaring Ruckus's way. He motioned to the guards. "Let's go already." He looped her arm through his and waited for his order to be followed.

Delaney took a deep breath and held it as the doors slowly slid open before her. Within, the ballroom was packed with people dressed in bold greens and golds. There were a few Kint blues, but she didn't focus on anybody. She was too busy concentrating on placing one foot in front of the other.

She'd dressed in a skintight gown that trailed some three feet behind her on the ground. Fortunately, putting it on hadn't been complicated, and she'd managed to do it on her own. It was a weave of both Vakar colors, shots of deep green and flashy gold sparkling on her body. It tied around the neck and left little to the imagination as far as her chest size was concerned, and while the back was superlong, the front stopped above her thighs. She really wanted to know what was up with the Vakar and their issues with covering their knees.

The heels she'd been given were a high four inches, and she'd wobbled when she'd first put them on. She'd never had a problem walking in stilettos before, so luckily it'd only taken her a couple of paces before she'd gotten the hang of them. Still, she was a bit concerned about tripping in front of the thousand or so aliens all staring at her.

From the door a gold carpet stretched forward twenty or so feet before veering off to a sharp right. The crowd stayed on either side of it, and once they'd turned, she saw it led to a dais where both the Basileus and Basilissa were currently sitting.

They were in chairs—thrones, really—a little ways back from another set, which took up the center. A man stood next to one of the empty seats, holding a metallic device she didn't recognize. He was older, with gray hairs mixed in with his chestnut-brown ones, and wrinkles at the corners of his eyes.

"Breathe, Lissa," Trystan whispered down at her as he began leading them toward the dais.

"Distract me," she pleaded before she could think better of it. She'd done a few pageants as a kid, thanks to her mom's insistence, but there had never been this many people watching her before in her life.

The corner of his mouth turned up, but he didn't laugh. "You look very lovely."

No, Olena looked very lovely. She was sure if he could see her, red hair and all, he'd say she looked like a Christmas tree threw up on her. But she took it anyway.

"Thank you."

He waited a moment and then, "This is the part where you return the compliment."

She snorted under her breath, just loud enough for him to hear but no one else. "I've been under the impression since we met that you know exactly how attractive you are. My telling you won't do anything but boost your already massive ego."

This time he grinned. "You think I'm attractive, huh?" Canting his head, he pretended to think. "What was that old nickname you used to have for me? Tryst, was it?"

Her eyes widened a fraction before she could get her reaction under control. Poor Olena. He'd known about her crush, and he still treated her like this? For what seemed like the millionth time since her arrival to Xenith, Delaney felt a pang of sympathy for the alien princess.

"Remind me, what does *tryst* mean on Earth, again?" he teased, tugging her a little closer to him by the arm she still had linked through his.

She gritted her teeth. "Pretty sure you know."

"I'd never contemplated having one with you before," he continued. "A tryst, that is. But now . . . I'm considering it."

"Seeing as how we're already betrothed," she stated sarcastically, "I'm honored."

The dais was fast approaching now, despite the fact that he'd been leisurely leading her. Her heart pounded away in her chest, and she actually found that this time her arm was the one clenching tighter around his.

"I'm thinking of having your head of guard replaced," he said then, successfully dashing away some of her trepidation about the ceremony.

"What?" She whipped her head toward him, almost stopping in the process. If not for the fact that he had a hold on her, she probably would have. "Why?"

"He's become a bit too close to you." He shrugged, not bothering to spare her a glance.

"Why do you care?" He couldn't be serious, could he? She'd assume her spending so much time with Ruckus would be a good thing in his mind. It meant less time the two of them had to be together, keeping up appearances—aka trading insults.

Part of her was momentarily worried that he was serious, before she recalled he thought she was someone else. Ruckus knew the truth, though, and there was no way he'd allow Trystan to separate them. Hell, she didn't think the Basileus would, either, knowing that she was walking a thin line as it was, pretending to be his daughter. He wouldn't want to risk her slipping up and blowing Olena's cover.

"I'm not sure," Trystan surprised her by admitting. "That's why I said I'm only thinking about it. You'll know when I decide."

"You'll tell me?"

"No." He looked at her intensely. "Because you'll never see him again."

She inhaled sharply at the truth in his eyes. He *was* serious. Could he actually do that? Did he have enough power here to convince the Basileus to take the risk anyway and fire Ruckus?

A new kind of panic settled in her bones, and she felt sweat trail down her back. Ruckus was the only thing keeping her together on Xenith, the only person she could be herself with. If he got taken away . . .

They came to a stop at the foot of the two steps that led up the dais, cutting off any response she could have given—not that she had one. The older man stepped toward them, holding out his hands to quiet the surrounding onlookers before motioning for her to move closer.

Trystan helped steady her as she moved up a single step, still one below the man leading the ceremony. Then he let her go and she felt him move a few feet away from her, but she didn't turn to see exactly how far.

"We come here today to honor the traditions of our Vakar creators," the man said, voice rising strong over her. "On this day one of our own rises up to take her place among the great rulers, past, present, and of the future. Your hand, if you would."

She dutifully lifted her arm, settling her palm up in his larger one like Ruckus had instructed. She knew what was coming next, braced herself for the cool touch of metal right below the curve of her right elbow. He'd warned her it would sting a little, but had sworn it wouldn't be anything like what she'd experienced during her fitting.

Apparently, every ruler of Vakar got signified thus with a tattoo of sorts or, in her mind, a brand. The metal device he was holding to her flesh would deliver the mark by transferring a design straight into the layers of her skin using microscopic lasers.

Ruckus had explained it as sort of a more advanced version of a tattoo gun.

"With the oath given before all, do you hereby accept your fate as Vakar royalty?"

The speech she'd been rehearsing the past few days ran through her mind on repeat, and she struggled to catch up, blurting the words out as quickly as she could to be done with them.

"Of my own volition, yes, and I also hereby accept the responsibilities and the sacrifices that will be expected of me as an Uprisen member of Vakar society, and citizen of Xenith. I vow to always do my best to protect my people, no matter the personal cost to myself, and to always uphold my word given here."

The metal device was pressed down harder against her, and she bit the inside of her cheek at the burning sensation. It felt like someone was shredding her skin at first, but Ruckus had been right: It wasn't as bad as the head pain from her fitting had been, and it only lasted a minute at most.

When the device was removed, there was a tiny forest-green *V* no bigger than a dime at the top center of her forearm. When she moved it under the light, it sparkled like there was glitter in the ink.

She'd been seriously upset about this part, the part where she had to get a tattoo. It looked like Olena's body on the outside to all of them, but later, once she was home, her friends and family would see the real her. And now the real tattoo that would make no sense to them. She didn't even know anyone with a name that started with *V*.

At least it was small. She decided the first thing she'd do when she got back to Maine was hit up a real tattoo parlor and get it covered. She didn't even really care with what at this point.

Cheers rose up around her, the entire audience roaring their approval with laughs and incessant clapping. She wanted to tell them all to shut up, biting down on her lip to keep from doing so. To her, this whole thing was a major sham, one she'd been dragged and threatened into. To them, they'd just witnessed their Lissa get named the next Basilissa of Vakar.

In the next moment, Trystan's hand settled on the curve of her elbow, and he escorted her up the last step and over to the throne on the right. He eased her into it, being more gentle here than he'd ever been with her before, and then took the seat next to hers.

She couldn't help the twist to her mouth, and she sent him a sideways glare, which he noted and actually chuckled about.

They weren't kidding anybody. The whole planet knew they hated each other.

Sitting rigidly, she scanned the room, letting out a small sigh when her gaze locked on to Ruckus. He was moving toward them, heading to one side of the dais, where he stopped and stood sentry. His hands were clasped before him, and he held her eyes for a long moment, a comforting half smile on his lips.

"Why the two of you insist on insulting my intelligence is beyond me," Trystan said harshly under his breath. Around them the festivities were starting up, people moving around and heading toward the buffet tables that lined the entire left wall.

"I don't know what you're talking about," she snapped back at him, keeping her voice low, same as him.

"We've established that I caught you at the pool the other day."

"You didn't *catch* me at anything." They were receiving a lot of stares, but no one had approached them yet, so fortunately no one was close enough to overhear their conversation. She rubbed at her temples, sorely wishing for a hot bath and her bedroom back home.

"We're betrothed, Olena," he sneered, gripping the sides of the chair so tightly, it was a wonder the arms didn't snap off. "How do you think it looks to others? Your gallivanting around with the Ander?"

"Um." She rolled her eyes. "Like we hate each other? Which we do. It's no big secret."

"Do we?" He'd been watching the room up until this point, but now his heated gaze swung her way, settling on her unflinchingly.

Not wanting to decipher that, she turned her head, feigning fascination with the food on one of the golden trays a waiter was carrying around the room. Oddly, he was dressed the same way the wait staff on Earth would be, only in traditional Vakar colors. And with more poise.

"I certainly don't get the warm fuzzies when I'm around you," she said, managing to keep her tone steady, bored, even. She knew he wouldn't like that, but she wasn't too concerned about pissing him off at the moment. They were currently surrounded by thousands of people, after all, and the crowd both terrified and emboldened her.

"*Warm fuzzies* isn't quite the term I think of in your presence, either." It was the way he said it, voice dropping down to a huskier timber, that got her attention. He'd angled his body closer, leaning on his arm across the rest so that they were mere inches apart. There was a look in his eyes, almost like he was waiting for something, and she wondered if this was just another way of goading her for a response.

Deciding she preferred self-preservation over her pride, she moved to lean on her right armrest, quickly placing more space between them. It was as far as she could get while remaining in the chair, and something told her she didn't want to attempt getting up and leaving.

"Where are you going?" he purred, smirking when she noticeably bristled. "Interesting."

"Stop."

He canted his head in response.

"This morning you admitted to trying to kill me, remember?" she snapped. "Guys who've attempted murder don't get to look at me like that."

"And how am I looking at you, exactly?" he asked.

"Delaney," Ruckus's voice flowed through her mind, deliberate and strong. *"Are you all right? Should I come up there?"*

She appreciated the fact that he was asking, though also noted it meant they were seriously being monitored. If she didn't want to risk causing a scene, that meant sitting there was still very important, even though the official part of the ceremony had ended.

"I'm fine," she sent back, not wanting to get him into trouble. The Basileus and Basilissa were still seated behind them, neither having said a word to her yet. She wanted to keep it that way.

"He's dangerous. If he tries anything—"

"I'll call you," she stopped him. *"Until then, I've got this."*

Trystan was still waiting on a response, eyeing her curiously.

If he guessed she was having a private conversation with Ruckus, he didn't show it.

"You're looking at me like you know something I don't," she answered. What she really wanted to say was that he was staring at her like he had the right to it, but she was smart enough to know that would only serve to open another set of doors. She didn't want to bait him. She just wanted this whole ceremony bullshit to be over.

"I know lots of things you don't," he said. "I guarantee it. Some of them concerning you. Like the date of our binding, for instance."

She tried not to let those words get to her, yet her heart tightened and she realized she was inadvertently holding her breath. To give herself a moment, she sought out one of the waiters, motioning him over. She had no idea what was on the tray, but accepted with a polite smile.

It was circular and a toasted white color that sort of reminded her of custard. There was a small golden fork on the platter already, and she took it up and cut a small edge off what she assumed was a dessert.

She practically gagged when she placed it on her tongue. The texture was sort of akin to scrambled eggs, but the taste was a mixture of sweet and bitter, emphasis on the latter.

At her side, Trystan laughed. "I told you to ask for the pumpkin pie. You should have taken my word for it."

"Is there a problem, Lissa?" The waiter hadn't moved away, and now addressed her with a sharp frown. He glanced between her and the plate in her lap. "The Basilissa informed us that gremming was your favorite. If it's not to your liking, we can have another batch made up right away."

"Oh"—she gulped—"no. It's not that. . . . My tastes have just changed, I guess. Sorry." She was painfully aware that Trystan had stiffened and was staring at her differently now. Gone was the teasing glint; it'd been replaced with that calculating look that always sent chills up her spine and sent her into flight mode.

Self-defense was all well and good, but really what they should have done was teach her about Olena, testing her on the ins and outs of what the Lissa liked and hated. She should have pressed more for it herself, but in the beginning she'd been in denial that this would go on so long. A few weeks could easily turn into a few months.

What if she really was stuck here forever?

Her chest pinched painfully, and she lifted a hand to press against it, focusing on keeping her breathing even. Having a mental breakdown here was *so* not a good plan. She needed to stay vigilant. Fortitude would get her through this. She couldn't wait for the day when looking back on this would be a laugh.

Or, at least, a slight chuckle.

On the upside, how many people got to say they'd been to another planet? Or that they'd made out with an alien? Her gaze wandered over toward Ruckus, and she smiled. A very hot alien, too.

He stood with his feet apart, shoulders back. His traditional outfit was snug enough that she could see the curve of his spine, wanted to trail her fingers all the way up it and delve them into his dark locks. She'd never really been one for touching, but as she sat there, her mind couldn't help but wander over all the ways she'd love to feel him up.

Which was ridiculous.

But it was certainly more stimulating than trying more of the gremming, that was for sure.

She was so distracted with her perusal that she almost didn't recognize the pinging sound for what it was. It whizzed through the air so fast, she barely even had enough time to pick up on it, the heat searing past her cheek the only initial sign the shot had missed. With a frown, she spun her head in the direction of its origin.

Everything seemed to still, people moving in slow motion as her breath felt like it eased out of her lungs instead of burst. The shooter was staring right at her, standing clean across the room in front of one of the gaming tables. He was dressed up like everyone else, wouldn't have stood out in the crowd if not for the weapon in his extended arm.

The one pointed at her.

She didn't recognize it, so it wasn't a fritz, but that was only a small comfort. His finger moved on the trigger. Considering how time seemed to lapse, she probably could have attempted to move out of the way, but she was frozen to the spot.

She must have blinked, for the next instant something heavy was pushing her against the back of the throne, cutting off her air supply so that she gulped desperately in a poor attempt to breathe.

It took her a moment to realize the object was actually Trystan, and that he'd turned himself into a solid shield around her smaller form. His head was up higher, above her own, leaving her face pressed against his steely chest so she couldn't make out his expression. When he didn't move, she tried to wiggle her hands free from where they were caught between them. She wasn't able to get them far, shifting them up only half an inch or so.

Her fingers instantly touched something wet, and she stilled.

She was touching the spot directly below his right pec, the part of him that happened to be positioned right in front of her chest where her heart would be. Where the shooter had been aiming.

"Oh my god," she said, the words rushing out of her, and she felt renewed panic. With more force, she tried to shove him away so she could get a look at the wound. Was he dead?! Concentrating proved otherwise, for she was able to separate the pounding of her own heart in her ears from the clear deep gasps coming from him above her.

Then the surrounding screams reached her. She couldn't see it, but it was obvious the room had spun into a panic.

"You're bleeding out!" she told Trystan as loudly as she could, her face buried the way it was. "You need to get off so we can stop it!"

He didn't respond, and there was no way she was strong enough to budge him, so she did the only thing she could. Pressing her palm flat against the wound, she attempted to stanch the blood flow.

"This was supposed to *help*," she rambled through clenched teeth. "That's what you both said! This was supposed to make things better—not get you shot! What happened to their not risking another assassination attempt? I frickin' *hate* this stupid planet and you stupid ali—" She cut herself off abruptly, realizing what she'd been about to do.

No way would Olena call her own people aliens. She just had to hope that Trystan was too out of it to have really heard anything she'd said. He had yet to acknowledge her at all, so . . . that was a good sign.

Right?

"Olena!" Ruckus was suddenly at her other side, and she could sort of peek out from beneath Trystan's left arm and see him. "Are you all right?! Are you hurt?!"

"I'm fine," she said, voice shaking slightly.

"Zane," Ruckus said, directing his comment toward the massive paperweight holding her down, "we've got the shooters. It's all right. You can move now. We need to get that wound of yours treated before it's too late."

Trystan shifted and let out a sharp breath, stilling instantly.

"Did I crush you?" he asked her, and she could barely make out the words.

"You *are* crushing me," she told him, her tone completely lacking bite. She swallowed and pressed her other hand against his chest more lightly. "Thank you."

It didn't seem like he could attempt talking a second time, and she felt him nod. When he went to lift himself again, she held perfectly still.

She could practically hear Trystan grinding his teeth, gearing himself up for the clear pain that would come with moving. Sure enough, he let out a low growl as he shifted, attempting to regain his footing but failing at the last second.

She reached for him as he toppled, unable to hold even part of him up despite clinging to his arm. She watched as Ruckus motioned for the five nearby Tellers to assist him, one of whom was Trystan's right-hand man, Brighton. They lifted him, and his head lolled. He'd passed out.

"Delaney." Ruckus's hands moved all over her, testing her for breaks. *"Tell me again you're all right. You weren't hurt?"*

"No," she said aloud, "Trystan took the bullet."

"We don't have bullets," he whispered to her, pressing his cheek against hers. His body surrounded her, gentler than the Zane had been. "They're called zees. They are fire-pressurized rounds, small, no bigger than a pea from your planet. They're easier to aim, and to pass through a crowd to successfully hit a target. We scanned everyone for weapons at the doors, but three shooters must have slipped through."

"Three?" She pulled back to frown at him. When he motioned over her shoulder with his chin, she turned to see the Basileus stooped over his wife.

There was blood trickling from her leg, but aside from that she seemed okay. She was gritting her teeth, her blond curls somehow still in a perfect array around her oval-shaped face. She caught Delaney's eye and actually tried to force a comforting smile.

For some reason, it actually worked. She'd yet to have a real conversation with the Basilissa, but in that moment, it didn't feel like it. It felt more like they understood each other, that the queen was assuring her of much more than just her own bill of health.

Or she was reading into it way too much. Which was also a likely possibility.

"They didn't just target you," Ruckus told her when a group of Tellers came to help escort the Basilissa and Basileus away, presumably to get the Basilissa medical attention. "They went after the entire royal family. If you hadn't reached for me, we probably wouldn't have noticed in time."

"What?" She hadn't done anything but freeze.

"You signaled the telepathic connection," he explained. "I felt the pressure on my neck and turned when you didn't immediately say anything to me. The shooter aiming for the Basilissa was on the balcony above you, and I spotted him. I was able to contact my men and have them take him out at the last second. The other shooter got spooked and tried to flee without even attempting a shot at the Basileus after that."

She'd thought of Ruckus when she'd seen the gun aimed at her, but she hadn't realized she'd opened a connection. Thank goodness she had.

"So much for them not risking killing off their leaders, huh?" she griped, feeling sick to her stomach as she began to descend from her adrenaline high.

"There's no way these were Vakar," Ruckus disagreed. "We must have been mistaken. The Tars must not be made up of equal parts Kint and Vakar. If they've even really got Vakar involved at all."

"What do you mean?" She shook her head. "Lura was definitely one of yours, and she definitely tried to kill me. Plus, her whole spiel about how I'd ruin you guys? She was Tar, without a doubt. Admitted to it, even."

"Yes," he said, and nodded, "but what if she'd been fed that spiel? What if that was something she and a few others were told by the Kints in order to get them to work with them? It wouldn't be hard. Lura was young, easily manipulated. And those soldiers who you fended off in the bunkers? We checked them; their identities were fake. They joined the Vakar army under false pretenses about a year ago. That's around the time we discovered the new weapon in the Kints' arsenal."

"You think they were planted?"

"I know so."

She had to admit that sounded pretty legitimate to her. It put the pieces snugly together, that was for sure, and after everything, it was sort of nice to have bits fitting. Except there wasn't any proof to back his theory, and she didn't know how to go about getting any. There was also the issue of the massive assassination attempt that had just taken place.

Had the Tars gotten sick of always missing her as their mark? Had they decided to cover all their bases and take out the whole family instead? With Magnus, Tilda, and Olena Ond out of the picture, there'd be no one Uprisen to take the crown.

Who would get control then?

CHAPTER 21

've got to make sure the rest of the castle is secure," Ruckus told her, hand at the small of her back as he urged her down the hall. "Pettus is going to stay with you."

They'd exited the ballroom, but everything after the moment Trystan had passed out and her quick talk with Ruckus about the Tars was one big blur in her mind. She'd thought all those other occasions had been close calls, yet this . . . If the Zane hadn't thrown himself into the line of fire, she'd be dead right now. No questions about it.

His blood was still drying on her dress, a huge burgundy stain at the center of her chest. She needed to change immediately.

With a sick twist in her gut, she realized where they were headed, and stopped in her tracks. The image of Lura with the hole in her back filled her mind, and bile rose up the back of her throat.

"I can't," she whispered, hating the frantic note in her voice but unable to do anything about it. "I can't go back to that room. Not after what happened."

Ruckus glanced between her and Olena's bedroom door at the center of the hall. Then he shifted on his feet, bringing his body closer to hers. He reached for her hand, gripping it tightly. "Delaney. Look at me."

"I don't want to go back there." She met his gaze. "I'm *not* going back there."

"All right." He smoothed the hair away from her forehead. "I'll take you to the science wing. Pettus will bring you a change of clothes. And something to eat."

"I'm not hungry."

He began pulling her down the opposite direction from Olena's rooms, and she fell into step with him. The relief she felt at not having to deal with Lura's death this afternoon on top of what had just taken place in the ballroom was overwhelming. "You need to get me out of here."

"I know, Delaney."

"No, you don't—"

He paused, cutting her off. "I'm doing everything I can. I swear it."

"Why do you think Trystan saved my life?" she blurted, instantly regretting doing so.

Ruckus's expression tightened, and then they were moving once more, this time at an even quicker pace. "We can't talk about that here. I need to get you somewhere safe."

She'd been removed from the ballroom along with the other three regents. From what she'd gathered, the rest of the guests were being kept there until Ruckus's soldiers were certain that the shooters had all been accounted for.

Pettus was already waiting for them outside the science wing, a bundle of clothing neatly folded over his arm when they got there. When he spotted them, he bowed his head, and the look of pity on his face made her want to throw up for what felt like the millionth time that day.

Delaney hated feeling like this, scared and weak.

They wordlessly entered one of the large workrooms, and Pettus handed the clothing over to Ruckus. Afterward, he moved toward two metal doors and exited, leaving them alone.

"Here." Ruckus held out the bundle and then spun pointedly on his heel. "I won't look. Dress quickly."

She couldn't get out of the bloodied clothing fast enough, and yet her fingers shook around the zipper, unable to hold it steady to get it down more than an inch. After the fourth attempt, she closed her eyes and took a deep breath, nearly jumping out of her skin when she reopened them to find Ruckus had turned around and was now less than a foot away.

"Apologies," he mumbled, then motioned for her to turn. "Let me."

He slid the zipper down and then stepped back.

"Thank you." She dropped the dress to the floor, never wanting to see it again, and slipped into a pair of black pants and a brown shirt that exposed her midriff. Done, she barely resisted the urge to kick the dress under one of the heavy metal tables.

Instead she stepped closer to Ruckus's back and eased her hand into his from behind. When he started to turn, she rested her head against the side of his arm. She was shaking and trying really hard to get a handle on herself. The horrible things that had happened that day kept replaying in her mind, and she just wanted it all to stop.

He reached around until he was holding her waist and hugging her gently to his front. The smell of firewood surrounded her, and for a moment neither of them spoke, giving her a chance to pretend that she was somewhere else. That they'd met somewhere else.

That they were even a remote possibility.

"Gibus believes he's completed the machine to reverse the effects on your appearance," he told her, breaking the silence and forcing her back to reality. "And the last report we received from Earth stated they were close. They're going to find Olena soon."

"Not soon enough." She took a deep breath and repeated, "Why do you think he did it?"

Ruckus didn't need her to elaborate, but when he didn't initially respond, she looked up to catch him glaring off into the distance. "Haven't you noticed the way he looks at you?"

She blinked. "Are you . . . You sound jealous. Of Trystan. Who is psychotic."

"Of Trystan," he corrected, "who just saved your life. He took a zee for you, Delaney. I've never seen him—" He clenched his jaw, tried again. "He's the only heir of the Rex of Kint, and he put his life in jeopardy to protect you."

"Olena, you mean." She wasn't sure how she felt about his odd reaction toward the Zane.

"No." He shook his head. "I mean you." His shoulders slumped almost imperceptibly. "I might not be the only one who can see past her face. He's trying to see you, and maybe he already has."

"Ruckus—"

He stepped back, running a hand through his dark hair in a poor attempt to smooth it back down. "I am jealous."

She frowned at him. "You're jealous because he took a bullet for me and you didn't?"

At her pointed look, he sighed, the corner of his mouth just starting to twitch upward. "And you were saying he's the psychotic one?"

"Oh!" The sound of Gibus's excited voice interrupted them, putting an abrupt end to their conversation. He appeared across the room behind one of the large metal workbenches, grinning ear to ear at them. "I thought I heard you! Come in! You've got to see this!"

Cautiously, they made their way closer. There was nothing on the table to indicate what he was talking about, and their gazes swept around, searching out anything of interest. Seeing them, Gibus shook his head, sending long tendrils of his brown hair around.

"No, no." He angled his body toward the right, through the door he'd just entered. "This way."

Pettus had a hip propped against the side of a table, idly flipping through a book of some sort. He straightened when they entered the room. "They're ready for you, Ander."

Ruckus nodded. "I'll leave in a moment."

Ignoring their exchange, Gibus continued leading them over toward one of the glass cases, then he stooped down, blocking their view. A hum started up at the back of his throat, a tune that Delaney didn't recognize, and he bounced a little on the balls of his feet. Obviously the assassination attempt against the royal family an hour ago had done nothing to damper the Sutter's mood.

"Look, look." He wiggled two fingers at Delaney without even turning to her.

Awkwardly, she stepped up, curiosity getting the best of her. Stopping close enough that their shoulders brushed, she bent down so that her face was at eye level with the glass. It was basically a twenty-gallon fish tank, only with a glass covering that had tiny pinpricks drilled into it.

The tank was filled with weird plants she didn't recognize, some with spiky bright red leaves, others with vibrant green ones that appeared to have a waxy texture. They'd been planted in a fine two-inch-thick layer of dark soil, and twisted every direction, obscuring anything else that could be hidden within.

"What am I . . ." Her words trailed off when she caught sight of a marble-sized eye. It peeked out from beneath the tip of one red leaf, blending in so much in color that she almost hadn't noticed it.

For a second all it did was stare at her, but then a head eased its way out from under the foliage, exposing bright neon-pink scales. The creature had a box-shaped head, with two large, glassy red eyes, two slits for a nose, and one for a mouth. It gaped a little, exposing a row of pointy teeth and a long curled brown tongue.

It pulled more of itself into view, so that she could see the long double-jointed legs on either side of its low oval-shaped body. A tail tipped with tiny razor-sharp pricks that mirrored its teeth flicked from under a green vine, clinking against the glass.

It took her a moment, but she realized with a start as it continued to tap its tail that it was doing so to the beat of Gibus's humming.

"Please tell me that's not a crumvit." She gulped, recalling the name of the breakfast she'd been served that first morning on Xenith. Even though she hadn't tried it, the idea of a dead version of this creature on her plate still made her queasy.

"What?" Gibus dropped his tune and gave her a disgusted look. "No. This is a spinik. Duh."

"Human here, remember?"

"You don't make it easy to forget," he said, and snorted. "Anyway, I named her Missy."

"Seriously?"

"Where'd you get a spinik, Gibus?" Ruckus asked, leaning on the side of the tank so he could get a look now as well. "I thought they all died off a few years ago?"

"They did," he affirmed, beaming. "I created her."

"You cloned her?" Delaney pulled back, eyes wide, and stared at him with a new appreciation. They could do stuff like that back on Earth now, sure, but it was still pretty cool to see it up close and personal. Even if she had no idea what a spinik was.

"I *improved* her," he corrected her. "You see these?" He pointed to the teeth on her tail. "The originals didn't have them. That's probably why the progos picked them off so easily."

"It's like a type of bird," Ruckus filled her in telepathically, because the Sutter was continuing and there was no way to get a verbal word out with him talking a mile a minute.

"Once I've tested her out, we'll be able to see if this new version of spinik can be released into the wild. If they can survive a progo attack—their number one predator—at least two out of three times, I'll have successfully raised Missy's species from the dead."

"Honestly, you sound a bit crazy . . . but I can see why you're so excited," she told him.

"Well, of course you can." Apparently he didn't know what modesty was.

She didn't know why his weird genetic experiment surprised her; he had been the one to create the device that allowed Olena to do this to her. Maybe part of her had assumed he'd learned his lesson. Then again, he was trying to save a species. That couldn't be bad, right? A bit mad scientist, but not necessarily bad . . .

Ruckus took a step back from the glass. "Make sure you don't let that thing out. If anything happens to Delaney, I'm going to hold you personally responsible."

"That's not fair," Gibus said, and spun on his heel, almost knocking into Delaney in the process. "Pettus is the Teller here, not me."

"And you're the genius who got me into this mess," she stated, a bit annoyed that he hadn't even apologized for it.

"Hey." Having noticed the slump to her shoulders, Ruckus gripped her hand once more. "I'll do this as quickly as possible and be back for you. Then you can get some rest."

She nodded, and for a moment it looked like there was something else he wanted to say, but he must have changed his mind, for he leaned in and kissed her cheek before turning to go. The second he was gone, she felt the panic from earlier seep back.

"Delaney." Pettus stepped over to her. "We won't let anything else happen to you."

She glanced over at Gibus, who was wiggling a finger at the spinik like one might to a goldfish. Lifting a brow, she returned her attention to the Teller.

He winced, playing up his reaction in an attempt to make her smile—which oddly worked. "Try not to think about it."

"Almost getting shot or"—she pointed at the Sutter—"*that?*"

Pettus laughed lightly, and she was momentarily caught off guard by how comfortable she felt around him. Now that she'd had a few minutes to adjust to Ruckus's leaving, she realized she wasn't as terrified as she would have been without him a few days ago. She didn't know the Teller as well as she did his commanding officer, but she trusted that he'd do his best to keep her safe.

And he was right. As badly as she wanted to curl into a ball and weep right now, where would that get her? She was still shaken up, but a distraction might do her good.

"Ruckus says you figured out how to fix my face situation?" Delaney addressed Gibus then. "Want to show me how it works?"

"I can't show you," Gibus said, "because there was only the one prototype. So reversing what was done to you can't be redone. However, I can explain it." The spinik forgotten, he dashed over to the other side of the vast room, snatching something off one of the tables among a pile of metal scraps.

Pettus leaned in and stated dryly into her ear, "This should be interesting." When she looked at him, he winked.

"Here it is!" Gibus was holding a small device about the size of a pencil and one-inch thick. It had a blue light tip that flashed every three seconds, and four silver buttons.

"That kind of looks like Doctor Who's sonic screwdriver," she mused, and when the two of them frowned, she heaved a sigh. "Never mind. When this is all over, remind me to loan you the DVD set." She tilted her head at the device. "How do you know this is going to actually work?"

If there'd only been the one prototype, and Olena had it, how could Gibus be sure this thing would do what it was supposed to? What exactly had he tested it on? The last thing she needed was for something to go wrong, and instead of looking like Olena, she'd end up looking like a spinik, or worse, an ung.

"I've done experiments," he said vaguely. "It'll work. Trust me."

"Pretending for a second that we actually do"—Pettus quirked a light brown brow—"*how* does it work?"

"Simple, really." He tilted the device so that the blue end pointed at Delaney. "You aim, and then twist at the center, like this." A slow hum emitted from it as he demonstrated. "And you hit the third button."

"Why the third button?" she asked. "What do the others do?"

"Nothing." He shut it down and slipped it into the pocket of his light green lab coat. "I just thought it looked more aesthetically pleasing this way. Only one button made it seem kind of quaint, you know what I mean?"

"I don't believe either of us do," Pettus answered for her, "no."

IF SHE STOPPED moving, for even a second, flashes of Trystan's body crushing hers, his blood on her hand, and Lura raced through her mind. After she'd almost slipped into her second panic attack, Pettus had caught on and gone out of his way to keep her distracted.

They spent the next three hours teaching her how to play a card game.

The game was called topsy and involved a deck of triangular cards that were held point down. Each player received a chunk of the deck, in their case a third, and all of them would flip a card from their hand at the same time, placing them faceup in the center for everyone to see. It was sort of like the game War, in that it was a game of chance, with certain cards trumping others. Once she got ahold of what each image was and which were the highest ranking, she started having a lot of fun.

It was actually very relaxing, doing something so normal, so mundane, and she got swept away in it. For a while, she was able to forget she was sitting across from a Teller and a Sutter, instead of a soldier and a scientist. She was able to forget that they were aliens, and simply enjoy their company.

This was even more impressive because of their topics of conversation. Throughout the games, they both took turns asking her questions about her life on Earth, what it was actually like there and some of the things she hadn't seen yet but would really like to when she went back.

Instead of feeling sad and hopeless when they mentioned this, she felt uplifted, like they knew for certain she'd get back there even though she had her secret doubts. And that was enough. Neither of them had taken their denzeration, opting out of them to kick-start their careers early. Apparently, it was a common decision among the Vakar and the Kints.

So she told them about baseball and cheesecake and Rollerblades. Some stuff they knew about, but mostly just from hearsay. It was interesting, how much aliens knew about her species as a whole but how little firsthand experience any of them had with it.

After about an hour and a half, she started dipping into more personal things, like stories about stupid adventures with Mariana, and how her parents had raised her with a certain image of who she'd become. How she didn't exactly own up to that. She was in the middle of describing *Doctor Who* to them—a show that had somehow become more popular after the discovery of Xenith—when Ruckus returned.

He looked haggard, with heavy purple splotches under his eyes. His hair was still slicked back, but the strands didn't quite stick together, insinuating that he'd been repetitively running his fingers through it. His uniform was a bit wrinkled, and there was a distinct smear of blood on his left arm, right below the elbow.

His tired eyes sought her out and he sighed, and some of the tension seemed to ease out of him with his slow exhale. Standing there, he was like a beacon of warmth, and she found her heart skipping a beat and her face stretching into an even bigger smile.

Waving the cards in her hands, she glanced over at the two men across from her teasingly. "You're just in time to see me kick their asses again."

"Oh, is that so?" Gibus laughed and slammed another card

down, whooping when it was the image of a large red lizard creature complete with fangs, five legs, and large, shiny wings. "Beat that, D!"

She'd discovered that she wasn't the only one there with a penchant for nicknames, and within the first half hour, Gibus had given her that one.

She and Pettus flipped theirs at the same time, and she scanned the three cards, grinning ear to ear when she realized she'd won the hand. On her card there was a crocodile-type creature with dark blue-black skin and sharp bloodred eyes. Initially, she'd been confused how this card could trump the red creature on Gibus's, seeing as how that one looked equally, if not more, terrifying, but they'd both insisted that the creatures were no match in a fight.

Pointing at Pettus's card, which had a fluffy pink creature resembling a cotton ball with googly eyes and antennae, she feigned fear. "Oh no! Not the rush bug!"

"Shut up," he mumbled, swiping his card off the surface with more force than necessary and flicking it across the table at her.

She caught it, letting out another laugh, and slipped it into the pile before her. Now she had almost the entire deck—so close to winning. There was an empty chair across from her between Pettus and Gibus, and she angled her head toward it.

"Want to join?" she asked Ruckus, who'd remained standing a few feet away.

"As much as I like seeing you actually having a good time," he admitted, rubbing at the side of his face, "honestly . . ."

"You're exhausted," she finished for him. As she stood, the sound of her chair legs sliding against the hard floor mingled with the others groans of disapproval. "Sorry, boys, looks like we'll have to pick this up another time. I've got to get the Ander to bed."

They blinked at her.

"Dirty minds, dudes." She rolled her eyes.

"How are you not exhausted right now?" Ruckus asked her, seemingly genuinely curious about the answer. He reached for her hand when she came close, linking their fingers naturally while keeping his yellow-green gaze steadily on hers.

"I just finished my last year of high school, remember?" she said. "Try studying for a biology midterm three nights straight, then you'll understand. I suck at science. Seriously, suck."

"That's what I'm here for, D." Gibus collected all the cards back into a deck. "I'm going to hold you to that rematch. I was really close to getting the upper hand."

"No." Pettus shook his head. "You were not."

"I was!"

"Get some rest," Ruckus ordered them, tugging her gently toward the doors.

"Yes, sir!" they both said mockingly, laughing afterward.

"You understand that's not what I meant," Ruckus said once they'd entered the hall. "When I left earlier, you were—"

"A mess?" She shrugged. "I still am."

"You're hiding it well."

"Isn't that the point?"

His hand tightened around hers. "Not with me, Delaney. You don't have to hide anything with me."

"I don't have to fall apart, either, no matter how badly I want to." She leaned her head against him. "But thank you."

For a moment she allowed herself to bask in the contentment, and even contemplate how it was possible for her to feel so relaxed after a day like she'd just had. There was still that underlying sense of fear, but it'd dimmed some over the past couple of hours. Pettus and Gibus had really gone out of their way to keep her mind off the Uprising. Friends really could get you through anything. And that was when she realized that was what she considered them now. Friends.

Weird.

"I never thought I'd be here," she said softly, breaking the comfortable silence they'd been walking in. "That this type of thing would happen to me."

"What type of thing?" he asked.

"Being let into your crazy world." She glanced up at him.

"You mean being forced into it," he reminded her.

She shrugged again. "Maybe that's how it started, but I can't regret everything. Some really amazing things have come out of your kidnapping me in that alley. I know about things that I never would have otherwise, seen things people back home will never have the chance to." She made a face. "Tasted some things, too, but we won't talk about that."

He chuckled and turned them down a corner, bringing them to the opposite end of the hall that led to her room. Stopping before a different door, he glanced at her frown, the only response the curving of his lips as he pressed his palm against a flat panel at the right of it.

A green light passed under his hand, followed by a quiet buzz and a clicking as the door latch undid itself. The heavy gray door swung inward half an inch, exposing a swath of darkness within.

Instead of opening it the rest of the way, Ruckus turned to her, a seriousness having come over him.

"We've swept your room and it's safe," he began tentatively, "but as you've pointed out, I'm exhausted, and I'd much rather not spend the rest of the night attempting to remain on my feet, worrying that something's happening to you in that room despite all the precautions my men and I have taken. And you made your stance on going back there very clear.

"So"—he inhaled deeply, bracing himself—"will you stay with me tonight?"

Suddenly she was very nervous, and unable to trust her voice, she managed only to nod. She allowed him to push the door all the way open and lead her inside, adjusting to the darkness for a second before the motion-sensored lights activated.

While he shut the door and entered a code into a similar pad on the right wall, she scoped the place out, increasingly more curious with every second.

His room wasn't as large as hers, or even as Trystan's, but there was a homier feel to it. The bed was still massive, yet the comforter was a deep brown with golden highlights that depicted a warm invitation. The pillows that peeked out were a muted gold as well, and silk. The headboard towered a good four feet up the beige wall.

Her eyes lingered on the bed a second too long, and she quickly forced her gaze away, pretending not to notice the pounding of her heart. Palms suddenly sweaty, she rubbed them against her thighs as she moved around the room, feigning a calm about being here that she didn't feel. She'd agreed before really considering what spending the night with him meant. Would they be sharing the bed? Was she ready for that?

This room was also shaped like an octagon, but instead of a balcony, the entire left wall caved outward, creating another sitting area complete with a couch under a bay window and a ceiling-high bookshelf on either side. Some shelves housed books of various sizes; others contained gadgets and trinkets she didn't recognize.

The door to the bathroom had been left open, so she could see all the similar appliances as the ones back in her own bathroom, but the closet door to her right was shut.

A comfy leather chair was tucked against the small wall between the sitting area and far wall, the crater-shaped center a dead giveaway that he sat there often. There was an end table to its left, a half-read novel on the edge as if to supply further proof. His smell was everywhere, that thick fire pit scent, and she breathed deeply. He didn't have a skylight, but a concave dome ceiling that was painted black.

Moving over to the side of the bed, Ruckus flicked his finger over the edge of what she'd assumed was just another end table. At his touch, a screen appeared, hovering a centimeter above the faux wood surface. After touching a sequence of buttons, he tipped his head back and stared up.

Following suit, she gasped when suddenly the ceiling came alive, billions of glowing dots appearing as if by magic. They flickered and sparkled like the real thing, surrounded by swirls of purples and bold oranges. It was like looking through a telescope and seeing everything more intensely.

"Sky roofs are a bit of a risk," he told her, coming up to her side to watch it with her. He rested a hand against the small of her back almost absently, as if instinctually needing to touch her. "I had this made instead. I tried to get Olena to follow suit, but she can be stubborn."

"This is so much better," she said breathlessly, finding it hard to concentrate with him near like that.

He smiled and glanced down at her. "I'm glad you like it."

"You'll have to install one in my room back on Earth," she joked, frowning when he tensed.

Swallowing sharply and licking his lips, he took both of her hands and eased Delaney and himself back toward the edge of the bed. Sitting down, he moved her so that she was standing between his legs, the position putting them almost at eye level.

"I have to tell you something," he said softly. "It's good news, but I don't want you to get too excited yet, all right?"

"Sure." She nodded.

"They found Olena. They've got her, and they're on their way here. It's a three-day journey."

A lot could happen in three days. Like, for instance, one of these murder attempts could be successful. Unbidden, she conjured memories of the attack in the ballroom. The heavy feeling of Trystan's body practically crushing her, the smell of his coppery blood, how it'd all happened so fast . . .

As if seeing the train of her thoughts, his grip tightened and he shook his head, gaze hardening some. "Nothing's going to happen to you. I'm going to keep you safe, and in three days I'll bring you home like I promised. Just keep up this charade a little longer, and you'll be home free."

If anything, she was more confused now than before. Lifting a hand to his cheek, she traced the line of his jaw with her thumb, reveling in the feel of him. He'd shaved, but there was still a hint of coarse hair beneath the pad of her finger.

"Then why are you so down?" she asked, pushing those dark thoughts aside to focus on him. "Like you said, this is good news, right?"

This was what they'd been waiting for, what she'd wanted since the first day she'd woken up on his ship. Magnus had predicted they'd have his daughter in custody by now, and they did. As soon as Olena got here, they could make a switch and

Ruckus and Delaney could head back to Earth. She'd be able to see Mariana again, her parents.

And then he'd leave. Because Earth wasn't his home; Xenith was.

"I've been thinking about you going," he whispered, clutching her hip to bring her closer, "and every time I do, it's like a piece of me gets torn out. I knew this wasn't permanent, that all you've ever wanted was to get back home. I just wish there was more time, that's all. Selfish." He smiled and dropped his gaze in embarrassment. "I know."

The problem was, if he was being selfish, then part of her was as well. She'd come to the realization that she was going to miss them. Not just Ruckus and the way he made her feel, but Pettus and Gibus also. She wished there was a way she could have her real life back with them in it.

Mariana would find Pettus funny and Gibus adorably strange, and if they'd liked the stories Delaney had told them during cards, they'd *love* the ones her roommate could share. She could see it now, the five of them sitting around the dining room table, talking about this whole crazy experience. Laughing about it, because by then it would be over and Delaney wouldn't be scared anymore.

Except, that couldn't happen, because they literally lived in different worlds. She belonged on Earth, and they belonged here. She couldn't stay, and they couldn't go. Leaving Xenith was all she'd wanted since her arrival. She'd never even contemplated that she might end up not wanting to leave them with it.

Delaney lifted Ruckus's chin and kissed him. It wasn't gentle, or slow, but a rough claiming of his mouth that she couldn't quite control.

Because he was right: She did want to go home, and she was

ecstatic that it now seemed truly possible, but she didn't want to leave him, either. It was hypocritical and confusing, and she didn't know how to explain it without botching it up and hurting his feelings.

She just kissed him, putting all those emotions into that one act. Pouring herself through him and clutching him close in a desperate attempt to hold on to him a little longer. She didn't know what this was between them, wasn't sure she could call it love yet, but it was something and it was strong.

She didn't want to give him up.

And she also didn't want to give up her freedom.

CHAPTER 22

She woke up in his arms.

He had them wrapped around her waist, holding her back to his front. His soft breaths fanned against her neck from where he'd buried his head against her in his sleep. They were still clothed, him in sleep pants similar to sweats, and her in one of his large T-shirts.

They'd made out for a long time last night, clinging to each other as if the only source of oxygen came from the other's mouth. Then they'd silently changed and slipped under the covers. He hadn't pressured her for more, hadn't said a single word. Instead he'd held her close and they'd dozed off like that, content to simply be in each other's presence. Not needing any confirmations or promises.

There was a certain freedom in that she'd never felt before, and now in the bright light of day, the reality of that hit her.

Carefully easing out of his hold, she tiptoed around the bed to the bathroom. A mirror stretched over the sink, and she stopped when the lights flickered and she spotted her reflection.

Olena's almond eyes stared back at her, set beneath dark brows that almost appeared painted on. The Lissa didn't have so much as a blemish, just smooth, milky skin.

Delaney pressed against a high cheekbone, picturing the smooth curve of her own, the freckles she had. On her real face, there was also a thin scar at the corner of her right eye that she'd gotten as a child.

And Ruckus didn't know any of this. They'd fallen asleep in each other's arms last night, were sort of unofficially dating, and yet he didn't even know what her actual hair looked like. He'd told her not to let it bother her, and she'd tried, but it was hard not to second-guess what was between them, especially now that she was in so deep. Questioning how badly she wanted to go home because it meant leaving him behind? What was that about? People didn't try to kill her there, for one, and two, she could actually be herself.

On Xenith she was Olena Ond, Lissa of the Vakar, and that was all she'd ever be. If they did discover she wasn't really who she claimed, a war would start, and she'd probably be murdered for real. The attempts could only fail so many times, after all.

Besides, she couldn't stay even if she wanted to—which she didn't. Not unless she wanted to be forced into marrying Trystan and ruling the Vakar—which she also didn't.

Yet, even knowing all this, when she thought about never seeing Ruckus again, her heart twisted painfully. She'd developed an attachment to him here because of the secret they shared; did that mean there was a chance it would dwindle once she was back among people who knew the real her? Or would this stick with her? Would she be forced to miss him for the rest of her life?

She rolled her eyes, annoyed that she was being so melodramatic. People had crushes all the time, and those crushes ended.

This was no different. She wasn't an idiot; it wasn't like she was madly in love with the guy or anything like that. She couldn't be.

And more important, he couldn't be with her for all the reasons she'd already noted. Sure, physical appearances weren't everything, but anyone who thought they weren't at least slightly important was either an idiot or a liar. Chemistry was nature's way of drawing two likely spouses together. Pheromones and all that jazz held at least some sway over attraction.

People could grow to love one another despite outward appearances, of course, but she was selfish. She wanted it all. She wanted Ruckus to be attracted to her outer self as well as her inner self. What would happen if he wasn't? What if the second they used Gibus's device, he took one glance at her and threw up?

It was easy to say there was a bond between them now, here on Xenith, where their lives and the lives of millions of people—earthling and alien alike—hung in the balance. They needed to rely on each other, get close to each other in order to protect themselves and the secret. It was a lot of pressure, and situations like that had a tendency to rush connections and speed up feelings that otherwise might take months or years to form.

Under normal circumstances, would Ruckus even be interested in her? If they'd met at the club, his knowing she wasn't Olena, would he have noticed her? Would she have caught his eye, at the very least, or would he have overlooked her the same as he no doubt had every other human in the room?

She knew she still would have been attracted to him; without a shadow of a doubt, back home his face would be plastered all over billboards and magazines.

She would have missed out on knowing a really great guy. And he was. He was kind and thoughtful and caring. He was also a soldier who'd dedicated his life to protecting people, and had been given a high-ranking position at a very young age. He had dedication, passion, determination, all things she found very sexy.

"Don't do that," his voice cut across the large bathroom then, causing her to jump. He was standing in the open doorway, arms crossed over his bare chest. He hadn't bothered to put on a shirt, or change out of the low-hanging pants.

Unable to help herself, her gaze shifted lower, roaming over the sharp V formed by his hip bones and the trail of dark hairs that disappeared down his center. His muscles were well defined, and she shivered at the reminder that all that had been wrapped around her only ten minutes ago.

She should have stayed in bed.

"Do what?" She had to clear her throat in order to get the words out, eyes still trailing the contours of his six-pack.

"Judge what's going on here." He stepped forward suddenly, forcing her to raise her gaze and look him in the eye. "Whatever is between us, it's real. I don't need to have seen your face for that to be true. Don't you realize how insulting it is to me for you to constantly think otherwise?"

A bit too late, she figured out he was angry.

"What kind of a person do you think I am, Delaney?" He was rushing on before she could answer. "I wouldn't care if half of your face was scarred. Or if you were missing a finger, or had no hair at all. I'd get past that, because how you look isn't all of you."

He had the uncanny ability to leave her speechless, something her parents would no doubt love to learn the secret to.

She must have kept quiet too long, because he let out a frustrated sigh and ran a hand forcefully through his already unkempt hair.

"If I were missing an eye, would you no longer be attracted to me?" he presented. "Or what if I was short?"

"How short?" It wasn't the right thing to say, but the words slipped out before she could stop them. Once they were out there, it wasn't like she could take them back, so she elaborated. "I just mean, if you only came up to my ankles or my thighs, then honestly? I probably wouldn't be as attracted to you. No. At least not physically. I'd still like you, though. The truth is, as much as people want to believe otherwise, stuff like that does really matter."

"Then can we at least agree that it's not everything?" he asked. He covered her hand on the counter with his own, staring at where they touched for a moment. "I promise, who you are means more to me than what you look like. Can you do the same? Or is that really so important to you? If I did get hurt, if I lost an eye or a limb, or got horrible burns," he said, and licked his lips, "would you still want me?"

Guilt flooded through her at the questioning, insecure look in his eyes. She'd inadvertently hurt him with her doubts, planted some of his own. She hadn't meant to. It was so easy to forget that insecurities could be passed on, like a disease, and she'd stupidly allowed hers to affect what was between them.

Her fears had caused him to second-guess her feelings the same way she'd feared his not knowing her actual face would affect his feelings. He was right; it wasn't very fair.

"I'm sorry." She moved closer, wrapping her arms around his waist, and pressed her cheek against his chest. His heart pounded a steady rhythm beneath her ear, kicking up a notch with each passing second. The fact that she could do that to him, affect him so much, caused her to smile.

"I'm being an idiot," she continued. "I'm just afraid of losing whatever this is, that's all. Of getting too deep only to have it ripped away."

"I am, too," he told her, tilting her chin up so that he could catch her gaze. "But we can't push each other away or be afraid of how the other really feels. I care about you, no matter what you look like. That's not going to change."

"I care about you, too." She grinned, knowing full well how stupid she probably appeared, but she was unable to hold it back. "So you're totally cool with me shaving my head, huh?"

He flashed a mock-terrified face. "Uh, let's not get carried away now. I like your hair. I'll like it when it's red. But yes, I'd rather you kept it. On your head." He paused and frowned suddenly.

Knowing that it meant he'd gotten a telepathic communication, she pulled away and activated the sink so that she could quickly wash her face. It was odd how comfortable she was doing it in front of him. She didn't feel like there was any reason to hide, especially after their talk.

Though, admittedly, despite that, it did still help that she didn't actually look like herself. If she looked stupid, it was Olena looking stupid to him.

"That was Trump Fendus, the Basilissa's personal royal adviser. The Basilissa has requested you." He glanced down at what they were both wearing. "We should probably change. And stop by your room. Quickly," he promised when she opened her mouth to argue. "This might surprise you, but I don't have any makeup here."

"That does surprise me," she said, feigning shock. "This whole time I thought mascara was how you got your lashes so long!"

"Come here, you." He grabbed her and began tickling her until there were tears in her eyes, which he effectively kissed away.

DELANEY TOOK A deep breath and braced herself before the doors to the Basilissa's personal chamber. Though, it wasn't technically hers, but a special room made out of the hospital wing of the castle. She was healing from her wound at a quicker rate than any human would, what with their advanced medicines and technology, yet she was apparently still pretty weak after the ordeal.

Trystan was supposedly in a private room as well, somewhere nearby, but Delaney wasn't going to ask anyone which one specifically, and had no intentions of visiting. Part of her felt guilty about that, considering he was there because he'd saved her life. The other part recalled all the times he'd threatened that same life, which eventually won out over the guilt.

She'd thank him eventually anyway. He'd be healed before the next two and a half days passed and the real Olena got here, which meant she'd be forced to see him again before her departure.

Upon seeing them, the guards stationed at either side of the doors to the Basilissa's room readied themselves, bowing slightly and avoiding eye contact. At her almost imperceptible nod signaling she was ready, they tugged the heavy golden doors open.

Inside didn't seem anything like how Delaney would have pictured an alien hospital room to look. For one, instead of all the high-tech science-fiction-like gadgets she'd imagined, there was just the one glass tablet resting on a metal side table. It was no bigger than an original iPad, and the only thing flashing across it was a squiggly neon line that moved with the Basilissa's breathing.

The Basilissa was seated upright, propped against a foam pillow that cradled her body perfectly. There was a thin white blanket over her lower half, and her loose-fitting shirt was a mint shade. Her hair was down and curled lightly around her shoulders, giving her a relaxed air Delaney hadn't expected to come from a queen.

The entire left wall was one massive window, letting in a stream of sunlight that warmed the room and set all the gold accents glittering. The place was big enough to fit another three beds at least, with an attached bathroom twice the size of Ruckus's.

There were currently four other people in the room, three of them obviously Tellers, the last an older man she assumed was the Trump.

"Ander Ruckus." The older man with sandy hair addressed him politely then turned her way. "Lissa Olena. Basilissa Tilda asked us to give you privacy. If you need anything, just call. My men and I will be right outside the door."

"Understood, sir," Ruckus said.

"Thank you," Delaney added for good measure, which might have been a mistake, for she caught the incredulous look that passed over his face before he quickly exited.

No one liked Olena. Not even the people who were supposed to protect her.

"Hello, Delaney." Tilda's voice was soft and almost lyrical. She smiled, and even that was delicate and ethereal in its own way.

"Hello." Really, what else was there to say?

Ruckus stood in the corner of the room, close but not intruding. Apparently he hadn't been asked for this meeting but was there merely as her bodyguard.

"How are you feeling after yesterday?" Tilda asked. The room smelled like a mixture of sweet roses and eucalyptus. The scent strengthened the closer she got to the Basilissa. "I'm sure the ceremony was hard enough for you without it being crashed by terrorists."

"It was, yes." This was awkward.

Tilda seemed to think so as well, because her smile wavered and she dropped her gaze to her folded hands in her lap. She'd pulled herself together a second later, though, and attempted conversation again.

"I'm sorry I haven't been more attentive," she began. "Being here must be very hard for you, having no prior knowledge of us or our customs. We didn't even bother trying to school you in our ways, just tossed you out into our world blindly. I'll forever regret that. Seeing how close you came to dying last night . . . I just want to formally apologize on my daughter's behalf."

Well, that was sweet and unexpected. Considering the way the Basileus had always treated her, she'd sort of just assumed his wife was on the same page.

"I appreciate that," she told her, smiling herself for good measure. She was standing next to her bed, and lowered her arms to her sides. She'd been a bit afraid that this talk would be negative, maybe even about Olena and something happening to her.

What would they do if something did? If her ship didn't make it here or she simply died somehow aboard it? If there was no longer a real Lissa, would they force Delaney to remain here and play the part forever? Her gaze shifted over toward Ruckus, who gave her a reassuring stare. He'd never let that happen to her. He'd already said as much.

"I know how it was done," Tilda said tentatively then, inspecting her face, "but it's uncanny how much you look like her. I haven't seen my daughter since she left for her denzeration. Unfortunately, Olena isn't the type of child who enjoys calling home."

"That must be hard for you, being apart from her for so long. Having to see me instead," Delaney offered.

"It is," she agreed. "That's part of the reason I've stayed distant and allowed Magnus to strong-arm you. To me, you look just like Olena, and it's a constant reminder of what she's done to you and to our people. She risked the lives of everyone to save herself." She squeezed her eyes shut, and it was clear she was holding back tears.

Instinctually, Delaney stepped closer, dropping a comforting hand to her arm. "You aren't responsible for the things she's done."

"But I am," she disagreed, "at least partially. We are created by the things people do and say to us. I'm her mother; I should have done a better job, should have paid more attention to her and to the type of woman she was becoming. It's no secret she isn't well liked or respected."

"She isn't a coward," Delaney surprised herself by saying. "Yes, she did a horribly selfish thing and put a lot of people in jeopardy, but you and I have both met Trystan. Add that to the fact that you can have children with only one person. . . . She did save herself at the expense of everyone else, but who's to say her life is less important? It was wrong, but it was also understandable."

"You surprise me." Tilda tilted her head. "She's the reason you're here, after all. Actually, ironically enough, Trystan is the reason. He did save your life yesterday, didn't he? I must admit, that shocked me. I almost didn't feel the wound in my leg because of how much so. In all the years I've known him, I've never once seen him put someone else's well-being before his own. Except, of course, for his people.

"That's the major difference between my daughter and him, you see. They're both well-known for their attitudes and disregard. My daughter might not be feared in the same ways the Zane is, but she's feared nonetheless. Yet where she cares only for herself, Trystan has always had a heart for the Kints. He might prefer war over peace right now, but that's merely because he feels it's the best course of action for his people. He'll make a great leader, unlike Olena, which is why, after much debate, Magnus and I decided to agree to the betrothal."

She thought about whether her own mother would make that choice, if she'd sell her to the highest bidder if it meant keeping their town together. What if an outside threat came and wanted to destroy it and all the people she'd grown up with? What would she do?

It was a hard scenario to play out, and she feared the only way anyone could truly know the answer was if it actually happened to them. People rarely knew what they were capable of until they were forced into a corner. The unsettling thing was, with the discovery of Xenith, a threat like that was possible.

Hell, if any of the Kints discovered where Olena really was, everyone was pretty sure they'd start attacking Earth so . . .

"What happens when she's back?" Delaney asked. "The Tar attacks probably aren't going to stop anytime soon."

"We don't think so, no," she agreed direly. "And unfortunately we're no closer to discovering where they congregate, or who their real leader—if they even have a set one—resides. Until then, I fear there's really nothing we can do except triple security and hope for the best."

"We've confirmed there isn't as strong of a Vakar presence in the Tars as we were led to believe," Ruckus spoke then. "Someone went through a lot of trouble, and used a lot of patience, to convince us to distrust our own."

"That's unsettling," Tilda acknowledged. "I assume the Basileus has been given this update?"

"I spoke to him about it last night, Basilissa."

"Good. Well, that's something then. At least we can rule out most of our people stabbing us in the back."

Seeing how the darker turn of conversation caused her shoulders to slump slightly, Delaney drew her attention back her way.

"I didn't ask how you were doing," she said. "You are the one currently in the hospital."

"Thank you. I'm doing well. I've actually been healed since this morning, but my nerves were a bit frazzled, and frankly this is the safest place for me until the castle is deemed one hundred percent secured. It's my understanding that we're running a few last-resort drills to be sure?" She directed this last part to Ruckus, who nodded.

"Yes, ma'am, we are. They should be finished with that within the hour."

"Maybe you'll get to try enjoying some of your day then." Tilda patted her hand. "Only two left before you leave and get to go back home. You should try to enjoy all the things Xenith offers while you still can. I've been thinking about making my way down to the pools all morning. I could use their healing properties right about now."

She felt a bit guilty about that, because the only reason Tilda hadn't been able to use the advanced healing pool, the Alter Pool, was that she'd just been Uprisen. Of course, that really had nothing to do with Delaney. It was their tradition and laws that deemed it so, after all.

"It was nice speaking with you," Tilda told her. "Thank you for allowing me to apologize. Hopefully last night will be the last of the unfortunate events that befall you during your stay here."

She had to agree with her there.

CHAPTER 23

They stepped out of the Basilissa's room at the same time Brightan entered the hall a few doors down. He froze, glaring their way before straightening and taking position against the wall.

She followed Ruckus, but as they were passing the room the Kint had just exited, she stopped. The only reason Trystan's Sworn—the Kint equivalent of an Ander—would be guarding this door was if it led to the Zane. Despite her earlier thoughts on the matter, now that she'd been spotted by Brightan, she thought it'd be really wrong of her to leave without at least stopping in quickly.

She could do that, pop her head in, call out a thanks if Trystan was awake, and be on her way. The whole process would only take a matter of seconds, and afterward she wouldn't feel so in-debted. Hopefully. Probably not—he had saved her life, evoking a slew of uncomfortable and confusing emotions in her—but at least she'd be closer to putting it behind her.

"That's not a good idea," Ruckus told her, clearly able to pick up on where her thoughts were headed.

"Everyone has seen us," she pointed out. *"I think it'd be a bigger*

deal if I didn't go in there. They're betrothed, after all, and he did just save my life. Even Olena can't be that coldhearted."

"Would it actually surprise you if she was?"

Sadly, no. But Delaney wasn't that person herself, so she stepped toward the door, bracing when Brightan threw an arm before it faster than a snake could strike.

"The Lissa would like to thank the Zane," Ruckus said, voice steely. "You will let her pass."

"I am under no obligation to your Lissa," he sneered.

"So long as you remain in Vakar"—Ruckus took a threatening step closer—"I disagree."

"Disagree all you like, Ander. I will not—" Brightan clamped his mouth shut and canted his head, the same way the rest of them did when they received a telepathic communication. A moment later his hand gripped the silver door handle so tightly, his knuckles turned bone white.

Without another word, he shoved the door open a few inches, immediately turning back to his post. He refused to look either of them in the eye, but when Ruckus moved forward, his arm was back and he shook his head once.

"She goes alone." It was obvious Brightan didn't like this scenario any more than Ruckus did.

"It's fine." She rested a hand on Ruckus's arm before he could argue, and turned to smile at him, despite how nervous she suddenly felt. This had been a bad idea after all, but it was too late to go back now. "I'll be quick."

"See that you are," he told her, then sighed. "I'll be right here."

Straightening her shoulders, she inhaled and then pushed the door open the rest of the way. Stepping inside, she almost jumped when Brightan snatched the handle and tugged it shut once more.

"I heard you in the hall." Trystan's voice yanked her attention to the other side of the room. He was lying in a bed similar to the one the Basilissa had been in. White bandage tape was wrapped tightly around his upper body, and he was propped up in an almost sitting position.

"I didn't think you'd come," he added when she continued to stand in front of the door and stare. "Are you here to see for yourself that I'm still alive? I'm sorry to disappoint."

"No, I—" She realized she'd been wringing her hands, then dropped them, forcing herself to take a determined step closer. "Can we drop the sarcastic act for one second?"

He lifted a single blond brow. "I wasn't being sarcastic."

"I'm here to thank you," she said, and waved at him, "for, you know. Getting shot. Saving my life. Does it hurt?"

Trystan seemed just as surprised by her question as she was by asking it. His gaze swept over her, a frown forming and deepening the longer he looked. He was a very pale color, and when he shifted on the bed, he couldn't quite cover up his wince in time.

"I hardly notice," he lied, and they both knew that he had, but he didn't recant.

"That was your chance," she said, the words rushing from her lips before she could help them. "No one could have implicated you if you'd just let him shoot me." She recalled what he'd said to her after the teekee had spilled. "That was your chance to be free. Why didn't you take it?"

Trystan watched her silently, and just when she'd started to believe he wasn't going to give her an answer, he murmured, "Olena never was very perceptive."

It almost sounded like he was speaking to himself, though, and when she locked her eyes on his, he was looking at her differently. Almost like he was confused about what he saw. The calculating expression was one he'd used against her before, and it made her spine stiffen.

"I'm trying to match the girl before me with the one I've known," he told her. "But you keep changing."

"Trystan." She retreated a step.

"Stop." His tone was harsh, and she found herself obeying. He contemplated his next words and ended up telling her, "It hurts when I move."

"I'm sorry." And, a bit uneasily, she discovered that was the truth. She didn't like him, but she also didn't like that he was hurt because he'd been protecting her. No matter what his reasons for doing so were.

"You are, aren't you?" He lifted a hand and curled his fingers toward her. "Come here."

Her survival instincts snapped back into place, and this time it was easy to ignore his command. She had her hand on the doorknob and was in the process of opening it in a matter of heartbeats.

"Thank you again, Trystan," she told him, meeting his gaze over her shoulder before quickly leaving the room.

Ruckus appeared very worried, reaching for her before she'd fully entered the hall. Seeing that she was all right, he led her away, waiting until they were out of the hospital wing before asking how it had gone.

"Fine," she said, barely holding back a shudder. "Strange. I don't know."

He pursed his lips, clearly not satisfied with her responses. "I don't like that you were alone with him."

"*I* don't like that I was alone with him." Delaney bumped her shoulder against him. "There's got to be something else we can talk about."

"I have a plan for when Olena gets here," he divulged, obviously just as eager as she was to end the Trystan topic. "The Tellers who have her in custody will arrive two hours before dawn, when the rest of the castle is still asleep. We'll sneak down to the loading dock to meet them, and do the exchange there. Let me show you."

They wound their way through the halls, passing his room first so that she could see the actual path they would be taking tomorrow night. Most of the passages they moved through were empty, and it was currently the middle of the day. There shouldn't be any problems for them when it came time to leave for real.

"Fawna, the pilot who helped us remove you from Earth, will be down there," Ruckus said.

They stopped at the base of a large white hallway, and she recognized the massive doors that she'd been led through upon first entering the castle weeks ago.

"She'll have the ship ready to go, so as soon as you and Olena switch off, we can leave. Gibus and Pettus will be coming with us as well," he continued, turning toward her once he was finished. He frowned. "Are you all right?"

"Yeah," she said, and cleared her throat. It was just hitting her how real this all was. There was a plan and a time frame and everything. "This is really going to happen, right? Because I don't think I'll survive another assassination attempt, and I'm not just being facetious when I say that."

"Delaney—" Ruckus cocked his head, holding out a hand to

keep her back as he stepped forward to glance down both ends of the adjacent halls. "I think I heard footsteps."

"We should go." She wanted to reach for his hand, but if he really had heard someone, they couldn't risk it. Instead she settled for keeping as close to him as possible as they began the walk back toward his room.

They'd only taken a few turns when they came upon Brightan briskly walking in the opposite direction. It was impossible to tell where he'd come from, whether or not it was the hallway they had just been in or the opposite one. Brightan's harried pace didn't help any, either. If the Kint was aware of their presence, he didn't let on, instead moving on his way until he'd disappeared around another corner.

"Do you think he was following us?" Delaney asked, nervous all over again. What other reason could Brightan have for being this far from Trystan's bedside? And if he had been stalking them, how much had he overheard?

"He could just be checking on the Zane's ship," Ruckus posed. "I've heard that Trystan doesn't trust many people with it. I guess the mechanics are complicated, and Brightan is one of the few who've learned how to operate and handle them."

The walk to his room was only about ten minutes, and it wasn't until they were safely inside that she pressed.

"You honestly believe that he was there to check on a ship, not us?"

"We don't know for certain he was even near the hangar." Ruckus ran a hand through his dark hair and eased down to the edge of the bed. "But no, I doubt it was a coincidence that he left Trystan at the same time we did. Could be he was attempting to follow us and got lost. Either way, he wasn't close enough to overhear anything, not if I was able to pick up on his approach."

Frustrated over the whole thing, Delaney dropped down next to him, sprawling out on her back so she could stare up at the ceiling. When he shifted so that he was lying as well, she rested her forehead against his shoulder.

"What was it like," she asked, "growing up here?"

"I'm not sure how to answer that," he admitted, then thought it over. "We're encouraged to pick a path at a young age. And position, as you've discovered, still holds a lot of weight in our society. How many life options you have is closely related to your social standing, unfortunately."

"So . . ." She moved onto her side so that she could wrap an arm around his chest, trying to ignore the increasing tempo of her heart. "The same as on Earth, is what you're saying."

"Am I?" He lifted a hand to her hair and began running strands of it absently through his fingers. "What was it like growing up there?"

"I'm not sure how to answer that," she joked, laughing when he poked her in the side. "I come from a small town and a well-known family, so I was always expected to be on my best behavior. It was important for me to correctly represent the Grace name."

"Let me guess," he said, and chuckled, "you were purposefully awful at it. That explains your issues with authority."

"You mean why I'm always snapping back at the Basileus?"

"I mean why you're always putting your life on the line with the Basileus," he corrected, though not nearly as seriously as he might have even a week ago.

Delaney didn't want to think too much about what that meant, or how she would feel once she was back on Earth for good and he was here, lying in his bed, alone.

"Tell me something else," she insisted.

"What else do you want to know?" The corner of his mouth curved up, and it took her a moment to figure out why.

"Whatever you want to tell me," she told him. After the Tandem game and her fitting, he'd attempted to distract her with questions about her life. They'd been interrupted by Trystan before they could get too far into it, however.

"I'll tell you mine if you tell me yours," he parroted, and her own words said back to her sounded odd coming from his lips.

She sort of liked it, though.

"All right," she agreed, settling more comfortably against him.

Amazingly enough, this time they managed the entire conversation without a single interruption.

DELANEY WOKE UP on her final day on Xenith, nervous. There were seemingly a million and one things that could go wrong, and suddenly they were all playing through her head like a horror movie she couldn't shut off.

Because he was going to be escorting her all the way back to Earth, Ruckus had a lot of loose ends to tie up before their departure. After he'd told her as much, it'd been her decision to come to the science wing. Hanging out with Pettus and Gibus had worked in calming her emotions before, and she'd hoped that it would again.

They'd quickly fallen into the same camaraderie they'd developed while playing cards, which made it easy to forget that this was her last day. Every time one of those thoughts slipped past her defenses—like when Pettus said something particularly funny, or Gibus told her something scientific and crazy—she'd immediately suggest they show her something else.

The idea of leaving them, of never seeing them again, was starting to make her chest ache and she didn't like it. It was to the point that, as the day waned, growing closer and closer to the end, she started missing them. Even though they were still standing right in front of her.

Gibus was in the process of showing her how to use one of his inventions when Ruckus finally came back almost eight hours later.

"Hold it here"—the Sutter adjusted her grip on the maroon metallic device shaped sort of like a banana—"and then squeeze."

Delaney did as told and sucked in a breath when a burst of neon-yellow goo shot out of the top of the device and flung straight across the room. Pettus had set up a row of thin glass jars on one of the workbenches, which she was supposed to be aiming at. The goo smacked into one of them, effectively shattering it and bursting bits of yellow all over the nearby ones.

"What exactly was the point of this thing?" she asked, still laughing, as she lined up her sight and let loose another goo ball. "It reminds me of this game back home, paintball. Is that what this is?"

"No." Gibus waved a hand at her like she was ridiculous. "It was meant for tagging oompha, of course."

"Of course." The corner of her mouth twitched as she held back a grin, and she glanced sideways at Pettus, who was staring back at her and doing the same. "Gotta tag those oomphas. Wouldn't want them getting out of hand."

"Definitely not," Gibus agreed with a curt nod.

"It's a fish." Ruckus made his presence known and stepped up to her, dropping a kiss to her cheek.

Before she'd met him, she would have thought the gesture too sappy for her, but now . . .

"A very large one that often jumps so far, it can be misconstrued as flying. They're fast, so hard to tag with traditional means. The science department in charge of monitoring underwater life requested that Gibus come up with a solution."

"And what did I get for slaving away for five weeks?" Gibus chimed in with a disgruntled look. "They went with someone else's invention. Morons."

"Want to get out of here?" Ruckus leaned closer and whispered against the curve of her ear, effectively sending her body into a heat wave. "It's late, and there's something I want to show you."

She nodded and they said their good-byes, heading out of the room, her arm linked with his.

"Shouldn't we be more careful?" she asked as they walked leisurely. Whatever he wanted to show her, he wasn't in any rush to get there. "What if someone spots us?"

"I know when all the guards do their rotations, Delaney," he reminded her. "And all the schedules. I am the one who made them. There are certain perks involved with being an Ander."

"Hmm," she said, acting impressed, "perhaps I'll try out for the role then. How hard can it be to become an Ander anyway?"

He mock-glared and then before she knew what he'd intended, picked her up and tossed her over his shoulder. She barely had a chance to inhale before he was moving down the hall at such a fast pace that the floor blurred beneath his feet. That was all she could currently see in her position, and she fought down a wave of vertigo.

Fortunately, he stopped them just in time, slipping through a doorway so that within moments the hard floor turned to curly grass.

"Are we at the pools?" she asked even as she pressed against his back to lift herself and take a look. Sure enough, she was met with the stony interior of the room they'd swam in over a week ago.

"It's about to happen," he told her excitedly, slipping her down his front but keeping a firm arm wrapped around her waist to keep her to him.

Her feet touched the ground, and she glanced around at the tiny white-and-yellow star-shaped flowers and the dark green climbing vines. It was just as peaceful and exotic here as she remembered, with the trickling of the water. She couldn't see the falls from here, being blocked off by a thick rock column, but she remembered how beautiful they were. The smell was a mixture of salt, sweetness, and an added tangy hint.

"What's about to happen?" she asked. Above them, the sky was darkening. In less than a minute it'd be completely black. She was so busy looking up that she almost missed it.

"Look." Ruckus breathed against the curve of her ear and she turned her head down.

Gasping, she pulled away from him and rushed over to the nearest batch of climbing flowers. They were starting to glow, one after the other lighting up like a string of Christmas lights. One strand of them would burst into a vibrant neon-greenish white or pale yellow, and then the next, until the entire place was lit up.

"Holy shit," she whispered, awed by the beauty of the place. "You weren't kidding. This is gorgeous." She reached for one and paused. "Can I?"

"Go ahead." He motioned her onward. "They aren't poisonous.

Only pretty. But don't pick them; they'll stop glowing immediately if separated from the vine."

She stopped herself from doing that just in time, changing tactics and stroking the soft petals instead. It felt the same as it had the last time she was here; only at her touch, they sparkled like she'd sprinkled silver and gold glitter on them.

"Whoa."

"Oh yeah," he added smugly, "they do that, too."

"I wish I could take some with me," she murmured, mostly to herself. When he remained quiet at her back, she glanced over. "It's not the only thing, you know."

He canted his head, suddenly serious. "Are you saying you'd take me home with you if you could?"

It was a weighted question, and for some reason she sensed there was more to it than she was getting. She didn't try too hard to decipher it, though, caught up in the serenity of the moment.

"Ruckus." She took a tentative step toward him. "I am going home, and we both know you can't really come with me. You have a life here, and I respect that. Despite the joke I made in the hall, I know how hard you've worked to get yourself here, to make Ander. I would never ask you to give that up."

"What if I want to?" he whispered, the words almost lost over the sound of running water. His yellow-green eyes had darkened, and he was so still in the dim lighting, it was almost as if he wasn't even breathing.

Did she want that? She certainly didn't want things to end with him, liked being around him, but she'd thought these thoughts before. The idea of leaving him behind was upsetting, yet she also meant what she'd told him. How could she expect him to leave everything he'd ever known and come with her to a foreign world?

"How would that even be possible?" she asked. "How would you explain away leaving? And what about your family?"

"They're dead," he admitted, continuing before she could utter an apology. "They died during the war with the Kints. I have an aunt, and we're close, a cousin as well, but they'd understand."

"And what about your position? I have a life back there, on Earth, but you, your life is here."

"I didn't ask you to list all the ways it wouldn't be plausible," he stated. "I asked whether or not you'd want me to. Will you miss me when you're back on Earth? Or was this"—he pointed between them—"merely a matter of circumstance?"

"Of course not!" She wanted to touch him, reassure him, but his demeanor kept her at bay. He was too still, too distant. She got the distinct impression she'd somehow hurt his feelings, but she couldn't place her finger on how. She was only trying to be honest, and keep her own emotions safe at the same time.

"Of course I'll miss you," she said softly. "And of course I'd love it if you came with me. We just both know that's not very realistic, and pretending otherwise . . . I don't want to get my hopes up for something that can't actually happen. No matter how unique this"—she mimicked his motion with a finger—"is. I wouldn't ask you to go any more than you would ask me to stay."

He deflated all at once, shoulders slumping even as he removed the space between them, cupping her cheeks in his strong hands. The glow from the flowers reflected phosphorescent yellows and whites off his lightly tanned skin, making him appear even more alien than ever before.

And even more beautiful.

"Apologies." He pressed his forehead to hers. "I didn't think of it that way. I didn't take raising your hopes into consideration. Forgive me?"

She pretended to think it over, then smirked up at him. "Sure. Just promise me one thing?"

"Anything."

"There's less than a day left," she reminded him, "and then I'm gone. I want to enjoy the rest of the time we have left together."

Wrapping an arm around her shoulders, he turned them toward the pool and then over to the edge. When he sat, he brought her with him, settling her on his lap so that his booted feet came close to being lapped at by the water.

"I'm going to miss you, too," he said against the crown of her head. "Fiercely."

She burrowed closer against his chest, breathing in deeply the fire pit smell. She was never going to be able to go to a bonfire again without thinking about him. It'd be a constant reminder of what she'd left behind. Of what she'd lost.

And she was starting to think of it as that. Even taking into account everything she'd been torn from, everything waiting for her back on Earth, the thought of being so far from him caused devastation. She wanted to cry like that first night in Olena's bedroom, screaming into her pillow so that no one would hear.

"Comfortable?" he asked, breaking into her thoughts. She felt him laughing quietly when she smiled against his chest.

"You hear me complaining?" she joked.

"Usually when I don't hear you saying something, it's a bad sign." He tightened his hold around her arms to keep her in place as he leaned closer to the curve of her right ear. "I'm not sure if anyone's ever told you this before, but you're kind of a loudmouth."

"I am not!" She swatted the back of his arm and shifted enough to glare up at him. "I'm vocal when it's called for, that's all. And you can't tell me that if our situations were reversed, you wouldn't be the exact same way."

"You're right," he agreed, not even bothering to think about it. "I'd probably be five times worse than you, even. You're actually handling all this pretty amazingly. I would have flipped a long time ago."

"Broken something, I remember." She recalled his saying something similar to that before. It felt like a lifetime had passed since. "You know, you were a lot tougher in that alley. Making all kinds of threats, speaking in that gruff voice I haven't heard you use since. Putting on a big show for the Lissa when in actuality you're just one big soft teddy—"

He rolled her so suddenly, her words cut off, and in the next second he had her pinned to the curly grass. Through the skylight above, the millions of stars winked, accompanied by the glow of the flowers and the lulling of the water.

"You were saying?" Ruckus lowered his head to the curve of her jaw, planting a kiss there and then nipping lightly. The move forced her to turn, curving and exposing more of her neck to him in the process. "I'm not gruff; I'm effective."

She had to agree with him there. When she tilted back even more to better accommodate him, she caught sight of the glass walkway above. Part of her froze, and she felt the moment begin to slip away. This was reckless; they weren't out of the woods yet, not when Olena was still at least a day away.

Last time they'd been in there Trystan had caught them. . . .

"We can't." She lightly pushed at his shoulders, not stopping until he finally took the hint and lifted himself off her, frowning. "Anyone can see."

He followed her gaze up to the glass then settled back onto the grass, his expression defeated. Running a hand through his hair, he heaved a sigh and took a moment to regain composure.

"I should be the one saying that," he stated. "I'm the one who's supposed to be protecting you, not losing my head. Ever since you arrived, I've done a terrible job showing you I'm actually good at being Ander. There's got to be a way the Tars are moving around my security teams. An inside man of some sort. I just haven't been able to find him yet."

Because initially they'd both believed it was Trystan, but after the other day . . .

"Trystan's saved my life more than once now," she pointed out, knowing by the harsh twist of his mouth that that was where Ruckus's mind had taken him as well. "He took the bullet—the zee," she said, correcting herself before he could. "Jumped those guys during the bombings."

And she still didn't quite understand why. Her feelings for Trystan were complicated, in the sense that while he still terrified her—and ultimately pissed her off with his arrogance—she also felt a little in his debt. Despite all the hatred between him and Olena, when it'd come down to it, he'd protected Delaney.

"I've seen him act," she added. "It's not his strongest suit. He was legitimately pissed off when Lura tried to poison me. And taking a zee? The guy is still in the hospital."

"He was released, actually." Ruckus curled his fingers around a tiny golden stone no bigger than a quarter and tossed it from palm to palm. "A couple of hours ago, if I got the information right.

The wound was all but healed, and he insisted on returning to his own rooms." He paused, held her gaze as if unsure whether or not to continue. "I'm surprised he didn't try to see you."

She snorted. "I'm not."

"You don't mean that," he scolded, seeing right through her. "He said something to you when you saw him, something that unsettled you."

He'd said a few things, all of which had made her infinitely uncomfortable. He had that way about him, the cold, calculating way that could turn a girl's insides to barbed wire all while twisting her heart with his devilish smile. It was eerie and terrifying. Whenever he paid attention to her, she felt like a rabbit trying to claw its way out of a collapsed burrow, the beautiful yet deadly fox hot on her heels.

"Why are we talking about Trystan?" she asked, sliding closer across the grass so their knees bumped.

"Because you were right before. The attacks won't stop once you leave; they'll just start happening to Olena. She's a pain, and a spoiled brat, but I've known her all my life. I don't want to see her dead, Delaney."

"I understand that." And she did. That jealousy she'd felt before was gone. Maybe she was actually starting to believe his spiel about being attracted to the real her, and not her outer appearance. "I don't want that, either. She might have done this to me, but it's how I ended up meeting you. I keep trying to hate her like I did those first few days here, but I can't.

"Still," she said, and rested a hand over his, stopping his fidgeting with the rock, "we won't figure this out tonight. You're having every single one of your men screened right now, right? And Tilda said she sent most of the staff home, so . . . the suspect list has dwindled down considerably. If there's a traitor still here, someone Lura didn't know about, you'll find him."

He smiled at her, lifting her hand up to plant a kiss across her knuckles. Then he stood and tugged her up with him, catching her around the waist and spinning them dramatically until her laughter filled the cavernous room.

"Did you want to go for a swim?" he asked once he'd placed her back on her feet, tilting his chin over her shoulder toward the water.

"No." She shook her head. "Let's go back to your room. I'm tired of being out in the open, and I want to kiss you again."

CHAPTER 24

Delaney, wake up!" Ruckus was shaking her roughly, and she groaned. "Wake up now!"

Coming out of sleep, she bolted into an upright position, instantly recalling the last time he'd woken her like that. Wide eyed, she scanned his bedroom, noting that they were alone. When she listened for the sounds of bombing, there were none, and her fear started to ebb into confusion.

She hadn't even meant to fall asleep, not when this was supposed to be their last night together, so she couldn't have been out very long at all.

"What's going on?" she asked, watching as he scrambled toward the leather chair in the corner, where a large black duffel bag was resting. It was already mostly filled, and he shoved in a couple more clothing items as he spoke.

"We need to leave the castle," he told her hurriedly. "Now. Quickly, get dressed."

She glanced down at the large shirt she'd fallen asleep in only a few hours ago, a bit of the sleep haze still fogging her brain. The frantic way he moved, so different from the lazy way he'd been before she'd fallen asleep, caused her chest to constrict.

Outside, the sky was still dark and foreboding.

"Is it time already?"

"Olena's ship has been discovered. No one was supposed to be monitoring the atmosphere, but somehow one of the Zane's men got in. Change of plan. We need to go now."

The upside to dresses was they were easy to put on, so she was ready within a minute, and stepped out of the closet in time to have him thrust his hand toward her. There was sweat already beading at his brow, and his mouth was pinched into a tight line.

"What are we going to do?" she asked, taking his hand.

"The Kints are trying to board Olena's ship." He rushed out, yanking her forward so she was forced to fall into step at his side as he moved them into the hall and headed right. "The Basileus is stalling. Won't let any of them into our airspace."

Seeing as how he knew his daughter was on that spaceship, that made sense.

"We should be fine then, right?" There weren't many Kints here in Vakar, only two dozen or so having been sent with Trystan in order to help protect him. Olena's ship was over the Vakar territory of the planet, so it wasn't like the Rex could order his men to travel there and delay her.

He wouldn't have a reason to, anyway. They had no way of knowing who was really up there.

"Trystan is missing."

"What?" Okay, that could be a problem.

"We have Tellers searching, including some of his own people."

"Yeah, a lot of good they'll be," she said, and grunted. "Bet they know exactly where he is, and what he's up to."

"Exactly," he agreed. "Our best chance is slipping away unnoticed and meeting up with Olena's ship in space instead. I've got Pettus and my pilot, Fawna, preparing the ship as we speak. Hopefully they'll have her up and running once we get there. We'll have to go fast, before the Kints realize what we're doing or who's on board."

This wasn't good. They'd had it all planned out before; making the switch would have been simple, but this . . . If the Kints were trying to find a way up, it meant they were congregating around the hangar. The matter was only made worse when she started thinking up all the reasons they could want to meet that spaceship so badly.

Ruckus glanced around a corner and then swore under his breath, pulling back quickly. "It's Brightan."

"He must be looking for Trystan down here," she surmised.

"We've got to go another way." He started for a narrower hallway across from them.

Delaney started to follow, but in the next instant a body slammed into her from behind, sending her sprawling onto the ground. Her head smacked against the floor, ears ringing as her vision blurred.

She wavered a bit as she got to her feet, and needed to brace herself against a wall. When she glanced up, it was to find four Kint soldiers surrounding them.

Ruckus slipped a knife from his boot, holding it at the ready.

A bunch of murdered Kints probably wasn't the best way to go, but it wasn't like there was a choice. Delaney wondered if they were even really Kint soldiers, or if they were actually Tars in disguise.

Springing forward, she used her entire body to slam into one of the four Kints. He didn't fall, but it was enough to have him smack into the wall face-first. Before he could recover, she kicked his feet out from under him, bringing her heel down against his head once he'd hit the ground.

One of the others was already pulling her back, and she brought her elbow up, snapping his nose.

A blond soldier punched her across the jaw, and her head whipped to the side. The sting was immediate and harsh, turning to a burn that had her tongue feeling three times its normal size. And her anger growing just as much.

"Delaney, we have to get out of here! Pettus says Kints are closing in on the hangar!" Ruckus's frantic voice filtered through her mind, momentarily distracting her.

A Kint had a knife out as well, and he slashed forward, almost nicking her right arm. She pulled back just in time, barely avoiding the curve of the blade. He came forward again, and this time she would have been too slow if not for Ruckus.

The whizzing sound of his fritz going off filled the air, and before the Kint could gut her, the shot hit the back of his head.

Bits of blood and gore splattered across the width of the hallway, hitting both walls and even leaving tiny droplets on the front of her dress. For a second, she stood frozen, unable to take her eyes off the slumped, headless body at her feet.

Ruckus's voice pulled her out of it, and she turned to find that he'd given in and shot the other three Kints as well.

"They'll know it was you," she said, a new kind of fear gripping her. They could track the weapons.

"It doesn't matter." He reached for her hand once more. "We have to get going. If we don't hurry, they'll have blocked off all the entrances."

"Why are they doing this?" Did they assume that Olena was trying to escape for some reason? Why? What would have given them that idea? "Do you think they were Tars? They looked like—"

"Regular Kints?" he cut her off as they ran. "Yeah, to me, too.

But remember, those Tellers who attacked you in the shelter appeared to be Vakar and weren't."

They took one last turn, and at the end of the hall were the two large frosted-glass doors that led to the hangar. As they approached, the doors began to slide open. A second later Pettus stepped through, and Delaney started to feel a modicum of relief.

Which didn't last.

Three Kint soldiers came at Pettus from behind; they must have found another entrance into the hangar in order to sneak up on them. She cried out a warning, but the Teller was already spinning on his heel to dodge the sharp edge of a long dagger. He fought them off, and before she and Ruckus could reach him to help, the sound of pounding footsteps from the other direction filled the corridor.

The approaching footsteps beat in time with her racing heart. It was one thing to shoot a hologram, another to hit a live target, so she was jittery. The idea of hurting someone wasn't appealing, but when it came down to protecting herself and Ruckus against an a-hole trying to kill them, there was really no competition.

Two Kint soldiers came around the corner, and she fired before she could allow emotion to get in the way. She felt a burst of air sail past her left ear as one of them fired back, and felt a twist of satisfaction when he was blasted off his feet by her shot. She didn't, however, watch to see where exactly she'd hit him or the kind of damage she'd done.

She shot the other one down a second later, but not before he'd managed to get her on the thigh. Fortunately, he wasn't using a fritz, and the zee merely grazed her, leaving a shallow cut instead of a gaping hole.

She had less than a second to freak out at the sight of the blood dripping down her leg before she heard Pettus grunt in pain.

He'd taken out the last of the three Kints and was moving to stand next to Ruckus, who was facing down more approaching soldiers. There was a large gash trailing from Pettus's right temple to his chin, but if it hurt, he didn't show it.

"Take her to the ship," Ruckus ordered, just as five of the Kints reached them. He'd been shooting them down with his fritz, picking them off, but there were too many. Now that they were so close, he was forced to switch back to the knife. "Pettus, go!"

"I'm not leaving you," Delaney argued, yanking her arm out of Pettus's grasp when he grabbed her.

"*I'll catch up,*" he promised through the fitting, already fending off a few of the Kints in hand-to-hand combat.

"If they catch you," Pettus reminded her tersely, tugging her back, "we're all dead."

She didn't need him to elaborate. He wasn't just talking about the three of them in this hallway. With a growl, she spun on her heel and allowed him to lead her through the two doors, trusting that Ruckus would follow shortly.

The ship that had taken her from Earth was all the way across the hangar, and they quickened their pace the second they were in the room. Movement from the corner of her eye had Delaney turning her head, just in time to spot Brightan.

He'd been standing behind a stack of white crates, out of sight long enough for them not to notice. Now, however, he was close, and before she could alert Pettus, Brightan had his hand wrapped tightly around her throat. He tossed her against the wall of crates, hard enough that her already aching skull began pounding with renewed vigor.

She could see Ruckus coming through the doorway now, still shoving off a couple of Kints, and Pettus was in the process of lifting his weapon. Everyone froze the second Brightan activated his fritz, pressing it against the soft flesh beneath her chin.

For a moment time stood still, even the remaining Kints who'd crowded around Ruckus coming to a stop.

Her mind fuzzed over, fear tightening around her heart, blacking out everything but the wild look in Brightan's eyes and the feel of the icy metal against her flesh. A secret part of her had actually convinced herself she wouldn't be as afraid during the next assassination attempt.

No bigger lie had ever been told in the history of the world. Her world, anyway. She couldn't really attest to the goings-on of Xenith.

"You should have died at the Tandem, Lissa Olena," Brightan told her in an even tone. It would have been less scary if he'd been enraged or even cocky. The casual way he spoke was an indicator that he wasn't worried about being stopped at all. "It would have saved us a lot of trouble, and me a lot of men."

"Seems to me Trystan is the type to do his own dirty work." What possessed her to taunt the guy was beyond her; the words just sort of slipped out, and once they had, her only option was to stick with them. Steeling her gaze, she made sure he knew exactly how she felt about him, effectively covering up most of her fear in the process.

"You don't want to do this, Sworn," Ruckus growled.

"Because I won't make it out of here alive?" Brightan remained calm as ever. "I won't anyway, not after openly threatening the Lissa. I kill her now, and at least I'll be taking the poisonous bitch with me."

At least there was one constant in her otherwise completely

insane life, Delaney thought to herself a bit hysterically. *Everyone* hated Olena.

"This is insane," Ruckus hissed, his frustration and panic evident.

"No," Brightan stated, "this is war. She should have stayed on Earth with the vermin where she belongs. Whatever she said to him, whatever she did, she'll pay in blood."

She blinked. Wait, what?

"I didn't do anything to anyone," she said, clenching her jaw when he pressed the fritz closer.

Lifting her own fritz in her defense was out of the question. Doing so would take too long, and he'd guess her end game before she got very far. Stalling him seemed like the only choice, but for what?

It wasn't like anyone other than the Basileus himself would even care, and he pretty much only did out of proxy. No, the only friends she had on this planet were standing less than ten feet away, just as powerless as she was.

"The Zane hated you a month ago." For the first time a flare of something entered Brightan's dark-brown-and-silver eyes, cracking the chilled exterior. "Now he's letting you live? He called off the bounty on your head; you can't tell me his throwing his life away has nothing to do with you."

She couldn't help it—her brows rose in mock surprise. "Are you in love with him, Brightan?" She made a tsk sound with her tongue. "Falling for your boss? Wow, man. Cliché."

"*Delaney, don't.*" Ruckus set his glare on her this time, and said aloud, "Why do you always have to bait them?"

"Genetics?" The sound of more approaching footsteps from

down the hall to her right had her close to breaking. It took everything she had in her not to let the fear and desperation show. If she was going to die, she was going to do it as the strong person she'd always been. No exceptions.

Brightan opened his mouth, hand tightening around the fritz, but just before he was about to say something, another burst of sound came from the other end of the hall. He didn't even have enough time to turn toward it.

One second he was standing in front of her; the next he was a pile of writhing fire. His screams filled the air, and he rolled around, flailing his arms and legs even as the flames spread, consuming him from sight. It was almost a slow burn, the screams lasting far longer than she imagined they would on a normal victim.

Brightan rolled closer to her, and with a yelp she leaped over him and toward Ruckus, practically toppling into his arms.

He pulled her close, backing them even farther away from the still-dying Sworn. Amazingly enough, the rest of the Tellers who'd been attacking them only moments before moved out of their way, their eyes glued to the same horrendous scene.

Delaney's gaze was suddenly drawn up, away from Brightan, and her breath caught in her throat.

Trystan was staring back at her from the doorway, an odd weapon she'd never seen before in his right hand. It was long, almost like a rifle, and made of a dark black metal. He was holding it down at his side now, but a smoky trail floated upward from the bottom of it. There were over a dozen Kints at his back, yet none of them had their weapons at the ready.

He'd shot Brightan. His right-hand man. He'd *barbecued* him.

She'd be frowning in confusion if she weren't still so shocked.

"Come on!" Pettus's voice pulled them all out of their daze. He was in front of the ship now, frantically waving them through. "Fawna's all set!"

Ruckus turned and began dragging her away, shoving the Kints who were still too shocked by Brightan's death to move. He had them halfway to the ship with little to no resistance.

And then all hell broke loose.

"Lissa!" Trystan's voice cut across the expanse, a loud furious roar that instantly had her heart stopping.

She turned to look at him over her shoulder, but she couldn't get a great visual because Ruckus didn't miss a beat. He kept pulling her along, moving faster now that the Zane had spoken.

Trystan called her again, moving across the room, his men doing the same. The ones who were closest to them who had stopped shot back into action, spinning on their heels and dashing after them.

The towering ceiling of the hangar was already in the process of opening up. The metal panes twisted in a circular motion, caving inward toward the wall until the gap there was large enough to fit the massive spacecraft through. The side compartment of the black craft was also lowering, sending down a set of steep stairs for them.

Pettus was already scrambling up them, turning to take aim at the approaching Tellers once he had. He didn't, however, fire, gritting his teeth in annoyance at having to hold back.

If Trystan was with them and they weren't Tars, they couldn't very well go around shooting them. Especially when no one was firing at them, either. The order clearly hadn't been given, and though they quickened their pace, trying to stop them from boarding, the command never came.

They reached the stairs, and Pettus helped tug her up and through the doorway. The second Ruckus was in as well, he twisted around and slammed a palm against the side panel of the inner ship. The staircase disappeared, and the doors began sliding shut.

Trystan was close now, only ten or so feet away. He shoved his own men aside, calling her title as he went. There was the same anger in his icy blue eyes that she'd seen after Lura's murder attempt, and she shivered.

Try as she might, she couldn't tear her gaze off him, though. It was as if he held her trapped, a deer in headlights with no way to break the spell. Part of her wanted to thank him for saving her life yet again, but she couldn't get any sounds past her lips, and they were out of time.

He must have realized he wouldn't make it, for he stopped less than three feet away. Staring up at her, unblinkingly, she got the distinct impression he was trying to tell her something.

And whatever it was, it wasn't good.

Even after the doors had fully shut, blocking him and the rest of the hangar out, she could still feel his gaze piercing her soul.

CHAPTER 25

Wht are you going to say?" Delaney trailed Ruckus down the familiar white halls of the spaceship. Ironic that she was back where she started. At least this time she'd boarded of her own free will.

"I'll tell them we assumed it was another Tar attack," he answered. "Considering they did, in fact, come after us, there's enough proof for it to be believable. And when Olena returns later today, there'll be nothing that Trystan can say. She wouldn't run just to come back within twenty-four hours."

"What if she gives us up, though?" Delaney was shocked that she hadn't thought of that sooner. "She's got to be seriously pissed off at being caught and dragged here. What makes you think she'll suddenly fall in line and play along?"

He sighed but didn't stop his descent through the ship. "She's immature and self-centered, but she's not a murderer. She knows what will happen to Vakar if she tells the truth."

"She knows what will happen to her, you mean."

He pursed his lips. "That, too."

"Well," she said, shrugging a shoulder, "if there's anything I know to be true about her, it's her knack for self-preservation." That took care of one problem then. What about the rest?

"Oh, there you guys are!" Gibus turned a corner suddenly, almost slamming into them in the process. Which seemed to be his MO. His lab coat billowed behind him, and his hair was in major disarray. "I've been searching the entire ship!"

"I highly doubt that," Ruckus claimed, moving past him and picking up speed once more, forcing the Sutter to fall into step at Delaney's side, a pace behind.

"Most of it, anyway," he admitted, unconcerned at being caught in an overexaggeration. "I managed to grab the device before being rushed off by Pettus, along with a few other things you might end up needing while you're—"

"We can talk about this later."

Delaney frowned between the two of them. Why did she get the distinct feeling something was going on here that Ruckus didn't want her to know about?

"I suppose you're right," Gibus agreed absently. "We do have three whole days to go over everything before reaching Earth. Our layover time with the Lissa will only put us behind schedule by twenty minutes, an hour at most."

"Isn't an hour a long time? We aren't switching ships with her, are we?" she asked.

"And trust someone else with mine?" Ruckus said, and grunted. "Not likely. We do have to talk to her, though, see her firsthand and make sure that they got the right girl this time."

"The device was broken," Gibus said. "She wouldn't have been able to reset it. I programmed the prototype to work only the once. If they say they have Olena, it's really her."

"I'll believe it when I see it." Turning down one last corridor, they finally came to the front of the ship, and Ruckus slammed his palm against a pad positioned at the side of the two metal doors. They whooshed open, and he walked through quickly.

"What's the rush?" Delaney still wasn't sure why he was in such a hurry. It wasn't like they could reach Olena any faster.

"Just have a lot to do," he told her over his shoulder, heading straight for a chair at the front left of the room.

It was the cockpit, with a curved ceiling and walls lined with different computer stations. The center of the room was empty, and so were the extra three seats in front of the weird setups, with buttons and technology she didn't understand to the left and right. At the head, there was a large glass window that exposed what she'd expected to be a vast black, but was actually a swirl of rushing deep blues and purples.

"We're already in fouge," Gibus informed her. "That's faster than the speed of light."

Two leather chairs were positioned in front of a console that took up that entire space, one of which was occupied by a woman with sandy-blond hair. She wore it up in a tight bun at the back of her head, and when she glanced Delaney's way, she gave a friendly smile and even lifted a hand to wave. Her eyes were a vibrant fuchsia with a deep blue rim, a bit eerie at first but then beautiful.

"Hi," the woman said after a moment had passed in silence. "I'm Fawna. It's nice to finally meet you, Delaney."

It was strange that they'd never met before. Where had she been the whole time they'd been at the castle?

"I don't work for Vakar royalty," Fawna answered, as if having read her mind. "I'm a private blaster hired by Ruckus. Which means while you all had to play nice, I got to head into town and get drunk."

Her odd mixture of both Vakar terminology and American momentarily had Delaney confused. She didn't think she'd ever get used to the weird assortment of words. Then she pieced together that *blaster* was probably their title for *pilot*. Guess that meant Ruckus seriously trusted her, if she wasn't even part of Vakar military. He'd allowed her out of his sight with the massive secret of who Delaney really was, after all.

"Well then, when this is all done, I'll buy you a beer," Delaney joked.

Fawna smiled, but it was obvious from the look in her eyes that they were both really thinking the same thing. That neither of them expected to see the other ever again once this was over with.

"Have you signaled Olena's ship yet?" Ruckus asked. His hands deftly moved over the panel in front of him, flipping black switches and pressing different-shaped buttons. "They know we're coming?"

"They were surprised to find we're ahead of schedule," she answered, "but yeah, they know. Sounds like Mazus can't wait to get rid of her."

"That's the Lissa," he stated, "always causing trouble."

Turning toward Delaney, he smiled, though it didn't quite reach his eyes. "I've got a lot to take care of here. Can Gibus show you to your room? You should get some rest; you barely got three hours."

Not really having anything to do there, she nodded and motioned toward the Sutter to lead the way.

"So," Gibus said the second they were back in the halls, "I was thinking, instead of showing you to your rooms, we could head to my lab. Some of that stuff I managed to sequester away?" He leaned in close conspiratorially. "Yeah, you might be interested in seeing it."

THEY SPENT THEIR time going over some of the gadgets he'd been able to grab, and the ones that he had permanently stowed on board. There were some pretty interesting things, including a jet pack, boots that adjusted to different gravitational pulls, and a plant that shrank instead of grew as it aged. Why he thought they'd ever need the latter was beyond her, but she had to admit it was cool.

There were other things, smaller things that reminded her of spy gear from the movies, and others that were so scientific in explanation, with big words like *norepinephrine* and whatnot, that she gave up trying to comprehend them half a sentence in.

She was nervous about being back in space, about having to see Olena . . . about how she'd left things with Trystan. The way he'd looked at her in the end, she was certain he was trying to tell her something, trying to promise something. She knew him well enough now to know that any promises he made were really threats in disguise.

The only reprieve from her fears was the fact that he couldn't follow her, and once she was on Earth, she'd never have to worry about seeing him again. He'd go back to being Olena's problem, and Delaney could go back to living her life, without looking over her shoulder every two seconds.

At some point the exhaustion must have gotten the best of her and she'd fallen asleep, for one minute she was sitting down in the corner of Gibus's lab on one of his soft chairs, and the next she was waking up in an entirely different room.

With a frown, she blinked, slowly slipping out of her sleep state. The room was white, and similar to the one she'd woken in upon being kidnapped, though it was almost three times the size. Instead of a cot there was a bed, a king-sized bed if she had to guess, and so comfortable, it was almost like she was lying on a cotton ball.

"You're awake," Ruckus's gruff voice came from the other side of the room, and when she sat up, she saw he was sitting at a desk built into the wall. He turned in the chair to better face her, resting his arms on his knees.

"How long was I out?" She glanced around. "And how did I get here?"

"Less than an hour," he told her, standing, "and I carried you."

When he didn't approach, merely stood there with his hands clenched at his sides, her chest tightened in worry. Brushing the blankets off her, she got to her feet, remaining on the side of the bed and awkwardly crossing her arms.

"What's wrong?" she asked.

"Nothing." He shook his head, but it was hard to believe him when he dropped his gaze in the process.

"Ruck," she said, waiting until he met her eyes once more. "Tell me."

He seemed to think it over for a moment before finally coming to a decision. He was just about to open his mouth when the door across from him slid open and Pettus popped his head inside.

"They're boarding now, sir." He nodded her way with a small smile. "Morning, Delaney."

She wasn't so sure it was actually morning, but she greeted him back.

"Let's go." Ruckus moved over to the door, holding his hand out to her once he got there. Whatever weirdness he'd been experiencing a second ago was gone, shelved more than likely because of Olena's arrival.

She hesitated, and he turned toward Pettus.

"We'll be there in a moment," he told him, waiting until they were alone before stepping close enough to her that she felt his body heat. Taking both of her hands, he rubbed his thumbs over her knuckles comfortingly. "Are you ready for this?"

"To see the person who did this to me?" She sighed, embarrassed that she was torn between wanting to cry and scream. The emotions had hit her so suddenly, she was a bit blindsided by them. "I can't tell. On the one hand, I hate her. Yet, on the other . . . I wouldn't have met you if she hadn't done what she did."

She'd voiced that opinion to him before, but now that they were actually so close to meeting with the Lissa, she felt herself flip-flopping between understanding where Olena's actions had stemmed from and wanting to rip her face off.

"Her face, huh?" Ruckus grinned even while she groaned. "You haven't made a slip like that in a while."

That was true; she'd gotten a hang of the whole telepathic thing rather quickly. "I'm going to miss being able to do that," she admitted, meeting his gaze. "Having secret conversations with someone is kind of awesome."

His mirth dropped away. "Delaney—" Swearing, he stopped abruptly and cocked his head. He'd steeled himself all over again when the conversation in his head ended. "They're here. It's now or never. If you don't want to do this, you can always stay here. There's no real reason for you to have to see her."

As tempting as that option was . . .

"I'm not going to hide out like I'm afraid of her," she told him firmly. "She did this to me; now she has to deal with me."

The corner of his mouth turned up slightly, bringing back a little snippet of his good mood. "That's my girl."

Her heart panged in her chest at the comment, but he was already turning away, so she brushed it aside. In little more than two days, he'd be dropping her off in Maine, and they'd go their separate ways. Her fingers tightened around his instinctually.

When he frowned over at her, she pretended not to notice.

She half expected to find Olena in the four-way stop, the same place Trystan had ambushed them with his guards on their first trip, but when they reached it, it was empty. They continued on and came to a stop in front of a wall that was mostly made up of a large metal door. She assumed that was where the other spaceship attached, allowing passengers to safely pass through both structures.

Ruckus opened the door, a loud grinding sound filling the room and adding to her discomfort. Not soon after, five figures appeared around the bend, heading toward them.

Delaney wasn't ready for what she felt when her eyes finally locked on to the Lissa. She'd been expecting anger, disgust, even pity, but she hadn't been prepared for the regret.

Pettus was standing tall next to four other Vakar Tellers, all men.

One of them had his hand wrapped tightly around Olena's right arm. His chin was up, shoulders back, and there was a tight expression on his face that instantly told everyone around him that he was done playing games.

Olena herself was in a pair of blue jeans and a loose-fitting white T-shirt. The logo for some band was written across it in green and black, the material too faded to make it out. Her nails were painted in dark pink polish that was chipped; gray sneakers covered her feet. Her black hair was longer than it had been when they'd bumped into each other, just a ways past her thin shoulders now.

"You look like you just came from club Star Light." Delaney wasn't sure why she said it; the words just sort of slipped out. Really, though, what was one supposed to say to the girl who'd stolen her life?

"And you look like me." Olena seemed like she was thinking about leaping out of the Teller's hold to attack Delaney but was holding back. Even through the fury, it was hard to miss the lingering fear in her eyes.

It was a bit strange that Delaney still appeared like Olena, but they couldn't risk using the device to reverse the process until they were 100 percent certain they'd gotten the real Olena Ond this time.

"Do you know how many lives you put in danger?" Ruckus demanded. "Including the ones you wanted so desperately to live among back on Earth. If Delaney hadn't agreed to play along with your ruse, we'd probably all be dead now."

The Lissa looked at him, and a range of emotions played across her pale face. It was so obvious that she'd missed him, and that she was hurt knowing he was partially to blame for her being dragged back here. Yet the anger was there as well, the arrogance. When she spoke, her voice dripped with venom.

"I saw an opportunity to be free, so I took it," Olena stated. "And I don't regret a single day I spent there instead of here. I tried to tell you what I wanted, but you wouldn't listen to me. You remember, don't you? I asked for your help, and you refused to give it."

"That's not what happened," he argued. "You asked me to betray the Basileus, knowing full well what the consequences of that betrayal would be, not just for the both of us, but for everyone else." He shook his head. "You still don't get it, do you? What you put everyone through? What you put Delaney through?"

"She looks fine to me." Olena stared at her. "You're lucky, you know."

"Because you turned me into a princess?" she asked incredulously.

"No." She blinked back obvious tears. "Your picture's all over the news in Maine. Has been since your disappearance. Your parents really love you."

Delaney stilled, feeling sick to her stomach for multiple reasons. She was immediately excited that she'd get to see them soon. At the same time, she understood what Olena was trying to tell her, after having been in the company of both of her parents.

"Your situation isn't ideal," she agreed. "That doesn't make what you did right."

The Lissa clucked her tongue, the sound somehow coming off malicious instead of childish, like it would on anyone else over the age of five. "It was *right for me*, and that's the only thing that matters." She turned to Ruckus suddenly, clearly dismissing Delaney. "Tell your man to let me go. I'm starting to bruise."

"Good," Pettus said, and snorted, immediately clearing his throat when she set her glare on him.

"You're not even sorry a little bit, are you?" Delaney wasn't exactly surprised, but it would have been nice to see some regret. There was only the bitterness and the fear.

"Why are you even still here?" Olena took a threatening step closer, only to be yanked back. "You've used up your usefulness. Someone"—she addressed the room with an air of misguided authority—"get her out of here."

"My thoughts exactly." Ruckus motioned toward the guy holding her. "You know what to say when you get there, Mazus?"

"Yes." The man nodded. "I'm more concerned with whether or not she does." He shook Olena hard enough that her teeth clattered for emphasis.

"What I'm going to say," she threatened, "is that you lot kidnapped me and placed an imposter in my stead!" She waved her entire hand at Delaney.

"Hey." She crossed her arms over her chest, not the least bit offended. "You chose me."

"You're the person I happened to run into," Olena corrected. "That's all."

So, basically, it'd been a matter of coincidence that had gotten Delaney into this mess. Great. Somehow, hearing aloud that Olena hadn't planned this all out, hadn't selected Delaney and watched her or followed her or any of that, helped drive home what everyone had been telling her from the very start.

"You're not very clever," she asked rhetorically, "are you?"

"No, she isn't." Ruckus stepped forward, ignoring the reddening of Olena's checks. "If she were, she would already know by now that saying anything about where she's actually been—or about your having to take her place this whole time—would be suicide."

"My parents would never—"

"But Trystan would." Delaney watched the first shimmer of panic enter Olena's dark eyes. "If Trystan ever found out that you deliberately tricked him, he'd be furious. If he ever found out that other people knew, meaning he'd basically embarrassed himself by believing it this whole time? He'd be murderous. You and I both know it's true."

"Mazus is going to take you back to Vakar, where you are going to pretend like none of this ever happened," Ruckus said, drawing the attention back his way. "You were here the whole time. Someone will brief you on your way there so that your lies can hopefully be somewhat feasible. For once."

"What do you mean, Mazus is bringing me?" Olena said, and huffed.

"I'm staying here."

"You're not coming with me?!" A panic settled in her high-pitched voice. Olena was clearly frantic now. "You can't be serious! I need you!"

"That's not what was implied when you sent a stranger in your place to trick me," Ruckus responded in an almost bored tone.

Absently, Delaney shifted closer to him, stilling when Olena's eyes homed in on the move and darkened even more. If she wasn't mistaken, the girl's bottom lip was quivering. Much of the earlier bravado the Lissa had been trying to give off was slipping away.

"You are *my* Ander," Olena reminded him, poorly attempting to keep it together. "It'll be suspicious if you're not with me when I return to Xenith. You have to escort me back. You don't have a choice."

"Actually," Delaney said, "he has to escort *me* back. To Earth, that is." She turned to Ruckus. "You do have a choice, though. I mean, if you'd rather—"

"I told you I would get you home," he interrupted. "That was always the plan." Then to Mazus: "That's definitely Olena. You can take her now."

"You have got to be kidding me!" Olena yelled. The Tellers began dragging her back toward the doors, and her expression turned more frantic. "You can't do this! Ruckus! Ruckus, I can't go back there! Ru—"

"Lucky travels, Ander Ruckus," Mazus said respectfully, though his voice was barely heard. The whooshing of the metal door opening mingled with Olena's loud and vocal struggles as they headed back to the other spaceship.

Once the sounds finally stopped, Delaney let out a breath she hadn't noticed she'd been holding. Beneath her, the floor vibrated, and she assumed that was a sign the other ship was detaching from theirs.

"We'll be on our way in a moment," Pettus told them. Then he asked her, "Do you need anything?"

She shook her head, still trying to sort through her feelings.

"I'll be in the cockpit," he informed Ruckus, waiting for the Ander to nod his agreement before moving off.

Once they were alone again, Ruckus took her hand and squeezed. "How are you doing?"

"I guess I just feel a little bad for her," she said softly.

He quirked a dark brow. "Even after meeting her?"

She thought about it, then said, "Yes. She's awful, don't get me wrong, but I did spend some time with Trystan and Magnus, and they aren't great, either. And now she won't even have you there with her as a buffer."

He frowned down at her. "Did you want me to go with her?"

"Absolutely not." Her fingers tightened around his. Just the suggestion made her stomach twist painfully.

"Good." He let out a relived sigh but seemed unsure all of a sudden. "As soon as we're close to Earth, we'll use the device to change you back. Then Fawna will drop us off. Pettus and Gibus will return to Xenith, and hopefully once they get there, it'll be to find that Olena has successfully reintegrated."

Delaney paused, thinking she must have misheard him. When he only stared back at her, waiting, she blinked.

"I don't . . . ?" She let her words trail off, not wanting to jump to conclusions. "Drop *us* off?"

"Unless, of course, you object?"

"I . . ." She shook her head, stopped, and inhaled before trying again. "You want to come with me, to Earth?"

"Yes."

"Like, to make sure I make it home?" That sounded strange, even to her own ears. That couldn't be it, not unless he was interested in wasting his time. The other option, however . . .

"No," he said, and licked his lips, "to stay with you. Hopefully at your home, but I could always rent an apartment, if you'd rather."

"You want to stay with me? On Earth?" The corner of his mouth twitched and she realized how ridiculous she sounded, practically repeating herself. "How? Don't you need to go back to Xenith? Won't you get in trouble?"

"Actually, no," he said. "I never took my right of passage."

A moment later it clicked, and her eyes widened. "You want to go on your denzeration."

"I do," he said, holding her gaze, "but only if you want me to. If you don't, I'll go back with Pettus and Gibus. And I'll understand, Delaney. After everything you've been through, if you never want to see another alien again, including me, I'll under—"

Her mouth smacked against his, cutting him off. He was so tall, she'd had to leap a little just to be able to kiss him, her arms locked around his neck to hold them close even as his circled her thin waist. She felt him smiling against her a second before he moaned as she deepened the kiss.

"You probably should have waited," she said then, but she couldn't get the right amount of seriousness in her tone. He was coming with her. She didn't have to say good-bye.

"For what?"

"You know what." She pulled back and gave him a blank look. "Is this a bad time to tell you I'm horribly disfigured?"

He chuckled. "You're making jokes about it now. That's good. Does this mean you finally believe I'm interested in the *you* you?"

With a huge wave of relief, she realized it did.

"READY?"

"Are you ready?" She took a deep breath. They were back in Ruckus's room, the one she'd woken up in, just the two of them.

Gibus had handed over the device and gone back to working on some invention in his lab. He'd clearly wanted to stay and see his handiwork in action, but one pointed look from Ruckus had changed his mind.

Ruckus was currently aiming the silver contraption at her. He'd been shown how to get it to work, and seemed pretty confident in his abilities. Yet as badly as she wanted to be herself again, that old nervousness had returned tenfold. She believed that he meant it when he said he wanted her, but . . .

"Last chance," she warned.

"To do what?" he countered. "Not know what my girlfriend actually looks like? Delaney, if you can't trust me enough to really see you, we don't need five years to figure us out."

He was right, which made her stick her tongue out at him like a child. Sometimes a little humor went a long way, and when he rolled his eyes with a smile, she felt some of the tension ease.

"All right." She took another deep breath and squeezed her eyes shut. "Do it."

It wasn't supposed to hurt—hell, she wouldn't feel a thing, seeing as how, physically, nothing had really changed about her. She felt a slight breeze burst her way, and then nothing. After a moment she began shifting her feet impatiently. When nothing else happened, she popped open an eye, then both when she realized he was staring at her.

"What?" She gulped. "Did it not work?"

"No," he croaked, clearing his throat immediately and rushing on before she could get the wrong idea. "I mean, yes, it worked. It's just . . . wow." He slowly made his way to her, as if afraid to spook her, and lifted a hand to her head. He took a strand of her hair and ran it between his fingers.

When she glanced down and saw that the locks he held were red, she almost wept with joy. Fortunately, she'd done enough crying, and not so much as a single happy tear slipped by.

"I know you're not used to redheads where you come from," she said nervously. "Hell, even where I come from we tend to fall into a taste category." She tugged her hair loose when he didn't respond, and took a deliberate step back.

He looked at her, and the breath whooshed out of him all over again. "Your eyes."

"Nothing like Olena's. I know." She made a face. "Also there's the whole single-color thing."

"They're beautiful," he said breathlessly. "*You're* beautiful. I know I told you that didn't matter to me, and it didn't, but . . . wow."

"You said that already."

"I'll probably end up saying it another couple hundred times," he confessed. He ran both of his hands through her hair, cupping the sides of her head and urging her closer. Just as their lips were about to meet, he paused, staring into her eyes intently.

She held her breath and waited, not sure what she expected him to say. It certainly wasn't what he did.

"I want to go bowling," he said.

She blinked. "That's . . . random."

He shook his head. "I want to try it, with you. I want to experience all the things you love to do. I want to understand firsthand why you love what you love." He paused. "But maybe not the bungee-jumping thing."

"Wait." She pulled her head back and gave him an incredulous look. "You can't honestly be afraid of heights, can you?"

The concept just seemed a bit ridiculous to her, considering all the dangerous things he did as an Ander. Like searching for bombers when bombs were going off, and being shot at with weapons that blast holes through people. Or Olena. Just Olena. No other description necessary.

"Of course not," he countered. "I don't have any problem with being up high. It's the falling I take issue with."

She laughed and then laughed even harder when she saw how serious he was.

"I don't know," she said, and clucked her tongue, once she'd calmed down, "you never did take me to that 3-D movie."

He pressed a kiss to the curve of her jaw. "I'll make it up to you."

"Impossible," she joked. "The 3-D movies on Earth are still played on a flat-screen. Now I'll never see one in actual 3-D, and it's all because you never bothered to take me to one."

She met his gaze, only to find he wasn't smiling anymore. Instead he was staring at her intently, yellow-green eyes roaming across her face as if trying to commit every line and contour to memory.

"I see you, Delaney," he whispered. "I see all of you."

The fact that he was looking at her like that made her breath catch. It wasn't Olena that he was staring at like he never wanted to stop. In a few hours they'd be on Earth, both of them, and neither of them would have to pretend to be someone else there. For the first time, there was nothing between them, no reason she had to hold back.

"Not all of me," she said. A sudden burst of confidence hit her, and she reached for the hem of his shirt. "Not yet."

He blinked, then captured her mouth in one swift move. Together they toppled onto the bed, his heavy weight pressing her against the soft mattress. Allowing her to tug his shirt over his head, he reached for the silky material of the dress she'd thrown on, stopping with it already shoved up past her hip.

Ripping his mouth away, it took him a moment to even his breathing enough to speak. "Are you sure?"

Wrapping a hand around his firm neck, she eased him back down toward her. "You just gave up everything to give us a shot," she reminded him, nipping at his bottom lip. "How could I not be sure?"

He let her press their lips together once more before pulling back yet again. "Isn't there a term for this back on your planet?"

She frowned. "What?"

"Sex on a plane?"

"The mile-high club," she said, and laughed. "This isn't a plane, and we're not in the sky. We're in space."

"So . . ." He pressed his mouth against the bottom of her jaw, each word punctuated with another kiss as he trailed his way up toward her ear. "What you're saying is, we're starting our own club?"

"We certainly have a unique situation," she mused, moaning at the end. "Okay." She redirected his lips to hers. "No more talking."

As their bodies came together, all her fears and doubts melted away. None of the negative stuff that had come along with this situation mattered; all that mattered was that it'd led her to Ruckus.

They were somewhere in space between Xenith and Earth, and yet here she felt more at home than she ever had on any planet.

EPILOGUE

FIVE WEEKS LATER

Delaney!" the high-pitched cry reverberated through the apartment.

Snapping instantly awake, she rolled out of bed, practically tripping down the hall. A thousand different nightmarish scenarios filtered through her mind as her name was called again. The second she got to the living room, she came to a sudden standstill.

And cursed.

Her roommate stood next to the couch, still in her pink pajama pants with the tiny koalas on them. Her dark hair was a little messy from having just gotten up, and her eyes were hard and glaring.

"Do you have to scream so loud this early?" Delaney rubbed at her temples, a headache sprouting.

"I don't know," Mariana stated. "Does your boyfriend *have* to always forget where wet towels are supposed to go?" She lifted her right hand, the large, damp green cloth grazing the ground. "I stepped on this and nearly had a heart attack!"

"You mean like the one you almost gave me with your screams?" she said. "I thought something seriously wrong had happened."

For a second she was about to argue, but then it must have hit Mariana what she meant and she deflated, guilt crossing over her face. "I'm sorry. You thought something alien had happened." At the confirmed nod, she sighed. "Hun, it's been over a month. It's safe to say you're in the clear. Olena didn't give you up. Besides"— she wagged her brows—"if I had a hot alien boyfriend to protect me, I certainly wouldn't worry."

"Um." Ruckus cleared his throat from the doorway. "Thank you?"

"Thank me by not leaving your disgusting used towels lying around!" Mariana shook the cloth again and then tossed it at him. Crossing her arms, she stared him down, clearly waiting for a response.

Delaney had to hand it to her: She'd taken the whole thing really well. More so than her parents initially had.

After two fantastic days with Ruckus—mostly spent in bed— they'd arrived to chaos on Earth. Olena hadn't been kidding: Delaney's face was all over the news, constantly being flashed as a missing person. Kidnapping was the main theory. Obviously, this posed a dilemma for them. All that time she'd spent wanting to get back home, and she'd never once thought about what she'd tell everyone once she had.

Fortunately, considering Ruckus's position, it was fairly easy to get government backing on their story. All he had to do was contact the liaison between Vakar and Earth, Trump Lorus, and explain the situation and how important it was to their people. He'd probably only been on the phone with the guy a total of five minutes before a couple of officers dressed in black and wearing badges had appeared at the Vakar embassy building, where they'd had Fawna drop them off.

Her parents had flipped when she'd shown up at their house, new boyfriend and government officials in tow. There'd been no good way to tell them the truth, so they'd come up with a believable story. She opted to give as many real details as she could, including that she'd accidentally been taken by aliens.

Of course, she'd left out the parts about being dragged to another planet, being mistaken for a princess, and all the times she'd almost died. Instead they'd spun a web of lies about being dragged down to Arizona, where she'd been interrogated—yet treated incredibly fairly—by members of the Vakar.

The two agents who'd been sent with them amazingly carried on the ruse rather convincingly. By the end of it, after all her parents' insane questions, even Delaney herself was starting to believe she'd been in Arizona that whole time.

They'd even helped quiet the media reports so that they disappeared, the only explanation to the public being that she'd been "found."

Of course, her parents had bought it, but Mariana was another story entirely. Not two seconds after the same agents who'd convinced her parents had left, she was jumping down Delaney's throat to know what had really happened. They knew each other far too well, and Delaney had been forced to tell her the real story.

Ruckus had given them space during the conversation, which she was grateful for, because a third of the way in, she burst into tears. There were times over the next three hours when she would laugh, others when she'd tear up all over again, and Mariana would hold her hand and listen without judgment.

"I apologize," Ruckus was saying to Mariana now, begrudgingly clutching the damp towel. "Won't happen again." He went into the other room to hang up the towel, then returned to the kitchen.

"Oh, you're damn right it won't," Mariana stated, moving her hands to her hips, "'cause if it does, I am never making you tamales again."

Delaney held in a laugh when Ruckus's face fell. "All right, guys, I think we get it."

"Good. Now"—Mariana's eyes sparkled with excitement—"get dressed."

"Why?" She glanced between the two of them, frowning when he held up his hands.

"Don't look at me." He moved toward the fridge. "I just live here."

He'd offered to buy them their own place—apparently being Ander paid well. Like, *really* well—but she'd declined. They'd been through a lot together, yet he was right about taking a denzeration first. They needed to make sure that they could be happy without all the adrenaline highs that came with being almost murdered.

So far, things were going well.

"We are having a girls' day," Mariana announced. "Just you and me, sista. No offense, Ruck."

"None taken." He smiled at Delaney over the rim of his glass of orange juice. His hair was still wet from the shower he'd taken, and while he'd thrown on a pair of light gray sweatpants, he hadn't bothered to put on a shirt.

The ripple of his muscles in the morning light made her think of other things she'd like to do that day instead.

"Uh-uh." Clearly noting her train of thought, Mariana tugged on her arm and moved to block her line of sight. "You did plenty of that last night." She mock-glared over her shoulder at him. "Thanks very much, by the way. You do realize we have thin walls, right? Anyway," she said then, looking back to Delaney, "after that, you owe me."

She wrestled between being embarrassed and finding it oddly amusing, settling on a place in between. "All right, what did you have in mind?"

"We haven't done anything awesome for the summer yet, and it's already halfway over, so beach day!"

"Why can't Ruckus come to that again?"

"Because I want to boy-watch and flirt, and there's no way anyone is going to approach us when Commander Tall, Hot, and Lethal is with us." Mariana looked at him a second time. "Again, no offense. You're just way too intimidating."

"Honestly," he said, and settled more comfortably against the edge of the counter, giving them a better view of his chest in the process, "after that kind of description, I'm not offended at all."

"Great." Mariana headed toward her room. "I'm going to get ready. We leave in twenty, Delaney!" At the last second she popped her head back around the corner, narrowing her eyes at them. "That means you do not have time for another make-out session, got it?"

They both held up their hands in surrender.

"So," Delaney asked once they were alone, moving over to settle in front of him, between his legs, "what are you planning on doing with your day?"

"Without you?" He winced. "Weep, mostly."

Playfully, she shoved his shoulder. "I'm serious."

"I don't know." He shrugged. "Maybe learn how to play the guitar?"

"Really?" Her eyes widened.

"I heard about them and I've been curious. Just never had the opportunity. We don't have them on Xenith. I saw a small music shop in town the other day. I think I'll stop by there to pick one up—maybe a couple of music books as well. Try my hand at it."

"Literally." She lifted onto her toes and pressed her lips against his, feeling the zings all the way down her spine at the contact. Forcing herself to pull back, she put a few feet of distance between them, and turned toward the hall herself. "Enough of that, or Mariana will kill us."

"You forget already?" he joked. "You're pretty hard to kill."

DELANEY WAITED AS Mariana licked the last drip of ice cream from the side of her hand before tossing the bottom bit of cone into the trash. Above, the sun was just beginning to set, the warm glow still lighting up the busy streets. They'd decided to leave now so that they could make it home by dark and have dinner with Ruckus.

"You sure about this?" Mariana asked her as they began walking once more. They'd parked a few blocks away because the beach lot had been so crowded. Even now it was still pretty packed. "We could always grab something quick and not tell him."

Ruckus had called about an hour ago to tell them he'd decided to cook dinner. He was good at many things; unfortunately, so far, cooking wasn't one of them. He still had a hard time figuring out what all the different ingredients were. Last week he'd made cookies but had mistaken the salt for sugar.

"No." She sighed. "Let's just give him another shot."

"Fine." Mariana adjusted the straps of her ruby-red bikini. "But you're trying it first."

"Deal."

They were both wearing jean shorts and their string bikini tops. Their shirts were stuffed into the tote bags on their arms, along with their towels. After a day of lounging in the sand—Mariana shamelessly checking out guys—they were both relaxed and at ease.

"I really needed this," Mariana said, bumping shoulders with her lightly. "Time with my girl."

"I'm sorry I've been spending so much time with Ruckus." With him sharing her room, it was kind of hard not to.

"That's not what I meant," she assured her. "I just missed you, that's all. And, well, normal."

"Trust me," Delaney said, and laughed. "I know what missing normal is like. I'm glad we did this, and that you like Ruckus, wet towels and all."

She'd initially tried to slap him after hearing he was the one who'd taken Delaney in the first place, but she'd eventually calmed down and given him a chance. Friends like her were next to impossible to find, the kind who stood by you no matter what, who understood crazy things happened, accepted that, and chose to ride the crazy with you.

"I don't know what I'd do without you."

"Well," Mariana said, "I know what I'd do without you, having experienced it recently, and that's totally freak out. So," she said, and sobered some then, "don't disappear on me again, okay?"

"Okay." Delaney linked their arms together.

They were only a block away from the car now, the beach-going crowd having thinned slightly, only to be replaced with the nighttime partiers. Most of the shops were still open, so it wasn't a big surprise, and Delaney absently scanned the people as they passed. Neither of them was in much of a hurry to get back for Ruckus's cooking, sadly. And it was nice enjoying the weather.

They turned the corner and had just started down the block when a man across the street caught her attention. He wasn't looking at her, and was dressed casually in a pair of blue jeans and a black T-shirt; nothing about him really stood out. Except for the fact that he was at least six-three and had blond hair.

Shaking her head, Delaney mentally scolded herself. She was about to let Mariana in on her crazy new irrational distrust of blond men when another man stepped out of a shop only twenty or so feet from them.

This time her breath caught in her throat, and her stomach twisted painfully. It took all her strength not to stop dead in her tracks. In the middle of the crowded walkway, that would draw way too much attention, not to mention her friend wasn't known for being quiet. Mariana had the kind of voice that carried.

For a split second she tried to convince herself that she was hallucinating, that her paranoia was getting to her and making her see things that weren't there. There was no denying it though; he was very real.

Trystan was here. And they were headed straight for him.

Completely unaware, Mariana continued to lead them down the street, intent on getting to the car. She was people watching as well, and when her gaze landed on Trystan, she stared a little too long before a girl's sharp laughter to the right caught her attention and thankfully held it.

Delaney wasn't sure what she'd do if her friend tried to flirt with him. She thought about reaching out to Ruckus telepathically, but that would only freak him out as well, and he was too far away to do anything anyway. Besides, it wasn't like the Zane was here looking for her.

And even if he was, he had no idea what she looked like, anyway.

With a slightly relieved breath, she realized that was true. He'd never seen her real face, and now that the effects of the device had been removed, he certainly wouldn't mistake her for Olena. She was in the clear; all she had to do was walk past him like he was merely another stranger on the street.

She could do that. Hell, she'd pretended to be an alien princess for weeks and he'd bought that. Mostly.

He was dressed just as casually as the first guy she'd seen, blending right in. The only difference was he'd chosen a navy T-shirt, a dead giveaway for someone who knew Kint colors. It was strange seeing him in casual clothing from her world, especially when the way he wore them made them seem just as dignified as the traditional uniform he usually wore.

She counted the steps it took to reach him, keeping her gaze straight ahead when he suddenly turned and began striding in their direction. From the corner of her eye, it didn't appear as if he was looking at her, and when they finally reached each other, he walked by without a single glance in her direction.

The breath she'd been holding slowly slipped past her lips, and she resisted the urge to check over her shoulder just to be sure. Instead she kept walking, keeping her pace even and her body relaxed.

Still, she couldn't help but panic over why he was here. On her planet. In her state.

When the car finally came into view, it was all she could do not to run toward it, throw herself inside, and lock the doors. Because that wouldn't be suspicious at all. Tugging the keys out of her bag, she clenched them tightly in her hand, the jagged metal biting into the flesh of her palm almost unnoticeably.

"Oh crap." Mariana stopped abruptly with less than five feet between them and the car. "I forgot to grab shampoo."

"What?" It took Delaney a moment to process her friend's words through the rushing of blood in her ears.

Mariana was already pulling away, eyes locked on the store they'd just passed. The one right next to the one Trystan had been in.

"Forget it. You can borrow mine." Delaney reached for her, but Mariana was moving too quickly and had already turned. She wanted to call her back, but irrational fear kept her from doing so. Mariana was tiny but fast, and with her already halfway to the store, she'd have to raise her voice to be heard.

Not that Mariana had a problem with that, for she waved a hand without glancing around and called, "Be back in a sec!"

The parking lot they'd chosen was smaller than the one at the beach and only had about a dozen other cars in it now. Still holding tightly to her keys, she moved over to the driver's side, slipping the car key into the lock. She'd wait in the car and hopefully realize she was overreacting by the time Mariana came back.

Her phone went off in her back pocket, and she nearly jumped out of her skin. Yanking it out, she heaved a sigh of relief when she saw it was Ruckus calling. Hitting answer, she brought the device up to her ear and twisted the key to open the door.

"Hey," she said breathlessly, "we're heading back in a minute."

"You sound funny," Ruckus said, concern in his voice. "What's wrong?"

"Nothing," she told him. "We can talk about it when I get home. What are you making, anyway?"

"Delaney . . . something's happened. Pettus got ahold of me. They know who was leading the Tars."

She paused. "Who?"

"Brightan. When Trystan said he hadn't tried to kill you those other times, he was telling the truth. He'd only discovered Brightan's betrayal that night we left."

"That's why he shot him."

"And saved your life," Ruckus confirmed, "yes."

"How did Pettus figure this out?" she asked.

"Trystan admitted it." He paused, continuing before she could feel any sort of relief. "Delaney, the Basileus is dead."

The fear returned tenfold, and she wished more than anything that they were together. She'd been trying to keep the fact that Trystan was here from him so that he wouldn't worry, but now . . . If Magnus was dead, who'd killed him?

"Ru—" She reached for the handle then glanced at the window. Her reflection wasn't the only one staring back at her. Before she could react, the tall blond image in the glass moved.

She was vaguely aware of Ruckus's voice calling through the phone as it dropped from her hand and hit the gravel. The sharp sting in her neck lasted only a heartbeat, and then the world fizzled out and everything went dark.

ACKNOWLEDGMENTS

I WAS VERY tempted to just write, "Thanks, everyone I know!" in this section, partly for fear that I'd forget someone, but mostly because acknowledgments are hard. That being said, if I did end up forgetting you, I am so sorry! It's just, there are a lot of people and if I listed every single one of you this would end up longer than the actual book!

First and foremost, I'd like to thank everyone over at Swoon Reads. All of you are amazing, and I will forever be honored that you believed in my book enough to let me be a part of the Swoon Reads family. Holly, thank you for all of the work you've done, and all of the amazing notes and suggestions you've given. This book is a million times better now because of you. Also, the little notes you left about Trystan (Team Trystan, huh?) always helped alleviate some of the stress during the editing process, which I really appreciated, more than you know! Thank you, Emily, for really making me feel welcome to the team by emailing with me about our mutual love for Luke Mitchell. And of course, thanks to Liz D. for this epic cover!

To all of the other spectacular Swoon authors, thank you for being so supportive and welcoming, as well!

Thanks to my parents, for making books such a huge part of my life from the very beginning. You guys have always been very supportive of my crazy dream, and your belief in me means the world. Mom, you're the best. Thank you for letting me ramble on about potential plots and characters, and for always seeing something within that jumbled nonsense. Dad, thank you for passing on your love of reading (even if you did name me after a character who dies). To my siblings, Kim and Daniel, thanks for understanding every time I pretended to listen to you tell me something, even when I was clearly typing away and not hearing a word.

To my best friends, Josie and Jon. Josie, you are always the first person I want to share something new with. Thank you for your support, and your feedback, and for thinking every new book I write is the best book I've ever written. Thanks for your honesty when certain things don't seem to work, and for standing by me during those low periods (which everyone who writes knows about) where suddenly I start believing I am the worst writer on the entire planet. Just a heads up though, you're still going to have to read my stuff even once I'm old and senile and none of it makes any sense. So ha! Jon, thanks for all the coffee, and for being the only person brave enough to pull me away from my computer when I've been writing for hours on end. I love you guys.

Thank you to all of my professors at Johnson State College, and my classmates for helping me grow and improve as a writer. Kat, Whitney, Stephanie, Ben, thanks for not completely tearing me down during workshops! And to my teachers from high school (Ms. Hinkle, you are the best!). Thanks to Mrs. DeToro for story time in the fifth grade, which was how/when I realized I wanted to be an author.

Thanks to Matt and Lisa, two people who aren't here to see it finally happen, but whose unwavering belief that I could make it helped me believe it, too.

And finally, thank you to everyone who has ever read one my books before, and everyone who is reading this now. The only reason any of this is even remotely possible is because of all the feedback—good and bad—readers have given me over the years, and I truly appreciate each and every one of you.

FEELING BOOKISH?

Turn the page for some

BONUS SCENE

BOWLING

You're sure this is what you want your first real Earth experience to be?" Delaney glanced around the tacky room, wincing when an arcade machine went off a few feet away. It twirled flashing lights and emitted a clown cackle. "I did offer to take you anywhere."

The six-year-old who'd won the clown game leaped up and down, almost spilling his tiny paper cup of coins on the ground.

After everything they'd been through, all of this—the bright neon, the bad nineties music, the ancient arcade games—seemed less than impressive. Maybe she should have taken him bungee jumping after all, or, at the very least, to the zoo to see some lions.

"Mariana insists that I try the nachos," Ruckus said distractedly, eyes roaming over everything. He held her hand in his, their fingers loosely linked. Casual, comfortable.

There was an excitement radiating off him that Delaney used to feel when she came to these places, and some of her reservations dwindled. He'd been pressing her since their arrival last week to take him bowling, but there just hadn't been the time yet with dealing with her kidnap scare and reestablishing a connection with her parents.

Not to mention moving him into their apartment.

He'd only brought a single duffel—the same one she'd seen him packing that night in the bedroom before they'd run off toward the hangar—but she and Mariana had learned rather quickly that his belongings tended to spread. . . . When they'd left twenty minutes ago, she'd spotted one of his shoes by the couch, an old Vakar uniform shirt across the dining room chair, and one of his extra daggers on the kitchen counter.

She'd thought military men were supposed to be, well, organized.

This particular bowling alley was small, with only seven lanes, five of which were occupied. He was watching a couple college guys nearby, and frowned when after a strike one of them let out a "Whoop!"

"All right." She rubbed her hands together and waggled her eyebrows at him in the worst evil-villain rendition she could muster. "Don't say I didn't warn you."

"Warn me about . . . ?"

"Losing?" Mariana walked up, juggling three pairs of old blue-and-red shoes. They each showed a certain amount of wear. She held the largest out to him. "Because you're gonna, just FYI."

"I still don't understand why you need to borrow shoes," he told them. "And what is that an abbreviation for?"

"*For your information*," Mariana pointedly emphasized, grinning. "You rent shoes because they have a smooth surface at the bottom. That way we don't scuff up the floor. And you get better *oomph* when you roll."

"Come on." Delaney tugged on his sleeve and moved them

down the aisle to the very last lane. Then she dropped into one of the seats and began removing her shoes.

"Yes!" Mariana made a beeline for the console at the center, already clicking away at it. Less than a minute later, she clapped her hands and their names appeared on the electronic scoreboard hanging overhead.

"Did she—" Ruckus started at the same moment Delaney scolded, "Mariana!"

"What?" Her friend shrugged, flicking her dark hair over one shoulder. "It's true."

She'd made their names Ander Hotness, Lissa Badass, and Lissa Dominate.

"What's with the last one?" Delaney finished lacing her shoes and angled her head, as if by doing so she'd somehow figure it out. She was glad her friend was in a place where she could make jokes about the kidnapping, but that didn't mean she was, too. Some nights she still had nightmares about bombs going off and Tars lurking in dark hallways.

Before Mariana could explain the name, Delaney corrected the board so that it displayed their actual names. When she turned, Mariana was already sticking her tongue out at her.

"I should have put 'Lissa Buzzkill.'"

"Didn't you promise Ruckus nachos?" she countered.

"Oh right!" Mariana leaped into action, darting for the concession stand all the way on the other side of the building.

Ruckus blinked after her. "I think she's more excited for me to try these than I am."

In his nifty blue-and-red shoes, he stepped to her, wrapping an arm around her waist. Absently, he brought her against him while still staring off after Mariana, who was currently bouncing on the balls of her feet as she leaned over the counter and pointed to the menu.

"Best thing about Earth?" Delaney said, lifting onto her toes so she could bring her face closer to his.

He glanced down at her and then smirked when he saw her expression. "No risk of being caught by angry regents?" He shook his head. "No. No Tar terrorists?"

"I was *going* to say"—no she hadn't been—"I get to teach you how to do something for once. And kick your ass at it. There's also that."

He lifted a single dark brow. "Confident, aren't you?"

"Have you ever been bowling before?" She already knew he hadn't, and when he shook his head she pulled back and went to select a ball. "Then, yes. Yes, I am."

Delaney had him follow her toward the start of the lane and demonstrated how a bowling ball was properly rolled. Or tossed, in her case, because she always threw it with a bit more force than necessary. She knocked down all but two pins with her first roll, and then got them with her second.

She spun in an excited circle and did a little dance. He was staring at her, trying to hold back a laugh when she finally stopped.

"That's a spare," she said, then waved him onward when the pins had reset. "There's no way you're going to do better than that on your first try, so don't feel bad."

He glanced over his shoulder at her hand when she patted him. "You're competitive, aren't you?"

"Of course not." She didn't bother hiding the sarcasm, winking to further the effect.

He lined himself up, positioning his body the same way she'd shown him. He inhaled, pulled back, and then let the ball go with a snap of his wrist.

The large, green bowling ball traveled down the lane almost faster than her eyes could follow, whipping against the center pin with a sharp *crack*. Within a split second all ten pins were lying in a pile.

"What's that called?" he asked, the grin across his face cluing her in that he already knew it was good, whatever it was.

"A lucky shot."

But by the time Mariana returned—and not just with nachos but with one of everything off the menu—Ruckus had already had ten "lucky shots."

"You played a whole game without me," Mariana whined, hitting the reset button and snatching a ball before either of them could speak. If she'd noticed the score, and that he'd gotten strikes in all ten frames, she didn't comment.

Mariana swung back and let the bright-pink ball she'd chosen go. It whacked against the floor and rolled almost immediately into the gutter. Unaffected, she practically skipped back over and selected another, retaking her position to try again.

"She's terrible at bowling," Delaney said, as if Ruckus hadn't figured that out for himself already.

"But I'm not."

"No," she grumbled. "You're some freakishly-good-for-no-reason bowler."

He linked their fingers and then tugged her across the booth so that she was almost in his lap. "Well, what do I get for winning?"

The whizzing sounds from the arcade and the clattering of pins faded into the background when she leaned into him. Over the heady smell of fried dough and melted cheese she caught a whiff of sparking embers and ignited firewood.

She pressed her mouth against his, not concerned with who was watching, and nothing else mattered in that moment but kissing him.

When she pulled back, his yellow-green eyes trailed over her face. He tucked a strand of red hair behind her ear, letting his fingertips linger there a second longer than necessary.

"You, then?" His voice was low between them. "I'll take it."

"Guys!" Mariana called, and they both grinned but didn't look away from each other. "Delaney, you're up!"

She untangled herself from him and made a big show of stretching. "This game, I am definitely beating you. So, what do I get when I win?"

He got to his feet, the move bringing his body back up against hers. His lips fluttered over the curve of her jaw promisingly before he finally met her gaze and offered, "Me?"

She smiled like an idiot, and she didn't even care. "I'll take it."

A COFFEE DATE

between author Chani L. Feener
and her editor, Holly West

Holly West (HW): What was the first romance novel you ever read?
Chani Feener (CF): The first was actually three in one and was *Mysterious* by Nora Roberts. Looking back, I was probably way too young to be reading that at the time. I think I was eleven. I immediately fell in love with her specifically and read everything else by her I could get my hands on for the next few years.

HW: I LOVED Nora Roberts growing up, especially her Chesapeake Bay series. Who is your OTP, your favorite fictional couple?
CF: This is a tough one, but I absolutely love Khalid and Shahrzad from *The Wrath & the Dawn* by Renée Ahdieh. They both go into their relationship thinking they're going to have to kill the other and they end up connecting. Theirs is the kind of empowering love that makes both of them want to be better people. Throughout the story, you sort of fall in love with them while they fall in love with each other, which was great.

HW: Do you have any hobbies? Other than writing, of course. Writing doesn't count as a hobby when you are a published author.
CF: I love drawing. For the longest time I thought I was going to grow

up and be an artist. Now I just draw portraits on the side for fun. I also collect Funko Pop. I got addicted to the Game of Thrones line two years back, and somehow it escalated. I have a little over four hundred right now. . . . Yikes.

HW: That is an impressive collection! I've barely started mine. ☺ And my favorite question, if you were a superhero, what would your superpower be?
CF: Transmogrification. I'd love to be able to transmogrify items, which is transforming one thing into another. I've tried writing a superhero story about this, but I never seem to get it right and always give up. As a superpower, I think it'd be amazing, like I'd be able to turn a rock into a cell phone to call my sidekick. Or I'd be able to turn the villain's gun into plastic flowers. It would certainly make changing into my superhero costume easier! I could be in sweatpants and then just touch them with my fingers and change in a second.

HW: How did you first learn about Swoon Reads?
CF: I believe it was through Goodreads.com. I'm on that site all the time so I'm pretty sure that's where I would have first heard about it. I thought it sounded like an amazing opportunity and immediately added the site to my favorites list.

HW: What made you decide to post your manuscript?
CF: I waited a little longer to actually post a manuscript after discovering the site. I'd been trying to get an agent for a while and wasn't having any luck, so I decided to try other options. I loved what Swoon was, how they made their selections, and how open it was for the readers. It seemed like a great opportunity, and I figured why not give it a try. So glad now that I did!

HW: What was your experience like on the site before you were chosen?

CF: I absolutely loved how interactive the site was/is. I think it's such a great idea to give readers the ability to comment and help choose what gets looked at. I also love how interactive it still is after a book has been chosen. Letting people vote on covers and giving them blog posts by authors is such a great way of keeping everyone involved and letting readers be a bigger part of it start to finish.

HW: Once you were chosen, who was the first person you told and how did you celebrate?

CF: My best friend, Josie. I immediately called her. She was driving and had to pull over because she was screaming and crying even more than I was! I was still trying to remain somewhat collected, so I remember saying, "I just got off the phone with them and I'm getting published!" and then her excitement made it impossible for me to contain it anymore. I celebrated afterward by buying myself bookshelves! I had these awful ones that were falling apart. It might not seem like a big way of celebrating, but it was a huge deal for me!

HW: Congrats! Proper bookshelves are always a big deal for book people. Speaking of, when did you realize you wanted to be a writer?

CF: When I was nine or ten. It was story time in fifth grade, and my teacher was reading *The BFG* by Roald Dahl to us. I was brought up surrounded by books, so it really shouldn't have been a huge revelation to me that people actually had to write them, but somehow it clicked in that moment. People wrote stories for a living and got to bring others into that world and make them forget about their own reality. All of a sudden I realized writing was something I could do with my life.

HW: Do you have any writing rituals?

CF: Not really. I guess if there are people in the room I'll put headphones in and play the same song on repeat so that they and the music don't distract me. Other than that I don't really have any rituals. I can pretty much sit down and write wherever I am.

HW: Where did the idea for *Amid Stars and Darkness* start?

CF: My brother hates when I answer this question because he thinks my response is always very lame. However, sticking with honesty, it sort of stemmed from an episode of that show *Ancient Aliens*. The people on this show are very convinced that aliens are real, and that they're capable of all these advanced things. I just started thinking about how a person with that kind of belief might react if they actually came face-to-face with an alien. Delaney's character started there as just a girl who knows aliens exist, but has always sort of distanced herself from learning more about them. Then I realized a story that takes place on another planet would be even more interesting, and the Vakar and Kint came into existence. Ruckus was, for the most part, planned, but Trystan sort of came out of nowhere. He practically wrote himself and forced his way into a bigger role. It's not surprising, really; we all know he's a bully.

HW: Do you ever get writer's block? How do you get back on track?

CF: Yes, and it is awful. Usually though, it passes on its own and I don't have to do much of anything. If I don't feel particularly inspired one day, I'll watch a movie, read a book, catch up on a TV show, etc., and the next day suddenly I'll be back into it. When that doesn't happen, however, if I've gone days without being able to jot down anything, usually that's when I'll force it. I'll sit down and just write anything and everything that comes to mind. These pages tend to get deleted from the book later on, but they help me clear my head and get back to the usable stuff. Pushing through it always works—it's just a matter of how many crappy pages/scenes I have to write first.

HW: What's the best writing advice you've ever heard?

CF: To just do it. I can't remember who specifically I heard it from. I believe it was a few years ago in an author interview, but it stuck with me. Life is hectic and busy and it's never going to not be those things. I try not to let myself go too long without writing anything, even if it's just a sentence of dialogue or description. If writing is really important to you, you've got to make time for it. If it's something that you want to do with your life, again, you have to find a way to fit it into your schedule. The notes on my phone are pretty much all small paragraphs/bits of dialogue that I thought up randomly while shopping or waiting in lines or even at work. More than half of them aren't usable, but I still feel good at the end of the day knowing that I got something down on "paper."

HW: On the site we have something called the Swoon Index, where readers can share the amount of Heat, Laughter, Tears, and Thrills in each manuscript. Can you tell me something (or someone!) that always turns up the heat?

CF: I like a little banter between characters. When they can tease one another and play off of one another it keeps things interesting. I also like reading books where there's a little mutual possessiveness going on.

HW: What always makes you laugh?

CF: I have a very dry sense of humor, so sarcasm and puns always make me laugh. I know it's supposed to be a very low form of humor, but it works on me.

HW: Makes you cry?

CF: People being compassionate. Every time I see someone do a good deed or go out of their way to help someone else, I start immediately tearing up. For example, there was a commercial where a woman didn't have anyone over for Thanksgiving and her neighbors saw and brought her all this food and spent the holiday with her. I cried a little. Every time I saw it. Don't even get me started on those videos where a loved one has come home from the military as a surprise.

HW: Sets your heart pumping?

CF: I love romances that start as one thing and evolve into more; that's really what catches my interest and keeps me reading. When I get invested in their relationship like it's an actual relationship taking place in reality, my heart starts pumping and I flip pages wildly.

HW: And finally, tell us all what makes you swoon!

CF: Little things. I'm not really into big grand gestures or cheesy romance moves. Remembering how I take my coffee is one of the sweetest things anyone can do, in my mind.

DISCUSSION QUESTIONS

1. Do you believe in aliens? Why?

2. Delaney goes dancing to celebrate a big moment with her best friend. What do you do to celebrate, and who with?

3. Olena put Delaney in a hard position. Do you think you would be able to pretend to be someone you're not if you had to? Do you think you'd be believable?

4. The aliens have different colors to symbolize whether they're Vakar or Kint. It's always one solid color, like blue or green, and then one metallic, gold or silver. If you ran an alien population, what colors would you choose to symbolize your people and why?

5. How do you feel about the way Magnus and Tilda treat Delaney? Do you think they went about "asking" her to stay the right way?

6. If you were looking for a job on Zenith and could shadow either Pettus, who is a soldier, or Gibus, who is a scientist, for a day, who would you choose and why?

7. If you had a device that could make you look like anyone else in the world, who would you pick and what would you do as them?

8. Delaney had to try a lot of new foods, some of which were very strange colors. Are you adventurous when it comes to food? Why or why not?

9. Delaney doesn't know much about aliens going into this, other than knowing that they exist. If you knew aliens were real, would you be fascinated like Mariana or distance yourself like Delaney?

10. If you could have dinner with either Ruckus or Trystan, who would you want it to be with and why?

When Delaney is kidnapped by aliens—*again*—she finds herself at the center of both a tense political battle between two alien kingdoms and Trystan's romantic attentions. Can she get back to the life she's built for herself on Earth?

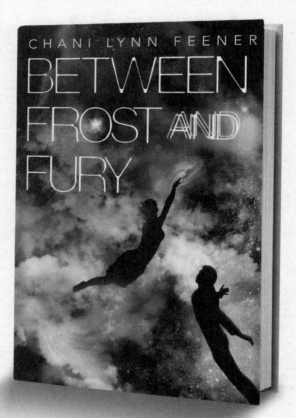

KEEP READING FOR AN EXCERPT.

elaney?!" Ruckus gripped the phone tighter in his hand. Fear was threatening to cloud his judgment, and he forced himself to still in the center of the living room. Inhale slowly until he stopped seeing black spots.

There'd been an odd note in Delaney's tone when she'd picked up a few minutes ago, a hint that something was already wrong before he'd told her about the Basileus's murder. Considering her plan had been to spend the day at the beach with her best friend, Mariana, there was no reason he could see for her to be nervous.

She'd been in the process of saying his name, which meant something had to have happened. There were any number of things that could mean—most of them bad—but until he got more information, he couldn't panic. Panicking meant making mistakes, and he couldn't afford any, no matter what was going on.

Ruckus hung up and dialed again, setting the phone on speaker and putting it aside while it rang, retrieving the clear device he'd left on the kitchen counter. He cursed when Delaney's voicemail started.

Ended the call.

Tried again.

The forgotten device in his other hand made a beeping sound suddenly, a row of tiny yellow lights flickering at the top. He drew his attention away from the phone long enough to tap the center button. A second later Fawna's face filled the palm-sized screen, the concern in her eyes apparent.

"We might have a problem."

"Something's happened to Delaney," he said, that tightening feeling in his chest getting worse when her phone went to voicemail yet again.

"There's a Kint ship," Fawna told him, momentarily glancing away to use the control panel in her own craft. He couldn't see it from the small screen, but the sound of her clicking keys gave it away. "I don't know how long it's been here. It was doing a very good job cloaking its presence. Could be they arrived before me."

His stomach bottomed out and he gripped the edge of the counter to keep himself from visibly swaying.

He and Fawna had only just ended their conversation moments before he'd phoned Delaney to fill her in. Because Xenith and Earth were in different galaxies, communications were limited to a certain range. Fawna had come all the way to tell him about the political unrest in Vakar, which meant she was still directly outside Earth's orbit.

And apparently she wasn't alone.

"Whose ship?" Ruckus asked, though he was already rushing down the hall toward Mariana's bedroom, where he'd last seen the car keys. He'd drive down to the beach and find out what was going on.

Because he was being paranoid, and there was no possible way what he feared was happening really was. No possible—

"I believe it's the Zane's," Fawna confirmed, basically shattering any remaining hope he had left. "Wait." She paused then added, "It looks like a smaller craft is about to board. Ruckus . . . it's coming from Earth."

Without stopping, he swiveled on his heel, adjusting his course of trajectory. He snatched the phone off the counter just in case, and quickly checked to make sure his fritz was turned on as he headed toward the front door.

"Come get me," he ordered, holding the screen up so Fawna could see the moment he got outside. "Now."

"We don't know she's been taken . . . ," Fawna began, though he could tell she was already preparing to do as he'd said. The console before her began to whir, and a digital voice announced preparations to approach the planet.

"She's on that ship," he stated, moving past the driveway and around to the back of the apartment building. There was more space in the yard. "Just get here."

He disconnected the device before she could respond, shoving it into his back pocket so he could try dialing Delaney one last time, already knowing it was useless. There was only one reason for the Zane's personal ship to be hovering outside of Earth.

Ruckus struggled against the mixture of anger and terror that warred within him, trying to keep his mind clear enough to run the calculations. If they'd just taken her, Delaney wasn't too far ahead. He could board Fawna's ship and be close behind, arrive shortly after.

And then?

The sound of an engine roared above him and he tipped his head back in time to see the smaller craft drop its camouflage, seemingly appearing out of thin air. A small hatch at the bottom opened, and a metal bar dropped down into his already waiting hand.

And then he'd do whatever he had to do to get Delaney back safely.

Check out more books chosen for publication by readers like you.